I0788143

CHRISSY CURRY

"You Can't Help but Turn the Pages!"
- D.J. Maughan, Best Selling Author of Idaho Fall

OPEN

ENDED

The Echoes of Redemption

HEMINGWAY
PUBLISHERS

Author's Note

When I first brought Cora to the page, she was broken but brave, stitched together by fear and the fragile hope of stability. Over three books, I've watched her love deeply, lose painfully, and rise fiercely—again and again. Her journey wasn't just about survival. It was about how a woman can rise from wreckage and rewrite herself with grit, grace, and a stubborn heartbeat. This final chapter isn't just the end of a story. It's a reckoning, a renewal, and a quiet redemption for every scar she's carried.

To anyone who has ever felt undone by loss or questioned whether they could begin again—this book is for you. Cora's story may close here, but its message endures: You are allowed to be rewritten. You are allowed to RISE. Again and again, if needed.

Thank you for walking beside Cora, for seeing her, believing in her, and rooting for her. I hope these pages stay with you like echoes—soft but persistent, full of promise.

With all my heart,

Chrissy Curry

What Readers Are Saying

"I thought I knew where this story was going. I didn't. And that's what made it unforgettable."

– D.V.

"I read the last chapter three times, not because I didn't understand it, but because I didn't want it to be over."

– F.T.

"It's the kind of book that stays with you, the kind you find yourself thinking about at a red light or in the middle of the night."

– S.N.

"Cora made me cry, then laugh, then cry again — all in the same paragraph."

– M.B.

"The ending was perfect."

– C.R.

"I closed the book and just sat there. Breathing. Processing. Feeling everything."

– T.K.

"Currently searching for my very own Lincoln McAlister."

– S.R.

Table of Contents

Prologue

"In the silence of forgotten moments, echoes of redemption whispered that even lost time could lead to healing."

The snow had started to fall before they reached the bend. Cora tightened her grip on the steering wheel, her eyes flicking to the rearview mirror where Avalina's eyelids fluttered shut in her car seat. Her cheeks were rosy from the cold, a soft blanket tucked beneath her tiny three-year-old chin. One sock had slipped off. Cora had smiled earlier at a red light, reaching back to tug it over her daughter's toes.

The winding mountain road of Swan Range stretched ahead like a ribbon of slate, its edges buried beneath mounds of snow. Towering evergreens lined both sides, their limbs sagging under winter's weight. The engine hummed steadily and the heater ticked softly unamused. From the driver's seat, Cora whispered a tune under her breath—a gentle murmur, barely louder than the snow brushing the windshield.

"Do you remember when we used to sing? Sha-la-la-la-la-la, la-la, la-la-la-la tee-da..."

Van Morrison's *Brown Eyed Girl* tasted like childhood. Like sun-warmed backseats and cracked windows letting in pine-scented air, her grandmother's hand tapping the steering wheel. Simpler days. Safer and whole. Before the world got noisy and grief wore holes in her joy. Before good things started to feel temporary.

She reached for that fleeting moment in the music, letting it swell through her body, as if it could hold her together. Her breath caught in her chest, suspended in the stillness—just before everything unraveled.

Then came the curve. It was too fast. Too sharp. The illusion of control vanished, replaced by the sickening truth that gravity—and fate—had taken the wheel.

Avalina's voice pierced the air, high-pitched and raw with panic. "Mama!"

Her cry rose above the screech of tires losing grip.

The crash came instantly—thunderous and brutal. Glass shattered in a blinding explosion, the windshield bursting into glittering fragments. The frame groaned and folded inward like paper caught in a storm. The seat belt bit into Cora's chest, her body wrenched violently sideways as the car slammed nose-first into the embankment. Her head snapped forward, then back, white-hot pain blooming at the base of her skull.

The scent of scorched rubber and antifreeze filled the air, sharp and wrong. Snow flew in through the shattered window, stinging her cheeks like tiny needles. The dashboard lights flickered—then died. The world flipped with glass raining, tires thudding, metal shrieking as the car rolled once, then again. The roof crumpled, and a branch speared through the rear window.

And then there was stillness—unforgiving, absolute stillness.

The car settled at an angle, half-buried in the snowbank, smoke curling from beneath the hood. Silence spread through the wreckage, eerie and vast, as if the world were holding its breath. Cora couldn't move. Her fingers twitched against the wheel. Somewhere close, she thought she heard a whimper, soft and trembling, but she couldn't tell if it was Avalina or her own voice caught in her throat.

All she could feel was cold, seeping into her bones. All she could hear was silence—heavy, suffocating, endless. Then faintly, she heard her own heartbeat. Unsteady. But there.

She was alive.

When Cora opened her eyes, the world returned in jagged fragments—blurred, broken. Trees dangled upside down. Blood pooled. Smoke coiled across the vast mountain range. And—then her own voice, hoarse and trembling, whispered one word:

"Avalina..."

She woke again in a hospital bed.

The lights were too bright. Cora's head pounded and her limbs were heavy. But she remembered the weight of Avalina in her arms. She remembered her scent. The warmth of her skin. Her daughter was safe.

The antiseptic smell made her stomach turn. A monitor beeped steadily beside her, grounding her in a present that didn't feel real. Then the door opened and two figures rushed in. One was tall and broad-shouldered; worry etched into every line of his face. The other—familiar, heartbreakingly so—clutched a bag too tightly, her eyes rimmed red.

"Cora," the man said, voice thick with emotion—relief, fear, love.

She blinked, confused. Her mind scrambled for names, for something to anchor her. But her body knew. Her heart softened.

"Dad?" she whispered. The name spilled out like a secret she didn't know she remembered.

He was at her side in two steps, taking her hand. "I'm here, sweetheart. I'm here. Selah's here. Avalina is okay."

Cora turned toward the woman. "Selah," she said slowly, unsure how she knew. But she did. The warmth in her chest told her so.

Selah began to cry, silent tears sliding down her cheeks. "Oh, Cora. You scared us."

"I… I know you," Cora murmured. "I don't remember everything. But I know you. I trust you."

Dax's jaw clenched, his thumb brushing over her knuckles. "That's all that matters right now."

In the confusion, in the spinning mess of memory and fear, Cora clung to the only thing that made sense—two people who felt like home when everything else had been wiped away.

Selah moved into the guest room the day Cora was released, without needing to be asked. She unpacked quietly, folded laundry, and filled the fridge with groceries Cora might actually eat. For eight weeks, she became the quiet rhythm of the house.

Cora didn't remember everything. Some mornings, she woke disoriented, heart pounding from nightmares she couldn't explain. On those days, Selah lit the vanilla pine candle Cora used to love and made tea without a word. She never pushed. Never asked about the gaps in memory or the fear that clutched Cora's chest when the doorbell rang. She just stayed curled beside her on the couch with old photo albums, softly narrating their past like fairy tales.

"This was when we tried to dye your hair blue and ended up with green. You cried for two hours, then wore it to class like a crown."

Cora would smile, unsure if the memory was real or just beautifully told. But she trusted it. She trusted her.

— x —

Some nights, when Cora couldn't sleep, she'd wander into the kitchen to find Selah already there with two mugs of warm milk in hand. They didn't talk much. Selah simply filled the silence with presence instead of pressure. And slowly, some pieces returned. Not just the painful ones, but the beautiful ones too—Selah dancing like a maniac in the car. Stories of Jensen and MJ. The ridiculous nickname they gave themselves in college: *Vodka Vixens*, coined by flamboyant MJ after a wild night on the quad. That time they ran out of gas on a back road and laughed until they cried. Some memories came back slowly, stitched together by the woman who never left. But the last five years were missing. Love. Heartbreak. Endings. Beginnings.

Gone. Like pages ripped from a book she hadn't finished reading.

Earlier, she had sat by the window, watching the storm roll in, the sky darkening with every passing minute, mirroring the weight pressing against her chest. Now, in the bedroom, she held Avalina close. Her daughter's small fingers curled around hers, grounding her in the present. Avalina's hair, still wild from her afternoon nap, stuck out in gentle curls, and her socks—one striped, one plain—peeked from beneath the hem of her pants.

The memory lapses were constant. Conversations, faces, and entire events slipped just out of reach, like trying to hold water in her hands. She'd wake in the night, drenched in sweat, screaming without sound. Visions of fire and faceless shadows that vanished when the light returned. It wasn't just confusion. It was fear. Her mind was hiding something. And it was starting to surface.

The worst part wasn't the forgetting. It was the *knowing* that just beneath the surface, something waited. Sometimes, Cora would freeze in a room, unable to remember why she walked in, or stare at a photo that should mean something and feel only a hollow ache. Avalina would ask about places they'd been, people they'd met, and Cora would smile and nod, pretending until guilt gnawed at her insides.

The dreams grew darker and the nights became longer. Cora stopped sleeping. She stopped believing the doctors when they said it was just a concussion. Something had shifted. Something had broken open. Still, Cora smiled through the pain. She told everyone she was fine. She focused harder. She dug deeper into motherhood. Because Avalina needed her—she needed normal. Needed steady. So, Cora chose to build her days around routine—packing lunches, walking to preschool, story hour at the children's boutique. She performed happiness with practiced grace. Every whispered *"I love you,"* every dance class, every bedtime story became her anchor. If she couldn't trust her mind, she'd trust her love. And maybe if she pretended hard enough, the holes would stay buried. Maybe the truth would never come for her.

That night, as the rain traced rivulets down the glass, Cora whispered the only truth she could hold:

"I don't know who I was before this. But I know who I am now. I'm Avalina's mother. A daughter. A friend. And that has to be enough... until the rest comes back."

Chapter 1

Unfolding the Forgotten

"I am pages torn by time, scattered by fate—yet in her eyes, I find verses of myself, unfolding softly in the margins of motherhood."

Morning sunlight spilled through the tall windows of Cora's house, warming the hardwood floors and casting soft light across scattered toys, a half-finished puzzle, and a well-loved armchair by the bookshelf. Her home wasn't just where she lived. It was her sanctuary. A space built on second chances and quiet strength. A place of comfort, of memories, of love. A fresh start.

It had been two months since the accident.

Cora often felt like she was running, though she couldn't say from what or why. A heaviness clung to her chest, something fresh air and clean slates couldn't shake. She had created a new life built on routine and smiles, but beneath it all simmered a quiet panic, clawing at the edges of her mind. Some mornings, she'd catch herself staring into the mirror, trying to recognize the woman behind her own eyes. She had suffered a concussion severe enough to cause retrograde amnesia.

"It's not uncommon with this level of head trauma," the doctor had explained gently to her father. *"She's lost the last five years. Her mind essentially wiped everything beyond that point to protect itself. We don't know if those memories will return. Some patients recover them slowly... others never do."*

He'd let the silence stretch before continuing, watching Cora search his face for something solid to hold onto. *"The brain blocks the most recent memories first—ones not fully cemented. It's frustrating, I know. But this isn't necessarily permanent."*

She had blinked, lips parted, trying to grasp the shape of five lost years.

"The good news," he had added glancing at Cora, *"is that memory often returns gradually. Especially people—your child, your close friends, your family. Even if the memories feel out of reach, they're not erased. Think of them as buried under fog. With time and the right support, that fog can lift."*

Then, even softer: *"You might start to recognize voices, gestures, or small routines before the full memories return. Don't force it. Your mind knows how to find its way back."*

Today marked Cora's first day back at work after eight long weeks. She paused at the front door, hand lingering on the knob, as if the threshold itself were asking if she was ready. After dropping Avalina off at the neighbor's, she made the short drive to the clinic—just six blocks, but it felt like crossing into a life she'd nearly forgotten. The streets rolled by in a blur of the familiar and the foreign, as if everything had shifted slightly in her absence.

Now, back under the sterile lights and quiet hum of the clinic, the reality of returning settled in her chest like a weight she hadn't anticipated. Cora sat stiffly on the edge of the exam table, fingers twisted in her lap as Dr. Bronson flipped through the latest scans.

"No new damage," he said, tapping the screen. "But your brain's still showing signs of post-traumatic swelling. It's minor but enough to explain the lingering gaps."

He looked at her kindly but cautiously. "The memory loss is still limited to the five years before the accident. That kind of amnesia can be stubborn. Sometimes pieces return with triggers. You may remember familiar places, smells or people. But forcing it won't help."

Cora nodded, though frustration bubbled beneath her skin. "So, I'm stuck?" she asked quietly.

"Not stuck," he said. "Healing. And healing doesn't follow a schedule." He leaned forward, a gentle curiosity in his tone. "You mentioned once that you kept journals. Have you looked at them?"

She shook her head. She'd kept them close since coming home but hadn't dared to open them.

"Sometimes the mind buries what the hand has already written," he said. "Your journals might hold the pieces you're looking for. Triggers, memories, even names that feel like strangers now. They could help you remember who you were."

Outside the clinic, Cora stood on the curb, keys clenched in her hand as the wind tangled her hair. The world around her shimmered with an eerie familiarity. *"Five years,"* she whispered.

The warm scent of sugar and butter greeted her as she stepped into *The Cookie Cove*. The woman behind the counter smiled. Cora's body responded instinctively, guiding her to the glass case, but her mind remained blank. Rows of cookies stared back: chocolate chip, snickerdoodle, lemon drop, birthday cake, red velvet, raspberry jam thumbprints. She searched for a spark. Something that would tell her which was Avalina's favorite.

Nothing came.

"I'm sorry," she murmured to no one in particular. *"I don't remember."*

"You okay, hon?" The clerk asked gently.

Cora nodded, forcing a smile. "I'll take one of each." Her voice cracked with the effort. She left with a box full of sweetness and a hollow ache in her chest, hoping something—anything—would click into place when she opened it with Avalina later.

Who was she before the accident? Before the gaps. Before everything felt fractured and unfinished. Her reflection gave her no answers, only the echo of something lost. Was she hiding from someone? From something she did? Or something done to her? Every instinct screamed that the past hadn't been simply forgotten. It had been buried. And she feared that if she dug too deep, she wouldn't like what she found. The questions haunted her: What had she run from? Why did remembering feel more dangerous than forgetting? And why did it feel like time was running out?

Avalina didn't help, though she didn't mean to. *"Remember when we used to live near the water, Mommy?"*

But Cora didn't. She'd never told Avalina they had. And when she asked follow-ups, Avalina would just shrug, like it didn't matter. But it did. Every forgotten detail made her feel like she was living inside someone else's life.

And at night, when the world quieted, the truth pressed against her like a weight she couldn't lift. There was something in those five lost years—something terrifying. She could feel it—like a storm behind a locked door. Part of her wanted to face it. But another part, the one that flinched at shadows and woke up screaming, wasn't sure she could survive remembering.

The journals were always nearby. Cora kept them tucked in her bag, resting on the nightstand, or nestled in her arm. They were a lifeline. A reminder. A mystery. Some days, she imagined opening them, the words flowing like a river reclaiming its course. Other days, she feared the pages, as if they held truths she wasn't ready to face. But the faces were fading. Feelings slipping through her fingers like smoke. She knew she had to try.

One name came to her clearly: *Vinny.*

He came in dreams. Not as a whisper, but as a weight. First a shadow, then a voice. Then a nightmare. His presence turned sleep into torment. Each time Cora woke, the chill lingered, like part of him had followed her into the light.

She sat in her car outside *The Cookie Cove*, hands trembling as they rested on the journals in her lap. Her breath became shallow and uneven as she opened the cover. Page after page blurred past entries scrawled in grief, in love, in fury. Until she saw it. And then she stopped breathing altogether.

Declan.

There was that look in his eyes…that apology that always came too late. I wanted to believe he could be different, but how do you rewrite a man already written in ink?

Cora blinked. Declan. Avalina's father. She'd heard her father mention him. But his face remained a blur.

She turned the page.

They took him. I didn't think they would, but they did. The charges stuck. I don't know how to explain this to Avalina. She keeps asking when she's getting a daddy. I told her not everyone gets to see theirs. God, did I lie to her? Did I do the right thing?

Her hands trembled. Declan was in prison. What had he done? Why couldn't she remember? Why was his name written with both longing and fear? And why hadn't anyone talked about him?

She reached for another journal.

I told Avalina her daddy is somewhere safe. I couldn't tell her the truth. Not yet. Not when she still carries his dimples and that laugh that sounds like it could undo the whole world. How do you tell a little girl the truth about the man who gave her life but couldn't live his own without destroying others?

Tears slipped down her cheeks. She had protected Avalina. Or lied to her. Maybe both.

She whispered, *"What else did I forget?"*

She kept flipping until her eyes landed on an early entry. It was dated the day Avalina was born.

She's like a tiny little bird, she had written. *Always hungry, always searching. Her mouth clicks softly as she looks for the next thing to fill her. So small, so delicate. I think I'll call her Wren. She's my little Wren.*

Cora smiled. The name stirred something warm and familiar. She remembered calling her that when the world felt too big, when Avalina felt too small. A little bird in the vast sky.

She closed the journal slowly, pressing her palm against the cover as if to quiet everything it had stirred. With a steadying breath, she started the car and pulled away from *The Cookie Cove*, the memory of her daughter's laugh guiding her back.

She tugged her cardigan tighter as she stepped onto the porch of the neighbor's house. Sunlight bathed the quiet neighborhood. She could hear Avalina's giggles before she even knocked.

The door opened before she had to.

"Perfect timing," Josie said, hip propped on the frame, Avalina peeking from behind her with a half-eaten cookie.

"Mama!" Avalina launched into her arms.

Cora crouched, heart swelling at her daughter's warmth. "Did you have fun with Miss Josie?"

"I watered the flowers and gave her cat two snacks even though he was only supposed to get one," Avalina whispered like a secret.

"Oh no," Cora teased. "Guess we're banned from next door now."

Josie laughed. "Anytime. You know that." Then, with a glance at Cora's face, her smile softened. "Everything okay?"

Cora hesitated. "Just the usual," she said softly, brushing a curl from Avalina's cheek.

Josie stepped down beside her. "I don't know what kind of heavy you're carrying today but just remember—you don't have to hold it all at once. Let the good moments in, too, even the small ones. Especially the small ones."

Cora's eyes misted. She nodded, not trusting her voice. And for a second, the weight didn't feel quite so crushing.

Back in the car, Cora caught her reflection in the rearview mirror. The doctor's appointment had left her with more questions than answers. But Avalina's smile anchored her, like always.

As they turned the corner, the front of her boutique, *Huckleberry Wonders*, came into view. The soft lilac awning fluttered in the breeze, and the sign above the door read in delicate script: *Whimsy lives here.*

Avalina gasped, like she always did. "Look, Mama! The new window!"

The welcome back display was storybook-themed with a cardboard castle that stood tall beside twinkle lights dripped like stardust. Plush dragons curled around stacks of books, and tiny dresses floated like clouds in a fairytale sky.

Cora parked slowly, her eyes lingering on the window. "Did… did I put that together?" she asked, more to herself than anyone else.

Avalina shook her head proudly. "Miss Harlyn did it. She said it was a surprise. She wanted you to smile when you came back."

Cora blinked, trying to recall the name, the face, the rhythm of their workdays, but it was like reaching for fog. "Harlyn," she repeated, tasting the name. "She did a beautiful job."

Avalina grinned. "She's really good at magic."

Inside, sunlight spilled through the windows as they rolled up their sleeves. Today was just for them. A quiet reset after chaos. They unboxed new shipments like they were unwrapping possibilities. They swept away cobwebs—literal and metaphorical. They rearranged displays, and laughter nestled all around them. And piece by piece, memory or not, they made space for something new.

Chapter 2

Little Voices, Dark Whispers

"The past always finds its way back. Sometimes in a child's voice."

The early light had filtered in through gauzy curtains, painting soft gold across the bedroom walls the next morning. Cora stood by the mirror, her hands trembling slightly as she ran a brush through her hair. Today was going to be one of those days. The kind that felt heavy before it even began. Behind her, tiny footsteps padded in.

"You forgot," Avalina said sleepily, holding up two satin ribbons.

Cora turned, her heart tugging at the sight of her daughter in fuzzy socks and a too-big pajama shirt. Avalina's small hands clutched the ribbons like they were a treasure.

"Oh, Wren," Cora whispered, kneeling. "I didn't forget. I just… needed you to remind me."

Avalina nodded with quiet understanding, stepping closer. "Brave Bows," she said with a seriousness far beyond her years.

They didn't need to say more. This was their new thing. They had made a pact that every day that mattered, they tied on courage together. Cora took the pink ribbon and gently smoothed it. "Ready?" she asked.

Avalina nodded. "You go first."

Cora tied the bow just above Avalina's ear, neat and snug. She gave it a final tap, like sealing a promise.

"Now me," Cora said, sitting cross-legged on the floor.

Avalina climbed onto the bed behind her and carefully tied the matching ribbon into her mother's hair. It was a bit crooked, but Cora wouldn't have it any other way.

"You're brave, Mommy," Avalina said quietly. "Even when you cry."

Cora blinked hard, turning just enough to scoop Avalina into a hug. "So are you, my love. Braver than anyone I know."

The ribbons swayed as they hugged, two threads of strength woven into the day. And when they stepped out the front door, hands clasped and heads high, the world saw just a pair of matching bows. But they knew better. They were brave. Together.

It was Saturday morning, the most cherished time of their week. Story hour. A tradition Cora had started when she first opened the shop, and today was her first official day back at it. Children and their parents were already gathering on the plush rug in the corner, where oversized cushions and a wooden rocking chair created the perfect nook for reading. Parents brought beautiful bouquets of flowers, chocolate-covered strawberries, and cards welcoming her back to the story time rug.

Cora stepped into the cozy warmth of the boutique, the old books wrapping around her like a forgotten song. Shelves of pastel toys and woven baskets lined the walls, and soft music played from somewhere unseen. A chalkboard sign near the counter read *"Story Hour with Miss Cora – Today's Book: The Curious Caterpillar."* The handwriting was looping and familiar. Hers, maybe. But it didn't feel like hers. Nothing did.

Her boots paused on the scuffed wood floor, and she looked around, hollowed out by confusion. The walls were painted a pale lavender, sunlight catching in the sheer curtains and turning everything soft. It should've felt comforting. Safe. But it didn't. It felt like stepping into someone else's dream.

A cluster of children sat crisscrossed on a carpet patterned with stars and moons, their tiny hands clutching juice boxes and stuffed animals. They were staring at her expectantly. A few grinned. One waved. A little girl in a pink jumper whispered, *"That's her,"* like she was a celebrity. Or a ghost.

Behind them, a few mothers and caregivers smiled from rocking chairs, their eyes warm and familiar. One of them mouthed *"You're okay,"* as if she could see the blank panic behind Cora's eyes.

But she wasn't. Because she didn't know any of them. Not the woman in the navy cardigan with the sleeping baby on her chest. Not the little boy clutching a book like it was a treasure. Not even the child who jumped up and ran to her, hugging her legs with a squeal of, *"Miss Cora!"*

Cora placed a trembling hand on the girl's back, her body moving as if on autopilot. She forced a smile. "Hi, sweetie…" Her voice cracked on the last word, foreign in her mouth.

The little girl looked up, frowning. "You look tired," she said.

Cora nodded once. "I am."

She stepped farther in, crossing the threshold like it might swallow her whole. The familiar layout of the reading area didn't spark anything. No memories, no comfort. Just the disquieting sense of having been carefully dropped into a life she couldn't remember living.

At the front of the carpet was a chair draped in a cozy crocheted throw blanket, a stack of children's books arranged beside it. She walked toward it, every step rehearsed and yet utterly unfamiliar. As she sat down, the chatter of the children quieted, and all eyes turned to her as she opened the top book. Her hands didn't shake, but only because she focused every ounce of herself on stillness. The title page read: *The Curious Caterpillar*. Her name was printed beneath it in neat serif letters.

Cora Atler. Her name. A name she suddenly wasn't sure how to wear. She cleared her throat, willing her voice to sound like it belonged to someone in control.

"Once upon a time," she began, as the room leaned in to listen, "there was a caterpillar who woke up one morning and didn't know who or what he was."

The children watched her, wide-eyed. And for a moment, Cora let the story carry her, even if she didn't remember writing it. She found a sense of solace in the room and loved watching the children—the anticipation, the quiet hum of excited little voices. Before she had ever dreamed of owning *Huckleberry Wonders*, she had been a storyteller, weaving whimsical tales late at night after Avalina was asleep, filling pages with adventure and wonder. The stories she wrote weren't just for children; they were for the little girl she had once been, the one who had longed for stories that made her feel safe, understood, and free to dream. And, today, after two months of grueling physical therapy, scans and doctor appointments, she was ready to dive back into the life she had seemingly grown to love.

As she adjusted herself in the rocking chair, Avalina climbed onto the armrest, her small fingers latching onto Cora's sleeve. *"Read my favorite one next,"* she whispered.

Cora smiled knowingly and reached for *The Starcatcher's Secret*, another one of her own books. It was a tale of a brave little girl who bottled stardust to light the way for lost travelers. It was the first book she had published under her name, a leap of faith that had led her here. She opened the book, the scent of its crisp pages familiar, comforting. As she began to read, the store seemed to hush, the world outside pausing for this sacred moment of imagination. Avalina leaned her head against Cora's arm, and for just a little while, they were wrapped in the magic of words, of stories, of a world they had built together.

After the story ended and Avalina cuddled herself into her lap, Cora's mind drifted off to the night before, when Cora had woken to the familiar creak of her bedroom door, soft footsteps padding across the floor like whispers.

"Ava?" she had murmured, rubbing sleep from her eyes.

Avalina had stood at the side of the bed, clutching her stuffed fox by its ear. Her curls were tangled, cheeks pink from sleep, her expression unreadable in the early gray light.

"I had a dream," she had whispered.

Cora had sat up straighter, then reached for her. *"Come here, Wren."*

Avalina climbed into the bed, curling into the warm hollow of her mother's side. She was quiet for a moment, her tiny fingers fidgeting with the edge of Cora's sleeve.

"There was a man," she had said finally, voice small.

A slow chill had crept down Cora's spine. *"What did he look like?"*

Avalina had looked up at her, serious in that eerie, too-old-for-her-age way she sometimes had in dreams. *"He didn't have a face, not really. But I could hear him smile. He had long fingers. He told me to go put on my jammies and meet him in the cemetery."*

Cora had blinked, heart knocking against her ribs. *"The what?"*

"The cemetery," Avalina had repeated, like it was the most natural word in the world.

But it wasn't. Cora had never once mentioned a cemetery. Avalina had never even been near one. There was no reason she should know the word, let alone use it like that.

"I asked where it was," Avalina had continued, *"and he said, 'You'll know.'"*

Cora had kept her voice calm, but inside, panic flared. *"And did you?"*

"No," Ava said, shaking her head. *"I tried to go, but I ran into a wall. The kind that's not really there. But I think he was still waiting."*

Cora swallowed. Her mind had spun—flashes of old nightmares, of people who watched too closely, of whispers behind her, too many shadows under doors.

"Did he say anything else?" she had asked gently.

Avalina nodded, her eyes suddenly wide and grave. *"He said, 'Look for the color red.' I'll try again tomorrow."*

Cora had pulled her closer, wrapping both arms around her daughter like a shield. *"You're not going anywhere, Avalina. Not tonight. Not ever. You stay right here with me."*

But even as she had whispered it, she knew the words weren't a promise. They were a plea. And in the quiet, just under the hum of morning, Cora could swear she had heard something else—something waiting. Cora didn't sleep after that. Once Avalina had drifted off, tucked beneath her arm with her stuffed fox pressed against her cheek, Cora had stared at the ceiling, eyes wide, heart steady only in rhythm but not in peace.

Cemetery.

She had mouthed the word silently, as if testing it in the air. The syllables didn't feel like something made up. They felt real. But she had never said that word around Avalina. And yet—there it was. Cemetery. Long fingers. Red. A smile in a voice. It scratched at something buried deep in her.

When the sun rose earlier that morning, she had made coffee with hands that wouldn't stop trembling. She didn't want to go digging. But she knew she had to. She slipped into the back closet of her bedroom, the one she kept locked. Behind a stack of old children's books and a bin of Avalina's outgrown clothes, Cora found it: a cardboard file box, sealed with yellowing tape and scribbled in black Sharpie:

DELAWARE // 2019 // DO NOT OPEN.

She had hesitated, then peeled the tape. Inside were old notebooks, newspaper clippings, and a worn paperback she once pretended to read just to keep her hands busy in group therapy sessions. At the very bottom, folded between files marked with initials and police case numbers, she found it. A composition notebook. She flipped through the pages.

March 7ᵗʰ, 2019 –

He followed me again. He wore the color red. He knew my middle name. Knew what I wore on Christmas Eve. He said he saw me when I was six. I told the police. They thought I meant Vinny. They told me not to worry.

Cora had blinked, heart sinking. She touched the ink, faded now. Her throat had closed. She hadn't remembered this. Not until now. Avalina hadn't just dreamed. She had remembered something Cora tried to forget. And Cora had no idea how.

After that, while Avalina napped on the couch with Bluey murmuring in the background, Cora sat at the kitchen table, the composition notebook still open in front of her like a wound. She had flipped through entry after entry. Half were nonsense, grief-pourings from a girl unraveling. She faintly remembered that part. The weight of stalking reports dismissed. The messy aftermath. But *this* was something else. The color red. She'd buried him deep. She turned the page.

April 2ⁿᵈ, 2019 –

He said he has always seen me. Truly seen me. I didn't take him seriously at first. I even laughed. He warned me that he remembers everything I have ever tried to forget. He knew about the night my mother drove off that cliff. Now, sometimes I wake up with the strange sense that I'm being watched. Not just a fleeting feeling but a presence, like someone is standing just outside the frame of my dreams, waiting for me to open my eyes. Sometimes, I swear I hear the creak of floorboards, or the soft breath of someone too close. He said I'd never be able to hide from him. Not really.

And now I believe him.

Avalina had stood in the doorway just as Cora stepped out of the shower. Her daughter had looked small there, framed in the soft morning light, curls tangled from sleep. One sock was bunched at her ankle, and in her hand, she dragged her spiral-bound art pad along the floor, its cardboard corner scraping faintly against the wood with every step.

"I made you something," she had said simply, her voice drowsy like this was just another Saturday and not a moment that would stay in Cora's bones. She had shuffled forward, arm outstretched, and handed over the page without ceremony.

Cora had taken the drawing with a faint rustle of paper. She forced a smile, trying to summon the warmth that usually came so easily with Avalina. *"Thanks, baby. What is it?"*

The picture was a child's swirl of crayons in bold strokes of red and green, and black. The lines were jagged in places, purposeful in others. It looked like a field. A stick figure in pink stood near what appeared to be rows of rectangles. Headstones, maybe?

Avalina had stepped closer, pointing with a crayon-stained finger. *"That's me,"* she had said matter-of-factly, tapping the pink figure. *"And that's the cemetery."* Ava's finger slid to a scribbled black shape in the corner. *"That's where The Teacher told me to meet him last night."*

The words had landed like a rock through glass. Cora's smile had faltered, then vanished entirely. Her mind tripped over the name *The Teacher* as if it were laced with something toxic. Her body went still, every maternal instinct tightening inside her like a coiled spring. She had stared at Avalina, searching her daughter's face for a crack in the story—a joke, a slip, a dream misremembered. Surely, she'd misheard. Surely Ava didn't say *that*.

But there was no flicker of uncertainty in her daughter's expression. Just the sleepy, solemn certainty of a child stating a fact.

The Teacher.

Cora's stomach had dropped with a quiet dread she couldn't explain. The name scraped against something in her memory. Something buried but not gone. And suddenly, the drawing didn't look like innocent crayon scrawls anymore. It looked like a message.

And Avalina was already on it.

Cora's fingers had tightened around the paper. Something cold stirred in her chest that morning. The drawing was detailed—too detailed. A wrought iron gate, hunched trees, crooked headstones. A long shadow in the distance. And the figure… faceless and towering. Hands too long, just like in her dream. She didn't even know how to draw a perspective like that. And the word *"CEMETERY"* was scrawled in block letters across the top—perfectly spelled.

Cora had gripped the table. Her hands had gone cold. *"You don't know that word, sweetie,"* she said, trying to keep her voice light.

Avalina had shrugged. *"I just do now."*

Cora was abruptly brought back to the present when a toddler tripped and fell over a chair, sending a chorus of gasps through the shop. She rushed forward instinctively, scooping the little boy into her arms before the first tear could fall. His wide, startled eyes blinked up at her, and for a moment, all the heaviness she carried melted into a soft, maternal calm. She smiled reassuringly, brushing the hair from his forehead.

"You're okay, buddy," she said, her voice a gentle promise, even as her own heart still raced from the sudden jolt.

The boy's mother appeared a moment later, breathless and apologetic, but Cora only waved it off with a smile. Setting the child back onto his feet, she watched him toddle back, and as she turned, she caught her own reflection in the window—haunted eyes, a tired smile, a woman still learning how to exist in a world that kept startling her awake.

Chapter 3

When the Past Whispers

"She thought she left it all behind. But the past doesn't always chase you—it waits in silence, then whispers when you least expect it."

The final page of the storybook fluttered closed, and the small circle of toddlers erupted into giggles and applause. Cora offered a shaky theatrical bow, earning a few gummy smiles and one sticky high-five. As the parents gathered up bags, the bell above the shop's front entrance jingled quietly. Mr. Zillman, the elderly mailman with his familiar wool cap and cheery grin, stepped inside.

"Well, if it isn't my favorite little ladybug," he said to Avalina.

Avalina beamed. "Hi, Mr. Zillman!" She chirped, hopping off the armrest to greet him.

"I've got something special for your mama today," he said, handing a small stack of envelopes to Cora. "And maybe, just maybe, there's a sticker waiting for you in my bag."

Avalina gasped with delight as Mr. Zillman pulled out a shiny butterfly sticker from his satchel, placing it carefully in her tiny hands.

"Say thank you, sweetheart," Cora reminded her, flipping through the mail absently.

"Thank you, Mr. Zillman!" Avalina said, admiring her new treasure.

Cora's fingers paused as she came to a thick envelope embossed with the University of Delaware's crest. She hesitated, heart picking up its pace as she carefully tore it open. Inside was an invitation printed on elegant cardstock.

University of Delaware invites you to the Class of 2021 Reunion— Come, celebrate with us back where it all began!

She exhaled slowly, the words blurring for a moment. Cora's fingers brushed over the embossed seal from the University of Delaware, the gold stamp catching the light just enough to shimmer. The second her skin met the ridged surface, something shifted. It was like the floodgates of her mind burst open. Suddenly, the campus sprang to life—brick paths winding under her feet, autumn leaves swirling in the breeze, the hum of students rushing to class. Laughter echoed in her ears. And then—MJ. MJ, with his dramatic flair and too-loud voice, strutting across the quad like it was his personal runway. Always in something sequined or scandalous, with sunglasses perched on his head, no matter the weather. His laughter, high and contagious, filled the space behind her eyes like a spotlight in the dark.

His voice rang out in memory: "Darling, if you're not causing a scene, are you even living?"

Faces she had forgotten began to surface. Friends. Moments. A life she once lived with color and chaos. All of it rushing back because of that simple, golden seal.

Selah.

Jensen.

MJ.

Back where it all began. Cora hadn't set foot on that campus since she left Delaware behind, determined to start fresh after her Gram passed.

The thought hit her like a quiet ache. Her Gram—her anchor, her constant—was gone. She hadn't let herself sit with that truth fully, not until now. Maybe because remembering meant accepting it. And accepting it meant letting go of the last part of who she used to be. Yet here it was. A thread pulling her back to a past she wasn't sure she was ready to revisit.

"Mommy, what's that?" Avalina asked, peering up at the letter in Cora's hands. "Is it a story?"

Cora smiled faintly, folding the invitation and tucking it back into the envelope. "Not quite, little Wren. It's an invitation."

"To what?" Avalina pressed, her big eyes filled with curiosity.

Before Cora could answer, Harlyn strolled in, her curls bouncing as she took in the scene. Harlyn, Cora's ever-loyal assistant at the boutique, had a knack for appearing right when she was needed most. Usually with coffee or tea in one hand and sass in the other.

"What's all the serious faces for?" she asked, appearing in the archway, holding two cups, steam curling upward from each.

Her copper-blonde hair was swept into a low, messy bun, wisps curling around her temples and neck like wild threads of sunshine. She wore a faded olive cardigan over a striped tee and worn jeans tucked into slouchy boots. There was something effortlessly earthy about her, like she belonged somewhere between a campfire and a rainy bookstore. Her freckles caught the light, and her soft gray-blue eyes held a steady kind of knowing.

"I made the chamomile one," she said gently, extending the mug.

Cora accepted it with both hands. Her fingers brushed against Harlyn's, and for a fleeting second, she wished the touch would unlock something—anything.

"Thanks," she said, her voice barely above a whisper. "For everything."

Harlyn settled onto the floor beside her, tucking one leg beneath the other, her own mug perched on her knee. "You're allowed to feel overwhelmed," she said after a quiet moment.

Cora turned to look at her, studying the face that clearly meant something once.

"Is it that obvious?" she asked.

"Only to someone who knows you."

Cora swallowed, the words thick in her throat. "I wish I remembered what that feels like. Knowing you."

Harlyn didn't flinch or shift uncomfortably. She simply nodded, like she had already learned to carry the weight of that gap between them.

"I remember you," she said quietly. "For both of us, if that's what it takes."

Cora looked down into her tea, letting the warmth rise into her face. "Avalina… she talks about you like you're a favorite part of the world. Like the day doesn't really start until Harlyn shows up." She glanced up, voice tightening. "That means everything to me. Even if I can't remember why."

A soft smile curled at the edges of Harlyn's mouth. "She's special. Brave and full of fire. Just like you."

Cora gave a broken laugh, wiping at her eyes. "You don't have to say that."

"I'm not saying it for you," Harlyn replied, the warmth in her voice unwavering. "I'm saying it for her—and for me."

Cora looked at her then—really looked. At the woman who had stepped into her chaos and stayed. At the hands that had probably braided Avalina's hair and stocked the boutique shelves. At the quiet strength she somehow knew had always been there.

"I must've trusted you with everything," she said softly.

Harlyn nodded. "You did. And you still can."

And even in the strange fog of lost memories, something in her began to settle. For the first time that day, Cora let herself lean shoulder to shoulder with the woman who'd once been a stranger, but now somehow felt like home.

Avalina squealed as Harlyn spun her around, the little girl's laughter filling the shop. "Harlyn! I got a butterfly sticker!" Avalina announced proudly.

"Ooooh, fancy!" Harlyn gasped, twirling Avalina again before setting her down. "You know, I think this calls for a celebration dance!"

Cora watched them with a soft smile, feeling the momentary weight of the invitation lift. Whatever the reunion meant for her, right now, in this space, she was exactly where she belonged.

Harlyn clapped her hands together suddenly. "Oh! Before I forget, I was thinking—why don't I take story hour this afternoon?"

Cora raised an eyebrow. "Really? You sure?"

"Absolutely!" Harlyn grinned. "I even brought the new puppets for the puppet show that goes with it."

Avalina's eyes widened with excitement. "New puppets?! What kind?"

Harlyn knelt to Avalina's level, her eyes twinkling. "A duck, a bunny, and even a zebra," she whispered dramatically.

Avalina clapped her hands, practically bouncing on her toes. "A zebra?! That's the best one! Can I help?"

"Of course, little ladybug," Harlyn said with a wink. "You can be my special assistant."

Cora laughed, shaking her head. "Looks like you've got this under control."

Harlyn gave a mock bow. "You just relax, boss. You look well today! I've got story hour covered."

As the children gathered for the second round of Saturday story hour in anticipation, Cora took a deep breath, grateful for the small moment of reprieve. The invitation and Avalina's dream still weighed on her mind, but for now, she let herself sink into the warmth of the present—

her daughter's laughter, the joy of storytelling, and the little shop that had become her new sanctuary.

Her phone buzzed in her pocket. It was Selah:

Reunion Time! Let's grab Jensen and GO! Give my love to my Avalina! Planning this trip to UD!!!

Though miles stretched between them and their lives had taken wildly different shapes three years ago, with Cora beginning anew in Montana, and Selah staying in Colorado, the thread of friendship between Cora and Selah remained unbreakable. Selah had blossomed into her own rhythm, running Golden Hour Gatherings with grace and grit after saying goodbye to the art world, transforming her love for beauty and order into a thriving event planning business. She was newly engaged to Max Colter, a professional golfer whose quiet steadiness grounded her in all the right ways. Yet, despite the miles and ever-evolving routines, she never missed a call when Cora needed to talk, or a chance to remind her she was loved. Their bond, once forged in college nights and heartbreak confessions, had only deepened with time. They celebrated each other's wins, carried each other's grief, and laughed in a way that made the years disappear. Different stages, different cities, but always the same love.

The scent of freshly brewed coffee and warm huckleberry cakes filled the shop as Cora carried in a tray, offering treats to the arriving families. "Coffee for the grown-ups, huckleberry cakes for the littles," Cora announced cheerfully, setting the tray on the counter. "And maybe an extra one for our fearless storyteller." She winked at Harlyn.

"Thank you, Cora," Harlyn said, accepting the coffee with a grateful smile.

She watched as parents settled onto chairs, their children eager and wiggling in anticipation of the afternoon story hour. Laughter and chatter filled the boutique, but Cora found her gaze drifting back to the invitation resting on the counter.

Class of 2021 Reunion—Come, celebrate with us back where it all began!

Back where it all began. Back to Delaware. Her stomach tightened at the thought. It wasn't just memories of old friendships and the dreams she once had. It was him. She traced the rim of her coffee cup, old fears whispering at the edges of her mind. Had time dulled his obsession, or would returning to Delaware stir it awake again?

"Hey, you." The voice was soft but grounding, and it tugged Cora gently from the fog of her thoughts. She blinked, eyes refocusing to find Harlyn standing a few feet away, one brow slightly raised, a crease of quiet concern between her brows.

Harlyn crouched down to her level, her cardigan sleeves pushed up to her elbows. Her eyes searched Cora's face with the familiarity of someone who knew what silence could hide. "You okay?" she asked, voice low and careful, like she was offering Cora a safe place to land.

Cora drew in a slow breath, her smile tugging at the corners with effort. "Yeah," she said, nodding faintly. "Just… lost in thought."

Harlyn's lips curved, but she didn't press. "Well, don't go too far," she said with a playful lilt. "We've got a zebra to introduce."

Before Cora could reply, Avalina burst forward with a gasp that was pure, delighted urgency. She clutched at Harlyn's sleeve with both hands, her curls bouncing, eyes wide with anticipation.

"The zebra puppet!" Avalina squealed. "Let's start!"

Harlyn laughed, and even Cora felt the warmth ripple through her. For a brief second, the fog lifted, and the room felt whole. Cora exhaled, pushing the past aside. Right now, she was here, in her shop, with her daughter and their little community of readers. She could deal with Delaware later. For now, there was a story to tell.

……

As the afternoon settled in, Cora began to mentally prepare for her busy week ahead. She had never dreamed of becoming a published author, and now, with the release of her new children's book series, that vision had fully materialized. Her debut book series had just hit the shelves, and the response had been overwhelming. To celebrate, her agent arranged a week-long book tour throughout the Midwest, giving her the opportunity to share her stories with young readers far and wide.

"Are you sure you're okay covering the shop all week?" Cora asked, glancing over at Harlyn as she stacked a few books on the front counter.

"Of course," Harlyn replied with a reassuring smile. "I've got everything under control. Besides, I think it'll be fun running things solo for a bit. Gives me an excuse to reorganize the front display the way I've been wanting to."

Cora paused mid-fold, the soft cotton of a display shirt tucked in her hands. Something outside the boutique's front window caught her eye—a flicker of unexpected color against the usual morning gray of Bigfork. She stepped closer, peering past the display. A woman stood across the street near the bench, her hair a wild, unmistakable shade of hot pink. It was striking, like a flame in the fog. She wore a patched-up coat, too big for her frame, and clutched a plastic bag with what looked like all her belongings. She didn't seem to notice the boutique or Cora watching her.

From behind, Avalina's voice chimed in, light and curious. "She has hair like mine, Mommy. Remember? When we dyed it fairy pink for my birthday?"

Cora blinked, the moment breaking like glass under the weight of memory. "I remember," she said softly, her eyes still on the woman who looked nothing like a fairy but everything like a sign.

Harlyn appeared at Cora's side, sipping her second cup of coffee, her eyes following Cora's gaze. "She must be homeless," she said softly, with a tilt of her head.

Cora said nothing at first. The woman didn't move. Just stood there like she was waiting. For what, Cora couldn't guess.

"I wish I could do more," Cora finally said, her voice barely above a whisper. "The homeless population in Bigfork isn't huge, but it's growing. People like her… they get invisible real fast in a town like this."

Harlyn nodded slowly, pressing her lips together.

Cora's chest tightened. She did what she could. She donated clothes and partnered with the shelter when they needed books for kids. But it always felt like tossing a pebble into a lake and hoping for waves. She wanted to help in a way that mattered. Something bigger. Something lasting. The woman across the street shifted her bag and walked on, the pink of her hair disappearing behind a pickup truck. Cora stood still for a moment longer; her reflection ghosted over the glass.

Cora was balancing a large cardboard box against her hip, which she had retrieved from her car a few minutes earlier, to prepare for switching out the window display. The cool air carried the scent of roasted coffee and crisp flowers, and the late afternoon sun cast golden hues along the bustling business district sidewalk. She shifted the weight of the box, struggling to peek around its edges as she made her way up the sidewalk.

She never saw him coming.

Lincoln McAlister had been preoccupied with a call, his deep voice rumbling as he navigated the sidewalk. His attention was split between his phone, a file folder held under his arm, and the to-go coffee cup in his hand. He didn't register the petite woman lugging a box directly into his path. Until it was too late.

They collided with an unceremonious oof, the force jarring Cora back a step as the box tumbled from her arms. A flurry of pastel tissue paper, tiny onesies, and miniature storybooks burst across the sidewalk like confetti at a surprise party. Lincoln's phone skidded across the pavement, his coffee tilting in slow motion before splattering onto the concrete, thankfully missing them both by inches.

"Whoa—" he breathed, instinct kicking in as he reached forward and caught her by the arms, steadying her before she completely lost her balance.

Cora looked up, momentarily breathless, not from the impact, but from him. Lincoln stood there in a crisp white dress shirt, sleeves rolled just enough to reveal tanned forearms and the sleek edge of a silver watch. His charcoal slacks were sharp, creased, tailored to perfection, and a loosened navy tie hinted at a long morning already behind him. His tousled blonde hair looked charmingly at odds with the rest of his polished appearance, like he'd run his hand through it one too many times between meetings. There was a faint stubble along his jaw, and a warmth in his piercing blue eyes that made it hard to look away.

"Are you okay?" he asked, voice laced with concern and just a trace of laughter.

Cora blinked, somewhere between mortified and amused. "I think so. My dignity, however, might need CPR."

Lincoln let out a soft chuckle, rubbing the back of his neck. "Pretty sure I just lost a battle with gravity, too. So, we'll call it even."

She glanced at the mess between them and let out a groan. "Great. Now my entire display is in the street."

Without hesitation, Lincoln crouched and started gathering onesies and shaking off stray leaves before stacking them neatly. "These are adorable," he mused, holding up a tiny pink bodysuit with the words *Little Dreamer* in golden script. "I don't suppose this comes in my size?"

Cora snorted, crouching to join him. "Not unless you can squeeze into six to twelve months."

"I like a challenge," he said, his grin disarming.

Cora took the onesie from his hands, their fingers grazing in the exchange. Warmth fluttered through her chest, unexpected but not unwelcome.

"I appreciate the help," she said, shifting to gather the rest of her things. "I own the boutique right here. I was restocking the display."

Lincoln glanced up at the shop's whimsical window display, soft pastel banners draped over the words *Curated for Little Dreamers*. "Right over there, huh?" He dusted off a tiny book before handing it to her. "I'll have to stop in sometime."

She arched a brow. "You shopping for a baby?"

"Nah." His lips twitched. "Just looking for another opportunity to crash into you. Maybe outdo this meet-cute?"

Cora rolled her eyes but couldn't help the grin that tugged at her lips. "Well, next time, try not to send my entire inventory flying."

"No promises." Lincoln stood, offering his hand to help her up. "But if I do, I'll make sure I'm holding two coffees."

She took his hand, his grip firm and warm. "I'll hold you to that, Lincoln McAlister," she said, her voice edged with mischief.

His brows shot up, and he grinned like the frontman of a glam band caught mid-encore. "Oh? Already know the name? Groupie behavior, if I'm being honest."

Cora smirked, brushing off her jeans with exaggerated flair. "Relax, Bon Jovi. Your name's stamped across that folder like an album cover. Hard to miss. And, it says 'Literary Finance Agent' in bold colors…so we are kinda in the same frame of work."

"Ah, my greatest hits," he said with mock solemnity, tapping his chest. "I only hand out the platinum editions."

She tilted her head, giving him a slow once-over. "Guess I'll see if you live up to the hype."

Lincoln laughed, hands sliding into his slacks pockets as he leaned back just slightly, like he had all the time in the world. "Oh, sweetheart," he said, eyes gleaming. "The tour's just getting started."

As he turned to leave, Cora watched him go, biting back a smile. Maybe spilling her inventory onto the street wasn't the worst thing to happen today.

Cora sat in the stillness of her boutique's backroom afterwards, the ticking of the old wall clock echoing like a heartbeat in her ears. She'd meant to restock the shelf of bedtime books, but her hands had stilled halfway through the motion, frozen by the weight of something she couldn't quite name. That uneasy feeling again. The sense that someone was watching.

It had become almost constant now, that crawling awareness on the back of her neck, like shadows that didn't belong to her own movements. She'd brushed it off as trauma—residue from her college years, where the memories were coming back in waves. But the doctor had told her something else.

"You're associating memory loss with danger," Dr. Bronson had said gently, eyes kind but firm behind thin glasses. *"And your anxiety about being watched…it's a survival response. Your brain is trying to fill in gaps, so it amplifies the threat. The fear is real. But it's not always true."*

Cora had sat there blinking, as if someone had turned the lights on in a part of her mind she'd tried to keep dim. *"So, you're saying I'm making it up?"*

"No," the doctor had answered with quiet certainty. *"I'm saying your brain is trying to protect you. You've lived through real stalkers, real trauma. But now, when your memory fails you even just for a moment, your mind panics. It assumes the worst. That someone else must be writing the parts you can't remember."*

Now, standing alone in the boutique, Cora ran her fingers along the spines of picture books, the familiar textures grounding her. She wasn't sure which part scared her more: the fear that someone was still out there, or the possibility that no one was and her own mind was conjuring ghosts. Either way, it didn't feel safe. But maybe now she understood why. Not just because of Vinny. But when memory vanishes, the mind creates a villain. And Cora had met enough real villains to believe every one her brain invented.

Night fell slow and heavy back at home with Avalina. Cora didn't turn off the lights. Avalina had gone to bed without a fuss. Her drawing still sat on the counter. Cora hadn't touched it. She paced the kitchen in silence, a carving knife in one hand, a flashlight in the other. It was a stupid pairing, she knew that, but it made her feel armed. In control. Like she could cut through whatever veil had slipped between her past and Ava's present.

Just after two in the morning, the house released a long, aching creak that echoed through the quiet. Cora stood alone in the kitchen, her hands wrapped around a lukewarm mug of tea, eyes heavy from the weight of another sleepless night. At first, she thought the sound was just the old bones of the house settling, as it often did during these cold, restless hours.

But then she heard it again. A soft shuffle, unmistakably the sound of bare feet brushing against the hardwood floor. She froze. There was a whisper next, muffled and fragile. A voice that sounded far away yet eerily close. Her breath stammered, and she strained to listen. More footsteps followed, small and light, moving in the direction of the back door. Panic bloomed in her chest.

"Avalina?" Cora called, her voice cautious and unsure. She placed her mug on the counter and hurried into the hallway, her heart hammering as she turned the corner. Her daughter was standing there.

Avalina stood motionless in the middle of the hallway leading into the kitchen, her tiny frame silhouetted by the pale yellow glow filtering in from the porch light. She was wearing her favorite pajamas. The soft pink ones adorned with little rainbows that had begun to fade from too many washes. Her curly hair was tangled from sleep, and her bare feet were planted firmly on the wooden floor as she stared, unmoving, at the glass-paned back door.

Cora's breath caught. *"Avalina?"* she whispered again.

Avalina didn't respond. She didn't even blink. Her lips moved in a hushed murmur, as if she were speaking to someone only she could see.

"I'm ready now," Avalina whispered. *"I have my jammies on."*

Cora's chest tightened. The chill seeped into her bones, and every instinct screamed at her to move, to wake her daughter from whatever spell she was under.

"No," Cora said, shaking her head as she stepped closer. Her voice cracked with fear. "No, no, baby—you're dreaming."

She lowered herself to her knees and gently reached out, trying to draw Avalina into her arms. But the child flinched and jerked away as if Cora's touch had burned her.

"Mommy?" she asked, voice groggy and small. "Why are we in the hallway?"

Cora couldn't speak. Her mouth opened, but no words came out. Instead, she held Avalina tighter, burying her face in her daughter's hair, rocking slightly on her feet as if it would keep them both grounded. The only sound now was the slow, rhythmic thump of her own heart and the soft, sleepy breath of the little girl she wouldn't let go.

Chapter 4

The Mother, the Echo, the Fight to Stay Whole

"What you can't remember can still hurt you. It waits in the quiet, in the corners of your mind, wearing your fear like a second skin."

Excitement buzzed in the air as Cora packed her suitcase the next morning, carefully folding her favorite outfits alongside stacks of her books, ready for signings and readings. But this journey wasn't just about her. It was a special adventure for her daughter, Avalina, too. It would be their first trip together on the road after her accident, just the two of them, a mother-daughter duo embracing the thrill of travel and storytelling.

In the quiet moments, when Avalina was asleep and the house finally stilled, Cora would sit at the edge of her bed, trying to piece her past together like a puzzle with too many missing pieces. She'd sift through her journals, her texts, and photos, searching for clues or dates that didn't add up, faces she didn't recognize, handwriting that didn't feel like her own. It was like standing in front of a half-finished painting she was supposed to have completed, but someone else had held the brush.

Some memories came back in flashes. Mostly scenes that felt more like dreams than truth. A man's voice. A screaming match in a hallway. The soft, eerie lull of a music box. None of it made sense on its own, but they left her shaken, as if some part of her knew exactly what they meant. Still, she kept digging, desperate for a thread that would lead her back to herself. The truth was hiding in plain sight. She could feel it. But each step closer brought a new ripple of dread, like something inside her was warning her not to look too deep.

At first, she brushed it off as anxiety, a trick of the mind still reeling from the accident, like the doctor said, but the feeling only grew stronger, more insistent. And somewhere deep inside, Cora couldn't shake the fear that it had everything to do with the past her injury wouldn't allow her to remember. What if someone from those missing years hadn't forgotten her? What if they were waiting for her to remember or, worse, to stay silent? The idea rooted itself in her chest, growing heavier with each passing day, until even the daylight felt slightly dimmer, like the truth was hiding just beyond the reach of the light.

Their itinerary was packed with stops in charming bookstores in cities like Chicago, Minneapolis, and Kansas City. Each venue was adorned with vibrant displays of her books, and eager young readers gathered with wide eyes and curious hearts. Cora loved watching Avalina interact with the children, sometimes sitting cross-legged among them during story time, other times handing out bookmarks with a shy but proud smile. Seeing her daughter so immersed in the experience filled Cora's heart with joy. This wasn't just her journey, but theirs together.

Along the way, they would explore new places, indulging in waffles at small-town diners and discovering local parks where Avalina could run free between events. At night, in their hotel room, they would curl up together, reading bedtime stories. Sometimes they'd read from Cora's own book, other times from a new favorite picked up at a store that day. It would be a whirlwind week of laughter, connection, and memories neither of them would soon forget.

The late afternoon sun cast a golden glow over the small Midwestern Park, its warmth stretching across the playground as Avalina darted across the soft mulch. Her blonde curls bounced with each step as she climbed the steps to the slide, her tiny hands gripping the rails with determination. Cora watched from a nearby bench. She had promised herself no distractions, but the vibration in her pocket had pulled her back into reality. One quick glance wouldn't hurt. A text came through from her agent:

Hey, Cora! Can you stay one more day? Final book signing at Wordsmith Bookshoppe—big turnout expected!

Cora sighed. She had been so ready to leave, to take Avalina home, where their quiet Montana life awaited. But one more day? It wasn't a huge ask, and yet it felt like a disruption to the life she was carefully building.

"Mommy, did you see me?" Avalina's excited voice snapped Cora back to the present. The little girl came running, her cheeks flushed from play. "I went down the twisty slide backwards!"

Cora tucked her phone away and smiled. "I saw! That was super brave of you. You're a little daredevil."

Avalina giggled, rocking on the heels of her sneakers. "I was like—whoosh—so fast!"

Cora reached out, brushing a curl from Avalina's face. "Hey, sweetheart, I need to talk to you about something."

Avalina grinned. "Is it about ice cream? 'Cause I was thinking we should get some."

Cora chuckled. "Not quite, but we can definitely get some later." She hesitated, then sighed. "I got a message from work, and they want me to stay here one more day before we go home."

Avalina's smile faded, her small brows knitting together. "But we're 'posed to go home today."

"I know, Wren. I was really excited too. But they want me to do one last book signing. Just for one more day. Then we'll go home for real."

Avalina scuffed her toe against the ground. "But my toys are waiting for me. And my bed. And Mr. Whiskers is lonely."

Cora's heart ached. She knew Avalina had been looking forward to home's comfort just as much as she had. She leaned in, gently tapping the tip of Avalina's nose. "I miss home too. But I promise we'll be home tomorrow night. And I'll make it up to you. What if we have a special adventure here tomorrow? Just me and you, before we leave?"

Avalina crossed her arms. "Like… what kind of adventure?"

Cora pretended to think, tapping her chin. "Maybe we could get the *biggest* ice cream cones in town. And we visit the bookstore together before my signing. You can help me pick out a new book just for you."

Avalina tilted her head, considering the offer. "Can I pick two books?"

Cora bit back a smile. "Two books. And we can even get Mr. Whiskers a new toy before we leave."

Avalina's pout disappeared, replaced by a mischievous grin. "Okay… but only if I get rainbow sprinkles on my ice cream."

"Deal."

Without warning, Avalina threw her arms around Cora's waist, hugging her tight. Cora closed her eyes for a brief moment, holding her daughter close, breathing in the familiar scent of sunscreen and sunshine. One more day—they could handle that, especially if there were sprinkles involved.

The next morning, Cora and Avalina stepped into Wordsmith Bookshoppe. The scent of old paper and fresh ink filled the cozy space, shelves stacked high with books that whispered stories waiting to be told. Avalina skipped ahead, her tiny fingers running along the spines of picture books, before pulling one out.

"This one's about a monkey! Can I get it, Mommy?" She asked, holding it up with bright eyes.

Cora smiled. "That looks like a great choice. You can pick one more, remember?"

As Avalina continued her search, Cora wandered toward the front counter, running her hand along the polished wood. She was about to reach for a book when something outside caught her eye. Through the large shop window, a man stood across the street in a red coat, partially obscured by a lamppost. He didn't move—just watched.

A chill ran up Cora's spine. Her fingers tensed around the book's cover. The man was too far to make out details, but something was unsettling about his stillness, the way he lingered as if waiting for something—or someone.

"Mommy?"

Avalina's voice pulled her back. She turned, forcing a smile. "Yes, Little Wren?"

"I found my second book!" Avalina held up a brightly colored story about a lost kangaroo, oblivious to the tension in her mother's frame.

Cora nodded, stealing one last glance out the window.

The man was gone.

A few moments later, Cora stood in the quiet corner of the bookstore, her back pressed against the cool wall as her hands trembled slightly. She couldn't let herself fall apart. Not now, not in front of Avalina.

Her small, innocent daughter was coloring in the front window, humming softly as she added strokes of pink and purple to her drawing. Cora watched her, a tightness in her chest. The world outside felt dangerous, unpredictable, and unkind at times. She had faced so many storms in her life, more than her fair share, but the thought of Avalina ever facing the same darkness broke her heart.

According to her journals, Cora had promised herself when Avalina was born that she would never show weakness in front of her little girl. No matter what she faced or how hard it got, Avalina needed to see strength. She needed to believe that the world was full of wonder, even if there were shadows lurking. So, when the weight of her worries pressed down on her, Cora would bury them deep, wear a smile, and show her daughter that no matter what, they would be okay. The notion of raising Avalina in a world that sometimes seemed full of dangers felt overwhelming. But Cora knew she couldn't let fear control her. She had to fight to create a space where Avalina could grow up strong, safe, and full of possibility. The thought of her daughter inheriting any of the burdens Cora had carried through life made her chest tighten with resolve. She couldn't let her little girl see the cracks in her armor. Not yet.

Cora took a deep breath and straightened up, her gaze softening as she watched Avalina with the innocent joy of childhood radiating from her. She might not be able to protect her from everything, but Cora would do whatever it took to carve out a world where Avalina could find peace, where the shadows wouldn't dim her light.

"Mommy, look!" Avalina's excited voice broke her thoughts as she held up the book, and Cora smiled, a soft, steady smile that said everything she needed it to say.

"I love it, sweetie. It's perfect." Cora's voice was full of warmth, the kind of warmth she wanted to surround Avalina with every day. And she would, for as long as she could.

Wordsmith Bookshoppe was everything Cora had hoped for when she'd imagined the perfect independent bookstore. Tucked away on a quiet street in a small Midwestern town, the shop had an old-world charm with towering shelves crammed with books of every kind and wooden floors that creaked with every step. The air smelled faintly of ink and paper, and the warm glow from the hanging Edison bulbs gave the space a cozy, inviting feel.

Cora stood behind a small table near the front; her book was stacked neatly for signing. Avalina was seated beside her, coloring in her favorite picture book while Cora greeted the few early arrivals who had come to meet her. She smiled as she spoke to a local woman who had just bought a copy of her latest release, but as she turned to sign the book, her eyes landed on a figure near the back of the store.

He was tall, with dark hair and a camera slung over his shoulder. Wearing a black jacket with a baseball hat looped through his jeans, he blended easily into the crowd, his posture relaxed as he scanned the room. But something about him felt familiar. It wasn't until he took a step closer that Cora realized who it was. The photographer.

Her heart skipped a beat. She remembered him in a completely different city, a different bookstore. He had quietly taken photos during her signing, never interrupting, always on the periphery. They'd exchanged only a few brief words, but she couldn't shake the feeling that he had been observing her more than he let on. Now, there he was—standing in the same bookstore—as if by some strange coincidence.

Cora quickly turned back to the woman in front of her, finishing the signature with a flourish, but she could feel the photographer's gaze still lingering on her, as if waiting for her to acknowledge him.

"Mommy, who's that?" Avalina's voice was soft, her small hand tugging at Cora's sleeve as she pointed toward the photographer.

Cora blinked, her eyes still fixed on the man in the corner. "I'm not sure, sweetheart. I think he's taking photos for the bookstore." She tried to sound casual, but there was something in her voice that betrayed her unease.

She could hear the photographer's camera click softly as he moved around the store, capturing candid moments of people browsing, the soft lighting, the spines of books stacked in neat rows. But Cora couldn't help but feel self-conscious, like he was trying to capture something more than just the store.

"You're doing great, Mommy," Avalina said brightly, her attention already shifting back to her coloring.

Cora smiled as she forced herself to relax, to concentrate on the people in front of her. But when she felt the photographer's gaze again, her hands went still for a moment, her pen hovering above the book's page she was signing. The last time she had seen him, in another city, she had told herself that it was just a coincidence. He was probably a freelance photographer or just someone who loved to capture book events. But now, the feeling in her chest tightened. What was he really doing here? Why had he followed her, seemingly from one tour stop to the next?

Before she could overthink it, the photographer approached the table, camera still hanging loosely by his side.

"Hi, Cora," he said, his voice smooth and calm. His eyes were warm, but there was an intensity to his gaze that made her skin prickle. "I'm Noah. I was at your last signing, in Chicago."

Cora blinked, trying to mask the surprise she felt at the familiarity in his voice. She had assumed their previous encounter was nothing more than a fleeting moment, a passing interaction.

"I remember," she said, offering a polite smile. "Nice to see you again."

Noah nodded, his fingers casually adjusting his camera. "I've been following your tour, and I have to say, you're doing an amazing job. Your energy—it's… It's really something."

Cora felt a flicker of discomfort at his words. She wasn't sure how to respond—was he complimenting her as a professional or just making casual conversation?

"Thanks," she said, her smile more strained now. "I'm glad you're enjoying the events."

There was a pause stretched between them. Cora could feel the weight of his gaze, but she couldn't quite read the expression on his face. Was he just doing his job as a photographer, or was there something more he wanted to say?

"She has your eyes," Noah continued, breaking the silence and glancing over at Avalina. "Would it be alright if I take a few shots while you're signing books?"

Cora hesitated for a moment, glancing over at Avalina, who was absorbed in her drawing. She wasn't sure why, but she felt uneasy about having him so close again. Something about his presence felt too observant, too focused.

"Of course," she replied, her voice a little more clipped than she intended. "Feel free."

Noah gave a nod of acknowledgment, raising his camera to capture the moment. The soft click of his lens was a constant as he moved around the space, snapping pictures of her, the fans, and the bookstore itself. Every click of the shutter seemed to echo in Cora's mind, and she couldn't shake the feeling that this time, the encounter was different.

She tried to focus on the fans who were waiting for her attention, on Avalina, who was still happily coloring. But a small part of her couldn't help but wonder—what was Noah really after? Why had he followed her to this bookshop, to this very moment? The one thing that used to anchor her—her ability to make sense of her unraveling life—was slipping away with each missing memory, and the safety net she once relied on was torn beyond repair. As the signing went on, she felt his presence like a shadow, always there, always watching.

"Here you go!" Avalina chirped as she handed a sticker to an elderly woman. "Mommy wrote the best book ever!"

Cora smiled, signing copies as she chatted with readers. The atmosphere was warm, filled with the quiet buzz of excited book lovers. She glanced up occasionally, catching the glint of camera flashes as Noah moved through the room, capturing moments with practiced ease.

But then—he paused.

Their eyes met briefly across the shelves, and something in his expression snagged her breath. There was a flicker—like recognition or memory, though they'd only just officially met. His gaze held hers—guarded yet knowing—as his eyes searched her face, as if he was trying to place a version of her she hadn't shown anyone in years.

Then, just as quickly, he looked away and disappeared through the back door.

Cora's pen hesitated over the next title page. A chill pricked along her spine, unshaken by the warmth of the room. She didn't know why, but in that brief exchange, something inside her whispered: *He's seen something you've forgotten.*

Her memory, once mercifully blank in places, was beginning to piece itself back together, but the pieces didn't fit neatly. They come in fragments. Sounds. Sensations. Smells. The flashbacks were brief but potent. Too broken to be trusted, too sharp to be dismissed. And the confusion left her unbalanced, like she was walking through fog with a compass that spun wildly, never pointing north. Everyone told her she was safe now, but Cora did not believe in safety. Not anymore. Not when her own mind was the most unreliable narrator she had. So, she stayed vigilant. Hyperaware and always scanning. Always bracing. Because being watched was not a feeling you imagine when you've lived it before. It was a truth your body never forgets, even when your memory does.

Two hours into her signing, her eyes drifted up toward the shop window. There he was.

This time, the man stood directly in front of the glass. He was tall, broad-shouldered, with a scruffy beard. His jacket was red and worn, the kind that had seen too many winters. The kind that triggered fleeting, half-formed memories. But it was his expression that made Cora's stomach twist. His gaze was locked on her—unwavering, laser-focused, as if she were the only person in the room.

Cora swallowed hard, her grip tightening on the pen. The cheerful chatter around her dulled, her pulse quickening.

"Mommy?" Avalina's small hand tugged at her sleeve. "Do you need a sticker too?"

Cora forced a smile, glancing at her daughter before looking back toward the window. But the man was gone.

"Mommy, where's Mr. Whiskers?" Avalina's voice rose in distress as she clutched the empty spot in her arms where her beloved stuffed fox should have been.

Cora's stomach tightened. "You had him when we came in, sweetheart. Let's look around."

Hand in hand, they searched the bookstore, checking beneath chairs and between bookshelves. Avalina's lower lip trembled, her small hands fidgeting. *"He's gone,"* she whispered.

Cora crouched beside her. "We'll find him, I promise."

Then Avalina gasped, her little hand pointing toward the front door. "Mommy! Look!"

Cora followed her gaze. There, on the front stoop outside the door, lay Mr. Whiskers. Carefully placed, as if someone had left him there deliberately. A shiver ran through Cora as she pushed open the door, the cool evening air brushing against her skin. She picked up the stuffed fox and placed it back in Avalina's arms. But as she looked around, scanning the street, the man was nowhere to be seen.

As the book tour came to an end, Cora felt an overwhelming sense of gratitude and equal amounts of distress. Her dream of starting over had expanded into something even greater: a shared adventure with her daughter, an experience that would shape both of them in ways she hadn't imagined. With the final signing complete, they headed back for one more night's stay in the hotel, hearts full, minds inspired, and the promise of new stories just waiting to be told.

When they found their way back to the hotel, Cora wrapped Avalina in a warm towel after her bath, scooping her up as the little girl yawned against her shoulder. Avalina's eyes were already drooping with exhaustion. Cora tucked her in, smoothing damp curls from her forehead as Avalina drifted off to sleep, clutching Mr. Whiskers tightly. With the room quiet, Cora settled at the small desk, pulling out her laptop. She wrote for a while, letting the words flow until fatigue crept in. Finally, she climbed into the king-size bed beside Avalina and let exhaustion pull her under.

Then, the night terror came. Cora jolted awake, heart pounding in her chest. The world around her was muffled, as if the air itself was thick with static. She tried to move, but her limbs felt heavy, like they were made of lead. Her breaths came fast, ragged, each inhale shallow, panicked. The room was dark, except for the faint glow of moonlight spilling through the window, but it didn't feel like her hotel room. The air smelled strange, a mix of damp earth and old wood. It was cold—too cold—and the weight on her chest felt suffocating, like a presence was pressing down on her.

Her mind was still tangled in the dream. A man's face, twisted in pain, his words echoing in her mind—*You belong to me, Cora.* He had said it over and over, and then the darkness had swallowed him whole, leaving her alone in a void of shadows—alone with a thousand voices whispering, *You can't escape.*

Her breath caught as the nightmare clung to her, pulling her under, pulling her back into the blackness. She squeezed her eyes shut, trying to will herself out of it, but the terror held her in its grip, refusing to let go. Suddenly, she heard footsteps—slow, deliberate, coming closer. Her pulse thundered in her ears. Someone was in the room with them, just out of sight, but she couldn't move. She couldn't scream. Her heart raced as the presence loomed nearer, its shadow stretching across the walls. She felt its coldness, its malice, as if they were feeding off her fear. No, no, no… this wasn't real.

"This isn't real," she told herself, forcing the words through her foggy mind. She focused on the feel of the blankets around her, the softness beneath her fingers. Her body responded, a slow shiver running through her as the nightmare faded, the oppressive presence

lifting. Her breathing steadied, and the room began to feel familiar again, the warmth of her hotel room returning. She reached for the bedside lamp, her hands shaking as she fumbled for the switch, flooding the room with light. Cora sat up, her skin clammy with sweat, her heart still racing, but the darkness had gone, and only silence remained. The nightmare was over, but the feeling of being watched lingered—a reminder that some ghosts don't fade as easily as the night.

And outside, beyond the curtain-drawn window, the night held its secrets.

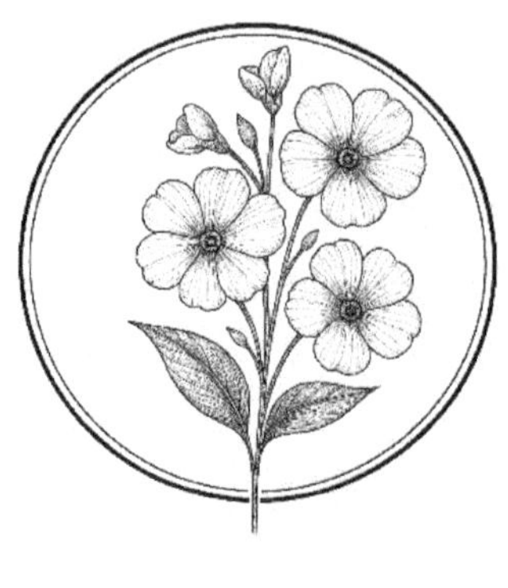

Chapter 5

Whispers in The Floorboards

"Sometimes the quietest voices speak the loudest truths—buried beneath our feet, waiting for someone brave enough to listen."

Cora sat at the small desk in the back of the boutique after they returned from the book tour, the soft hum of the town outside drifting through the open window. It had been three years since they'd moved to Bigfork, Montana, and now with the accident behind them, life had settled into a rhythm she hadn't realized she'd been craving. The boutique was thriving so much that she had considered moving Harlyn from a part-time assistant to full-time help with the influx of customers. The shelves—once bare—now brimmed with an eclectic mix of children's books, crocheted toys, and the occasional rare finds from her travels. Cora's memory was not fully back, but some spaces felt sacred, and the boutique was one of them.

Cora's display of children's clothes was a haven of whimsy and warmth, where every stitch told a story. Soft pastels, earthy neutrals, and pops of playful color filled the space, each piece designed with both charm and comfort in mind.

The infant collection was a dream of organic cotton rompers, adorned with delicate embroidery of tiny woodland creatures stitched along collars and dainty florals trailing cuffs. Hand-knit bonnets in muted tones of sage, blush, and ivory hung from rustic wooden pegs, their intricate patterns woven by local artisans. For newborns, there were footed sleepers in buttery-soft bamboo fabric, gentle against the skin, with tiny wooden buttons and fold-over mitts for added warmth.

For toddlers, the boutique boasted vintage-inspired pinafores with scalloped hems, paired with Peter Pan collared blouses. Soft linen overalls in warm caramel and dusty blue were a customer favorite, designed with adjustable straps and deep pockets for tiny treasures. Delicate lace-trimmed dresses fluttered from antique hangers, their airy layers of tulle and chiffon perfect for special occasions. On a lower shelf, tiny leather moccasins and soft, knitted booties sat in neat rows, waiting to begin their first adventure.

As children grew, so did the sophistication of their wardrobe. Twirl-worthy dresses in rich jewel tones lined one side of the shop, each with careful detailing on hand-smocked bodices, velvet bows, and pearlescent buttons. Cozy knit sweaters with playful woodland patterns with foxes, owls, and mischievous raccoons were stacked beside ribbed leggings in soft autumn hues. The boys' section featured classic suspender shorts and chambray button-downs, paired with thick cable-knit cardigans perfect for crisp fall days.

But it wasn't just the fabrics or the designs that made Cora's boutique special. It was the feeling woven into every piece. Every outfit told a story, whispered of childhood memories waiting to be made, of twirls in sunlit fields and laughter echoing down cobblestone streets. Cora had built more than a shop; she had created a world where the magic of childhood was sewn into every seam.

Every morning, after Avalina was dropped off at pre-school, Cora would sit down to write. She had fallen into a routine that soothed her soul. First, she'd spend an hour working on her latest book, *The Adventures of Ava and the Magical Forest*, a story she hoped would be as enchanting for Avalina as it was for every child who picked it up. She worked with care, tapping into her creativity in a way that felt as freeing as it was fulfilling.

But it wasn't just writing. She'd spend afternoons curled up with books, immersing herself in the stories she wanted to bring to life. She took inspiration from the world around her. The small-town charm, the warmth of the community, and even the occasional eccentric character who wandered into her store. It was a place of connection, where each person's story was as unique as the colorful books on her shelves.

The community had embraced her even more so after the accident, and she couldn't deny the sense of belonging she felt. Every morning, she greeted the somewhat familiar faces that passed by her boutique, exchanging pleasantries with the local coffee shop owners and the woman who ran the children's museum across the street. Her memory had trapped her in one space in time, yet she refused to yield her smile in any way. Her customers, a mix of young families and retirees, would stop in to chat, ask about her books, or simply admire the collection she had carefully curated.

Cora had become a beloved figure in Bigfork. Children waved to her when they passed by, their parents offering warm smiles as they picked out a new book for bedtime stories. She began reading her stories in classrooms around town, always leaving them with a surprise class set. It was everything she had hoped for, a chance to build a life where she was known for something good, something real. She was more than the woman running from a past she couldn't shake or a memory she couldn't keep. Here, in this sleepy little town, Cora had started to feel like she belonged. And yet somehow, with the uncertainty caused by the accident, she thrived.

But as peaceful as it seemed, there were moments when Cora couldn't escape the nagging feeling that something was just *off*. It was subtle at first. Strange, unmarked packages began arriving at the boutique. One was a box filled with old children's books, their pages yellowed and brittle. Another was a collection of vintage toys, a hand-carved music box with intricate detail. But it wasn't the items themselves that unsettled her—it was the note tucked inside each package:

I haven't forgotten about you, Cora.

The first note made her heart race. It was the kind of cryptic message that didn't just send a shiver down her spine—it settled like ice in her gut. She quickly tucked the note away in a drawer. It didn't take long before more packages arrived, each stranger than the last. A faded photograph of her from a few years ago. A tattered journal, its pages filled with scribbled, incoherent thoughts. She couldn't help but feel like someone was watching her, lurking in the shadows.

Then there were the fleeting glimpses. Faces Cora didn't recognize at first—until she did. They were people from her past, people who shouldn't have any reason to be in Bigfork. She saw one of them—a tall, dark-haired man—through the window of the bakery one afternoon. He was staring directly at her, his eyes cold and unreadable. She'd caught sight of him just as he disappeared around the corner, but it was enough to make her stomach turn. Another time, she spotted a woman in the park, standing under a tree, watching her with an intensity that made her skin crawl. But when she turned to look again, the woman was gone.

It wasn't just the strange occurrences. It was the feeling that they were connected. Someone was out there—someone who knew her past too well—and they were trying to send a message. But Cora refused to let fear take hold. She had worked too hard to build this life, to create a safe space for Avalina, to let shadows from the past destroy what she had worked for. She couldn't let herself live in constant fear, not when things were finally going well. She had to trust that, no matter what happened, she would be able to protect her daughter and keep their lives intact.

On the good days, when the sun was warm and the air smelled like fresh-baked muffins, she could almost forget about the lingering dread clinging to her. She'd meet with the other shop owners for lunch, chatting about the town's upcoming festivals, laughing with friends who had become as close as family. It felt like the kind of life she had always wanted.

As the days passed, Cora grew more vigilant. She'd scan the crowd whenever she left the boutique, watching for familiar faces in the distance. She had learned, over the months, how to stay alert, how to pick up on the smallest signs that something wasn't right. And even though Bigfork was becoming a place she still cherished, the quiet whispers of her past followed her, like shadows stretching long into the night. Still, she pressed forward, determined to carve out a life here, to make sure Avalina grew up in a world full of possibility and safety. And for all the unease the strange happenings caused, Cora knew she couldn't let them overshadow what she had worked so hard to build. Not yet. Not ever.

That night, sleep never came. Cora lay stiff beneath the blankets, eyes fixed on the ceiling as shadows crawled across the walls. Her heart thudded like a drum without rhythm, her thoughts looping endlessly between fear and disbelief after yet another sleepwalking episode with Avalina. By midnight, she abandoned the illusion of rest.

The next morning, Avalina settled onto the living room rug, legs tucked neatly beneath her in a practiced little pose that made her look older than three. The coffee table in front of her was a rainbow mess of crayons spilled like candy, their wrappers peeled, paper curling at the edges. Cora stood a few feet away in the kitchen, half-heartedly assembling sandwiches she couldn't bring herself to finish. Her gaze kept drifting back to Avalina.

Avalina's tongue poked from the corner of her mouth in concentration, but she wasn't humming like usual. No soft melody under her breath, no giggles when the crayons rolled away. Just silence, focused and eerie, like she was listening to something no one else could hear. Avalina reached for the black crayon with a slow, deliberate hand. Her fingers curled around it tightly, and she began to draw again. Slow arcs, controlled strokes—something curved and rectangular taking form.

Cora edged closer, wiping her hands on a dish towel.

"What're you working on, honey?" she asked, trying to sound light.

Avalina didn't look up. "The red box."

Cora blinked. "What red box?"

"The one under the floorboards," Avalina said matter-of-factly. "With the shiny letters and the pictures of you with the purple on your arm."

Cora's breath caught and the air thinned. The room began to tilt, a slow shift like gravity had betrayed her. She took another step forward and dropped to her knees beside Avalina. "Sweetheart… where did you hear about that box?"

Avalina shrugged slightly, still focused on her drawing. "I didn't hear it."

Her tiny hand added the last detail—a latch at the front. Then she looked up with eyes too wide, too calm.

"He showed me," she said softly.

Cora's voice cracked. "Who?"

Avalina turned the drawing around and held it up with a quiet kind of pride. "The Teacher."

Cora stared. It was an exact rendering. The red lockbox she hadn't seen in nearly six years. Every corner, every latch, every dent drawn with unsettling accuracy. The same box she'd buried beneath the loose floorboards of her old apartment in Delaware.

Unlike the rest of her past of fractured, forgotten, or forcibly erased moments, the red lockbox had remained—not in sight, but in memory. It was the one thing she'd allowed herself to keep—and to remember. A secret she never wrote down, never spoke aloud.

Her breathing slowed and her fingers tightened around the edge of the paper as a slow chill crept up her spine. But Avalina had no way of knowing about it. And yet, here it was. Drawn in her daughter's hand. A mark from a past Cora had buried under floorboards and time. Her pulse thundered in her ears. The room suddenly felt smaller, darker, as if the walls themselves were listening.

Avalina dropped her crayon. *"Mommy,"* she whispered suddenly, her face changing. *"He says I have to tell you something."*

Cora's heart stopped. "What is it?"

Avalina leaned in and whispered into her ear, soft as breath: *"He says you're the lesson. I'm just the echo."*

Cora recoiled.

Avalina blinked, confused. "Are you mad?" she asked.

Cora grabbed her and pulled her close, trying not to cry. "No, baby. No. You didn't do anything wrong."

But something was *very, very wrong.* Cora knew it wasn't just memory, it wasn't an imaginary friend—it was something reaching across *time.*

Chapter 6

A Slow Turn Toward The Light

"Redemption isn't a light switch. It's a slow turning of the soul towards something softer."

It was a quiet Tuesday morning when Cora first met Rowan. The sun was barely up, and Avalina had just been dropped off for pre-school. Cora was sorting through a stack of new books that had arrived the day before. She loved mornings like this, when the world felt still. It was the kind of peace she craved. A calm before the inevitable rush—customers, mothers with children in tow, curious book lovers, and the occasional neighbor looking for a chat.

Cora was halfway through unpacking a box of beautifully illustrated books about ancient myths when she looked up as a man stepped into the shop, a familiar warmth in his dark eyes. He looked out of place, at least at first. He was tall with shaggy dark hair that fell a little too carelessly over his forehead. But there was a kind of comfort in his presence, something grounded and steady that Cora couldn't quite place.

"Good morning," he said, his voice warm, like the kind of tone one would use when speaking to someone they knew would be a part of their day for a while. "I'm sorry to barge in. I heard about this place from a colleague, and I've been meaning to check it out. I'm Rowan."

Cora's smile was genuine as she set the book down. "No barge at all. Welcome to my little corner of the world. Do I know you?" She extended her hand, noting the way his handshake was firm but kind. There was a calmness about him, an air of reassurance she didn't realize she needed.

Rowan was the kind of man who walked into a room and immediately gave off a warm, grounded energy. He had tousled, carefree curls that fell just past his ears, like he forgot to get a haircut or maybe just didn't care to. His beard was thick and slightly overgrown, giving him a wild, almost mountain-man look, though it was more endearing than intimidating. Ink traced down his forearms, visible with the sleeves of his fitted Henley rolled up, and each tattoo seemed to hint at a story—some deeply personal, some probably spontaneous. He wore old Levi's that fit like a second skin, paired with boots that had seen their share of dirt roads and scuffs. Despite the rough exterior, there was a gentle edge to Rowan: a guy who would fix a bookshelf, quote ancient philosophers mid-lesson, and hold your gaze like he actually heard what you were saying.

"I don't believe we have met. I teach at the junior high," Rowan said, his eyes scanning the shelves before landing back on her. "I'm a history teacher. Figured a bookstore like this would be a good way to introduce my own kids to the magic of reading."

Cora nodded, her curiosity piqued. "That's great. We have a whole section for young readers, if you're interested in some recommendations for them."

Rowan smiled, but there was something in his eyes that made Cora pause. He had the look of someone who had been through more than his share of hardship. But that didn't seem to affect him in the way it had affected others she'd met. Instead of bitterness or weariness, there was a kind of quiet resolve in him, a determination to make the best of things and rebuild when things fell apart.

He glanced at her again, this time with a softness in his expression. "I lost my wife a year ago. It's just me and the kids now." He cleared his throat, almost as if he hadn't meant to say it, but the words were already out in the open. "I'm still figuring out what it means to raise them on my own. But they enjoy reading—always have."

Cora's heart twinged at the vulnerability in his words, the weight of his confession. She understood that kind of loss, the quiet ache that never completely left. She didn't ask for details, not yet, but there was something in his openness that made her want to know more.

"I'm sorry," she said softly. "It must be hard. Raising two kids on your own… It's not easy with one. I'm recovering from a car accident and lost some of my memory. It's been rough. And, I have a daughter named Avalina who keeps me on my toes."

As soon as the words left her mouth, Cora blinked—surprised by her own honesty. The admission tumbled out so easily, so openly, as if the weight of it had been waiting for release. She hadn't planned to say that. Not yet—and not like that.

He gave a small nod, his smile tinged with both sadness and warmth. "I'm not sure who trumps who here. It's definitely a challenge. But they're kids. They're resilient."

There was something about the way he spoke about his children. He had a deep affection for them—a devotion to making their world a stable, loving place. It stirred something inside Cora. She wasn't used to seeing a man so wholly dedicated to his family, to giving them the best life possible, even after everything he'd been through. It was refreshing, and it made her wonder how she might have offered Avalina a life like that if her circumstances were different.

Rowan shifted his weight, clearly looking for a distraction from the heavier topic. "Are you new to Bigfork?" His voice was gentle, as if he truly wanted to know.

Cora hesitated. She wasn't one to share her past openly, not yet, not with someone she'd just met. But there was something about him that made her feel, if not comfortable, then at least safe enough to offer the barest of truths. "I'm from Colorado. I needed a fresh start. My daughter and I… we were looking for a place to call home, somewhere we could settle and put down roots. Bigfork seemed like the right fit. Been here three years now."

He nodded, his gaze thoughtful. "Sounds like it's been a good fit for you. Your store's got a great vibe. The kids must love it."

Cora smiled, feeling a small sense of pride. "They do. And I love meeting all the parents, hearing their stories, and connecting with the community. It's been… healing, in a way."

"Good," he said simply, his eyes softening as he looked around the shop once more. "You're doing something great here. Not just for the kids, but for the whole town."

Cora felt a warm flush of gratitude. "Thank you," she murmured, not sure how to say just how much his words meant.

The conversation shifted after that, light and easy, as they both settled into the rhythm of casual chatter. Rowan asked her about her favorite books, and she shared a few suggestions for his kids. He talked about the junior high, his students' antics, and the little moments of joy that kept him going, despite the weight of responsibility on his shoulders. They spoke for nearly an hour before he finally realized the time.

"Looks like I've kept you longer than I intended," Rowan said with a rueful grin. "I'll let you get back to work. I'll come by again soon, if that's alright."

"Of course," Cora said, smiling as he moved toward the door. "It was nice talking to you, Rowan."

When he stepped outside, Cora stood there for a moment, watching him walk down the street, his figure fading into the morning light. There was something about him. Something kind, steady, and patient that felt different from anyone she had met in a long time.

Over the next few weeks, Rowan returned to the boutique, slowly but surely. Sometimes he came in alone, browsing for books for his kids. Other times, he brought them with him—an energetic boy with messy hair named Seth and a shy little girl who clung to his side named Tessa, both eager to choose a new book for their nightly reading ritual. Cora grew to enjoy their visits, each one adding another layer of familiarity to their budding relationship. They would talk about books, the town, parenting, and life in general. Rowan's warmth was comforting, but it was also his patience that struck Cora most. He didn't rush her, didn't ask for more than she was willing to give.

They began to share moments that hinted at something deeper, something beyond friendship. A casual touch on Cora's arm as he handed her a book, the way he'd smile a little longer when their eyes met, the way their conversations seemed to linger after the others had faded. Cora was cautious, careful. She had been hurt before, her memory was lapsed, and her heart had been broken in ways that still haunted her. But she couldn't deny the pull she felt toward Rowan. The way he made her feel safe, understood. She wasn't ready to open herself completely, not yet. But with Rowan, she found herself beginning to trust again. In the steadiness of life in Bigfork, a quiet romance began to bloom between them, one that didn't rush but instead took its time, like a flower growing in the sunshine. It was gentle, it was warm, and it felt like a new beginning, even though the past would always be a part of them both.

At home, Cora had set Avalina's art supplies aside, hoping the drawings and chatter about *The Teacher* would stop. Bigfork was home, and with each passing day, the walls she'd built around herself seemed a little less necessary.

It was one of those mornings when Gemma and Miles moved into the space next door to her boutique. The small, vintage storefront had sat empty for months, its dusty windows a quiet buffer between her world and the rest of the block. When the *"Opening Soon"* sign appeared in the window, Cora felt a twinge of curiosity. She was busy restocking shelves when in walked a woman with bright red hair and a sunbeam of a smile. Gemma radiated warmth, the kind that made people lean in before they even realized they were doing it. She had that magnetic, untamed energy that made it hard to look away.

"Hi! I'm Gemma," she said, stepping inside with the easy confidence of someone used to being welcomed. "I'm so sorry to interrupt, but we're just getting settled next door, and I wanted to introduce myself. My partner, Miles, and I just opened up the craft shop—*The Art Nest.* It's a cozy refuge for anyone needing to breathe again."

Cora blinked at the word *partner*, unsure why it snagged at her. Maybe it was the ease with which Gemma said it. Maybe it was how the word hung in the air, soft but charged. Or maybe it was just that when Miles walked in a moment later—tall, olive-skinned, effortlessly handsome—he didn't so much glance at Gemma as he did Cora. And something about the way Gemma noticed but didn't mind made Cora's skin prickle.

Inside *The Art Nest* was warm and dreamy, filled with little stations designed to draw you inward. Pottery wheels spun slowly in the corner, inviting hands to shape and mold. Collage tables overflowed with magazines, scraps of fabric, and trays of glue sticks. A curated bar lined with local wines and craft beers stood like a quiet companion, ready to loosen tongues and steady nerves. Everything about the place whispered intimacy, encouraged vulnerability, and offered quiet permission to release whatever you were holding in.

"We've heard a lot about your children's boutique," Gemma said, her eyes scanning the soft pastels and storybooks lining Cora's shelves. "We're really excited to be neighbors."

Cora offered a polite smile, but her hands stayed busy folding tiny shirts that had already been folded. Something about the couple—their seamless connection and subtle openness—unsettled her. It wasn't that they were inappropriate. Just…fluid. Unapologetically free. She wasn't sure whether she envied that freedom or feared what it might stir in her.

And just like that, the rhythm of her space had shifted. Cora couldn't help but smile, though it came with a soft hesitation. She wasn't used to immediately forming connections, especially not with couples, not after everything she had read about in her journals lately. She'd trained herself to keep things at arm's length, to remain composed and pleasant but unavailable. But Gemma's warmth had a way of reaching past that, uninvited but not unwelcome, like sunlight slipping through a window she hadn't meant to open.

She stepped around the counter and took Gemma's outstretched hand. "I'm Cora," she finally said. "Welcome to the neighborhood. I've heard a little about your shop. I'm sure it'll do great here."

Gemma's eyes lit up. "I hope so. We're still getting settled, but we've got big plans. Workshops, art nights, and maybe even a few open-studio evenings with wine and music. It's all about creating a space where people can come, make something beautiful, and… unwind and let go a little. I think this town could use more of that."

Cora nodded slowly, intrigued in spite of herself. "That sounds wonderful. I've been trying to find ways to get more involved with the community, too."

Even as she said it, Cora felt a slight tightening in her chest. There was something about the way Gemma spoke—so open, so easy. So free. It made Cora feel both drawn in and exposed, like standing too close to a flame she couldn't decide was comforting or dangerous.

Gemma lounged against the edge of the table, a loose-fitting tank top slipping off one shoulder, revealing the delicate line of her collarbone. The soft fabric clung just enough to suggest the curves underneath, swaying slightly each time she shifted. Her long silk skirt shimmered as she moved, split right up the center, exposing glimpses of smooth, tanned thigh when she walked. Everything about her felt effortless, like she hadn't dressed to seduce anyone, yet somehow she always did.

Cora wasn't used to women like Gemma. Women who took up space without apology. Women who looked at you too long, who touched your arm when they laughed, who carried a kind of sensuality that made the air between you feel too warm. It stirred something in her. Not quite envy. Not quite desire. Something unnamed. Something dangerous.

Just then, Miles stepped in, leaning casually in the doorway as if he'd been there the whole time. He had that relaxed confidence that didn't beg for attention but always got it anyway. His button-down shirt hung open, revealing a chiseled chest that looked like it belonged in a cologne ad or splashed across the cover of *GQ*. Tanned skin, defined lines, and effortless allure. He smelled faintly of sun and cedar, like he'd just returned from somewhere warm and far away. His dark hair was tousled in that intentional, careless way, and there was a faint stubble along his jaw that made him look both charming and just a little dangerous. His smile was easy as he raised a hand in greeting. It was like he was in on a secret the rest of the room hadn't figured out yet.

Cora felt her breath catch, not out of attraction exactly, but from the weight of his presence. The way he looked at her sent something flickering down her spine. He didn't have to say a word to introduce himself. The way he stood there said enough.

"Has Gemma been talking your ear off about our place yet?" he asked, his voice warm and low.

Cora let out a small laugh, brushing a strand of hair behind her ear. "Nothing wrong with that. I'm always happy to welcome new business owners."

But the way Miles looked at her, like he saw more than what she was saying, made her pulse shift, just slightly. And when Gemma glanced at him with a smirk, then turned back to Cora without the slightest hint of discomfort, something in Cora's stomach flipped. It was subtle. Innocent, even. But Cora had learned to trust the flickers. The charged silences. She didn't know if it was her past making her suspicious, or something real blooming quietly beneath the surface. Either way, she suddenly felt aware of the smallness of the boutique. Of how close they all stood.

They chatted for a few more minutes with Gemma and Miles sharing cheerful updates about their shop and Cora mentioning the community events she hosted at her boutique. They were friendly, almost *too* friendly, but maybe that was just Cora being cautious. Maybe she was overthinking it. After all, they seemed harmless enough. And that kind of easy connection? She hadn't felt in a while.

Later, after the introductions were over and the boutique was quiet again, Cora found herself standing at the front window, watching Gemma and Miles through the glass as they rearranged displays in *The Art Nest*. They moved around each other with a quiet ease, communicating in gestures and half-smiles, as if they spoke some language no one else understood.

She should've gone back to work. There were shipments to sort, shelves to restock, and invoices to check off. But instead, she stood still, arms folded, the hum of their connection pressing against something tender in her chest. It wasn't just that they were beautiful or artistic or unapologetically open. It was the way they seemed to invite others into their orbit. Gently, but with purpose. The same way others had before. And not just any *others*.

She tried to shake it off. The way Gemma's gaze lingered. The way Miles had leaned in when he spoke, like he already knew her somehow. Maybe it was nothing—maybe they were just artsy, kind and unafraid of closeness. But when the boutique door clicked shut behind them that morning, something inside Cora tightened.

The air felt heavier now, like someone had rearranged the room while she wasn't looking. She moved on autopilot, folding a onesie that didn't need folding, wiping a countertop that was already clean. But her thoughts refused to settle. A wash of memories hit—fast and uninvited.

Declan.

Not the Declan she sometimes allowed herself to remember. But the other one. The one who slowly bent the air around him until she couldn't tell which way was up. The one who made her feel chosen one minute and cornered the next. The one who blurred boundaries in the name of *"openness"* but only ever wanted control.

She suddenly remembered how she used to feel at those parties— like an accessory draped in charm. Like she was supposed to *"get it."* The couples they entertained always smiled too wide, spoke in riddles wrapped in compliments. She remembered the first time she'd laughed it off, brushing past the suggestion like it meant nothing. And the last time, she hadn't because by then, it had already gone too far.

The problem was the blurred lines, the unspoken expectations dressed up as liberation. It wasn't just the shared bottles of wine or suggestive glances. His version of love came with eyes that tracked her across the room. Freedom, but only for him. Her skin prickled now with that same old static. Gemma and Miles hadn't done anything wrong.

Not really. But the way they moved, the way they opened their lives so effortlessly, it stirred a place in her that was still trying to understand the difference between open and exposed.

She pressed a hand to her chest, grounding herself. *'This is different,'* she told herself. *'This isn't then. You're safe now.'*

But memory had a way of curling back in on itself, showing up when you least expected it. And even as she returned to the routine of the boutique, tidying shelves, updating the register, somewhere deep down, Cora knew the past had just knocked on the door again. And this time, it wore warm smiles and smelled faintly of wine and paint.

Cora pressed her hand to the cool glass, then turned away. She had spent so long building a life with clear edges. A business, a routine, a version of safety that left no room for other people's complicated intimacy. And yet here they were again. A new couple. A new current. And something about it made her uneasy.

Later that afternoon, Cora was kneeling beside a display table when she heard the front door open through the quiet boutique. She glanced up, expecting a last-minute shopper, but instead, she found Rowan standing there, his tall frame silhouetted against the glow of the streetlights outside.

He looked slightly out of place in the delicate, pastel-hued world of her shop, dressed in his usual dark jeans and a fitted Henley. But what really caught her attention was the massive canvas tote slung over his shoulder, the weight of it causing him to lean slightly to one side.

Cora stood, brushing her hands down the front of her sweater. "Rowan? What are you doing here?"

A slow, knowing smile spread across his face as he kicked the door closed behind him and strode toward her. "I come bearing gifts."

She narrowed her eyes playfully. "That bag looks like you're smuggling a whole Thanksgiving dinner in it."

He chuckled, setting the tote down with a dramatic *thud* onto the counter. "Close," he admitted, unzipping it. "But I had something a little more special in mind."

Before she could question him, he reached inside and began pulling out items one by one. First, he draped a folded cream-colored blanket over his arm. Then, a wooden charcuterie board wrapped in parchment paper, followed by a bottle of wine and two glasses. Next came a small lantern, already glowing with the soft flicker of a flameless candle.

Cora paused. "You—" She shook her head, a smile breaking through. "You planned a picnic? Good thing Harlyn is picking Ava up from school and taking her to dance class."

Rowan glanced up at her as he carefully stacked the items back into the tote. "It's your late night. I figured you wouldn't leave work early, so I brought dinner to you."

Warmth spread through her chest as she watched him, completely caught off guard by his thoughtfulness. "Where are we supposed to eat?" She asked, though she was already half in love with the idea.

Rowan lifted the bag and nodded toward the open area in the front. "How about right here. Seems like the coziest spot."

Cora laughed softly, unable to hide the way her heart fluttered at the sight of him standing in the middle of her boutique, determined to make her stop working for just one night.

"Okay," she said, giving in. "But if you get crumbs on my new shag rug, you're vacuuming."

Rowan grinned. "Deal."

With a shake of her head, she followed him through the shop after turning the sign on the door to *Closed*, her heart light and her steps even lighter. Maybe letting Rowan in wasn't as terrifying as she once thought.

Cora sat cross-legged on the thick, cream-colored blanket, watching as Rowan carefully arranged the items from his tote. The front room was bathed in a warm glow from the flickering flameless candles he had placed around them, their soft light reflecting in his hazel eyes. A gentle hum of instrumental music played from the small speaker he had pulled from the bag, filling the quiet shop with an intimate warmth. Then, reaching into the tote one last time, he pulled out something she hadn't expected—his guitar.

Her breath hitched. "You brought your guitar?"

Rowan smirked as he settled onto the blanket across from her, resting the instrument on his knee. "I figured a fancy dinner needed some live music."

Cora shook her head, biting back a smile. "You never stop surprising me."

"Good." He ran his fingers over the strings, adjusting the tuning, then, without another word, he started to play.

The familiar opening chords of *Wonderful Tonight* drifted between them, wrapping around Cora like a soft embrace. Her heart gave a little flutter as Rowan's voice, deep and smooth, filled the space.

"It's late in the evening... she's wondering what clothes to wear."

Cora exhaled softly, completely caught in the moment. His fingers moved effortlessly over the strings, his voice carrying the song with a quiet intimacy that sent warmth curling in her stomach. As he sang, his gaze never left hers. It was like he wasn't just playing—he was telling her something without words.

By the time he reached the chorus, he leaned forward, just slightly, the candlelight flickering between them.

"And I say yes, you look wonderful tonight..."

The final chords faded into the air, and before Cora could even process how much her heart was pounding, Rowan set the guitar aside and leaned in, his eyes locked on hers. The space between them disappeared, and as he tilted his head, his lips brushed against hers. The kiss was soft, unhurried, yet carried an undeniable intensity. The glow of the candles flickered against his jaw as he deepened the kiss, his fingers grazing along her cheek, sending a shiver down her spine. When he finally pulled back, his forehead rested against hers for just a moment, his breath warm against her skin.

Then, with that same teasing smile, he murmured, "Dance with me."

Cora blinked, still caught in the haze of the kiss. "Here?" she whispered, glancing around at the small space, at the blanket spread out between them.

Rowan nodded. "Right here."

Before she could overthink it, he stood, reaching down to pull her up with him. He grabbed the speaker, turning the volume up just a notch as *Desperado* by The Eagles began to play—slow, haunting, and a little too on the nose. Then, with one hand resting on her waist and the other lacing their fingers together, he swayed with her—right there in the middle of her shop, bathed in the soft glow of candlelight.

For three years, Cora hadn't dated—not once. She'd buried herself in motherhood, in writing, in the quiet safety of solitude. But something about Rowan felt different. Natural. Easy. For once, she set her conflicts aside and simply let herself be present, allowing herself the rare grace of the moment. The world outside faded, and for a moment, the only rhythm that mattered was the gentle sway of the music and the steady beat of his heart beneath her hand. Cora let her head rest against his chest, closing her eyes as he pressed a slow, lingering kiss to the top of her head. And in that moment, as they moved in gentle circles on the worn wooden floor, she realized this wasn't just a romantic gesture. This was Rowan showing her, in the simplest, most beautiful way, that he saw her. That he was here.

Outside, Lincoln McAlister slowed his steps as he passed by the children's boutique, his hands shoved deep into the pockets of his coat. The soft glow of the string lights inside bathed the storefront in warmth, a stark contrast to the crisp evening air around him. He hadn't meant to stop, hadn't meant to look inside, but his gaze was drawn in before he could help himself.

There she was. Cora. She was laughing, her head tilted back in a way that sent a pang through his chest. Her curls bounced as she moved, her body light and free, twirling in the center of the store. And she wasn't alone. Lincoln's stomach tightened as he watched the man— tall, confident, with an easy smile—spin her in a slow, playful dance. They moved together effortlessly, like two people who had done this before, who knew the feel of each other's hands, the rhythm of each other's steps. Cora's laughter rang through the shop, muffled by the glass but still enough to twist something inside him.

He should look away. He should keep walking. But he didn't. Instead, he stood there, watching, feeling the weight of what could have been pressing heavy against his chest. He'd never asked her. He'd never even let himself believe he could. And now, watching her in the arms of another man, he realized just how much he had let slip through his fingers. What would it have been like if he had asked? If he had taken that chance? Would she have smiled at him that way? Would she have let him pull her close, let him be the reason she laughed, the reason she danced without a care in the world? The ache was unexpected. Deep and lingering. Lincoln exhaled, finally forcing himself to turn away, but the image stayed with him. Cora, happy. Cora, dancing. Cora, with someone else. And him walking away.

Cora plastered on a smile as she entered Avalina's room later that night, smoothing the usual worry from her face like a mask. *"Hey, Little Wren,"* she whispered, crouching beside the bed. *"Still wide awake?"*

Avalina nodded, rubbing her eyes. "What if I have that dream again? The one where the man is standing in the flowers?"

Cora swallowed hard but didn't let her smile falter. "Well, that would be spooky. But guess what? Tonight's different. You're safe, I promise. And I was thinking…" She tapped her daughter's nose lightly. "How about we stay up a little late and play a game? Just you and me."

Avalina's face lit up. "Candy Castle?"

"Candy Castle it is," Cora said, even though she hated the game. But tonight it wasn't about fun. It was about *distraction.*

They spread the game out on the coffee table, the living room lit in soft lamplight, a candle still burning faintly nearby. Cora let Avalina shuffle the cards, making exaggerated "Ooooh" sounds every time she pulled a good one. She even let herself lose twice. She laughed at all the right moments, answered Avalina's questions with warmth, and tucked a throw blanket around both of their legs.

"I like when we do this," Avalina said mid-game, her voice drowsy now, eyelids heavy.

"Me too," Cora murmured, brushing a curl behind her ear. "Let's do it more often, okay?"

She cleaned up the game slowly, watching her daughter's head tip to one side in sleep. And when she carried her to bed, she held her tighter than usual, whispering promises she wasn't sure she could keep. Cora's hands trembled slightly as she pulled the blanket up to Avalina's chin, pressing a kiss to her forehead while forcing a smile. Her latest drawing still burned in her mind with crayon scratches of a tall man with hollow eyes standing in the cemetery, her hand reaching up. Avalina had said it was just someone from her dream, but Cora couldn't shake the tight coil of dread winding in her stomach. She lingered longer than usual by the bed, brushing back her daughter's curls, trying to quiet the thoughts racing through her head. Was it just imagination… or a memory Avalina didn't realize she'd made? How could she help her if she had no memory of her own? Cora turned off the light, but even in the dark, the image haunted her.

Cora couldn't sleep. Not even close. Her eyes swept the street outside, but the night stared blankly back. No footsteps. No figures. She locked the door. Twice. Then slid the chain across and twisted the knob again just to hear the mechanical *click*. Still, it didn't feel like enough. Cora paced the length of the living room, the paper clenched in her hand, crinkling with every step. She forced herself to toss it into the kitchen drawer beneath a pile of batteries and expired coupons—out of sight but pulsing like a bruise in her mind.

She turned off the porch light, made tea she wouldn't drink, relit the candle that smelled like vanilla and safety, and curled up on the couch with her legs tucked close. The TV hummed in the background, some mindless cooking show she used to love, but the host's laughter grated. She tried to focus on the warmth of the mug between her hands, the flicker of the candlelight against the wall, the weight of the blanket pulled across her lap. Normal things. Safe things. But her mind wouldn't still. It looped back, unbidden, to *another night.*

The first time.

It had been raining. Not a downpour, but that slow, relentless kind of drizzle that blurred the windows and made the world feel far away. She was younger back then—barely twenty, still in school but on lockdown during the COVID pandemic, renting the bottom floor of an old duplex with creaky pipes and a faulty lock she always meant to get fixed.

She had come home late, arms full of textbooks and a to-go container of food from the campus cafeteria. The door was closed when she arrived. Locked, even. Nothing seemed out of place. But when she stepped inside, she smelled it.

Cigarette smoke. Not fresh—but recent.

She didn't smoke. None of her friends did either. Her throat tightened as she set the books down and turned on the hallway light. A single photo was missing from the wall—the one of her and her mother at the lake.

In its place had been a note.

No envelope. Just folded once and tucked neatly between two nails where the frame had been.

"I came here for you."

She'd told herself it was a prank. A jealous ex. A sick joke. But that phrase, that handwriting—it had never fully left her.

Cora flinched, her tea sloshing over the rim and onto her wrist. She hissed and set the mug down with shaking hands, staring at the faint red burn blooming on her skin. The scent of vanilla had turned sour, thickening in the air. She blinked hard, grounding herself in the fabric of the couch under her thighs, the hum of the refrigerator in the next room, the distant tick of Avalina's white noise machine through the baby monitor. But the memory still clung to her like smoke.

She stood and double-checked the locks again, this time dragging a chair in front of the door like that would do something. She hated how paranoid she looked, how irrational it felt, but worse was the feeling of déjà vu that had wrapped itself around her ribs like a vice.

The drawer in the kitchen whispered to her. The picture, buried beneath junk and denial, still radiated something cold. Cora turned off the TV, and silence settled like dust. She padded down the hallway toward Avalina's room, needing to see her, needing proof that this night hadn't unspoiled everything she'd built. She opened the door slowly. There she was.

Tiny, safe, asleep with her little chest rising and falling beneath a blanket dotted with stars. Cora stepped inside, kneeling beside the bed, smoothing her daughter's hair off her forehead.

Please stay small a little longer, she thought. *Please never know what it's like to feel watched.*

Her eyes kept drifting first to the front door, then to the hallway, then back to the baby monitor. Still black. Still quiet. Avalina's room aglow in the soft, pink wash of the nightlight.

Just breathe.

She told herself that like it was a fact, as if it would ground her. But her chest was already tight, her pulse already ticking faster than it should.

It's nothing. It's probably nothing. Everything is fine. Everything is normal.

She kept saying it, but her body knew better. Her fingers felt numb as she walked into the kitchen and opened the drawer to pull out the folded scrap of paper. She didn't need to open it to remember what it was, but she did anyway. There it was, sharp and loud under the overhead light.

She set it aside and moved through the next steps without thinking— scooping coffee grounds, pouring water, pressing the button. The soft hiss and drip of the machine filled the silence like a clock ticking down inside her chest.

While the coffee brewed, her eyes landed on a worn hardcover of *Wuthering Heights* near the fruit bowl. It was one of Gram's old books, the kind with frayed edges and her name scribbled in cursive inside the front cover. Cora picked it up, brushing her fingers over the spine like it might warm her. She held it close, not for the story, but for the weight of memory it carried.

She stepped into the living room and sank onto the edge of the couch, curling in on herself with a blanket wrapped tight around her shoulders like armor. Through the window, the first pale light of morning stretched across the horizon, casting everything in a gentle hush. The world looked calm. Unbothered. But inside her chest, the ache gnawed—sharp and familiar, like a wound she kept pressing just to feel something.

Her coffee sat abandoned on the windowsill. She hadn't even noticed the taste anymore. She just needed something to hold, something to ground her while her thoughts spiraled. She'd read the same paragraph in her book three times. Words didn't stick. They hadn't for days. Beside her, Avalina's favorite stuffed fox had toppled off the couch sometime in the night. Cora reached down, gently set it upright, and exhaled slowly, as if that small motion could stop the trembling inside her.

She walked onto the back porch, the drawing clenched in her hand. Morning mist clung to the trees, wrapping the yard in a hush that felt too deliberate, like the world itself was holding its breath. The paper trembled, or maybe it was just her. She didn't know anymore. A crow cawed from the fence, loud and jarring, as if it were reminding her: this moment is real. Maybe Avalina's dreams weren't just dreams. Maybe the shadows Cora kept seeing weren't tricks of exhaustion or grief.

She took a deep breath, but it caught halfway down. The therapist at the campus wellness center had once told her to let go—*back then*, before the accident.

Before the lost memories.

Just a week ago, Jensen FaceTimed her. The name on the screen meant nothing at first, but the second Cora saw his eyes, something inside her shifted. Not a full memory. Not yet. But a feeling. A flash of warmth, like a room she used to live in. He'd smiled gently, not pushing, just asking how she and Avalina were holding up.

Selah had suggested therapy for Avalina. Jensen suggested simply throwing the art away. Her dad wanted them to come home to Pine Brook, to give Bigfork a rest. It all blurred together with voices from different corners of her fractured past. She couldn't tell if the confusion was from the memory loss or the sheer weight of it all, but her head was spinning. And none of it felt still enough to hold onto.

Cora stood, the chair creaking behind her, and paced to the edge of the porch. The drawing crinkled in her grip, damp from sweat or dew—she couldn't tell. She stared down at it again.

"I know what I saw," she whispered, more to herself than anyone else.

Only the wind answered, rustling the trees as if they nodded in quiet sympathy. For weeks, reality had felt unsteady—like being handed a story to finish without ever reading the beginning. A photo on the mantle she didn't remember placing. A whisper behind the shower curtain that made her question her own mind, like a memory just beyond her grasp. She told herself it was just the aftershock of memory loss.

She looked back down at the drawing. This was what they'd all warned her about. Slippery lines. Memory's betrayal. The thin thread between sorrow and madness stretched too far. But if she was unraveling, why did it feel like someone—or something—was tugging at the thread?

Her heart thudded hard as she stood, the heavy silence pressing in around her. Slowly, she crossed the porch, every step cautious, and crouched by the sliding glass door.

That's when she looked up—startled—to see Avalina standing there, framed in the dim light, her face unreadable and still as stone. No fear. No question. Just watching. But in a blink, Avalina's expression softened, just like that. She smiled, wide and sweet, pressing her palm against the glass.

"Mommy, look! The deer came back," she said, pointing to the far edge of the yard.

Cora swallowed hard, trying to shake the lingering unease as she opened the door. "Come inside, baby. It's chilly. Let's get you back to bed."

Once Avalina was back in the warmth of her bedroom like nothing had happened, Cora reached for her phone with shaking hands. She stepped into the laundry room, shut the door quietly behind her, and found her father's name in her contacts. It rang only once and the FaceTime call was picked up.

"Cora?" Dax's voice was alert, concern mimicking his expression.

She didn't try to explain it. Didn't mention the look in Ava's eyes or how it felt like something—or someone—was watching through her daughter.

"I need you," she said softly. "I don't know what's happening here, Dad. But something's... not right."

There was a pause. Not out of disbelief—but assessment.

"Walk me through the house," he said, his voice shifting into something sharper. Focused. "Windows, doors, anything broken? Any sign someone's been near the property? Gas smells? Burn marks? Anything out of place—no matter how small."

Her throat tightened. "No break-ins. Just... things that don't feel right. Like something's shifted."

Another pause. Then quieter, more personal: "Cora, I've seen a hundred scenes that didn't look like trouble until they were. Trust your gut. Lock everything. Keep Ava close. I'll be there late tonight—with my gear."

Tears welled in her eyes, but she let out a breath she hadn't realized she was holding. "Thank you."

When she hung up, the wind outside picked up, rustling the trees just beyond the fence line.

And for the first time in weeks, Cora felt less alone. Not safe. But maybe—just maybe—less alone.

Chapter 7

Shadows Behind The Glass

"Memories are rarely loud. They creep like dust and stay like the dawn."

The late evening sun cast a mellow, golden light over the quiet town of Bigfork as the SUV pulled up to the curb. Dax stepped out first, his shoulders tense beneath the weight of exhaustion, his usually sharp eyes dulled by hours on the road and too many sleepless nights. He ran a hand through his disheveled, silver-streaked hair and scanned the street like he was still chasing the embers of some unfinished fire.

Isla followed, slipping out of the passenger side with a restless kind of grace, her face pale beneath her sunglasses. Her dark curls were pulled into a loose bun that had lost its shape somewhere around the

Rockies, and the soft lines around her mouth held the tension that only comes from carrying too many worries and not enough rest. She tugged her sweatshirt tighter around her shoulders, despite the warmth, as if bracing for something colder waiting beneath the surface.

Cora gave a small smile. "Hi, Dad."

Then to Isla, polite but uncertain: "Hi. I'm sorry—I…"

"You don't remember me," Isla said softly, offering a small, understanding smile. "It's okay. Dax told me about the crash… about your head."

Before either of them could say more, Cora stepped off the curb and crossed the sidewalk in a few quick strides, pulling Isla in a hug. Isla stiffened at first, caught off guard—but then her posture softened, the tension in her shoulders loosening just slightly. Still, Cora could feel it—the quiet tremble beneath her ribs. A restlessness not entirely soothed by reunion.

Dax approached, his hand coming to rest on Cora's shoulder after taking Isla's hand in his. "It's good to see you," he said, but his voice carried a fatigue deeper than travel. He glanced at Isla, then back at Cora, his brow creased.

Cora nodded, her stomach tightening. "Can I get you guys something to drink?"

"Maybe we could just use a coffee," he said, rubbing his shoulders, straining.

Inside, Isla trailed her fingers along the edge of the bookshelf in Cora's living room, her touch slow and uncertain. Her eyes skimmed the titles, though none seemed to register. Her gaze paused on a silver picture frame nestled between two books. It caught the light just enough to draw her in. She leaned closer, her breath hitching as she took in the photograph inside.

Four college students stood on a grassy expanse, sunlight spilling like gold over their shoulders. The University of Delaware campus, with its elegant Georgian-style buildings, stretched out behind them. Brick buildings, maple trees in full bloom, students in the distance with backpacks and skateboards. The photo had been taken just after their visit to The Kissing Arches freshman year, where the urban legend states that young couples who were separated from the girls' campus and boys' campus, and kiss under the arches five times, will have good luck and a happy future. Their faces were carefree, frozen in a moment that still believed in luck, in love, and in the promise of forever.

Jensen—young and vibrant, his hair wind-tossed, a book clutched against his chest. Beside him stood a tall girl with honey-brown skin and box braids—Selah, based on what Cora had said earlier. Next to her was a guy with warm, playful eyes and a crooked grin—MJ, the kind of boy who probably made everyone feel like they belonged. But it was the last face that made Isla's breath catch.

A young Cora, with her short hair in a pixie cut.

She stood slightly apart, yet somehow tethered to all of them. She wasn't smiling like the others, just watching, as if even then, she knew something the rest of them didn't. A chill swept up Isla's spine. She had seen this girl before—years ago. She reached out and touched the edge of the frame, as if it might confirm the memory rising like a shadow behind her eyes.

"She was there," she whispered. *"She was the girl."*

Footsteps sounded behind her. She turned. Cora stood in the hallway, watching.

But Isla stared at her as if she were a ghost. "Delaware. 2018. The café across from campus. You had a black sketchbook. You used to draw people when you thought no one was watching."

Cora's blood ran cold.

"You… knew me?"

Isla's voice dropped, a tremor threading through it, as if she was reluctant to speak the words but couldn't hold them back any longer. "I saw you once in the stairwell of the wellness center. You didn't see me—I was there visiting my nephew." She paused, her breath catching, and Cora noticed the way her fingers tightened around the edge of her coffee cup.

Isla swallowed hard, the sound barely audible. "You were sitting on the steps, crying quietly—just…folded in on yourself. I didn't know what to do, so I just kept walking. But I've never forgotten it."

Cora felt the floor beneath her feet shift, as if the earth itself had suddenly tilted. The words stuck in her chest, thick and choking. Isla's gaze locked with hers—direct and unwavering—as the room seemed to shrink around them. Cora's body went ice-cold, her pulse stuttering in her veins. She could almost hear the echo of it, as if the word itself had a pulse, a life of its own.

Her thoughts shattered as a bright, innocent voice cut through the tension.

"Mommy! Look what I drew!" Cora's heart lurched. She turned slowly, her legs heavy, as if the weight of Isla's words had seeped into her bones. Her chest tightened, her breath shallow as she looked toward the living room, where Avalina stood holding a piece of paper. Her heart was lodged somewhere in her throat.

Avalina sat cross-legged on the rug, her tiny frame haloed by the late afternoon light filtering through the curtains. A violet crayon was clutched tightly in her hand, her knuckles pale from the pressure. Her expression was disturbingly serene. Her eyes were focused, lips slightly parted, as if the chaos in the room had never touched her, as if the words she'd spoken moments earlier had simply drifted away, harmless.

Before her, the drawing lay still and ominous on the floor.

Thick lines cut across the paper in sharp, deliberate strokes, carrying a sense of purpose far beyond a child's whim. In the center stood a figure—tall, looming—his shoulders boxing in the space around him, too broad, too straight. His face had been drawn with chilling clarity: slitted eyes, cold and reptilian. Unfeeling and unblinking. His mouth was stretched into a grin that didn't belong in the world of the living. It was jagged, cruel, stretched too wide for his head, a smile that *knew* things. Beneath it, scrawled in bold, looping strokes of the same violet crayon, a name sat like a curse:

VINNY.

The letters shouted in silence. Not playful—not imagined. It was something else entirely.

Isla's breath caught. She staggered backward, one hand flying to the doorframe for support. *"Oh my God,"* she whispered, barely audible.

Dax stepped forward, his jaw tight, eyes locked on the page. "Isla—" his voice was rough, uncertain, "what is this?"

Isla didn't look back at the drawing. She couldn't. Her eyes darted to Dax, wide with disbelief. "That's my nephew," she said, voice thin, shaking. "That's Vincent."

Cora blinked hard, as if she could reset the moment—erase it. But the name, the face—it was all there. It was undeniable.

"What?" she breathed, her voice barely her own.

"Vincent Moretti," Isla said slowly, like saying the name might conjure him. Her voice was flat, stunned. "My sister's son. He disappeared in 2020 after some… trouble. I heard from him briefly a few years ago, but the call got dropped, and I never heard from him again."

Cora didn't breathe.

"He was obsessed with a girl," Isla continued, her eyes fixed on the drawing in front of her as if it might come alive. "We never knew who. He sent these strange letters—rambling, obsessive. My sister said he was sick. Delusional. She tried to get him help, but he just vanished. Got wrapped up in a life with bad men after that. The kind you don't come back from."

Cora's knees gave out beneath her. She collapsed onto the edge of the couch, breathless.

"It was me," she said, the words escaping in a whisper as her hands gripped the cushion beneath her. Her gaze went distant, hollow. "He was obsessed with me."

Isla covered her mouth, her face draining of color.

"No one believed me," Cora said, her voice cracking under the sharp weight of remembered fear. "I reported it to campus security more than once. They brushed it off—called him persistent, not dangerous. I never went to the police. He was my TA senior year, but it started way before that. All four years, it kept going. And because he was staff, they acted like he couldn't possibly be a threat." She paused, the next words catching in her throat. "I should've done more. But when he started leaving messages in blood on my dorm door…" She swallowed, her eyes flickering. "They told me I was overreacting."

Dax stepped closer, a tension building in his jaw. "Cora," he said carefully, though the storm in his voice was barely contained. "Are you telling me Vinny was the stalker?"

She nodded, dazed, eyes unfocused.

Isla sank onto the ottoman across from her, her movements slow and uncertain.

"He was one of the stalkers. But Avalina—" Cora turned sharply toward her daughter, who was still humming, still scribbling fire like it was a perfectly normal Sunday. "How could she… how could she *know*?"

Isla looked up now, her eyes wet and wide. "I don't think she does know. Not fully."

Dax ran a hand over his face, his voice lower now, steady but laced with something raw. "I spoke to the department's on-call psychiatrist. Just needed a second opinion on… what we're seeing with Avalina. She said it's not uncommon for young kids. Especially after a traumatic event like a car accident, to show signs of emotional spillover. At that age, the line between imagination, memory, and perception is pretty blurry. They absorb everything—tone, tension, even things we don't realize we're putting out there. If you're carrying trauma, Cora, even if you're not speaking it out loud, she's likely picking up on it. Kids are sensitive like that."

Cora swallowed, her throat tightening. The idea that her daughter's haunting dreams might be echoes of her own buried pain made her stomach turn. Had she passed something on without meaning to? Without even knowing it was still alive inside her?

"The doc said sometimes they dream in symbols that aren't even their own," Dax continued. "It's not literal, not exactly… but it can feel that way, especially when they're deeply bonded with a parent. She called it emotional resonance. Or even transference in extreme cases. And I asked her straight, 'Is it possible for a child to reflect a parent's buried trauma in their sleep?' She said yes. Not proven, but she's seen it. Said it's rare. Unsettling, but not impossible."

Dax exhaled slowly, like he didn't quite believe what he was about to say aloud. "And at first, I chalked it up to stress or coincidence, maybe even projection. But the psychiatrist… she didn't dismiss it. She said when people are emotionally close, it's possible for their subconscious to sync in strange ways. Like a mirror effect. Especially if they're under the same roof, exposed to the same emotional charge. She called it 'trauma transference.' Said it's rare, but she's seen it happen between mothers and children, twins, even partners who've experienced intense events together."

Cora didn't reply. Her body moved before her mind could catch up, propelled by something primal. She crossed the room in a few urgent strides and dropped to her knees beside Ava, the floor pressing cold through the fabric of her jeans.

"Sweetheart," she said, her voice low, careful, as if anything louder might shatter the delicate thread holding this moment together. "Can you tell Mommy where you saw this man?"

Ava didn't look up right away. The blue crayon hovered just above the paper, paused midstroke like a thought suspended. Then, slowly, she turned her head. Her eyes were wide, clear, unbothered, and so calm it unsettled Cora more than any scream ever could.

"I didn't see him, Mommy," she said with a small, tilted smile that didn't quite belong on her young face. "He told me."

Cora's breath snagged in her throat. Her stomach dropped as though the floor had shifted beneath her.

"Who, baby?" she asked, though she already feared the answer.

Ava leaned closer, her nose nearly touching Cora's. Her voice came in a soft, pleased whisper, like she was sharing a secret meant only for them.

"The Teacher," she said, then sat back on her heels with a satisfied little nod.

With one quick, unbroken motion, Ava pressed the red crayon to the paper and drew a tiny square door on the side of the burning house she'd been coloring. The flames she'd drawn licked upward, wild and chaotic, but the door… the door was precise.

She smiled wider, almost proud of it.

Cora turned her head, slowly, her pulse pounding in her ears, each beat louder than the last. Her eyes landed on her daughter, who now sat quietly, cross-legged once more, immersed in a fresh sheet of paper. She hummed to herself completely unbothered, as if nothing about this day had broken the ordinary.

But Cora felt the rupture deep in her bones.

The paper before her was scrawled with red and orange crayon, flames devouring a building in wild, chaotic streaks. Behind the windows, dark stick figures with jagged mouths seemed to scream. In the corner, Ava had drawn herself standing just outside the blaze, smiling as if nothing were wrong.

Cora froze.

Then Ava spoke, her voice soft and singsong, almost like a lullaby: "He said that's how we learn. He said fire makes the echo louder."

Cora's hands trembled as she turned the drawing over, but the image burned into her mind: a building on fire, her daughter smiling. And still, she couldn't breathe. This wasn't just about Cora anymore. This was about the twisted legacy stretching back to her college years, tangled with the years she had lost and the things she had tried *not* to remember. Her connection to Vinny, the violence, the threats, and everything that had followed—*Isla's nephew. Her stalker.* It wasn't just her ghost anymore. It was *their* ghost.

Avalina, so young, so innocent—she shouldn't even be here. She shouldn't be *involved* in this. But her drawings were speaking louder than words.

"Cora?" Isla's voice broke through the fog.

"I—I can't breathe…" Cora whispered.

Dax moved forward, his presence a solid anchor. He placed his hand on her shoulder. "We'll figure this out," he said, his voice gravelly but sure. "But we need to get ahead of it. We need to find him. If Vinny is alive…"

Cora flinched. *"Is he?"* she asked, barely able to get the words out. *"Alive?"*

Isla's face paled. She looked like she was going to say something, but then her eyes darted to Avalina, who was still humming as she colored.

Cora's stomach knotted so violently it felt like it might cave in. Her gaze locked onto Avalina, who sat peacefully cross-legged on the rug, her small hand moving rhythmically as she colored in a darkening sky. She hadn't even looked up.

Cora's thoughts stuttered. That image—*she knew it*. Not from dreams. From memory. Something buried deep. A flash of scarlet in a hallway. A figure watching from the edge of her vision. And now Avalina had seen him too.

Dax and Isla stayed for a few more hours, but neither could shake the gnawing sense of wrongness in the air. Isla had gone silent, her eyes distant, but her thoughts were too deep, too tangled to unravel. Cora could tell she was hiding something.

Dax said little, though he lingered longer than usual, checking the locks twice, walking the perimeter before finally coming back inside. There was something heavier beneath his silence, a truth sitting just behind his eyes. He kept glancing at Avalina when he thought no one was looking, like he was trying to connect pieces he didn't want to fit together.

He knew about a fire. About who started it. About the fact that Avalina's father had been the one to set the blaze that killed MJ. But Dax had decided, at least for now, that Cora couldn't carry that weight on top of everything else. Not yet. There were things Dax hadn't told her. Things about Vinny. His name had come up once in the early days of the investigation, linked vaguely to a stolen vehicle spotted near the building the night of the fire. At the time, it had felt like a stretch. But now, with Vinny suddenly edging his way back into Cora's life, Dax couldn't ignore the timing.

There were overlapping threads that connected in ways he didn't fully understand yet. Vinny and Avalina's father had never been mentioned together, not directly. Dax didn't have proof. But something told him the past wasn't finished unraveling. That the fire, the stalker, the whispers in Avalina's dreams—they weren't separate storms. They were all circling the same eye. And soon, Cora would be standing at its center. So, he said nothing, just kissed her on the forehead before he left and promised to call as soon as he crossed state lines.

Cora watched as they left the next morning, the door closing behind them with a soft thud. Avalina's eyes followed them, curious, but her gaze shifted, suddenly focused on the hallway inside. She reached unquestioningly for her daughter, but Avalina wasn't behind her anymore. She slammed the door shut so hard the frame rattled, her back pressed to the wood as if she could bar something unseen from slipping through the cracks. Her heartbeat thundered in her chest, each thud ricocheting through her ribs like a warning drum.

After they left, Cora turned the drawings over again and again, trying to make sense of them. The girl in the graveyard. The red coat. The burning building. But they didn't lead anywhere. There was no *map*, no answers. Just echoes. Just *fire*.

Later that night, she clutched the wall and watched as Avalina turned and climbed into bed like it was nothing. She sat in the hallway just outside Avalina's door, knees tucked to her chest, listening. Every rustle of the bed sheets made her tense. Every creak in the house felt louder than it should have been, like the walls were shifting around them.

Avalina had gone to bed, unusually calm. Too calm. She hadn't asked for a story or her nightlight. She simply curled under the covers, clutching her newest drawing, a red door, no longer part of the burning house but alone on a black background, floating.

At 3:12 a.m., Avalina giggled.

Cora was on her feet instantly. She cracked the door open, moonlight filtering in through the curtains. Avalina sat upright in bed, her eyes open, but blank. She was facing the corner, speaking to it in a low, steady murmur.

"No, I'm not scared," she said softly. *"You said it's just a lesson. That Mommy learned hers already."*

Cora's heart raced. "Avalina?"

Her daughter turned—slowly, too slowly. Her eyes refocused like something had to swim back into her. Then she smiled. "Hi, Mommy. I was just talking to the wall."

"To the wall?" Cora's voice wavered.

Avalina nodded. "The Teacher says that's where the echo lives. You can hear better at night."

Cora moved to the bed, kneeling. Avalina's skin felt cool. Her pulse, steady.

"Sweetheart, what does The Teacher say?"

Avalina yawned, already sinking back beneath the covers. "That you shouldn't have forgotten. He says remembering hurts, but forgetting is worse."

Then she rolled over, already slipping into sleep.

Cora backed out of the room, heart in her throat, and blood buzzing in her ears. She closed the door and leaned against it, as if her weight alone might hold the world together.

From behind the door, Avalina's voice whispered once more, barely audible:

"Echoes never die, Mommy. They just wait."

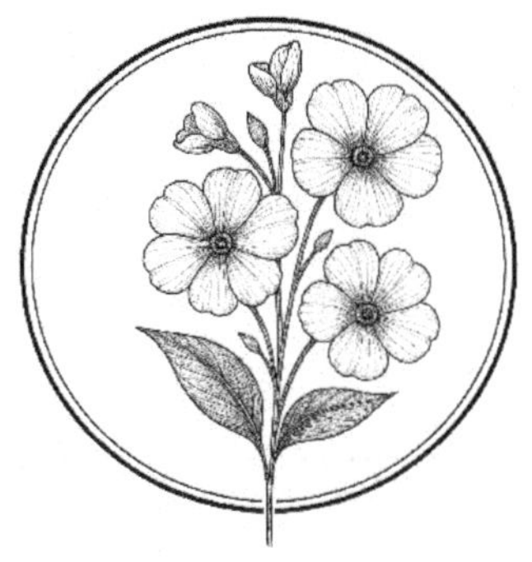

Chapter 8

What The Silence Remembers

"Some names echo long after they're spoken—haunting, hollow and hungry for closure."

The house was still, wrapped in the hush that came just before sunrise. Cora sat curled on the couch, her robe pulled tight. Upstairs, the cries had finally quieted. Avalina had woken again—the third time this week. Another nightmare. Another frantic search for her mother in the dark. Cora didn't go back to bed. She never could after those.

Soft footsteps echoed on the stairs. "Mommy?"

Cora turned, setting her tea aside just in time to open her arms. Avalina crawled into her lap without a word, her cheek resting against Cora's chest.

"I hate the dark dreams," she whispered.

"I know, Wren. Me too."

They sat like that for a long time. Breathing and listening to the quiet that followed the storm.

Eventually, Avalina stirred. "Can we wear them today?"

Cora paused. "Our brave bows?"

A small nod. "Just in case the dreams try to follow us."

Cora smiled softly and brushed the hair from Avalina's face. "Of course we can."

They climbed the stairs hand in hand, the morning just beginning to brighten the sky. In Avalina's room, the drawer of the special things creaked open, and two worn ribbons waited. They didn't match perfectly anymore. One was fraying at the edge, the other had a faint hot cocoa stain. But they were sacred.

Avalina held hers out to her mother. "You first."

Cora knelt, bowing her head. Avalina's fingers worked carefully, tying the ribbon into her mother's hair with focus and a little bit of hope.

Then Cora turned to her. "Your turn."

She tied Avalina's ribbon with the same care, anchoring it just above her temple. She gave it a gentle tug to make sure it would hold.

"There," Cora said. "Extra brave today."

Avalina's smile returned, sleepy but sure. "Maybe we can beat the dreams this time."

Cora kissed her forehead. "We always do. One bow at a time."

The bell above the door chimed softly as Cora stepped into the boutique. It was quiet, just like most mornings. The smell of fresh-brewed coffee from the corner café mixed with the sweet scent of baby powder and pastel fabrics. She'd spent years making this place a sanctuary—a safe haven for herself and her daughter. The cozy little corner of the world where they could escape the outside.

But now? Now, there was no escaping.

Avalina, skipping alongside her mother, pulled a colorful stack of picture books from the shelf. Cora watched her for a moment, her heart heavy as she noticed Avalina's usual joyful energy had been replaced with something else. An almost… *knowing* look in her eyes.

"I want this one, Mommy," Ava said, her small voice bright and sure as she held up a picture book. A soft pink bunny danced across the cover, its ears flopping in mid-hop beneath a sky of watercolor stars.

Cora smiled, a tired warmth tugging at the corner of her mouth. "Of course, honey. We can take it home."

She reached out to take the book, crouching beside the display, but just as her fingers brushed the glossy cover, a sudden chill prickled across the back of her neck. It slithered down her spine like ice water, invisible but undeniable.

She drew in a shallow breath. Something wasn't right.

The air shifted—subtle but charged. Cora slowly lifted her head, a thread of dread unspooling in her chest. Her gaze moved past Avalina, past the rows of carefully arranged shelves and the soft string lights twinkling above, to the large front window of the boutique.

It had always been her favorite part of the shop—the big pane of glass that let in the morning sun and made the space feel open and welcoming. But now it held something else. In the reflection, just beyond the safety of the store's soft glow, a figure stood. It was a man—motionless, like he had been carved from stone. He faced the glass directly, his presence stark against the morning.

He was tall, lean, his posture stiff with intention. The glare blurred his face, but the coat he wore was unmistakable—deep crimson, like wet blood on snow. The collar was turned high, the buttons fastened to the top. And though his face was cloaked in shadow, Cora felt the weight of his gaze like pressure on her chest.

Cora froze, every muscle seizing beneath her skin as if her bones had turned to iron. The boutique suddenly felt hollow. The pastel displays blurred at the edges, the soft spines of children's books seemed too bright, too staged. Even the warm scent of vanilla and old paper, once comforting, now clung to her like something artificial—masking a rot beneath. It was as if the room itself had exhaled and gone still, waiting for something to break.

Behind her, Avalina giggled, the sound light and unbothered. She clutched the bunny book to her chest, her joy pure, untouched by the chill curling through the air. But Cora couldn't turn. Couldn't speak. Outside the glass, the figure didn't flinch.

He stood just beyond the sunlight's reach, framed in the reflection like an afterimage burned into the world. His posture too still, too certain. Though Cora couldn't see his face, she felt his stare—

unblinking and deliberate. Not like someone passing by. Not like someone curious.

No.

He was waiting.

And he was watching her.

His face was hidden beneath the brim of a dark hat, but Cora could see enough. The broad shoulders. The deliberate stance. The way his body seemed to *loom* in the cold light of morning.

A chill crawled up her spine and her lungs seized. Before Cora could so much as blink, Avalina's voice rang out—bright, innocent, slicing through the thick tension like a bell in a graveyard.

"Mommy, look! The man in the red coat! He's outside!"

Cora's heart plummeted, a cold thud in her chest. Avalina had seen him, too.

A slow, crawling dread crept up her spine as she spun toward the window, eyes wide, pulse roaring in her ears. But the figure was gone. The glass reflected only the street, empty and sunlit—as if no one had ever been there.

No trace.

No coat.

No man.

And yet… the air hadn't shifted. The heavy, invisible presence still pressed in around Cora, thick as smoke. The warmth of the boutique now felt like a trap. Something unseen lingered—close, just out of reach, like the echo of a scream she hadn't heard yet. She stepped quickly to the window, peering out. There was no sign of him. Just the quiet street, bathed in the soft light of the morning. But something told her he was still there. Somewhere. Watching.

"Mommy, he's coming. The man in the red coat. " Avalina's voice was quiet, almost as if she were speaking to herself. "He's here to talk to you."

A wave of nausea washed over Cora. *Talk to her?*

"Ava," she said, voice strained. "Honey, go to the back of the store and sit down with your books, okay?"

But Avalina didn't move. She simply stood there, staring out the window, her small hand pressed against the glass.

"Mommy, don't let him in."

Cora's mind raced. Was she hallucinating? Was this a break from reality?

No. The feeling in her gut told her this was real. And this man was not just a figment of her imagination.

The boutique pressed in on her like a shrinking box, every corner suddenly too sharp, every pastel hue too loud and false. What had once felt warm and whimsical now throbbed with unease. The air had thickened, as if she were breathing through gauze soaked in syrup. Her chest tightened, ribs cinching inward as though the walls themselves were inhaling, preparing to swallow her whole.

Cora's eyes flicked to the front door—the pale blue one with the brass bell that used to make Avalina laugh. She had locked it. She remembered locking it. She could still feel the chill of the key in her hand. But now, doubt slithered in, oily and insistent.

Then she heard it.

A sound that didn't belong.

Footsteps echoed in the stillness. Not hurried. Not uncertain. Just… slow. Deliberate. Each step landed with the weight of finality, like a heartbeat made of stone—steady and unrelenting. They grew louder, closer, each one stripping away the illusion of safety she had wrapped around herself. The silence didn't break; it deepened, stretched taut like a wire about to snap. Whoever was coming wasn't lost. They weren't hesitating. They knew exactly where they were going. And they were heading straight for her.

Her breath snagged, catching in her throat like a thread pulled tight. She didn't move. Her body froze, caught between instinct and disbelief, as the sound came again—measured, confident, and terrifying in its steadiness.

The door handle trembled, a soft metallic rattle that shattered the silence. It wasn't a knock. It wasn't a mistake. It was a test. A threat.

Someone—*he*—was trying to get in. And in that moment, the boutique stopped feeling like a shop. It felt like a real trap.

Her mind raced. Was this the same man who had been following her for years? Or was it someone—or something—else entirely?

She needed to *know*. But how could she face it when she was so unsure of everything?

Avalina turned toward her, expression unreadable.

"Mommy," Avalina whispered again.

Before Cora could respond, the doorbell jingled again. The door creaked open, and a faint whiff of smoke drifted in—sharp, familiar, and entirely out of place. It hit her like a memory, sudden and unwelcome. For a moment, she wasn't standing in her boutique; she was back in Delaware, the night air thick with the scent.

"You always did have that cautious look in your eye, Cora. That flicker of recognition, like your mind almost remembers something your heart won't let in. I've watched that hesitation grow. I've seen the way you flinch when someone gets too close. The way you smile like you're trying to convince yourself it's safe. But you already know it's not, don't you? I've been watching you for a long time—long before the boutique. Before Bigfork."

He stepped inside like he belonged there. Like he always had.

"You look just like her when you're afraid," he murmured, almost fondly. "But you're not her, are you? No. I made sure of that."

Cora's pulse thundered in her ears. Her feet refused to move, planted in the hardwood as if her body understood what her mind still couldn't fully process. A memory stirred—hazy, fragmented. The smell of smoke. A red jacket. A voice whispering her name through a keyhole. It flashed, then vanished, leaving behind only the hollow ache of something lost and dangerous.

Her breath came shallow, her hands trembling at her sides.

"You don't have to say it. I know you don't remember everything yet. But I do. Every detail. I watched your whole life through windows and keyholes. I saw what she did to you—how she twisted love into punishment. How she called it protection while she tried to destroy you."

His eyes gleamed, not with rage, but devotion.

"I saved you, Cora. Don't you see that? I was the only one who saw what she really was. The way she locked you up inside yourself. The way she lied to everyone, even you. I got you out. I made sure you could become something else—someone else."

He took another step forward, slowly, reverently.

"I've always kept watch. From the shadows, from across the street, even when you moved again and again—I never stopped protecting you. Even when you stopped needing me. Or thought you did."

He paused, gaze settling on Avalina.

"I let you have this little life. I let you believe it was yours. But we both know it was borrowed. I gave it to you. All of it. Because I love you. I loved you enough to take you from her."

His smile was soft now. Familiar and devastating.

"And I'd do it again. For you both."

Cora's breath caught in her throat as the man in the red coat stepped back over the threshold, the air growing colder with each inch he retreated onto the street. Something in the way he lingered—like he hadn't finished what he came for—sent a ripple of unease through her chest.

Avalina remained eerily still, her small hand coloring at the table in the back, as if she were no longer afraid, but waiting—waiting for something that hadn't yet come.

Waiting for what? Or who?

Cora's eyes darted between her daughter and the door, a hollow chill settling in her spine.

He had said *both.*

But who did he mean?

Both what?

Both who?

Her mind spun, reaching for answers that refused to take shape. The word echoed, sharp and unfinished, threading into all the dark corners she'd tried to forget.

The door clicked shut behind the man when he left, the sound too final, too intentional. His eyes met Cora's through the window—cold and empty. The smile on the man in the red coat faltered for the briefest of moments before he fixed his gaze on her one last time.

The door handle jerked again—harder this time—and Cora took a single step back, her heart pounding so violently she could feel it in her throat. Avalina clutched the bunny book to her chest, blinking up at her mother with that same eerie calm.

Cora's hand moved slowly toward the counter, where her phone lay just out of reach. Another rattle. Another pause. The shadows outside shifted.

And then—

BANG!

The front door burst open with a screech of wood and brass.

Cora gasped, stumbling backward as two figures rushed in, breathless and wide-eyed.

"Miles?" she rasped.

"It's us!" he said quickly, scanning the room. His dark curls were wind-blown, cheeks flushed. "We saw someone outside—he was standing at your window, just watching. Gemma thought it looked off."

Gemma pushed past him, her keys still in her hand, her eyes darting toward Avalina and then to Cora. "Are you okay? You look like you've seen a ghost."

Cora tried to speak, but no sound came. Her hand hovered in the air, trembling. The boutique—though technically secure—felt like it had already been breached.

Avalina broke the silence. "The red coat man came in," she said dreamily, returning to her drawing as if nothing had happened.

Miles turned sharply to Cora, concern darkening his features. "What the hell is going on?" He asked.

And Cora—finally—could only whisper, *"I am not sure what is going on."*

Cora exhaled shakily, brushing a hand through her hair as she sank onto the bench beside the boutique's story-time nook. The cheerful pillows and pastel rugs looked absurdly innocent now, like relics from another life.

Miles crouched beside her while Gemma locked the door behind them and drew the curtain. Cora stared down at Avalina, who had gone back to drawing without a care in the world, her tiny fingers smudged with crayon. Then she looked up at her friends.

"It started when I was nineteen," she whispered, her voice brittle and barely above a breath, hoping Avalina couldn't hear. "University of Delaware. I had a stalker." Her fingers fidgeted in her lap. "I was unraveling—panic attacks, sleepless nights. I ended up checking myself into the campus wellness center for a few days. I just needed to escape, to catch my breath." She paused, eyes distant. "I've never told anyone that before."

She paused, remembering the sterile scent of eucalyptus oil and detergent, the way the windows didn't quite open all the way.

"There was a stairwell," she continued. "Between the second and third floors. I used to sit there at night, just to feel… out of view. Safe."

Her voice cracked on the word.

"That's where he found me," she whispered. "Not at first. But eventually. He said my silence reminded him of something sacred. That I was 'receptive.' I didn't know what he meant."

Gemma slowly lowered herself onto the rug, listening intently. Miles didn't speak.

Cora swallowed hard. "He left letters. Strange, rambling things. Pages taped to my dorm door. Phrases like 'the lesson begins in sleep' and 'fire births the echo.'"

"But it got worse?" Miles asked as his voice tightened.

Cora nodded. "Much worse. He left a trail—chalk markings, burned flowers, one night a dead bird in my shoe. When I went to campus security, they said I was dramatizing. They thought I was spiraling again. Over-medicated. Unreliable."

Gemma leaned in, her voice gentle. "Did you know him?"

Cora's gaze dropped, her fingers curling tightly in her lap. Her eyes welled, but she blinked quickly, pressing it back.

"I didn't know his name then," she said carefully, her voice tight with the effort of keeping steady. "Not until later, after everything had already started."

She hesitated, her gaze dropping to her hands as she picked at an invisible thread on her sleeve, choosing her next words with care.

"He was around a lot. He was actually my TA during senior year. Always lingering near the lecture halls, the common areas. He volunteered at the wellness center, too." Her throat tightened. "That's… where we crossed paths. Where it really began."

She left it there, not willing to say more. Not yet. Some truths still felt too heavy to drag into the light.

"And before that—this. A man in a red coat keeps appearing in my life."

Gemma reached for her hand. "We're not letting anyone hurt you, Cora."

Cora nodded slowly, but her gaze lingered on the front door. On the lock. On the quiet. Because something in her bones whispered the door had already opened.

She turned her thoughts to the very first time she met Vinny.

FLASHBACK — University of Delaware, 2019
The Wellness Center — Third Floor Lounge

The hallway smelled of lavender diffusers and lemon floor polish, with soft instrumental music piped faintly through the ceiling speakers. It was the kind of place meant to soothe, where everything came in hushed tones and pastel hues.

Cora sat curled in the corner of a well-worn loveseat near the lounge window, knees tucked to her chest, a chamomile tea cooling on the windowsill beside her. It was close to midnight, and the center had grown quiet, except for the occasional creak of old pipes and the echo of distant footsteps.

The common room was dim, lit only by the flicker of a salt lamp on the windowsill and the occasional flash of headlights bleeding through the blinds. The floral couch beneath her creaked each time she shifted, its cushions worn and sagging from years of sleepless students seeking refuge. Cora sat hunched in the far corner, legs tucked beneath her, wrapped in the same oversized gray hoodie she'd worn for the past three days. The cotton carried the faint scent of lavender mist she sprayed on her pillows to sleep. The sleeves swallowed her hands completely, and she twisted the fabric in slow, anxious knots every time her thoughts began to rise and crash in waves she couldn't quiet.

Somewhere down the hall, a door clicked softly. Then came the footsteps muffled against the industrial carpet. She lifted her head just enough to see the outline moving toward the room.

The door creaked open, its hinges groaning against the stillness of the room. Warm fluorescent light spilled in from the hallway, casting a long rectangle of brightness across the floor and outlining the figure who stepped through. He was tall and neatly groomed, with a calm, professional air that seemed to precede him. A clipboard rested in one hand, held with casual authority. His navy fleece bore the embroidered crest of the university's counseling program—familiar, official, trusted. The kind of emblem meant to put you at ease. But something about the way he moved—the silence in his steps, the precision in his posture—made her skin crawl.

Vinny Moretti. The name meant nothing to her then, but her stomach knotted instantly, a cold, instinctive twist that made her sit up straighter without meaning to. The air around her felt suddenly different— heavier, like the pressure had dropped in the room. Her breath stalled in her chest, shallow and silent, as though her body recognized something her mind hadn't yet caught up to.

He stood there blinking as if he hadn't expected anyone else to be here. His dark eyes scanned the room, pausing on her curled form near the window.

"Oh," he said lightly, like an accidental meeting in the dining hall. "Didn't think anyone else was up. Couldn't sleep either?"

His voice was smooth—warm in tone, but something about it scraped against her skin. Not the words, but the familiarity behind them. The way he said "either," as if the two of them shared something—a late-night secret. A cracked piece of something private.

She didn't move. Only watched. And something—something small and sharp—twitched deep in her gut.

His voice was low and smooth as he walked with that quiet confidence of someone used to being unnoticed until he chose otherwise.

Cora gave a small, barely perceptible nod and dropped her gaze to the frayed edge of her sleeve, her fingers still twisting the cotton in slow, nervous loops. Her shoulders curved inward, as if trying to make herself smaller, less visible. The soft hum of the vending machine filled the silence between them.

Vinny took a step closer, the clipboard still tucked under his arm. His shoes made a faint scuff against the linoleum.

"Mind if I sit?" he asked, voice easy—too easy.

Cora paused, her pulse thudding a little harder. She didn't look up, only gave a tight shrug, her voice thin as paper. "Free country."

He sank into the chair across from her, setting his clipboard on the floor. "You're in Professor Hale's class, right? Social Psych?"

"Yeah," she said warily.

He smiled—a little too long, a little too knowing. "Didn't expect to see you here. But I guess none of us really expect to end up here, do we?"

Cora didn't respond.

"I volunteer," he added casually. "A couple nights a week. Keeps me grounded."

She looked out the window. The trees swayed outside in the lamplight. "Didn't realize students had the time."

"I make time," he said. Then he leaned forward, resting his elbows on his knees. "You always sit in the first row. Quiet. Observant. I notice things like that."

She blinked, unsure how to respond.

"I'm glad you're here," he added softly. "Taking care of yourself. A lot of people don't."

There was something in the way he said it—gentle, almost admiring—but underneath it, a sharpness. Something less about her and more about control.

Vinny leaned back in the plastic chair, one arm draped casually over the backrest, his smile stretching in a way that felt too relaxed for the sterile, midnight quiet of the wellness center. "I was thinking," he said smoothly, "maybe when you're out of here, we could grab a coffee. No pressure. Just two people who understand the mind a little better than most."

Cora's brows drew together. She angled her head slightly, her voice flat. "You're... asking me out? While I'm admitted here?"

He chuckled, a soft, practiced sound that echoed faintly off the tile floor. "I know how it sounds," he said, leaning forward with his elbows on his knees, his voice lowered like they were in on some kind of secret. "But this place… it's just a pit stop. Not a permanent label. You're still you, Cora. Still sharp."

She finally looked up at him—really looked. His eyes were a deep, unreadable brown, warm on the surface, but behind them, something flickered. Cold. Controlled. Like he was holding a mirror, carefully angled to reflect whatever he thought she needed.

Cora's stomach tightened. She swallowed and gave a noncommittal nod. "I'll think about it."

Vinny stood, slow and casual, brushing at his jeans like he'd just done something strenuous. "No rush," he said, flashing another one of those too-wide smiles. "I've got all semester."

He turned to go, his footsteps soft against the floor. But just before he reached the door, he looked back. That same grin on his face— familiar now, but no more comfortable than the first time.

"Sleep well, Cora."

The door clicked softly shut behind him, the sound unnaturally loud in the silence that followed. Cora didn't move for a long time, still wrapped in her hoodie, still twisting the sleeves, as the quiet around her grew oppressive.

……

Cora snapped back to reality after Gemma and Miles left when the faint creak of the door opening broke through the silence. A gust of cool air swept in behind it, tugging at the hem of a display curtain. She looked up, startled. At first, she barely registered the figure in the doorway. Her mind was still clouded—fixed on the tension that clung to the room, on the lingering dread of the man in the red coat who had vanished as suddenly as he appeared.

A woman with dark, wavy hair and an effortlessly chic style appeared in the doorway. She smiled warmly, the kind of friendly smile that felt like a glimpse of sunlight after a storm.

"Hey there," the woman called out cheerfully. "Everything okay in here?"

Cora looked up, startled, though her mind was still racing with what had just happened. The woman's voice, casual and light, seemed to cut through the heaviness that had settled around her.

"Oh, uh—yeah, just…" Cora trailed off, unsure how to explain the strange events of the morning.

The woman stepped in, her eyes scanning the room with that casual curiosity Cora had grown used to from regular customers. She paused when she noticed Avalina in the back of the shop, humming to herself in a strange, soft tune. It was as if the woman's eyes sharpened for just a moment before her smile returned, unfazed.

"I was just next door," the woman continued, as if they were catching up after a long weekend. "I thought I'd pop in and see how things were going. Letty, by the way," she said with a little tilt of her head. "I've got a place just down the way. I like to wander in from time to time."

Letty. Cora blinked, trying to place the name, but it didn't quite register. Maybe she'd seen her around town before? Known her before the accident?

"Letty?" Cora repeated, trying to sound friendly but still distracted.

Letty's gaze shifted to Cora like she could read what was humming beneath her skin. She moved forward with an easy grace, the soles of her boots whispering against the wooden floor. Her smile remained, but its warmth had thinned, stretched into something more careful. With a flick of her wrist, she dusted off a nonexistent speck from her sleeve, her bangles chiming in a soft metallic murmur as she drifted toward the center of the room.

"You know," she said, her voice dipped in that syrupy calm only fortune tellers and liars seem to master, "some children… they carry echoes. From before."

Cora's jaw tightened. "Before what?"

Letty tilted her head, considering. "Before they were born. Before we tried to forget. Same thing, really."

She walked over to a nearby display of storybooks, running her finger along the spines.

"I was just pulling tarot," Letty said. "Cards were jumpy this morning. The Tower flipped three times. Reversals and all. A warning, maybe. A collapse. Something old clawing its way back up."

She turned slowly, her gaze locking with Cora's.

"I don't tell people everything I see. Most wouldn't believe me. Or worse—they'd remember."

Cora's heart thudded. "Remember what?"

Letty stepped closer now, her expression unreadable, her voice low.

"That you didn't just run from something, Cora. You were delivered. Snatched from a life you were never meant to finish."

Cora flinched. Something about the word *delivered* made her stomach turn.

"Saved, some would say," Letty added, watching her carefully. "From your mother. From the legacy she didn't survive."

Cora's mouth went dry. Her mother? That wasn't something she talked about. Hardly thought about. How would Letty—

"I don't need your story," Letty whispered. "I already know it. The red thread between you and that little girl of yours… it's tangled. And something—someone—is tugging at it."

Avalina had stopped humming. The silence from the back room was louder than any noise. Letty began walking away from the counter, as if the wind had changed and she knew it was time to leave.

"If she starts speaking in riddles," Letty said without turning back, "don't dismiss her. Children always see the spirits first. They don't know how to lie to themselves yet."

Before Cora could reply, Avalina's voice rang out from the back of the store, still humming that eerie tune. Letty's gaze shifted toward the little girl, her eyes narrowing ever so slightly. There was something about the way she looked at Avalina that made Cora's heart skip. Letty nodded slowly, though she didn't look convinced. She leaned in slightly, lowering her voice just enough for Cora to catch it.

"You might want to keep an eye on your little one," Letty said softly, though there was an unmistakable seriousness in her tone now. "Things aren't always as simple as they seem, and when the past comes back to visit, it's never just a visit."

Cora froze. The words felt like a chill down her spine, and she couldn't quite place why.

Cora's breath hitched as she watched Letty step back toward the door, her tone light again as she gave a little wave. "I'm sure you've got it all under control. I'll see you around, Cora."

Cora's eyes flicked to Avalina, who had stopped humming and was now staring blankly at the back wall, her expression vacant and distant. Then, from somewhere deep within, the faintest flicker of realization started to surface. Something was happening—and it wasn't good.

Letty's easy, casual smile lingered in the air as she moved toward the counter, slipping a business card with an elegant swirl of lettering onto the wood surface. The card was thick, with a shimmering finish that caught the light—a subtle touch, making it seem almost out of place in the otherwise ordinary shop.

"I'm down the street, just in case you need someone who knows how to… read between the lines," Letty said with a wink, her tone dripping with something Cora couldn't quite decipher.

Cora opened her mouth to reply, but before she could say anything, Letty glanced over her shoulder at Avalina. The little girl was still humming, her back turned to them as she absently fiddled with a plush toy in the corner. Letty's expression softened, and she walked toward Avalina as though drawn by an invisible thread. Cora's heart skipped, a strange feeling of unease creeping up her spine.

Before she could stop her, Letty leaned down, her hand brushing through Avalina's hair with a tenderness that felt strangely intimate. The way her fingers lingered in Avalina's curls, the way she leaned in so close, it felt—wrong. It wasn't just a casual gesture. It felt like an unspoken connection, like something that shouldn't be happening, something that Cora wasn't prepared for.

Cora's breath caught in her throat. "Hey!" she snapped, her voice much sharper than she intended. "What are you doing?"

Letty straightened up, her fingers lingering for just a moment longer than necessary, before she turned to face Cora with an almost unbothered smile. "Oh, just thought I'd give her some good energy, you know? Children are so sensitive to that kind of thing."

The words hit Cora like a punch in the gut, her stomach tightening into a knot. The way Letty had said it, the way she *looked* at Avalina—it felt like something more than just a kind gesture.

"Don't touch her," Cora said, her voice low, her hand instinctively reaching out as though she could physically pull Avalina away from the moment that had just passed. Her heart was pounding in her chest, and the air in the shop suddenly felt too thick—suffocating.

Letty paused, giving Cora an appraising look, as though sizing her up. For the briefest moment, Cora thought she saw something—just a flicker of something dark—pass over Letty's face, but it was gone before she could make sense of it.

With an almost imperceptible shrug, Letty gave a soft chuckle. "Don't worry, I'm harmless."

She stood straight, dusting off her jacket as though nothing was amiss, her smile returning to its previous warm, but too-perfect form. "I'll leave you to it, Cora. You've got a lot to figure out."

Cora stood frozen, watching as Letty turned for the door.

"Take care of yourself," Letty added over her shoulder. "And remember—sometimes it's the things we can't see that matter most."

As Letty stepped out, the doorbell jingled again, leaving Cora standing in the middle of the shop, her mind reeling. What did Letty mean by that? Why did she seem to know something Cora didn't? And most unsettling of all, why had she been so focused on Avalina?

The silence that followed was thick and oppressive. Cora stood there for a long moment, her hands trembling, her eyes flicking to the counter where Letty had left the business card. She couldn't seem to breathe, her thoughts spiraling. Slowly, Cora turned toward Avalina, who was still lost in her world, seemingly unaffected by the strange encounter. But Cora's heart was pounding. She couldn't shake the feeling that something had shifted—something dangerous had just passed between Letty and Avalina.

A shiver ran down her spine as she crossed the room and knelt in front of Avalina, placing her hands gently on her daughter's shoulders.

"Avalina," Cora said, her voice soft but firm. "What did she say to you?"

Avalina didn't answer at first. She simply looked up at Cora with wide eyes, still humming under her breath. Then, she spoke in a tone that sent chills down Cora's back.

"Mommy," Avalina whispered, *"she told me not to put my jammies on. She said I'd see her soon."*

Cora's breath hitched. "What? Who?"

Avalina's eyes seemed distant for a moment, as if she were seeing something far beyond Cora's reach.

"Miss Letty," Avalina said, her voice dreamy. "She said we'd all be together."

Cora's heart dropped hard, leaving her frozen. Thought scattered, unreachable. The walls seemed to press inward, and every nerve in her body screamed the same truth—something was terribly, irrevocably wrong.

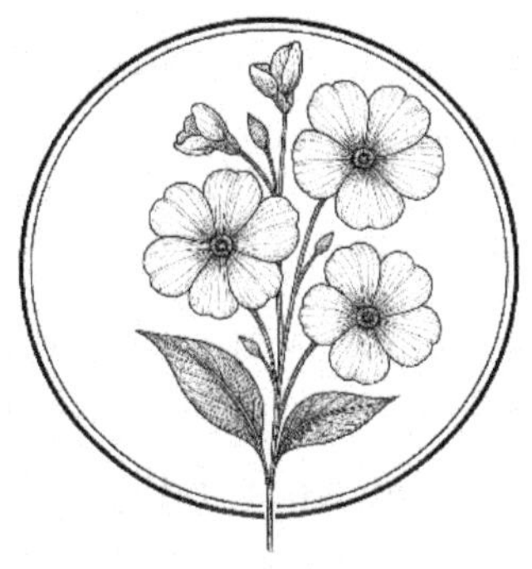

Chapter 9

Behind Closed Doors

"Even the most broken voice can still echo if it's speaking from the right place."

Lincoln McAlister had always believed in the power of books to shape young minds. As a successful entrepreneur and literacy advocate, he had spent years funding reading programs in schools, but something still nagged at him—what about the homes of these children?

He believed that love for reading didn't just start in the classroom; it started in the quiet corners of a home, in bedtime stories whispered under blankets, in books worn soft from eager little hands flipping through their pages over and over again. But too many children lacked even a single book of their own. That's where his new initiative, *The Home Library Project*, came in.

Lincoln's goal was simple but ambitious: to ensure that every child had access to books at home. He envisioned a program where families, regardless of income, could start their own home libraries with books that sparked imagination, curiosity, and joy.

There was one person he knew he had to reach out to—Cora.

Cora had built her boutique around fostering childhood wonder, authoring books that spoke to young readers and creating a space where children could gather, listen, and fall in love with stories. She understood the importance of books in a child's hands. More than that, she lived it.

So, Lincoln made the call.

"Cora, I have something I think you'll want to be part of," he said, his voice full of bright, undeniable energy over the phone.

She tucked the phone between her ear and shoulder, smiling at the sound of it. "Oh yeah? That confident, are we?"

"Well," he said, "I wouldn't call it overconfidence. Let's just say… I'm channeling the leadership energy of a guy with a clipboard and a perfectly feathered 80s mullet."

She laughed. "That's a very specific vibe."

"It's the best vibe," he replied. "The project's called *The Home Library Project*. We're building personalized libraries for families who don't have access to books at home. Shelves, stories, the works."

"That actually sounds… incredible," she said, her tone softening.

"I was hoping you'd think so. And if it helps sway you, there may or may not be themed playlists involved. Possibly including Journey and Whitesnake."

"You're really selling this."

"I haven't even gotten to the matching volunteer t-shirts yet," he teased. "But hey, no pressure."

She laughed again, already knowing she was going to say yes.

And just like that, *The Home Library Project* had its first real champion.

Cora listened as Lincoln outlined his vision, her mind already spinning with possibilities. She had spent years fostering a love of reading in children, first through her boutique and story hours, then through her own books. But this? This was something bigger.

"You want to put books directly into homes," she mused, excitement creeping into her voice. "Not just in schools or libraries, but where kids can reach for them anytime they want—even at 6 a.m. in pajamas with cereal stuck to their cheeks."

"Exactly," Lincoln said. "Schools do what they can, but not every kid can walk to a library. I want to remove the obstacle. I want them to read because they want to—not because it's homework."

Cora leaned back in her chair, glancing toward Avalina, who was sitting cross-legged on the floor, completely absorbed in one of her favorite books. It struck her then—how different her daughter's world would be if stories hadn't been within reach every day of her life.

"I'm in," she said without hesitation.

Lincoln let out a satisfied little laugh. "I had a feeling. You've got the voice of someone who reads dramatic bedtime stories with full character voices and probably throws in accents."

Cora smirked. "Only for the villains. And maybe a really judgmental squirrel."

"Oh, good," he said. "We're gonna get along just fine."

Cora smiled, but there was something beneath it. A flicker of warmth that hadn't been there before. She told herself it was admiration—nothing more. Just respect for a good man with a big heart and a vision that mirrored her own.

And yet, as Lincoln spoke more, eyes alight with passion for the project, she felt it again. That quiet pull. That soft thrum beneath her ribs. It wasn't just the idea that excited her. It was *him.* The way he saw the gaps, no one else seemed to notice. The way he didn't just talk about change—he *made* it happen. The way he spoke, like he already knew she'd say yes, not because he was arrogant, but because he *understood* her.

Cora tried to brush it off. To tuck it away in the same place she stored the rest of her wishful thinking. After all, she wasn't looking for anything. Not really. Not now. And something had begun to bloom with Rowan. But there was something different about Lincoln. Something that didn't scream or demand or ask too much of her. He was just *there.* Dreaming big and inviting her in.

But it was *something.* A feeling Cora hadn't named. A comfort she hadn't expected. He was a man she didn't see coming and as she listened to him talk through logistics, Cora realized with quiet certainty: whatever this was—this flutter, this spark, this *something*—it wasn't going away.

They spent the next hour brainstorming—fast, focused, and a little chaotic in the best way. Cora suggested incorporating local authors, making sure the books reflected diverse experiences so every child could see themselves in the pages. Lincoln threw out the idea of a subscription-style model, where families could sign up to receive books regularly at no cost.

"We could start small," he said, tapping a pen against his notebook. "Maybe a pilot program in Bigfork and a few surrounding areas."

"I can introduce you to some shop owners who might help," Cora offered. "And I know families who'd jump at this. I'd love to eventually reach the women's shelter and the homeless shelter, too. They need stories just as much as anyone else."

Lincoln grinned. "Perfect. This isn't just about handing out books—it's about building readers for life. Raising little story rebels."

Cora raised an eyebrow, smiling. "Story rebels?"

"Yeah," he said, eyes lighting up. "You know—kids who grow up devouring books and blasting Guns N' Roses like it's a personality trait."

Cora laughed. "So, what, we're raising future rockstars with library cards?"

"Exactly. Long hair, loud hearts, and a love for literacy. Like if Bon Jovi opened a bookmobile."

She laughed harder, the kind that made her shoulders relax. "I'd fund that tour."

Lincoln leaned back, satisfied. "This is more than a project. This is our backstage pass to change."

And just like that, *The Home Library Project* was officially in motion—equal parts mission, movement, and maybe a little *Motley Crüe*.

After hanging up the phone, Cora had walked Avalina to ballet class two blocks away, umbrella in hand, her daughter bouncing along in sparkly tights and oversized rain boots. The sidewalk shimmered with puddles, and the sky threatened more, but Cora didn't mind. She was still smiling—at the conversation, at *him*.

Lincoln's voice echoed in her mind, playful and disarming: *"Like if Bon Jovi opened a bookmobile."* She'd laughed out loud right there in the rain. The man was clever, quick, and had a brain wired for both community service and hair-metal metaphors. It was a dangerous combo.

Now, back in the boutique, the shop was quiet and closed after a long day. The lights were dimmed to a soft golden glow, casting cozy shadows across the room. Shelves of picture books and tiny dresses stood in gentle, tidy rows, like quiet witnesses to the day's joy and noise. Outside, rain pressed steadily against the windows, rhythmic and soothing. Inside, it was warm—a honeyed warmth, faintly scented with lavender, old wood, and the memory of little feet.

Cora stood behind the counter. Her fingers moved automatically, but her thoughts lingered on Lincoln, the way his words crackled with enthusiasm. She didn't know him well yet—but she liked how he made her feel. Energized. Light. Like maybe the next chapter could be something entirely new.

She didn't hear the door open. But she felt it—the subtle shift in the air, the quiet current that rippled through the space.

Then Rowan's voice broke the hush. "I knocked," he said, setting a gloved hand on the counter. "Twice."

She looked up, surprised. "You didn't text."

"I wanted to see your face when you weren't expecting me."

She smiled, slowly and tired, but it reached her eyes. "Well, mission accomplished."

Rowan stepped closer. He leaned across the counter, brushing his fingers along hers, ink-smudged from unpacking. "You've got marker on your cheek," he murmured.

Cora reached up to wipe it, but he stopped her. His thumb moved gently across her skin, his touch lingering. The moment stretched, warm and quiet and taut with something unspoken.

"You always smell so good," he said.

She looked down, suddenly aware of how fast her heart was beating. "And you always say things that make it hard to breathe."

Rowan came around the counter. He didn't rush. He just stood there, inches away, and when he pulled her into him, it was slow. His hands settled at her waist, hers at his chest.

"I've been trying not to fall for you in the middle of all this," she whispered, her forehead resting against his collarbone.

"I know," he said, holding her tighter. "But I want you to know that if you do fall—I'll be here."

His lips found hers, not demanding, but sure. It was the kind of kiss that didn't ask for more, only promised to be present. But even as Cora's eyes fluttered closed, something flickered in the back of her mind—*Lincoln*. The memory of their phone call still buzzed faintly beneath her skin. The way he'd made her laugh, his passion, the rhythm of his ridiculous hair band metaphors. It wasn't romantic. Not yet. But it was something. And this kiss—Rowan's warmth, his steadiness—it should've settled her. Instead, it stirred everything up.

When they pulled apart, Cora rested her head against his chest, steadying her breath. He ran his hand down her back, slow and grounding.

"Stay a little longer?" she asked.

"I'll stay as long as you'll let me."

She nodded, exhaling softly, then pulled back just enough to glance up at him. "I started a project with a guy named Lincoln—he's helping launch this thing called *The Home Library Project.*"

Rowan raised an eyebrow, intrigued. "Sounds like something you'd be amazing at."

"It's about getting books into homes that don't have them. Not just schools or libraries—actual shelves in kids' bedrooms. We're starting small, but it feels… big. Bigger than me." She paused. "It's probably nothing, but—I can't stop thinking about it."

He smiled gently. "Sounds like it's already something."

As she stood there in Rowan's arms—comforted, cared for—her thoughts kept drifting to that unexpected burst of energy from earlier. That laugh she didn't see coming. That *voice* on the other end of the line that had sparked something different. Something she hadn't figured out yet.

And still, here was Rowan—steady and tangible, like the solid weight of a familiar anchor in a restless sea. Loyal without conditions, present without demands, offering a quiet reassurance that wrapped around her like a well-worn sweater. Yet despite his calm presence, a strange tension twisted inside her chest, tightening with each breath. It was suddenly harder to breathe evenly—as if the air itself had grown thick with questions she wasn't ready to ask. With feelings she couldn't yet name.

The air between them held a kind of stillness, not uncomfortable, but heavy—like both of them knew there was more to be said and neither wanted to speak first. The usual rhythm had softened, replaced by something more introspective. Outside, the rain tapped gently against the windows. Cora tucked her legs beneath her, watching Rowan out of the corner of her eye, sensing the shift in him before he even spoke. Whatever this was—whatever had brought that furrow to his brow—it wasn't casual.

They sat on the small velvet couch in the reading room, a half-finished cup of tea resting on the table beside them. The dim lighting cast soft shadows across Rowan's face, his usual easy confidence replaced with something quieter, heavier.

"I don't talk about my late wife," Rowan murmured, his fingers idly tracing patterns along his knee. "Not because I don't want to—but because I don't know how."

Cora shifted slightly, turning toward him. "You don't have to," she said gently.

He let out a slow breath, his jaw tightening for a brief second before he nodded. "I think I do."

For a long moment, he just stared down at his hands, as though sifting for the right place to start. When he finally spoke, his voice was quieter than she'd ever heard it.

"Vanessa struggled with depression. At first, it was little things—bad days that turned into bad weeks. Then, it became harder for her to get out of bed, harder for her to be the person she wanted to be. I tried. God, I tried to pull her out of it, to remind her that she wasn't alone, but…" He swallowed hard, shaking his head. "One night, I came home from work, and she was just… gone."

Cora drew in a sharp, unsteady breath.

"She swallowed a bottle of pills," Rowan continued, his voice hoarse. "Our daughter, Tessa, was the one who found her. She was seven." His face twisted with something between grief and guilt. "Seven years old, and she was the one who walked into that room first."

Cora reached for his hand without thinking, squeezing it tightly. He didn't pull away.

"The hardest part wasn't losing Vanessa," he admitted. "It was watching my kids try to make sense of it. Watching Tess struggle with nightmares, watching Seth ask why his mom didn't love him enough to stay." His voice broke slightly, and he exhaled sharply, running a hand down his face. "How do you explain to a child that it was never about them? That no amount of love could've saved her?"

Cora's heart ached for him. For his children. For the weight of loss he had carried for so long.

"You did the best you could," she whispered. "You're still doing the best you can."

Rowan finally looked at her then, his eyes searching hers. "Some days, I wonder if I'm getting it right. If I'm enough for them."

Cora held his gaze, her voice steady. "You are."

He let out a breath, his shoulders sagging slightly, as if the weight of his past had settled, if only a little. Then, he finally squeezed Cora's hand back. And in that quiet moment, surrounded by the books and the soft glow of the boutique, Cora realized something. Rowan wasn't just opening up about his past; he was letting her in.

The silence between them was heavy, filled with all the words Rowan couldn't say. He sat beside Cora on the couch, his fingers laced loosely with hers, his grip absentminded but steady, like he wasn't sure he wanted to hold on, but couldn't bring himself to let go. His gaze was distant, fixed on nothing in particular, but the weight of his grief pressed into the space between them. Then, without a sound, a single tear slipped down his cheek, tracing a slow path along his sharp jaw.

Cora didn't think. She just reached up, her fingertips brushing against his skin, catching the tear before it could fall any further. The warmth of his cheek and the vulnerability in his eyes were enough to make her chest tighten.

Rowan turned his face slightly, pressing into her touch, his breath uneven. When his eyes met hers, there was something there— something raw and real—and before she could stop herself, she leaned in.

Their lips met in a slow, aching kiss. Gentle, lingering and full of quiet understanding. Rowan exhaled softly against her, his hands sliding to her waist, pulling her just a little closer, like he needed to anchor himself to her—like they were both searching for something steady in each other.

Cora wasn't sure who deepened the kiss, only that it happened. Natural and inevitable. And for a moment, she let herself melt into it.

But then, when her eyes fluttered closed, it wasn't Rowan's face she saw. It was Lincoln's.

That crooked smile. Those blue eyes full of mischief and challenge. Cora's stomach twisted. She didn't understand it. Didn't *want* to understand it. Because this—Rowan—was supposed to be the safe place. The right choice. And yet, somewhere deep in her chest, something restless stirred.

Cora took a steadying breath, breaking the silence just as Rowan's hand lingered at her cheek.

"Hey," she said softly, "Harlyn's picking up Avalina from dance class tonight. She's taking her to the library, so… we've got the place to ourselves for a little while."

Rowan's eyes flickered with surprise, then softened. "Just us, then."

She nodded, a small smile tugging at her lips. "Yeah. Just us."

The boutique was quiet, cloaked in after-hours stillness. Moonlight poured through the front windows in silver streaks. Cora stood facing Rowan, her heartbeat quickening with every inch he closed between them. He reached for her slowly, brushing a strand of hair from her cheek. His touch wasn't rushed—it was reverent, like she was something sacred.

"Are you sure?" he asked, voice low, eyes searching hers.

She nodded, lips parted. "I need to feel something real. I need to feel you."

But even as the words left her mouth, doubt pressed in, quiet and persistent—like a draft sneaking through a sealed window. Because Rowan *was* real. The kind of man who showed up with warmth in his hands and patience in his voice. The kind of man who made sense after the chaos.

And yet, something in her eyes felt off-center. As if she were standing just outside of herself, watching a version of her play along. This should've been simple. But nothing inside her ever was. Even now, as Rowan's touch trailed slowly along her skin, it wasn't his presence that raised the goosebumps. It was the idea of someone else. Of *him.*

Not a memory because they had none. Not a man she'd known intimately, but one she felt.

Lincoln.

He lingered in the shiver beneath her ribs, stirring in the corners where certainty never reached. He was untamed in ways Rowan could never be—an unpredictable pulse she caught in her breath before she even realized it. She couldn't put the ache into words. It was a name she hadn't dared to speak aloud, yet one that filled her completely, like a question she wasn't ready to face.

And in the quiet of Rowan's tenderness, it wasn't desire she felt. It was an absence. The haunting space where *Lincoln* lived.

Why him? Why now?

She pushed the thought down. Hard. Because she wanted to want Rowan. She *wanted* him to be the one to soothe whatever had been clawing at her since the accident, since the dreams, since everything started unraveling again. Maybe if she let herself get lost in him, the noise would fade. Maybe if she chose what was good for her, the ghosts would finally be quiet.

And yet… the ache didn't leave.

Rowan leaned in, kissing her like he'd been waiting his whole life to do it right. His lips were warm and deliberate, coaxing hers open with quiet intensity. Her hands slid up his chest, finding the steady rhythm of his heart. He was solid, warm, grounding.

Their clothes came off piece by piece—shirts tugged over heads, buttons undone with trembling fingers, skin revealed in flickers between kisses. When Cora's bare back met the velvet of the settee, Rowan knelt before her, taking in every inch of her like a vow. He pressed kisses along her thighs, slow and unhurried, until her breath came shallow and her hands tangled in his hair.

When he rose and pressed into her, it wasn't a rush—it was a merging. Cora gasped softly against his neck, her body arching into him like a question finally answered. They moved together, slow at first, like waves pulling in and back, finding their rhythm. It wasn't just heat. It was history and healing and hunger.

Rowan cradled her face as he moved deeper inside her, his gaze locked on hers. *"I've got you,"* he whispered, over and over. *"I've got you."*

Cora held on tighter, willing herself to believe him. To stay in this moment. But somewhere in the silence between heartbeats, something shifted. She saw him—*Lincoln.* Not clearly. Just the shape of him. The idea. Eyes like storms. A mouth that didn't ask—it *took.* Hands that wouldn't tremble. For a breathless second, it was *him* moving inside her. Not Rowan. Not safety. Something else. Something that tasted like risk and ruin. Like the kind of love that left marks.

Cora blinked, swallowing the gasp that rose in her throat. Rowan's voice grounded her again—steady, loving. But the ghost of Lincoln lingered, just beneath her skin, in the goosebumps that refused to fade. And though she didn't speak his name, she felt it. Everywhere.

She turned her head instinctively, her eyes flicking toward the front of the boutique—and froze mid-inhale. Outside the large display window, just beyond the fogged glass and streaks of rain, stood Gemma, still as stone. Her arms hung loose at her sides, but her face remained rigid—expressionless, unreadable. Her gaze was locked on them, unmoving. She didn't flinch. Didn't look away. Didn't pretend she hadn't seen.

For a long, suspended moment, the world seemed to narrow to that single moment—Cora's heart hammering, the hush inside the boutique suffocating, thick with confusion and dread. Time collapsed in on itself, and all the warmth in her limbs drained into a cold, prickling awareness.

Her breath hitched violently, and panic sliced through the haze of closeness like a jagged shard of glass. Without thinking, without speaking, she shoved against Rowan's chest—hard—staggering a step back as though waking from a spell.

"Stop—" she gasped, scrambling for the throw blanket, clutching it around her chest. "Someone's out there—she's watching us—she was just *watching* us."

Rowan turned quickly, alarm in his eyes. "What? Who?"

Cora stood, her body trembling, the heat of the moment replaced with a cold that clawed beneath her skin. "Gemma. I saw her—she was just standing there. Looking right at us."

They both rushed to the window, but the sidewalk was empty now. Only rain drifted lazily down in the glow of the streetlamp. No figure. No shadow. No proof. But Cora knew what she saw.

She backed away slowly, the blanket still wrapped around her, her voice barely above a whisper. *"She saw everything."*

Rowan didn't try to calm her, didn't offer false comfort. He just stepped between her and the glass, shielding her with his body, his jaw tight. But the echo of Gemma's stare clung to Cora like smoke. Neither of them moved.

In that moment, the only thing that mattered was that they weren't alone.

Chapter 10

Echoes Of the Guarded Past

"The past still found a way in, cracking the heart in places even light couldn't reach."

Cora couldn't concentrate. The boutique smelled like sandalwood and fresh cotton from a new batch of candles she'd unpacked, but it didn't soothe her today. Her body still tingled from last night—Rowan's hands, the way they moved with need, but there was something else, something crawling just beneath her skin.

It wasn't Rowan.

It was the thought of Lincoln—the way his voice lingered in her mind long after their call ended, the way his passion for *The Home*

Library Project sparked something she couldn't quite get. Excitement? Hope? Or something deeper, more complicated?

She didn't understand it. How could she, when the feelings tangled inside her were both thrilling and unsettling? A mix of warmth and confusion, like a whisper she wasn't sure she should listen to. Yet, somehow, he unsettled her in all the right ways that made her heart race and her thoughts spin. And that scared her more than she wanted to admit.

And it had taken her all morning to admit it wasn't paranoia. It was knowing. Someone had watched. The memory came in flashes: her back arched on the antique velvet couch, her hand gripping Rowan's shoulder, the boutique dark but not completely, warm lamplight still pooling near the window display. She hadn't closed the curtains.

She had wanted to believe it was nothing. Until this morning, when Gemma from next door walked past her boutique with too much brightness in her smile, a glimmer in her eye, and an awkward comment: *"You two were really...connected last night."*

Cora had frozen mid-fold of a baby blanket in her hand. She was done pretending. She stormed out the front door, the bell clattering behind her, and stepped into Gemma's art shop, where soft jazz played and the scent of linseed oil and citrus cleaner mingled in the air. Gemma was behind the counter, paint-streaked apron tied over her long cardigan, head bent as she sketched

"Hey, Cora," she chirped without looking up. "Need another personalized print for the reading nook?"

Cora's voice was low. Sharp. "Did you watch us?"

Gemma's pencil stopped moving. "Excuse me?"

"Last night." Cora took a step forward, arms crossed. "You walked by. You saw me with Rowan. And instead of turning away, you stayed."

Gemma's face went slack for a second. Then a nervous laugh broke out. "Wow, okay. That's—dramatic. I mean, it's not like I—"

"I saw you." Cora's tone sliced through the room. "Don't insult me by pretending."

Silence stretched like wet paint between them.

Gemma closed her sketchbook slowly. "It was…an accident," she said. "I was heading home and I glanced in—like I always do—and I just…froze."

"You froze for how long?" Cora's mouth curled with something bitter. "Long enough to get off on watching?"

Gemma flinched. "It wasn't like that."

"It was exactly like that." Cora stepped closer. "You watched something that wasn't meant for you. Something private. In my store. My safe space."

Gemma's expression cracked. "I didn't mean to. I don't know why I couldn't look away."

"You violated me," Cora said, quiet now. "And I trusted you. We've shared coffee. Clients. Laughter. And now I feel like I have to second-guess who I am around you."

Gemma blinked fast, eyes glistening. "Cora, I'm sorry. I messed up. I don't know what's wrong with me."

"I do." Cora shook her head. "You think everything's yours to interpret. To twist into something that fits your aesthetic. But I'm not one of your ceramics. I'm not here to entertain your loneliness."

Gemma's mouth opened, but no sound came.

"I don't need your apology," Cora added. "I need distance. Clear lines. You keep to your art studio. You don't step into my store. Not for a while."

Gemma nodded, slow and ashamed. Cora turned and walked out, the bell clanging again behind her like punctuation.

Back inside her boutique, the couch where it all happened sat quiet and unbothered. She walked past it, took hold of the curtains, and this time, pulled them closed. Some things weren't meant to be seen. Some people didn't deserve a view in.

......

Over the next few weeks, Gemma and Miles kept their distance. But not entirely. They dropped by now and then, sometimes with awkward smiles and gentle attempts at conversation, other times with a shared look that said they weren't sure where they stood. Cora had been the one to pull away, pulling back behind her defenses, lashing out with fear and distrust that, in hindsight, had more to do with her own wounds than anything they'd done. It took time and quiet reflection for her to see it clearly. She wasn't angry at Gemma. She was scared. Just guarded. She always had been. But in pushing Gemma away, she realized she was driving away one of the few people who had genuinely tried to understand her.

One morning, without overthinking it, Cora opened the door when Gemma knocked, and she listened. Then she talked. It wasn't a full unraveling, but it was enough—a sliver of vulnerability she hadn't offered in a long time. And when she did, something shifted. They stopped being just neighboring shop owners. They became friends—the real kind. The kind that brought coffee without being asked. The kind that showed up even when you didn't think you needed them. The kind that slowly, quietly, reminded Cora what it felt like to belong.

Miles, with his now calm demeanor and thoughtful conversation, made Cora feel like she could breathe more easily. He was a man of few words, but when he spoke, it was clear he chose his words with care. Gemma, on the other hand, was a whirlwind of energy and ideas, the kind of person who could make Cora laugh even on the hardest days, and she always seemed to know just when Cora needed a distraction. Mostly, she was going out of her way to mend their friendship.

They invited her to dinners, movie nights, and even to some of the art workshops they held at *The Art Nest*. And she brought Rowan along to a few of those encounters. Slowly but surely, their presence filled the gaps in Cora's life, offering her a sense of family she had been missing. They didn't push her to open up about her past, respecting her space while also showing that they cared.

But despite their kindness, something in the air still felt off. Cora couldn't put her finger on it. It wasn't anything overt. Nothing that screamed "danger" or "untrustworthy", but it was there. An undercurrent that sent her heart into a quickened beat and her thoughts into a restless spin. There was a fluidity that Cora found unsettlingly familiar. They were clearly comfortable with one another, but sometimes the way they joked about past lovers or the dynamics of their bond made her feel like an outsider. Memories and details of Declan came flooding back daily. It reminded her of the kind of relationship she had once been a part of, the kind that had left her heart bruised and battered.

Gemma had stopped by her boutique a few days ago with a tiny, hand-painted bookmark for Avalina and a cheery question: "How are you really doing? Everything okay?"

Cora had smiled too quickly. Nodded too vaguely. Because the answer was: *no, not really.*

She still forgot things. But sometimes it was worse. Sometimes, the memory lapse was changing. Conversations with her daughter. Fuzzy flashes of nightmares that felt more like memories. A voice she couldn't place but somehow feared.

But Gemma and Miles didn't need to know that. They didn't need to know that Cora Atler, owner of the curated boutique with hand-labeled book bins and vintage blocks spelling *WONDER*, had once forgotten her own daughter's favorite cookies. They didn't need to know about the journal she kept under the cash register, where she scribbled quick summaries of each day so she could remember if it happened again.

They saw her as calm. Capable. The woman who ran story hour like it was Broadway. Who could recommend the perfect book for a shy toddler or pick the exact ruffle dress a mother didn't know her daughter needed? And she *was* that woman. Just not always. Not when it got quiet. Not when it got dark.

Outside, next door, laughter burst through the cracked window of the newly opened art shop. Gemma's voice was easy to recognize— breezy, elevated, laced with flirtation. Miles responded with a deep chuckle, the kind that reverberated through brick walls and maybe bones if you let it. Cora paused, her keys dangling from one finger as she glanced toward the art shop. They were good people. Kind, creative. They'd transformed their new space into something that felt like a cozy, chaotic studio-meets-gallery. Paintings leaned against the walls. Clay sculptures lined rustic shelves.

Down the sidewalk, Gemma stepped out of the art shop, her smock still speckled with streaks of paint. "Hey, Cora!" she called, waving. "We've got a little open studio night on Saturday night. Come by if you're free. I'll save you some wine."

Cora smiled, already half-raising her hand. "Thanks. I might stop in."

Gemma gave a thumbs-up and slipped back inside, the chime of the door quickly swallowed by the breeze.

Saturday evening, Cora approached *The Art Nest* with easy curiosity, drawn by the thought of wine, light conversation, and maybe a quiet glimpse of creativity at play. But as she reached the door, her steps slowed. The windows, usually flooded with sunlight and color, were blacked out with thick curtains. A handwritten sign taped to the glass read *Private Event* in looping red ink. Still, she knocked once and let herself in, the latch clicking softly behind her.

Inside, the air shifted. Warm, perfumed, and too quiet. The lights were dimmed, golden and soft, pooling around clusters of bodies. A nude woman stood calmly in the center of the room under a focused spotlight, her pose graceful, her expression distant. Around her, guests perched behind easels, wine glasses in hand, sketching with hushed intensity, the scratch of charcoal breaking the silence.

In the far corner, a couple knelt at a pottery wheel—both completely nude. Clay streaked their skin as their hands moved together, slow and sensual, molding a vase between them with a rhythm that felt too intimate to witness. His hands slid over hers; her fingers trailed back up his arms. Their bodies leaned in close, their breath mingling as they laughed quietly, as if the wheel was spinning something sacred between them.

Near the wall, a trio blurred together in the shadows—a man, a woman, and another woman—pressed close in the corner, mouths meeting, hands sliding beneath sheer fabrics and over bare skin. Their silhouettes pulsed with tension, a collision of mouths, hands and hunger.

Something about it all felt… off. Not just unexpected, but wrong. Like Cora had stumbled into a room where the rules had shifted and no one told her, the wine she'd imagined now tasted bitter in her throat. Something hollow pressed against her ribs.

And then, uninvited, the memory hit—Atlanta. Declan. The surgeon's conference was a blur of name tags and forced conversation. But the home—that home—was crystal clear. White curtains swayed gently in the hallway, leading to private doorways cloaked in gauze. She'd thought they were just part of the aesthetic until she realized they were windows. Viewpoints. Frames for people to watch each other. Couples observing other couples. Some participating. Some lingering in shadows.

Declan's voice had been velvet over ice: *"In our world, Cora…we can be whoever we want to be."* His hand firm at her back, guiding her forward. The blinds drawn tight. The weight of being watched settling over her skin like heat. She hadn't understood until it was too late— that this was his world. That trust, to him, meant surrender. She'd followed him to the sheer white curtains that swayed gently in the air-conditioned hush. Beyond them, not just a bedroom, but a corridor of other doorways, each veiled with the same translucent fabric—soft enough to give the illusion of privacy, thin enough to see the silhouettes moving behind them. Couples watching other couples. Paused moments of intimacy framed like a living artwork.

Now, standing in the art studio, surrounded by beauty twisted just slightly sideways, her breath faltered. Her body remembered what her mind tried daily to suppress and bloomed into a tight ache where breath should have been. It was like she'd stepped into a version of reality that didn't belong to her. Something hollow pressed against her ribs. And once again, she wasn't sure where the lines were drawn. Or if they ever had been. The longer she stood there, the louder her body screamed for distance. To her, this wasn't art. This was something else. Something that curled around her and clawed at the edges of her calm. Something that pulled the past too close.

Air snagged in her lungs, sharp and sudden. She didn't move, didn't blink, as her gaze swept the room again. This time, more slowly, more cautious, like walking barefoot over glass. The light felt too warm, the walls too close. Everyone else seemed at ease, as if this raw intimacy belonged here, as if nothing about it was strange. But to Cora, it was all tilted, off-kilter in some invisible way. Her fingers twitched at her sides, aching for something solid to hold onto. She should leave. Just turn around, excuse herself politely, and walk back into the cool night air. But her feet didn't get the message. They stayed rooted, while her mind started pulling threads loose—threads that led straight back to a hotel room in Atlanta—and to the man who once convinced her that surrender looked like love.

"Cora?"

She turned slightly at the sound of Gemma's voice, her expression caught somewhere between apology and panic. Gemma approached slowly, paint still streaked across her hands, a towel slung over her shoulder.

"You made it," Gemma said gently, like she already sensed something was wrong. "I was just about to bring out the sangria—are you okay?"

She looked past Gemma, toward the nude model still holding her pose, the couples tangled in color, the artists lost in strokes. It all felt too loud, even in silence.

"I shouldn't have come," she said softly. Her voice cracked around the edges, brittle.

Gemma's face softened. "It's not what I usually do for open studio, " she offered. "Tonight's more experimental. A few local artists pushing boundaries. I probably should've mentioned. Cora, are you really okay?" Gemma asked gently, her eyes searching Cora's face. "You've been a little… distant lately. Is everything alright?"

Cora hesitated, her instinct to push people away rising fast. But Gemma's tone wasn't prying. It was warm and sincere. Still, Cora couldn't ignore the tightness creeping up her spine. She hadn't shared the full scope of her past with Gemma or Miles. They knew pieces—fragments she allowed—but not the terrifying whole.

"I'm fine," she said quickly, flashing a tight smile. "Just… tired. The past few weeks have been busy."

Gemma exchanged a glance with Miles, who had just stepped closer behind her. "If there's something going on," she said gently, "you can talk to us. You're not a burden."

Cora's chest tightened. She appreciated the sentiment. But she couldn't lean. Not now. Not yet. Not with everything beginning to fray again.

"I'm okay, really," Cora said, her voice more clipped than she meant.

Gemma gave her a long, searching look, then nodded. "Alright. But just know we're here for you. We're not going anywhere."

Before Cora could respond, Miles' hand brushed the small of her back. It was a soft touch. Familiar and reassuring at first. The kind of gesture friends exchanged in passing—grounding, supportive. But it lingered too long. Then his lips grazed the side of her neck.

Cora stiffened instantly. The air in the room shifted, thickening with a sudden, uncomfortable weight.

"Miles..." she said, barely above a whisper—unsure if she was asking a question, drawing a boundary, or begging him to stop.

But he didn't stop. He moved with calm intention, stepping in front of Cora, closing the space between them, and kissing her full on the mouth. Slow and deliberate. Like this had been waiting just beneath the surface all along.

Cora froze. Her entire body went rigid, her arms stiff at her sides like they didn't belong to her. Her heartbeat surged in her ears, thunderous and erratic. Her mind blanked—white static crashing against her skull.

No. It isn't right—it isn't happening.

She started to pull away, but then Miles caught her hand. Gently but firmly. There was no space to resist before he guided it downward, across the space between them, and placed it deliberately, undeniably on Gemma's chest.

Gemma didn't flinch. She stepped in as if on cue, her lips brushing the edge of Cora's cheek, then slowly trailing toward her mouth.

"We just want you to feel good," Gemma whispered, barely audible. *"To feel safe... seen..."*

But Cora couldn't hear anything anymore over the rush of blood in her ears and the echo of a scream building in her throat.

No. No. No. Not again. Not like this.

The breath tore from her lungs like glass. She yanked her hand back as if burned, stumbling a step away. Her chest rose and fell in shallow gasps. The room warped—walls closing in, air thick and choking.

"Don't," she choked out, voice barely a thread. "Don't touch me."

Gemma's eyes widened, startled but calm, as if this reaction had simply not occurred to her. "Cora—"

But Cora was already moving and backing away, eyes wild with disbelief. Then she turned and walked out. The studio door slammed behind her, rattling the frame. She didn't care that she left the front door unlatched, nor did she look back to see if they followed. All she could feel was the panic pulsing through her limbs, the sharp tremble in her hands, and the hot sting of memory clawing up from the dark.

The night air hit her like a shock. Cora didn't realize how tightly she'd been holding her breath until she stepped outside. She didn't rush, didn't run—just walked slowly down the sidewalk, arms wrapped tightly around herself as if she were trying to keep from unraveling completely. The street was quiet, and her boots clicked hollow against the pavement. Under the streetlamp's glow, her car looked distant, like it belonged to someone else.

She slid into the driver's seat, shut the door, and stared out the windshield at nothing.

And then it came—without warning.

The first sob tore through her chest before she could stop it. Then another. Her hands gripped the steering wheel, white-knuckled, her forehead pressed to it as the weight of the night crashed over her. She wasn't crying over the studio or the paintings or even the memory of Declan, not exactly. It was everything tangled together. The discomfort. The confusion. The shame she didn't ask for. The way her body remembered things her mind was still trying to forget.

She wept because it felt wrong to feel this broken over something like this. She wept because she didn't know if the problem was the room or her. She wept because part of her still didn't know where the pieces of herself had gone. And when the tears finally slowed, when her throat burned and her breath came ragged, Cora sat in the stillness, her fingers trembling on the steering wheel.

As much as she wanted to focus on continuing to build a new life— on embracing the stability she had longed for—Cora knew that the fear would never truly leave her. And though she thought she had found something close to a family with Gemma and Miles and their daily presence, she couldn't shake the feeling that the past was still out there, watching, waiting. And until she could shake that fear, until she could feel safe again, her heart would remain guarded.

Cora had only just begun to lower her guard, to let herself believe that maybe, just maybe, she was building something steady again— friendship, safety, the quiet comfort of being known without being exposed. Gemma had felt like a small step toward normalcy, someone she could laugh with, lean on. But now, the rug had been pulled out from under her again, and she was falling through the familiar emptiness she thought she'd left behind. Her skin still buzzed, her mind echoing with the studio's too-bright lights and blurred lines. She didn't blame Gemma—not entirely—but it didn't matter. The damage was done. All she wanted was for situations like this to stop. To stop being surprised by the wrong things. To stop walking into rooms that felt like traps. To stop searching for safety and finding ghosts instead.

Later that evening, Cora was sitting on the window seat of Avalina's room. Outside, the wind bent the trees in gentle rhythm, and inside, the silence was a rare kind of peace. Her phone buzzed beside her knee. *Selah.*

She hadn't spoken to Selah in nearly a week. That kind of distance between them always made Cora nervous.

"Hey," Cora answered, tucking the phone between her shoulder and ear as she smoothed a ribboned hem.

"Hi," Selah said, a giddy edge in her voice. "Okay. Don't panic. I have a plan."

Cora paused mid-fold. "You say that like you know I'm going to panic."

"Because I do," Selah laughed. "But listen—this one's good. I planned the whole reunion thing. University of Delaware. A weekend escape. Me, you, Max, Jensen… and Brillia."

Cora blinked. "Brillia?"

"Yes! She's in. Max is bringing his camera. Jensen's been weirdly agreeable. I booked a lake house twenty minutes from campus. Rustic, charming, and allegedly haunted. I figured we could ease into the nostalgia with a view."

Cora's chest tightened. The word *Delaware* still tasted like rust in her mouth. *What about MJ?* The question slipped through her mind before she could catch it, sharp as a thorn.

She forced a smile. "That sounds… ambitious."

Selah didn't miss a beat. "It'll be safe. I already scoped it out. I checked every route in and out, even looked up local cops in the area. Nothing's going to happen. And you'll have us."

There was a pause. Cora sat down on Avalina's bed, holding a tiny lavender sock in her palm.

"And," Selah added, a little too casually, "you should bring Rowan."

Cora's head snapped up. "Rowan?"

"Yes. He clearly likes you. And seems calm. Solid. He doesn't flinch when things get complicated. That's rare."

"He has two kids," Cora said automatically.

"You have one," Selah said. "This isn't a competition. It's a reunion. Bring your maybe-person and let him see who you were before all the storm."

Cora leaned back against the headboard and exhaled. "You don't think it's too soon?"

"Too soon for what?" Selah asked gently. "For you to have a weekend with your friends, your daughter in safe hands, and someone who might actually hold your hand when it gets dark out? You've survived worse. This is joy, Cora. Claim some."

Cora stared at the ceiling for a long time before whispering, "What if I see *him* there?"

"You mean Vinny?" Selah's voice was steel now. "Then he'll see that you're not alone. He'll see Max, Jensen, and me. He'll see Brillia, who—by the way—boxed in college. And he'll see Rowan, who looks like he could break a man in half just by raising an eyebrow."

Cora smiled in spite of herself. "He does have a solid eyebrow."

Exactly," Selah said triumphantly. "We're doing this. Pack something wild. Something that makes you feel like her again—you know, college you.

College. Back then. Before everything cracked open. Before the night terrors. Before the missing pieces of memory. Before Declan and his ghosts. Before Delaware stopped being just a place and became a vault of shadows she'd never dared unlock. Even Selah didn't know it all—the fragments she had buried so deep they sometimes felt like they belonged to someone else.

Cora closed her eyes and nodded. "Okay. I'll talk to Rowan."

Selah squealed. "I knew it. I'll text you the Airbnb link. Get ready, Cora Jacobs."

Chapter 11

Where The Lines Blurred

"It lived in the space between impulse and intention, where clarity vanished and the lines blurred into something dangerously close to wanting."

A few days later, Lincoln and Cora met at Jimmy's Pizza, a staple known for its oversized slices and no-frills atmosphere. The smell of garlic and melted cheese filled the air as Cora slid into the booth across from him, shrugging off her coat.

She smiled, casual and practiced, but her eyes kept drifting upward, watching him. Measuring. She wasn't sure what she was looking for exactly. A shift in his tone? A different kind of glance? A trace of something hiding behind his easy grin?

And then the thought crept in—why was she even seeing Lincoln in this light anyway? She was with Rowan. Sweet, steady Rowan. The man who showed up when he said he would, who held her like he meant every second of it. She should be content. She *wanted* to be. But something inside her kept fidgeting, unsettled.

With Lincoln, it wasn't just the teasing or the tension. It was the way he looked at her, like he already knew the parts she kept hidden. Like he *saw* her, without her needing to explain. Maybe that's what kept pulling her in. Maybe it wasn't even about Lincoln. Maybe it was about the version of herself she became in his presence—the version that didn't feel like she was trying so hard to belong to something. But still… what kind of woman searched someone else's face for answers when she already had someone who swore he'd give her everything?

But Lincoln was just… Lincoln. Steady, relaxed and sitting there talking about their new literary adventure. Still, as she nodded along and picked at the corner of her napkin, goosebumps rose along her arms—subtle, uninvited, and impossible to ignore.

Was it just the way they teased each other? The familiar rhythm of their banter? Or was there something more pulsing beneath it, something neither of them had dared name?

She didn't know. She only knew that she was stuck somewhere between a normal business lunch and a question she was too afraid to ask. And that every time his knee brushed hers under the table, her body lit up with possibilities her mind wasn't ready to follow through on. Not yet.

"This place is great," she said, glancing around at the checkered tablecloths and old framed photos of Bigfork's little league teams.

"That's why it's the best," Lincoln replied with a grin, setting down the folder he'd brought. "Comfort food and big ideas—perfect combo."

A waitress came by, took their order, and left them with two tall glasses of sweet tea. Lincoln tapped the folder. "So, I've been running numbers and reaching out to potential sponsors. We'll need some serious funding to scale this, but I think we can start with community donations and local businesses."

Cora sipped her tea, nodding. "That makes sense. We could also do book drives—have people donate new or gently used books to get the program rolling."

"Exactly. And I want to make sure the books aren't just random. I'd love for kids to get high-quality stories that engage them, not just whatever people clean out of their attics."

"That's where I can help," Cora said, leaning in. "Between my boutique, my author connections, and your publishing world, we can make sure we're giving these kids books that matter."

Lincoln's expression warmed with appreciation. "See, this is why I called you first."

Their conversation was interrupted when their pizza arrived—a massive pepperoni and mushroom pie, the cheese still bubbling.

"You know," Lincoln said, reaching for a slice, "this pizza is basically the Bon Jovi of food—crowd-pleaser, a little greasy, and it gets better with age."

Cora smirked. "Please don't tell me you're about to compare literacy rates to Def Leppard album sales next."

"I wasn't," Lincoln said, mouth full, "but now that you mention it—both peaked in the 80s and deserve a comeback tour."

She laughed, shaking her head. "You're ridiculous."

"Ridiculously committed to this project," he said, raising his slice like a toast.

They ate between bursts of ideas. Cora suggested organizing reading events where kids could pick out books, and Lincoln mentioned the possibility of corporate sponsors—maybe even publishers willing to donate inventory. The pieces were falling into place, and the more they talked, the more *The Home Library Project* felt real.

By the time their plates were empty and only a few stray crumbs remained, Cora wiped her hands and looked at Lincoln. "When do we start?"

Lincoln smiled. "Now."

They clinked their glasses of sweet tea together, sealing the deal. *The Home Library Project* was officially underway.

......

Lincoln made the literary finance world seem anything but boring. With a third-floor corner office overlooking the city, he had built himself into a powerhouse in the literary world—sharp, strategic, and always five steps ahead. Underneath, he was pure rock-and-roll energy, with a playlist full of classic riffs and a personality to match.

He was sarcastic in the best way, throwing out sharp one-liners that kept everyone on their toes. Fun and flirty, he knew how to turn a business meeting into a stand-up routine and still walk away with the deal closed. Once, baseball was his destiny—he was a catcher with a real shot at going pro—until a brutal injury at 18 shattered that dream. Instead of wallowing, he pivoted, channeling his competitive drive into finance, where he played the game just as aggressively, only now the stakes were higher, and the scoreboard was his bottom line.

But deep down? That old athlete never left. The discipline, the swagger, the quick reflexes—it was all still there. And if you challenged him to a game of anything, from poker to pickup basketball, be ready. Because Lincoln never played to lose.

Cora leaned against the doorframe of Lincoln's office two days later, arms crossed, trying to stifle a grin. He was lounging in his chair, feet kicked up on his desk, twirling a pen between his fingers like he had all the time in the world. His office smelled like coffee and expensive cologne, the windows behind him framing the city skyline. A framed jersey from his baseball days hung on the wall, a reminder of what could have been—if life hadn't thrown him a curveball.

"Tell me something, Cora," Lincoln drawled, tapping the pen against his lip. "How does a woman who writes children's books end up being this terrifyingly good at negotiating?"

She smirked. "You think I'm terrifying?"

"Absolutely. You smile all sweet, make people think they have the upper hand, and then—bam!—they're signing contracts they didn't even know they wanted. I'm impressed but also mildly concerned for my own safety."

Cora laughed, shaking her head. "You're just mad I called your bluff in that meeting."

Lincoln pointed at her. "That was uncalled for. A man should be allowed to exaggerate his stock predictions in peace."

"You said, and I quote, 'This is a sure thing. Like gravity. Or the fact that Nickelback will always be unfairly slandered.'"

Lincoln put a hand over his heart. "And was I wrong? The market bounced back, and 'Rockstar' is still a banger. Admit it, I'm a genius."

Cora rolled her eyes, still laughing. "You are something, that's for sure."

"You like it."

"I tolerate it."

He grinned. "Same thing."

Cora shook her head, but her laughter lingered. Lincoln had a way of making her forget stress, making even the most mundane work conversations feel like an inside joke. And judging by the way he was looking at her—like getting a laugh out of her was his favorite part of the day—she figured that was exactly his plan.

But beneath the ease of it all, something heavier stirred. Cora felt ready to know more about him. Not just the surface-level stuff, but the layers he never offered up unless asked directly. She didn't know how to make that happen without breaking whatever delicate rhythm they'd found. But maybe this friendship, this comfort, was all it needed to be, especially now that life had thrown Rowan her way.

Still, a part of her hoped Lincoln would be the one to shift the current. That he'd send a message, give a sign, *say something* that told her she wasn't the only one wondering what this could be. Because no matter how much she tried to file it all away under the label of friendship, something in her kept turning back toward him.

Lincoln leaned back in his chair, stretching his arms behind his head, looking far too smug for Cora's liking. "You know, you laughing at my jokes like this? Dangerous territory."

"Oh yeah?" She arched a brow, arms still crossed. "And why's that?"

"Because now I know I can get to you." He smirked. "Means I'm winning."

She scoffed. "Winning what?"

"This ongoing battle we clearly have."

Cora let out a dramatic sigh. "Oh, of course. The very well-documented, highly intense battle where I… exist… and you annoy me for sport."

Lincoln pointed at her. "Exactly. And you just gave me a major advantage by proving you enjoy it."

She shook her head, biting back a smile. "Delusional."

"Strategic," he corrected, swinging his feet off his desk and leaning forward, resting his elbows on his knees. "Listen, Cora, I've been in high-stakes situations before—negotiating multi-million-dollar deals, catching fastballs from future Hall of Famers, even once talking my way out of a very questionable haircut in college—but cracking you? That's the real challenge."

Cora laughed again, and Lincoln's smirk deepened.

"See?" he said. "You *like* me."

"I put up with you," she corrected.

"You put up with me enthusiastically."

She rolled her eyes. "I should've never walked in here."

"Too late." He leaned back again, lacing his fingers behind his head. "You're in my domain now."

"Your domain?" She gestured around his office. "You mean this overpriced, testosterone-scented ego shrine?"

Lincoln gasped, hand on his chest like she'd personally wounded him. "First of all, rude. Second of all, I'll have you know this place is carefully curated. It screams 'literary finance genius with rugged charm.'"

"It screams *early* mid-life crisis, but sure."

He let out a sharp laugh. "Wow. Mid-life? That hurts, Cora. Really cuts deep."

"You'll survive."

"Barely." He studied her for a beat, then grinned. "You know, if you ever get tired of writing books, you've got a real future in roasting people for a living."

Cora tilted her head. "If you ever get tired of literary finance, you've got a real future in being roasted."

Lincoln clapped his hands together. "And she sticks the landing, folks! Truly, an icon."

Cora shook her head, fighting another laugh. She hated how easily he got under her skin—hated even more how much she enjoyed it. Lincoln had that effortless charm, the kind that could make a boardroom fun or turn a bad day into a bearable one. And, unfortunately, he knew exactly what he was doing.

Lincoln leaned forward, resting his chin on his hand, watching Cora with an amused smirk. "Alright, let's cut to the chase."

She narrowed her eyes. "Cut to what chase?"

He drummed his fingers against the desk. "You, me, lunch. Right now."

Cora blinked. "That's your big pitch?"

"You like efficiency," he said, pushing back from his desk and standing. "And I like winning, and this feels like a win."

She laughed, shaking her head. "I didn't say yes."

Lincoln grabbed his jacket. "You didn't say no either."

Cora was caught in an agonizing tug-of-war between two versions of herself—one that craved the fire and freedom Lincoln ignited in her, and another that found peace in the steady warmth Rowan offered. With Lincoln, she felt alive, untamed, like every nerve was on fire and every moment pulsed with possibility. But with Rowan, there was safety, a softness she could curl into, a future she could almost see clearly. The thrill and the calm. The chaos and the quiet. And in the stillness between them, Cora wondered if she had to choose—or if choosing one meant losing a piece of herself forever.

The literary project with Lincoln had started as a distraction. An escape from the heaviness of her life, but it quickly evolved into something lighter, freer. Their brainstorming sessions turned into comical banter, inside jokes, and easy silences that felt unexpectedly intimate. It was fun, uncomplicated until the night before, while flipping through her grandmother's old journals, Cora's eyes had landed on a line she hadn't thought about in years: *"Find love in friendship first."*

The words had struck a chord, humming beneath her ribs. She had frozen, heart caught between nostalgia and realization, suddenly unsure if her growing feelings for Lincoln were more than just creative chemistry. Could her grandmother have been pointing her toward something deeper—even now?

She huffed. "Fine. But if this is some overpriced finance-bro steakhouse where you talk about stock projections, I'm walking out."

"Wow. That hurts, Cora." He placed a dramatic hand over his chest. "You think so little of me."

"I *know* you."

He grinned. "Fair. But don't worry. I'm taking you somewhere *classy*."

Twenty minutes later, they stood outside McGillicuddy's Pub, an old-school Irish dive with weathered green paint and a neon shamrock blinking in the window.

Cora stared at the empty parking lot. Then at the door. Then at Lincoln. "Are they even *open*?"

"Oh, they're open," Lincoln assured her, swinging the door wide.

She stepped inside, and sure enough, the place was completely deserted. Not a single patron. Not even a bartender in sight. Just dim lighting, dark wood booths, and the faint sound of a classic rock station playing from the speakers.

Cora turned to him, arms crossed. "You lured me to an *abandoned* bar at noon?"

Lincoln let out a booming laugh. "Not abandoned." He gestured grandly around the empty space. "I bought out the whole place. Just for us."

Cora blinked. "You *what?*"

"Pulled a few strings," he said nonchalantly, strolling over to the bar. "Told them to clear out the lunch crowd. I wanted privacy. And, you know…" He leaned an elbow on the counter. "To impress you."

Cora shook her head, trying *really* hard not to laugh. "You seriously rented out an entire Irish pub just so we could have lunch?"

Lincoln shrugged. "What can I say? I go big."

She eyed him. "And let me guess, you ordered the most ridiculous drink possible just for the bit?"

He grinned. "I might have."

At that moment, the bartender—who had apparently been lurking just out of sight—appeared and slid a massive, absurdly pink frozen drink in front of Cora.

She stared at it. "A strawberry daiquiri?"

Lincoln lifted his glass, an identical monstrosity of blended ice and sugar, and took a triumphant sip. "Correction: a *never-ending* strawberry daiquiri. I made sure of it."

Cora finally lost it, laughter spilling out of her. "You're ridiculous."

"And yet, you're here." He clinked his glass against hers. "Admit it, Cora. You're having fun."

She rolled her eyes, taking a sip of the overly sweet, slightly ridiculous drink. "Like I said, I tolerate it."

Lincoln grinned. "And, like I said, it's the same thing."

A couple of hours later, the once full daiquiris had been refilled twice. Maybe three times. Cora had lost count.

Lincoln was leaning back in the booth, arms stretched along the top, looking way too pleased with himself. "So, let's review," he said, swirling his straw around in the slushy pink drink. "I've successfully lured you into a midday drinking spree, made you laugh at least fifteen times, and—if I'm not mistaken—you *just* told me I'm your favorite person."

Cora, who was mid-sip, choked on her drink. "I *definitely* didn't say that."

Lincoln smirked. "You *thought* it, though."

Cora shook her head, laughing, the buzz of alcohol making everything just a little bit funnier. The empty bar, the ridiculous drinks, Lincoln's insufferable confidence—it all felt light, easy, like a little pocket of escape from real life.

But real life had a way of creeping back in. There was Avalina and her absurd dreams and sightings… things Cora didn't quite know how to handle beyond just being there for her, grounding her, protecting her from what she could even if she didn't fully understand what she was protecting her from.

Then there was Rowan. Sure, he was charming. A good father. Dependable and generous in all the ways that looked right on paper. But something was missing. It was something Cora couldn't name without feeling guilty for even thinking about it.

And then came the odd, unspoken thing with Gemma and Miles. The night at the studio that left her feeling like she'd walked in on a secret too intimate to process. She hadn't dared bring it up, hadn't even figured out how she *felt* about it. It lingered like a shadow behind her thoughts, tugging at her curiosity and unsettling her calm.

But now—laughing with Lincoln, feeling light in a way she hadn't in years—she was enjoying herself immensely. It was rare, that feeling. And it left her wondering if this, whatever *this* was, could be the kind of normal she'd been craving. Something solid. Something that didn't carry a double meaning or a hidden cost.

Her phone buzzed on the table, and she glanced at the screen. A text from the Harlyn:

Ava just woke up from her nap! She's having a snack and watching her show. Everything's good.

Cora exhaled, relief settling in. Avalina was fine. Not that she expected anything else, but still.

"I'll be right back," she said, sliding out of the booth and grabbing her phone.

Lincoln gave her a nod. "Try not to miss me too much."

She rolled her eyes, but the grin lingered as she made her way to the ladies' room.

Once inside, she leaned against the sink and unlocked her phone, FaceTiming Harlyn. A moment later, Avalina's little face filled the screen, her curly hair slightly messy from sleep, her chubby fingers gripping a handful of crackers.

"Hi, baby," Cora cooed, her heart melting instantly.

"Mommy!" Avalina beamed, waving a cracker in front of the camera. "I'm eating snacks!"

"I see that," Cora laughed. "Are you being good for Miss Harlyn?"

Avalina nodded, her mouth full. "We're watching *Bluey*."

"Sounds like a perfect afternoon," Cora said, warmth spreading through her chest. "Mommy will be home soon, okay?"

Avalina nodded again, then squinted at the screen. "Where are you?"

Cora glanced at her own reflection—flushed cheeks, slightly tousled hair, and the unmistakable buzz of day drinking in her expression. "Mommy's... having lunch with a friend."

"Is it a fun lunch?"

Cora thought about Lincoln, his never-ending sarcasm, the ridiculous drinks, and the way he made her laugh even when she didn't want to.

"Yeah, little Wren," she murmured, smiling. "It's fun."

Avalina grinned, then promptly turned her attention back to *Bluey*, already losing interest in the call.

Cora chuckled, exchanging a few words with Harlyn before hanging up. She took a deep breath, steadying herself. And then, with one last glance at her reflection, she shook her head and laughed softly. Day drinking with Lincoln. What a ridiculous, wonderful afternoon. Cora stepped out of the ladies' room, still slightly buzzed, still smiling to herself from her call with Avalina. She wasn't expecting Lincoln to be standing just a few feet away, leaning casually against the wall, arms crossed over his broad chest like he'd been waiting for her.

Before she could say anything, he pushed off the wall and started toward her. But it wasn't just a walk. It was *intentional*. Determined. The kind of stride that made her pulse quicken, her breath hitch, her body go completely still as he closed the space between them.

"Lincoln—"

And then his hands were on her waist, firm but not forceful, his body crowding hers back against the wall. Before she could process the heat of his touch, his lips crashed against hers.

Cora sucked in a sharp breath, but the kiss swallowed any sound of protest or surprise. It was *hungry*, like he'd been holding back since the moment they met and finally decided he wasn't going to anymore. His hands slid up her sides, fingers brushing the fabric of her shirt, his body pressing into hers like he needed to feel all of her at once.

And God help her—she let him.

She melted into it, her fingers gripping the front of his shirt, her head spinning from alcohol and Lincoln and the fact that he kissed like he *meant* it. Like he'd been *dying* to. When he finally pulled back, just enough to look at her, his breathing was uneven, his eyes dark and searching. Cora was speechless, still trying to catch up, still trying to remember how to breathe.

Lincoln smirked, running his thumb over her bottom lip. "That shut you up real quick."

Her heart pounded. *"You—"* She swallowed, trying to sound unaffected. "You're so full of yourself."

He grinned. "Yeah, but you *like* it."

She stared at him, still pinned against the wall, still reeling, and she hated that he was right. But she didn't deny it.

Chapter 12

The Harbor and The Storm

"One steadied her trembling hands. The other set her pulse on fire. And somewhere between the calm and the chaos—she forgot who she was without both."

Cora didn't go home right away. She wandered through side streets and alleyways, through the quiet hum of the town's outer edges, past the bookstore, past Letty's window lit with candles and flickering shadows. Her feet moved on instinct, but her mind was a wreckage of questions and echoing touches she couldn't shake off.

Her skin still prickled, like it couldn't decide whether to leap off her bones or bury itself deeper inside them. Beneath the shock, beneath the silent grief she didn't yet have words for, another ache stirred—one that had nothing to do with what had happened and everything to do with who hadn't been there. Her heart tugged in two directions: one drawn to the comfort of Rowan's steadiness, the other pulled toward Lincoln's quiet gravity. And in the hollow space between them, she felt like she was coming undone.

Rowan. Lincoln. Two different orbits pulling her in opposite directions. Was she mistaking peace for boredom? Chaos for chemistry? Or was she simply too broken to know the difference anymore?

She found herself sitting on the curb outside a closed flower shop, arms wrapped around her knees, head bent low. The air smelled like lilac and rain, and she hated that it reminded her of both of them— Rowan's cologne after a long day, Lincoln tossing wildflowers into her passenger seat "just because."

They were both showing up for her. In their own ways. One like a shelter. One like a storm. And she didn't trust herself to walk into either.

Not yet.

Maybe not ever.

The past still haunted her, arriving in jagged flashes. It lived in the shadows between heartbeats and whispered warnings she couldn't quite silence. What if she misread the signs again? What if she opened the door to the wrong person… and the price this time was written in blood?

And still…

There was a part of her that wanted to call Rowan. To hear his voice and let it tether her to something good. Another part wanted to track

Lincoln down at that dingy bar he liked, slam tequila with him, and pretend for one night she could forget how heavy everything had become.

But for now, she stayed seated on the sidewalk, suspended between fire and water, craving both and terrified of either.

And for the first time in weeks, she admitted the truth—aloud, barely a whisper in the dark:

"I don't know who I am with either of them."

... ...

Cora stood in the kitchen that night, fingers wrapped around a chipped mug of ginger tea she hadn't sipped. The house was quiet, too quiet, except for the low hum of the fridge and the occasional creak of the floorboards upstairs where Avalina slept. Or tried to.

Cora stared blankly at the refrigerator, where Avalina's latest drawing hung crookedly—another one of the shadow man. This time, the figure had red around his hands and no eyes, just black hollows, and behind him, a tiny stick girl with pigtails, holding what looked like a teddy bear by one arm.

Cora hadn't asked about it. Not yet.

Would Rowan understand that? Or would he see it as too much? Would Lincoln think she was just crazy enough? Would he just walk away?

Cora sank into a chair, resting her forehead on her clasped hands. Rowan had two kids of his own—sweet, grounded children who liked puzzles and wore matching socks. What if this was the thing that made him pull away? What if seeing this part of Avalina—the darkness that sometimes slipped through her small frame—made him decide they were too broken?

Cora blinked back the sting behind her eyes. What scared her most wasn't losing Rowan. It was him seeing them and choosing to leave. The idea that someone could look into the corners of her life—the drawings, the nightmares, the way Avalina sometimes seemed to remember things that hadn't happened—and say, *"I can't carry this."*

She bit her lip and traced a finger along the edge of the table. Neither Rowan nor Lincoln had ever given her a reason to doubt their presence. But she knew too well that people stayed—until they didn't.

She thought of telling them. Of sitting across from them each and laying it all out—how her daughter spoke in her sleep, how she sometimes drew things years after they happened, how she once looked at a stranger and whispered, *"He smells like matches."* But then what? Would they look at Avalina differently? Would they look at her differently?

Cora let her head fall back and stared at the ceiling. Maybe not yet. Maybe not until after the reunion. After Delaware. The truth was that the trip wasn't just about catching up with old friends—it was about facing the ghosts she'd left there. Digging for answers to questions she'd never spoken aloud. Questions that belonged only to her. She needed to know which shadows were real and which ones she'd conjured in the dark.

And she needed to protect Avalina. Not just from the shadows but from the kind of people who promised light, only to disappear the second the room got dark. And to do that—to truly stand between her daughter and the darkness—Cora would have to come to terms with the secrets of her own past, the ones she'd buried so deep she sometimes pretended they weren't there at all.

......

Cora stood outside The Packinghouse restaurant the next day, her fingers tightening slightly around Rowan's as she glanced toward the parking lot. Avalina bounced excitedly beside her, her dark curls pulled into two messy buns, her little hands wrapped around her sparkly pink purse. Across from them, Rowan's kids stood watching the entrance, their expressions a mix of curiosity and uncertainty.

It felt like the next natural step—seeing how their worlds might fit together. Dating Rowan had been easy so far, but today was different. Today wasn't just about them. It was about Avalina meeting his kids, about testing the quiet, unspoken question hovering between them: *Could this work? Could we blend our lives without breaking anything precious?*

"You nervous?" Rowan murmured, tilting his head toward her.

She smiled, though her stomach fluttered. "A little. Avalina's never been around other kids for this long outside of school. She's... spirited."

Rowan chuckled. "Tessa's got her beat. And Seth's used to keeping her in line." He looked down at his son, giving him a light nudge. "Right, buddy?"

Seth, ever the quiet one, just shrugged. "I guess." But his gaze flicked toward Avalina, who was now fiddling with the charm bracelet on her wrist.

Tessa, on the other hand, was already watching Avalina with wide eyes. "I like your purse," she said finally.

Avalina beamed. "Thanks! It's my special dinner purse. It has ChapStick and a lucky rock in it."

Tessa grinned. "I have a lucky rock too!"

Cora met Rowan's eyes over their heads, and he gave her a reassuring smile. Maybe this wouldn't be so hard after all.

Dinner went smoother than expected, aside from the moment Tessa dared Avalina to try ketchup on her mac and cheese, which resulted in an exaggerated gagging display. Seth rolled his eyes at his sister's antics but cracked a small smile when Rowan gave him a knowing look.

By the time they made it to the mini-golf course, the kids had warmed up to each other. Tessa and Avalina had already formed some sort of secret giggling alliance, whispering between shots, while Seth took the game seriously, lining up each putt with careful precision.

"I bet you I can make this hole-in-one," Rowan said, aiming dramatically as Cora watched with amusement.

"You're going to embarrass yourself," she teased.

"Have a little faith." Rowan lined up his shot, swung—and the ball bounced off the side of the course, ricocheting off a rock before rolling straight into the water hazard.

Seth groaned, covering his face. "Dad…"

Tessa cackled. "That was so bad!"

Avalina giggled beside her. "You should let me teach you how to do it, Rowan."

Cora smirked, nudging him. "Looks like you've got a new coach."

Rowan huffed but grinned, looping an arm around Cora's waist as the kids ran ahead to the next hole. The evening air was cool, but the warmth in her chest was undeniable. As she glanced at the children and saw Avalina chattering excitedly to Tessa and Seth shaking his head but clearly enjoying himself, Cora felt something settle inside her.

After the final hole, where Seth won by a landslide and Rowan dramatically declared a *mini-golf rematch* in their future, the group piled into their cars and headed to Kastle Kreme, a small, locally owned ice cream shop shaped like a fairytale castle. Twinkling string lights wrapped around the faux stone walls, and a neon sign above the window glowed in whimsical pink letters.

As soon as they stepped out of the car, Avalina and Tessa gasped in unison.

"It looks like a princess castle!" Avalina whispered, wide-eyed.

Tessa grabbed her hand. "I bet they have sprinkles."

Cora chuckled as Rowan held the door open, ushering everyone inside. The scent of fresh waffle cones filled the air, and behind the counter, tubs of brightly colored ice cream lined the freezers.

"Alright, troops," Rowan said, hands on his hips. "What's everyone getting?"

Seth was the first to decide, ordering a classic chocolate cone. Tessa got cotton candy with extra sprinkles, while Avalina chose birthday cake with a swirl of whipped cream on top. Cora settled on a scoop of salted caramel in a waffle cone, and Rowan chose cookies and cream. As they found a booth by the window, Avalina and Tessa sat side by side, swinging their legs beneath the table as they devoured their ice cream.

"You have some blue on your nose," Avalina pointed out, giggling as she gestured to Tessa's cotton candy-covered face.

Tessa crossed her eyes, trying to see, before wiping it off with the back of her hand. "Oops."

Seth, who had been quiet for most of the evening, finally broke into a grin as he shook his head. "You two are a mess."

Rowan took a bite of his cone, glancing at Cora. "I think this went well."

She nodded, watching as Avalina and Tessa laughed together like they'd been friends forever. "I think so, too."

Rowan reached across the table, his fingers brushing against hers before lacing them together. It was a simple touch, but one that sent warmth spreading through her.

Tessa, catching the movement, pointed her spoon at them. "Are you guys, like, in love or something?"

Cora nearly choked on her ice cream, while Rowan let out a bark of laughter.

Seth groaned. "Tessa…"

"What? She's pretty!"

Avalina rested her chin on her hands, blinking up at them. "Yeah, are you?"

Cora opened her mouth, but Rowan squeezed her hand gently, his hazel eyes twinkling.

"I think we're working on it," he said, his gaze never leaving Cora's.

Her heart fluttered as she squeezed his hand back. The kids went back to their ice cream, giggling and making a sticky mess. As they sat in the cozy booth, surrounded by the sweet scent of freshly made waffle cones, Tessa happily scooped up another bite of her cotton candy ice cream, her face already covered in sprinkles.

"My mom used to take us to an ice cream place kinda like this," she said suddenly, kicking her legs beneath the table. "But she always got ice cream in her pink—"

Seth stiffened beside her. *"Tess."* His voice was quiet but firm, his spoon pausing mid-air.

Tessa blinked up at him, her mouth still half-open like she hadn't realized she'd said anything wrong. Rowan's jaw tightened slightly, and he set his cone down, rubbing his thumb along the side as if debating whether to say something. Cora glanced between them, feeling the shift in the air. Avalina, who had been happily twirling her spoon in her melted ice cream, tilted her head curiously, but she didn't say anything.

Tessa frowned. "What? I was just gonna say she got strawberry with those little chocolate chips in it."

Seth exhaled, shaking his head as he went back to his ice cream, muttering, "It doesn't matter."

Tessa pursed her lips, looking between her brother and her dad. "I didn't mean anything bad."

Rowan finally spoke, his voice gentle. "I know, Tess." He reached out, brushing her hair back from her face. "It's okay to talk about her."

Seth's grip on his spoon tightened, but he stayed quiet.

For a moment, Tessa looked unsure, then she gave a small shrug and went back to eating, as if the moment had already passed. But Cora saw the way Seth kept his head down, the way Rowan's fingers tapped absently against the table. She reached under the table and gave Rowan's knee a small squeeze. When he looked up at her, she offered a soft smile. They were still figuring this out—how to blend their worlds, their pasts, their pain.

The night air was cool as they walked toward their cars, the laughter of the kids still echoing in the distance. Tessa and Avalina were chasing each other near the ice cream shop entrance, their high-pitched giggles filling the quiet streets, while Seth and Rowan lagged, talking about the latest video game they'd both been playing.

Cora turned to Rowan as they reached her car, her fingers brushing lightly against his. There was something about the evening that felt… easy. Natural. Almost like they'd been doing this forever. But now, as she stood beside him, a knot formed in her stomach.

"I need to tell you something," she said, her voice just above a whisper, though she wasn't sure why it felt so difficult to say.

Rowan glanced at her, his brow furrowed slightly. "What's up?"

"I… I'm leaving for a few days," she began, swallowing the lump that had formed in her throat. "I've got a book tour coming up in Spokane. Just three days… I'm taking Avalina with me. I've never been away from her for more than a day, so I usually take her on my tours." She trailed off, unsure of how to explain the mix of excitement and apprehension she felt.

Rowan nodded, his face softening with understanding. "I get it. How's she feeling about it?"

"She's excited," Cora replied, her lips curling into a small smile. "She loves it. Loves the attention. I try to make it fun for her, though. We'll explore the cities we're visiting, maybe even take a little time to relax."

"I'm sure she loves it." Rowan reached out, giving her hand a reassuring squeeze.

Cora took a deep breath, pushing forward with the words she'd been holding back. "The thing is… I've got my college reunion coming up, too. It's been years, but I've been invited to go back, and I'm… I'm honestly not sure how I feel about it. It was a strange chapter in my life, and, well…" She paused, gathering her thoughts. "I'd love it if you could come with me. I know it's kind of last-minute, but it'd mean a lot to me. To have you there. To meet my friends from Colorado."

Rowan looked at her for a long moment, his expression unreadable in the dim light. Then, slowly, he nodded. "I'll go with you," he said, his voice steady, but there was something warm in it—something that told Cora he was serious.

It was in that moment that Cora realized how much Rowan had noticed—how he sensed the pieces of herself she kept hidden, the weight of unspoken memories she carried like glass in her pockets. He hadn't pushed, but he'd watched, waiting for an opening. This trip, he could tell, wasn't just about being there for her; it was his quiet way of wanting to know her better, to step inside her world and understand what shaped her. And Cora wasn't sure if that made her feel safe… or exposed.

Relief washed over Cora, her shoulders relaxing for the first time since she'd brought it up. She leaned in, brushing a soft kiss against his cheek. *"Thank you,"* she whispered.

Rowan smiled, a little crooked, but it was real. "Of course. Besides, I wouldn't miss it for the world."

Cora felt something shift inside her, a quiet peace settling into her chest. With Rowan by her side, she knew she'd be ready for whatever came next—whether it was the book tour, the reunion, or anything else life had in store. Still, a part of her couldn't help but drift to Lincoln. The thought lingered, uninvited yet undeniable, like a thread she wasn't sure she wanted to pull.

As she slid into the driver's seat of her car, Rowan lingered by her door for a moment longer, his fingers grazing the top of the doorframe.

"Drive safe," he said softly, his voice warm.

Cora smiled up at him. "I will. And you take care of the kids. I'll be back before you know it."

With one last lingering look, she pulled away, the gentle hum of the engine comforting her as she headed home. But as the miles slipped by, her thoughts refused to settle. Rowan—steady, familiar, safe—still lingered in her mind, his presence like an anchor. Yet it wasn't *only* him. She couldn't stop thinking about Lincoln. About the way he looked at her. About the kiss they shared—unexpected, electric, and utterly disarming. One made her feel grounded. The other made her feel alive. And somewhere in the space between them, she found herself wondering which version of herself was real.

Chapter 13

He Knows Her Name

"To redeem yourself, you must first step into the echo and listen to the truth it carries."

The first light of morning had just begun to filter through the blinds when Cora stood in the kitchen, packing the last of her things into her suitcase. Avalina was already dressed in her favorite little travel outfit—a colorful hoodie with stars, denim jeans, and mismatched socks she'd insisted on wearing. Her stuffed fox, Mr. Whiskers, was tucked under one arm, and her backpack stuffed with books and crayons for the journey hung from her small shoulders.

Cora paused for a moment, looking at her daughter. Despite the excitement in Avalina's eyes, there was a nervousness there, too. She could see it in the way her daughter kept glancing at her, as though checking to make sure she wasn't going to disappear.

"Are we really leaving today?" Avalina asked, her voice still a little sleepy but full of wonder.

Cora smiled softly, walking over and kneeling beside her. "Yep, we really are. Spokane, here we come."

Avalina grinned, her eyes bright. "Are we gonna see any cool places? Like… a zoo or a park?"

Cora chuckled. "Maybe not a zoo, you have a field trip to one soon! But we're definitely going to find some fun spots. I think you'll like the hotel we're staying in. They even have a pool."

Avalina's eyes lit up at the mention of a pool, and she bounced on her toes. "A pool! Can we go right after we check in?"

"We'll see," Cora said, zipping up the suitcase and lifting it off the bed. "But first, we have a few book signings to do, and then we'll have plenty of time to relax. What do you say, partner?"

Avalina gave an enthusiastic nod, clenching her stuffed bunny a little tighter. "I'm ready, Mommy. I'm ready for the adventure."

Cora smiled, brushing a lock of hair from her daughter's face. "Me too, kiddo."

The next hour flew by as they made their way to the airport, Cora double-checking the flight details while Avalina sat by her side, drawing in her sketchbook with intense concentration. Their bags were packed, snacks were ready, and Cora had taken care of every little detail to make sure it went smoothly. She had to admit, though, there was a nervous energy inside her, too.

But, as they walked through security and made their way to their gate, she could feel Avalina's excitement starting to lift her own. Cora let herself focus on the adventure ahead, rather than the nerves.

"Look, Mommy!" Avalina exclaimed, her voice filled with awe. "There's an airplane! We're gonna ride in one!"

Cora chuckled, feeling her heart lighten. "We sure are."

As they boarded the plane, the hum of the engines seemed to quiet the nervous thoughts in Cora's mind. Avalina curled up next to her, Mr. Whiskers nestled in her lap, and Cora smiled down at her, wrapping an arm around her shoulders.

"We're going on an adventure," Cora whispered, pressing a kiss to Avalina's head. *"And I can't think of anyone better to do it with than you."*

Avalina looked up at her, eyes wide and trusting. "We're gonna have so much fun, huh, Mommy?"

Cora nodded, squeezing her daughter a little closer. "We sure are. Let's make it the best one yet."

And with that, the plane began its ascent, lifting them both toward new experiences, new places, and new memories—together.

Emerald & Amethyst Bookstore was one of those quaint, off-the-beaten-path bookstores that felt like it belonged in a storybook. The exterior was painted a soft, inviting green, with ivy curling up the walls, and a sign above the door made of rich wood, etched with golden letters. Inside, the smell of freshly brewed coffee and old books filled the air, mixing in a comforting, cozy embrace.

Cora stepped through the door with Avalina by her side, her heart already lightening at the charm of the place. A few early birds were browsing the shelves, their soft voices blending with the low hum of classical music that played in the background. The store was small but had an air of quiet elegance, with polished wooden floors and shelves stacked to the brim with books of all kinds.

"Welcome to Emerald & Amethyst!" A cheerful woman with bright red glasses approached them from behind the counter, her eyes twinkling as she smiled warmly. "I'm Laci. We're so excited to have you here today, Cora. I hear you had an event at my sister's shop, Ink & Imprint!"

"Thank you, Laci. It's great to be here," Cora said, smiling back as she shook her hand. "Your sister? Small world! I'm really looking forward to meeting everyone here."

Laci led them to a cozy corner of the store, where a small table had been set up with copies of Cora's books neatly stacked, alongside a jar of pens for signing. There were some chairs arranged around the table, and a few people were already milling about, awaiting the event to begin.

Avalina immediately made herself comfortable on one of the chairs, flipping through a picture book she had grabbed from one of the shelves. Cora caught a glimpse of the cover showing a picture of a big purple dragon, and smiled at her daughter's choices.

As she set up and greeted a few early arrivals, Cora's eyes wandered over the crowd, her gaze flicking from one friendly face to another. Then, her heart skipped a beat.

Standing near the back of the room, casually leaning against a bookshelf, there was a familiar face. It was the photographer—the same one she'd seen during her Midwest tour. He was dressed in a simple black jacket and dark jeans, his camera bag slung over his shoulder, and his posture was relaxed but observant. His eyes met hers, and for a split second, Cora felt an odd rush of recognition and confusion.

She hadn't expected to see him here, not after the way their last encounter had ended. Back then, he'd snapped photos of her event without much more than a brief introduction, and they'd exchanged a few polite words before he disappeared into the crowd. But today… Today, there was something different in his gaze. Something more lingering. Everything inside her went still, and for a moment, she wasn't sure whether to approach him or turn away. It had been an innocent enough encounter the last time, but the memory still made her feel uneasy—almost like he knew too much about her, even though they'd barely spoken.

"Mommy?" Avalina's voice broke through her thoughts.

Cora blinked, shaking her head as she refocused on her daughter, who was now holding up a picture book with wide eyes. "Yes, sweetheart?"

"I'm done with this book! Can we pick out another one to read?" Avalina asked eagerly.

"Sure thing," Cora replied, her voice a little shaky as she tried to pull herself together. She turned to look back at the photographer, but he was already looking at his camera, his attention back on the room.

A part of her felt a strange sense of relief. Maybe he hadn't noticed her reaction. But another part of her couldn't shake the feeling that something had shifted. Something she couldn't quite place.

She focused back on her daughter, giving her a reassuring smile. "Let's pick out a book, okay?"

As she walked over to the children's section with Avalina, she felt the photographer's presence lingering at the edge of her awareness, but she pushed the thought away. This was about the book signing. This was about Avalina. She would focus on that.

When the event started, Cora greeted the small crowd with warmth, her nerves easing as the first few fans came up to have their books signed. But every so often, her eyes would flicker back to him standing there in the corner, patiently waiting for his turn, his camera never straying far from his side. And so, she signed books, chatted with fans, and tried her best to ignore the lingering sense of déjà vu that filled the air every time she glanced toward him.

The final signature smudged slightly on the inside cover of *The Moon Beneath My Boots,* but Cora didn't mind. Her hand ached from the looping script she'd written all day—*To Lily, Dream wild, For Evan, Keep going, To the reader who still believes in magic.*

She smiled at the last person in line, a teenager with chipped blue nail polish and trembling hands.

"Thank you," the girl whispered, holding the book like it might break if she gripped it too tight.

"Thank *you* for reading," Cora said gently. "It means more than you know."

When the girl disappeared through the glass doors of the small Spokane bookstore, Cora let herself exhale. The hum of the day still buzzed in her bones. Behind her, Avalina perched on a stool near the window, coloring a pirate owl on a takeout napkin and nibbling on a granola bar.

But Cora's eyes had drifted toward the corner of the shop. The flash of his lens always came at strange moments—when she wasn't speaking, when she was distracted, when Avalina's hand was in hers.

Cora watched as he fiddled with the camera settings, not even pretending to browse. She stood slowly, the chair legs scraping wood.

"Stay right here, love," she murmured to Avalina, and crossed the room before doubt could talk her out of it.

He noticed her halfway there, straightened like he'd been caught sneaking candy.

"Hey," she said, folding her arms across her chest, narrowing her eyes. "You've been at every stop. Noah, is it?"

The man blinked. "I'm a fan."

She lifted a brow. "A fan who never asks for a signature? Who only takes candid shots of me and my daughter? Unless you're doing an exposé on overworked moms, I'm going to need a better explanation."

He hesitated, eyes flitting to the side like a guilty dog. Then he said it—quietly, like he knew it would land wrong.

"I know you, Cora. We have a past."

Cora's stomach flipped. Her arms dropped to her sides, fists tightening.

"No," she said flatly. "We don't."

That made him flinch. "I didn't mean to make you uncomfortable."

"You did." She took a step closer. "Delete the photos. Of my daughter. Now."

He reached for his camera, jaw tightening. "I didn't mean any harm. I was just… I've been trying to figure out the right time."

She didn't blink. "The right time for what?"

His fingers shook slightly as he fished into his back pocket and pulled out a business card. He held it out like an olive branch.

"My father is Hudson," he said carefully.

The name meant nothing to her. It registered like static in her ears, familiar in a wrong-way kind of way, like a word heard in a nightmare and half-remembered at dawn. She didn't take the card.

He held it out anyway, arm extended. "You should call me. I think… I think there are things you deserve to know."

Cora took a step back, heart thudding louder than before.

"I don't know who Hudson is," she said, voice hardening.

Noah nodded, solemn. "You will."

With an awkward flick, he tapped at the camera, showing her the display. He hovered over the images—Avalina reaching for her water bottle, Avalina half-asleep on her coat, Avalina laughing while Cora signed.

Her stomach turned.

"Erase them. I'll watch."

He did. Each deletion made her stomach ease just slightly, but the feeling wouldn't fully leave until they were somewhere safe. Somewhere real. He placed his card on the table, and after he left, muttering apologies and avoiding her gaze, Cora returned to Avalina with a smile that didn't quite reach her eyes.

"Ready for our special date?"

Avalina lit up. "Pottery painting?"

"You bet."

They walked two blocks to a small art café tucked between a vintage record shop and a florist whose windows spilled over with blooms. Inside, the chipped tile floors carried decades of color stains, and pink chairs huddled around tables already dotted with paint-splattered palettes. Shelves along the walls held rows of unpainted ceramics—mugs, animal figurines, platters, and tiny houses—each one waiting for someone to give it life. The air smelled of fresh coffee mixed with the earthy tang of clay, and soft jazz hummed in the background. A long counter at the back displayed jars of paintbrushes and rainbow-hued glazes, while the owner—a woman in a denim apron streaked with cobalt and gold—waved them toward a sunny table by the window.

Cora helped Avalina pick out a wide-eyed ceramic fox, its tail curled neatly around its paws. She chose a simple mug for herself, the kind she could imagine holding on a quiet morning.

"Are you okay, Mommy?" Avalina asked as she dipped her brush in blue.

Cora looked at her daughter, all cheekbones and imagination. "I am now."

They painted in silence for a while—Cora's brushstrokes slow and steady, Avalina's chaotic and joyful, leaving pink streaks on the fox's paws and a smile too wide on its face. Afterward, they walked to the library. It was an older building with ivy climbing one side. They spent an hour curled up in the children's section, flipping through picture books and chapter titles.

The library stretched wide and endless, a cathedral of stories. Towering shelves rose in neat, shadowy rows, their spines a mosaic of color and age. Golden light filtered through high windows, casting long beams that caught on the dust drifting lazily in the air. The hush inside was alive, filled with the faint rustle of pages turning and the soft echo of footsteps between aisles. To Avalina, it felt like stepping into a treasure chest; to Cora, it was a sanctuary where the world slowed to a gentle, steady rhythm.

"Are you going to write about me again someday?" she asked, swinging her legs under the reading table.

"Always," Cora whispered. *"Every story I write… you're already in it."*

That night, back at the hotel, Cora double-checked the locks, the soft click giving her a small measure of comfort. She set Avalina's painted fox on the windowsill to dry, its glaze catching the glow from the city lights outside. The scent of chlorine still clung to Avalina's damp curls from their swim, mingling faintly with the hotel's clean linen smell.

Cora lay beside her, listening to the gradual slowing of her daughter's breathing. Avalina slept on her side, one small hand tucked beneath her cheek, the other curled loosely around the corner of the blanket. Her lashes cast delicate shadows over flushed cheeks, and now and then, her lips twitched as if she were still chasing something in a dream. The rhythmic rise and fall of her chest became the room's heartbeat, steady and sure. Only when Cora was certain sleep had fully claimed her did she slip from the bed, the quiet weight of her thoughts waiting in the dark.

Lately, something had opened inside Cora. She had become a woman with fire in her eyes, no longer the girl who flinched at shadows or second-guessed her instincts. She carried her boldness like armor now, polished by every scar and sharpened by every sleepless night. When she confronted Gemma, her tone was ice but her stance was blaze, calling out the manipulations that once would've paralyzed her. And when she faced the photographer, there was no tremble in her voice, only steel—protecting Avalina like a lioness who'd learned, finally, that surviving wasn't enough. She was done shrinking. Now, she burned—and she was ready to pounce on the demons waiting for her in Delaware, teeth bared and unafraid.

Chapter 14

The Scar That Wasn't Hers

"Some ghosts don't haunt houses—they haunt hands. And the only way to quiet them is to let go before they bury you."

When they arrived home, Cora was standing in her cozy kitchen, a steaming cup of coffee in her hands, watching Harlyn flip through the spiral-bound notebook she had put together. A mix of nerves and gratitude twisted in her stomach. Leaving Avalina, even for a weekend, felt like peeling off a layer of herself.

"I know it's a lot," Cora admitted, setting her mug down on the counter. "But I just wanted to make sure you have everything you need."

Harlyn smirked, tapping the cover of the notebook labeled *'Ava's Weekend Guide'* in bold, cheerful handwriting. "You're lucky I love you, because this might be more detailed than the owner's manual for my car."

Cora huffed a small laugh, but her fingers still twisted in the hem of her sweater. "I just—she has her little routines, and I don't want her to feel out of sorts."

Harlyn softened, reaching out to squeeze her wrist. "I get it, Cora. You've never left her overnight before, let alone an entire weekend. But we're going to be fine."

Cora exhaled slowly. "Okay, so… let's go over it one more time."

Harlyn rolled her eyes playfully but nodded. "Shoot."

Cora flipped to the first page. "Her bedtime is eight-thirty, but she usually needs at least one story. Sometimes two if she's feeling stubborn. I wrote down a few of her favorites, but 'Goodnight Moon' is a safe bet if you want an easy out."

"Got it. Moon book equals bedtime success," Harlyn said, miming writing notes in the air.

Cora smirked and continued. "She likes her milk warm, but not too warm. Think 'sun-kissed,' not 'boiling lava.' And if she wakes up in the middle of the night, just rub her back, hum 'Twinkle, Twinkle,' and she'll settle."

Harlyn nodded, flipping through the pages. "Meals are planned out, emergency contacts, backup plans… Cora, you covered everything. The only thing missing is a bodyguard detail."

Cora gave a wry smile. "That would be me, if I wasn't leaving."

A small, knowing silence passed between them. Harlyn closed the notebook and met her gaze. "I promise, I will take care of her like she's my own. You go, have fun, catch up with old friends, and try not to stress the entire time."

Cora bit her lip, glancing toward the living room where Avalina was twirling in her pink tutu, oblivious to the weight of this moment. "Okay," she finally said. "But if she so much as sneezes funny, call me."

"Obviously."

Cora pulled Harlyn into a tight hug, finally letting some of her tension melt away. "Thank you."

"Anytime," Harlyn whispered.

Cora sat cross-legged on the plush living room rug, her palms resting lightly on her knees as she studied Avalina. The last light of day streamed through the sheer curtains in soft ribbons, bathing the room in honeyed warmth. Avalina's brown eyes caught the glow and were wide with quiet wonder as she turned a stuffed bunny in her hands, its worn ears spinning lazily between her fingers.

"Ava, baby," Cora began gently, tucking a strand of Avalina's hair behind her ear. "Mommy needs to go on a little trip this weekend."

Avalina's tiny fingers stilled, her eyes widening. "A trip?"

Cora nodded. "Yep, I'm going to take a big airplane all the way to Delaware."

A slow frown formed on Avalina's lips. "But who is taking me on my field trip to the zoo?"

Cora smiled, pressing a kiss to Avalina's forehead. "You get to stay here with Harlyn. She's going to have a fun weekend with you—movies, pancakes, maybe even a dance party. She will take you to your trip to the zoo with your school on Monday, and then I will be home the very next day."

Avalina's brows scrunched in thought. "But you'll be far away."

Cora felt the familiar tug in her chest, the ache of leaving, even for just a little while. "I will," she admitted, "but only for three sleeps. Just three, and then I'll be right back."

Avalina held up two fingers. "Three sleeps?"

Cora nodded, taking Avalina's little hands in her own. "Three sleeps. And I'll call you every day. You can even tell me if Harlyn makes the pancakes just right."

That made Avalina giggle. "Harlyn says pancakes are circles of happiness."

Cora laughed. "She's not wrong."

Avalina's giggle faded, and she toyed with the ear of her bunny. "Will you miss me?"

Cora felt her throat tighten, but she kept her smile steady. "Oh, so much. I'll miss you from the moment I leave until the moment I come back. But I'll be back before you know it."

Avalina studied her for a moment, then sighed dramatically. "Okay. But only three sleeps."

"Only three," Cora promised, pulling her into a warm hug. "And when I get back, maybe we will go to the bakery and get those sprinkle cupcakes you love."

Avalina pulled back just enough to grin. "With extra sprinkles?"

"As many as you want."

That seemed to seal the deal. Avalina wiggled happily in Cora's arms before hopping up. "I'm gonna tell Mr. Whiskers that Mommy's going on a big airplane again!"

Cora watched her skip toward her room, her heart both heavy and light at the same time. Three sleeps. It wasn't long. But for a little girl and her mama, it was still enough to feel like forever.

The duffel bag was packed, resting by the door like a quiet countdown. Cora moved through the house with a practiced calm, but her chest was tight with a new ache—the one that came when she had to leave Avalina, even just for a couple of days.

Avalina sat at the kitchen table and leaned over a sheet of paper. A fox took shape in bright orange crayon, its tail curling through a forest of green and gold. The scent of sharpened pencils and waxy crayons lingered in the air. Beside the refrigerator, Harlyn stood with one hip against the counter, a mug of chamomile tea cradled in her hands. Steam curled upward, catching the light as she scanned the neatly written weekend schedule Cora had left—story hour at the library, ballet class at ten, Saturday pancakes circled twice as if to guarantee they happened. The hum of the dishwasher filled the quiet, steady and domestic.

Cora stepped into the room with something folded in her hand.

"Hey," she said softly, drawing both their eyes. "I have one last thing before I go."

Avalina perked up, setting her crayon down. "Is it a surprise?"

Cora smiled and opened her hand to reveal two ribbons. "It's our brave bows."

Avalina's smile stretched wide. "Because you're leaving?"

"Because we're being brave," Cora said, walking over. "You'll wear yours while I'm away. It'll be our way of staying connected. You tie mine before I leave, and I'll think of you every time I feel it."

Avalina climbed down from her chair, already bouncing with excitement. "Can I tie yours first?"

Cora knelt. "Go ahead, sweetheart."

With careful fingers, Avalina tied the ribbon in her mother's hair, slightly off-center, as always. Cora stayed perfectly still, like it was a sacred ceremony.

Then Cora tied the pink ribbon into Avalina's braid. "You wear this one while I'm gone. When you miss me, just touch it. It's like a whisper from me that says, 'I love you, I'm proud of you, and I'll be back soon.'"

Avalina beamed and touched the bow immediately. "I already heard it."

Cora turned to Harlyn. "Would you...?"

Harlyn stepped forward, a little surprised but smiling. "I'd be honored."

Cora tied a matching ribbon loosely around Harlyn's wrist. "You're part of her brave circle, too. Thank you for being here while I'm away."

"I've got her," Harlyn said warmly, squeezing Cora's hand. "She'll be safe and happy. We'll make it a fun weekend."

Cora kissed Avalina's forehead, then Harlyn gave them a moment alone.

"I'll miss you, Mommy," Avalina whispered.

"I'll miss you more. But remember—brave girls wear brave bows."

When Cora finally walked out the door, her steps were lighter. Because she wasn't just leaving—she was handing off a small piece of herself, tied up in a ribbon and wrapped around the heart of the little girl who wore it with pride.

As Cora stepped back, she took one last look at her daughter and inhaled deeply. For the first time in a long time, she was stepping away. It was terrifying—but maybe, just maybe, it was exactly what she needed. She needed to find that red box, and now was her time to do so.

......

The cool autumn air carried the scent of fallen leaves and nostalgia as Cora stepped onto the familiar campus grounds of the University of Delaware. The ivy-clad brick buildings stood tall, their windows glowing softly under the evening sky. Fallen leaves crunched beneath her boots as she walked past the student commons, where laughter and music drifted from inside. It felt the same, yet different—like a ghost of the past whispering in her ear, its echoes stretching through time, brushing against her skin like a memory trying to be remembered.

She had agreed to come because she had promised herself she wouldn't let fear dictate her life. Avalina was safe with Harlyn for the weekend, giving Cora the space to slip back into the past, if only for a few days. Max, Selah's new fiancé, had his arm slung casually around her shoulders, laughing at something she'd said. Jensen and his new wife, Brillia, walked ahead, their hands entwined, sharing a quiet conversation. Beside Cora, Rowan reached for her hand, grounding her momentarily.

As they slowed to cross the street, Jensen glanced back. A grin tugged at his mouth as he fell into step beside her, giving her a light nudge with his shoulder. "Feels weird, huh?" he said, his voice pitched low enough to keep it between them.

"A little," she admitted.

"You'll be fine," he said with quiet certainty. "You're with us." He gave her arm a quick squeeze, and the tension in her chest loosened just slightly.

She hesitated, her gaze flicking toward the side of his face. "Jensen… did you ever hear what happened to—"

"Hey, Cora!" someone shouted from across the quad. A small group waved, jogging over with the kind of energy that didn't leave room for half-finished questions. Jensen's attention shifted instantly, his easy grin sliding back into place.

And just like that, the moment was gone, swallowed up by greetings and chatter. The name she hadn't spoken out loud still burned on her tongue.

Cora stepped onto the campus sidewalks, her boots clicking softly against the stone path as she gazed up at the familiar yet unfamiliar skyline of the university. Buildings stood taller, glass facades reflecting the late-morning sun, while newer structures blended into the old with careful precision. The campus had changed, but the bones of it remained the same—the place where she once dreamed, once feared, once belonged.

She followed the tour group, a mix of alumni and a few curious students, led by an enthusiastic architecture professor who detailed the updates with pride. "The new Fine Arts building was designed to mirror the historic chapel while incorporating sustainable materials. And over here—" he gestured toward a sleek, steel-and-brick atrium "—is our newest student center, completed last fall."

Cora barely heard him. Her gaze lingered on the archways of the old library, the ivy creeping up its walls, and the intimate courtyard where she and her friends used to study, debate, and waste hours talking about everything and nothing. She could almost hear MJ's voice— *"It's not procrastination, babe, it's intellectual marination."*

Her lips twitched.

And then it hit her—like a sudden drop through the floor—MJ was gone. Gone. Not just missing from the courtyard or from her life these past years, but gone in the way that made the world quieter and colder. Dead. The echo of MJ's voice vanished just as quickly as it had come, leaving behind a silence that pressed in around her.

She blinked, the crisp air stinging her eyes. No one had brought him up. Not in the emails. Not in the reunion chatter. Not even in the scattered catch-ups with old classmates.

Why had no one said a word? How had he died?

The questions spiraled inside her, unanswered. Then a quiet thought settled in—maybe they were protecting her. Maybe they knew how fragile she was, how much she'd already lost. Maybe they thought shielding her from the pain was kinder than reopening wounds she wasn't ready to face.

She never asked. Maybe she didn't want to know. Or maybe she believed that if the details were important, someone would have told her by now. But the silence felt deliberate—an unspoken promise to carry the weight so she wouldn't have to, at least not yet. That absence weighed heavy on her, as strange and suffocating as the fact itself.

After the tour, lunch was set up in the faculty lounge, where familiar professors welcomed them like long-lost children. The scent of roasted chicken and fresh bread filled the room, but the real comfort came from the conversations, the easy way they slipped into reminiscing. There was a quiet stillness that hung in the air, a shared tenderness forged from surviving the Coronavirus Pandemic of 2020. Many had lost colleagues, mentors, even friends—professors and staff who never returned to campus. A memorial wall just outside the lounge displayed their names in gold lettering, framed by candles and student artwork. It was a reminder of everything they'd endured and the sacredness of being together again.

Cora's eyes lingered on the names, searching for a flicker of something. For MJ.

Maybe COVID had taken him. Maybe he got sick early on—one of the unlucky ones. That would explain the silence, wouldn't it? The lack of updates, the way no one ever said his name?

But then she remembered—she'd seen him at graduation. She was sure of it. She could still picture his arm slung around Selah, both of them grinning beneath their blue and gold gowns. That moment was burned into her mind, vivid and sharp.

So why didn't she know what happened after that?

Why hadn't anyone told her?

Or… had they?

A chill worked its way down her spine. Maybe the truth had come and gone, swallowed by the fog of everything she'd lost after the accident. Her memory still had holes—gaping, confusing blanks that no amount of time or therapy had fully patched. MJ lived in one of them now. And the not-knowing was starting to ache.

Professor Roberson, now retired but still sharp, peered over his glasses at them. "You were one of my most stubborn students, Cora."

She smirked. "And yet, you always gave me A's."

"You earned them. Argued your way into a few, too." He chuckled. "It's good to see you back."

Others chimed in with their own stories consisting of late-night debates, impossible deadlines, the ways they had challenged each other and, in turn, had been challenged by the world. It felt warm and safe, like, for a moment, they had never left.

But the real reason she was there loomed like a shadow pressing into her spine. It never left her, not even for a moment. As laughter echoed behind her and familiar voices blurred into the background, a flicker of something stirred—part memory, part longing.

She leaned over to Selah and whispered, *"Can you cover for me? Just for a bit—I need some air."*

Selah gave a subtle nod, no questions asked. Cora remembered her old apartment, small and sunlit, the only place that had ever felt like hers. She could see it across the way. The pull was quiet but certain, and before she could talk herself out of it, she slipped away, needing to see it again, to stand in the space where so much of who she was had unraveled—and begun.

The moment she quickly crossed onto Scholar Drive, her chest tightened. The building stood unchanged, a husk of the life she once tried to survive in. She saw the same cracks in the stucco and the same tangled vines climbing the walls like desperate fingers reaching for escape. Unit 2B was hollow now. Empty and forgotten. Except by her.

She crept around the back, her hands instinctively finding the window frame. It stuck stubbornly, just like it always did, but with a quiet push, she forced it open and slipped inside, her movement unnervingly smooth like smoke weaving through cracks, like someone stepping back into a crime scene long abandoned.

The apartment felt frozen in time. Every floorboard creaked beneath her feet, each groan a whispered reminder of days past. The carpet sagged with damp patches and curled at the edges, brittle as if begging to be forgotten. Yet despite the decay, it held a strange familiarity, as if it had been waiting—patient and unyielding—for her return.

In the bedroom, she stopped abruptly. That corner was etched deeply in muscle memory before her mind could even process it. The sudden sharpness of recognition struck like a pulse. Her knees hit the floor, rough and cold against her skin. She reached out, fingers trembling, to the warped wooden plank tucked beneath the closet shelf. It was loose, swollen at the edges, reluctant to move. She pried it up carefully, heart hammering against the silence.

There it was—the red lockbox. It sat in the hollow space like a relic from a life she had tried to forget, looking exactly as it had the last time she saw it. The metal was dented in one corner, rust crawling along its seams like veins, the surface powdered with a thick layer of dust. It was real. Terrifyingly real.

She stared at it, her breath shallow, her heart thudding in her ears. Every instinct told her to leave it closed, but her hands betrayed her. They moved with an unsettling familiarity, curling around the cold metal and unclasping the latch. A shiver rippled through her, sharp enough to rattle her teeth.

Inside were fragments—small, jagged pieces of a story she wasn't ready to read. A photograph lay on top: her face, caught mid-turn, shadowed and unguarded. The faint outline of bruises darkened her arms. The image pulled at something deep inside her, but her mind recoiled from it, as if trying to will it away. Her ribs ached faintly at the sight, a phantom pain with a clear cause.

Beneath the photo was a folded letter. Cora recognized the handwriting instantly, but the words blurred as her eyes moved over them. Her brain refused to register the sentences, sliding off each one like water off glass, as though it had been trained not to look too closely.

And then the knife. Cora stared at it. It meant something. She could feel that deep in her bones. A cold recognition without clarity. The handle fit too easily in her memory, like something she'd once relied on. Something that had changed everything. There was a stain. Faint, but still there. Blood? Her stomach turned, but the memory didn't follow.

The pieces were all here, scattered like a puzzle dumped from a box. But the picture was still trapped somewhere inside Cora—lodged deep, behind locked doors she hadn't found the keys for. Not yet. Maybe not ever. She pressed the lid closed with trembling hands. Something had happened. She knew that. But knowing wasn't the same as remembering. And some memories don't come until you're ready to survive them.

She left the way she came. And yet, every step back felt louder. She kept glancing over her shoulder—not at the path, but at the weight pressing into her chest. The past hadn't stayed buried. It never intended to. Halfway down the block, she stopped beside a rusted dumpster behind a boarded-up laundromat. Her hands trembled as she opened the box one last time. She didn't look at the photos. Didn't read the letter. She only stared at the knife—the one stained with a history she no longer wanted to carry.

Cora wrapped it in the same cloth and tossed it into the trash. The clang echoed like a verdict. She stood there for a moment, the chill of the afternoon air curling around her. Then she closed the lid, wiped her hands on her jeans, and walked away lighter in body, but not in spirit. Some things don't release you just because you've let them go.

Later that evening, they stepped inside *The Hollow Cave*, and for a moment, Cora felt the years peel away. To her friends, the bar had the same low lighting, the same mismatched barstools, and the same old jukebox in the corner, humming something soft and bluesy. The air smelled like aged wood, spilt whiskey, and time.

Cora hesitated just inside the doorway, her friends flanking her, each one caught in their small moment of disbelief. She wondered if this place had held them once on long, reckless nights and quiet ones too. Maybe it was where secrets were spilled, where hearts were broken, where MJ used to throw his arm around her and say, *"This bar's seen more truth than any confessional."*

But nothing came.

No flash of memory. No anchor to grab onto.

Just a blank stretch where something meaningful used to live.

Why could she remember the chipped paint on the windowsill of her old apartment on campus, the red lockbox hidden beneath the floorboards, but not this? Not the music, not the smell of beer and citrus and salt in the air, not Wes behind the bar or the worn leather booths that clearly meant something to the people around her. She *wanted* to remember. She *tried*. Her brain just wouldn't give it to her.

Behind the bar, a man looked up—and then grinned. "Holy hell," he said, tossing the rag over his shoulder. "If it isn't the Vodka Vixens & Crew."

"Hi, Wes," Selah said, smiling despite the lump rising in her throat as she turned to Cora to see if she had any recollection.

Wes stepped around the bar, arms outstretched. He looked older now—gray at the temples, a little slower—but his eyes were still sharp and kind. He pulled her into a hug, then made the rounds, greeting each of them like they were his family.

"I saw your name come through on the reservation list," he said, pointing a thumb toward the back. "Didn't believe it until just now. Figured maybe it was someone messing with me."

Jensen laughed softly. "Nope. Just us. All grown up, supposedly."

Cora gave a small smile, but her heart wasn't in it. The warmth in the room tugged at something just out of reach. She stood there in the noise, in the familiarity reflected on everyone else's faces, and quietly mourned the parts of herself that hadn't come back.

Wes shook his head with a low whistle. "Well, damn. I saved your spot—same table, back corner. You know, the one MJ always claimed as his."

That name hit like a thud in her chest, but it also warmed her in a strange, steady way. She glanced at her friends, and they all nodded—Selah and Jensen standing quietly beside her, their eyes quietly watching, waiting for her to catch the weight of it all.

"Thanks, Wes," she said.

He gave her a look—part understanding, part nostalgia. "Drinks on me tonight. First round, at least. For old times' sake."

Cora smiled, following her friends as they headed toward the back, past other tables filled with laughter and strangers who, like her, had no idea the kind of history that lingered here. The table waited for them like a time capsule—carved initials still etched into the wood, old candle wax hardened along the edge. She walked up to the booth and looked around at her friends. And just like that, the memory slammed into her.

MJ. The late-night talks and laughter. His voice sharp but steady. He was the only one who had ever really seen the cracks in her smile. Her knees weakened, a sudden tremor running through her legs, and she reached for the edge of the table to steady herself. Tears welled but refused to fall, burning hot, trapped by the shock clamping down on her chest.

It felt like he'd been waiting for her to come back—for her to see this, to remember.

A sudden image tore through her mind: orange light licking the night sky, the air thick and choking, the pop and groan of wood giving way. Heat against her face, too close, too real. Somewhere in the chaos, his voice—calling out—and then nothing but the roar. The silence after was worse. A kind of hollow that swallowed sound, breath, time itself.

Her body jerked, as if the memory had physically struck her.

Selah's gaze didn't waver, steady and patient. Jensen's hand rested lightly on her shoulder—a silent anchor, grounding her in the present while her mind teetered at the edge of the past. They were waiting. Waiting for her to open the door to what she had buried too deep, too long.

She whispered his name once, just to hear it. Just to make it real. *"MJ..."*

The sound barely existed, yet it seemed to echo before being swallowed entirely by the quiet.

Wes walked over, raising his glass. His voice wavered but didn't break. "To the ones who should still be here. To the memories that won't fade. And to us, for carrying them with us, always."

Glasses clinked, voices murmured soft tributes, and for a long while, they simply sat together, sharing stories, laughter, and grief. Outside, life carried on. But in that corner of the bar, for one night, the past and present existed as one. And in their hearts, so did the ones they had lost. Memories rushed in like a tidal wave. This had been their place. The spot where they'd celebrated victories, mourned heartbreaks, and, most painfully now, grieved MJ.

"Remember when MJ convinced the whole bar to do karaoke to 'Like a Prayer'?" Selah said, her voice tinged with fondness.

Wes chuckled, despite the ache in her chest. "And then demanded free drinks for his *'iconic performance'*?"

Jensen smirked. "He got them, too. No one could say no to MJ."

A quiet sadness settled over them. MJ had been the heart of their group—vibrant, unapologetic, and full of life. His laughter had been infectious, his presence larger than life. Losing him had shattered them all.

"I still think he's haunting you guys," Max mused, lifting his drink. "Especially you, Selah. Every time your playlist shuffles to Madonna, I swear it's him."

Selah rolled her eyes, but a small smile played on her lips. "He'd want us to be having fun tonight."

Before anyone could say more, Wes stood and strode over to the jukebox sitting in the corner. Fingers poised over the buttons, he hit play—and the unmistakable opening chords of *Like a Prayer* filled the room, weaving through the chatter and laughter. A spark ignited, and one by one, people rose from their seats. The sadness didn't vanish—it transformed. Friends took each other's hands, moving to the rhythm with laughter and tears intermingling. The dance floor became a tribute—a living, breathing celebration of MJ's spirit. Cora felt the weight in her chest shift as she joined the circle, spinning and swaying hand-in-hand with Selah, Jensen, and the others. For this moment, the memory wasn't a wound—it was a flame, burning bright and unbroken.

And as the chorus soared, Cora whispered, *"This one's for you, MJ."*

After the song had ended, the bar hummed with low conversation, the kind of energy that lingered in the space between grief and celebration. Glasses clinked, laughter bubbled up in quiet pockets, but at the heart of it all was the unmistakable absence of MJ.

Jensen stood on an unsteady chair, holding up his whiskey neat like it was some kind of sacred relic. The dim glow of the neon signs caught the moisture in his eyes, but his smirk was intact. Classic MJ—still making them feel everything all at once.

He cleared his throat. "Alright, shut up, everyone. I'm about to be poetic and shit, and MJ would never forgive me if I botched this."

The room quieted, every familiar face turning toward him. Some still had tear-streaked cheeks, others wore the kind of smiles that ached at the corners. They were here for MJ, because of MJ. And if that wasn't proof of the ridiculous gravity he had in their lives, Jensen didn't know what was.

But Cora barely heard the rest.

The sight of him standing there, so steady and sure, sent her spiraling into a memory she hadn't touched—one that didn't feel invited but forced its way in.

A vast kitchen at night. The press of curtains blowing in a breeze. The sudden, sharp sound of someone shouting her name. Then movement—fast, jagged—Jensen stepping in front of her before she even understood the danger. A woman's face twisted with fury. The glint of a blade catching the overhead light. And then Jensen's grunt, low and pained, as the knife found him instead of her.

The flash left her breathless, the present room around her tilting ever so slightly. She gripped the edge of her chair, grounding herself in the here and now, but the phantom thud of her own racing heart from that night still echoed in her chest.

Jensen's eyes flicked to hers mid-sentence, just for a second. There was no question in them, no demand for explanation—only the quiet recognition of someone who remembered too. The corner of his mouth twitched upward, not quite a smile, more a silent *I'm still here and you are ok.*

And then he went on speaking, as if nothing had passed between them at all.

He inhaled deeply. "MJ was, in a word… extra." A few chuckles rippled through the crowd. Jensen grinned. "And I mean that in the best way. The man had opinions on everything. Clothes? If you looked like a disaster, he told you before you embarrassed yourself in public. Music? If it wasn't on his playlist, it wasn't worth your time. Life? He didn't just live it—he choreographed it, full lighting design and all."

Someone near the bar let out a choked laugh. Jensen nodded. "He loved hard, danced harder, and if you ever had the privilege of being roasted by him, you know—without a doubt—he loved you."

He swallowed, his throat tight. "MJ was the kind of friend who made life bigger just by being in it. He'd hype you up when you felt like shit, drag you out when you wanted to hide, and he never, ever let you forget that you were worth something."

Jensen exhaled, then smirked up at the ceiling. "And if I know MJ, he is definitely judging my outfit from the afterlife right now."

A soft wave of laughter moved through the room, mingling with quiet sniffles. Jensen lifted his glass higher. "To MJ—I hope Heaven has unlimited WiFi, good tequila, and a dance floor big enough to contain his fabulous soul."

The room echoed back, voices thick with love. "To MJ."

Glasses clinked, the sound ringing out like a promise—he might be gone, but he would never, ever be forgotten. Cora nodded, raising her glass. "To MJ."

The others echoed the toast, clinking glasses before taking a sip. The warmth of the whiskey settled in Cora's chest, momentarily easing the unease lingering at the edges of her mind. But then, a flicker caught her eye. Across the dimly lit bar, a shadow detached itself from the crowd. She didn't want to see him, yet there he was—Vinny.

He wasn't just standing there; he was watching. Still and silent. Like a shadow that refused to fade. The years had etched lines into his face, but the cold, calculating fire in his eyes hadn't softened. A jagged scar traced the length of his cheek—a raw, angry slash that seemed to deepen the menace in his stare. A slow, creeping dread wrapped around Cora like a vise. Her pulse spiked, pounding in her ears, drowning out the music. She tried to look away, to disappear into the crowd, but the moment shattered—Vinny's gaze pinned her in place. And then, without hesitation, he began to move. Closing the distance—deliberate, measured steps.

Panic clawed at her chest as she slipped through the crowd, muttering excuses as she maneuvered toward the exit. The night air was sharp against her skin as she began to take a step outside, desperate for space to breathe.

He looked like time had dragged him behind it—unkempt, eyes bloodshot, jaw twitching like he hadn't slept in days. But the grip on her was steady. Purposeful and possessive.

"Cora," he breathed, yanking her a half-step toward him, away from her friends.

"What the hell—" she started, wrenching her arm back, but he tightened his hold.

"We need to talk," he said, eyes darting between her and the crowd. "Somewhere private."

Her friends were laughing at something behind her, unaware. The room spun a little, the lights blurring with memory—him outside her window, him behind her car, him after the body in the trunk that no one ever proved was real.

She planted her feet. "Let go of me, Vinny."

"I had to disappear," he hissed, a sick edge curling around his words. "It was out of my control."

"You stalked me," she snapped, her voice low and slicing. "You followed me. Harassed me. You *hurt* me. You don't get to pull me aside like we're some kind of unfinished story."

He blinked like the words didn't land, like he was still stuck in a version of their past only he remembered. "You owe me five minutes."

Cora shoved at his chest. "I don't owe you *anything.*"

Her friends finally noticed—Jensen stepping forward, brows drawing down, voice sharp. "Is there a problem here?"

Vinny looked between them—her, the circle closing in, the reality he never fit into. His hand fell away. But she could still feel his fingers on her skin long after he was gone.

"Step away from her." His voice was steel, unwavering.

Vinny scoffed. "Stay out of this, man. This is between me and Cora."

"No," Jensen said, stepping forward. "It's not. And if you don't back off right now, I'll make sure security throws your ass out of here."

Vinny sneered and shoved Jensen hard in the chest. In an instant, Jensen retaliated, grabbing Vinny by the collar and slamming him into the side of the bar, rattling the glasses. Chairs scraped back, voices shouted. Max lunged forward from the crowd, grabbing Vinny's arm just as he swung, yanking him backward and throwing a stiff elbow between them to break it up.

"Enough!" Max barked, planting himself between them like a wall.

Then Rowan appeared—calm but lethal—his hand curling around the front of Vinny's shirt. "You need to leave," he said, low, dangerous. Without waiting for agreement, Rowan shoved him toward the exit, his grip unrelenting, dragging the weight of the moment behind him.

Vinny hesitated, his jaw clenching. He glanced between Cora and Jensen, nostrils flaring, before spitting a curse under his breath. "This isn't over. See you around, Cora," he muttered, pointing to the scar on his face and slipping out into the crowd like a stain disappearing in water.

Cora didn't breathe until Vinny disappeared further into the night. Her legs felt like jelly as the weight of what had just happened crashed over her.

Jensen placed a steadying hand on her shoulder. "You okay?"

She nodded, though her hands were still shaking. "Thank you."

He offered a small, knowing look. "I can't believe he is here… out in public after what we saw that night, Cora."

The night air was still cold, but the warmth of his words settled deep in her chest. She kept her eyes locked on Vinny fading into the distance, refusing to flinch, refusing to give him the satisfaction of seeing her turn away first. Her pulse pounded, but her feet stayed planted, her spine straight.

For a long moment, it was a silent standoff—her breath visible in the chill, his gaze steady and unreadable. Then, without a word, he turned and walked away, his figure disappearing into the crowd.

She had faced her fear. And she won, at least, on the outside.

Her gaze dropped to her hands, trembling despite her will, and she quickly curled them into fists before anyone could notice. *If only you knew the whole truth,'* she thought. The truth that only she carried. The truth she had never spoken aloud.

The truth that no one else saw.

That she didn't just run that one night—she *froze*. That part of her had wanted to scream, but couldn't even find breath. That the look on Vinny's face wasn't just familiar, it was *intimate* in a way that made her question what was real and what had been warped by fear and trauma.

There were things she remembered now that she wished she didn't. The way his voice changed when they were alone. The smell of rust and sweat. The soft click of the lock turning behind her.

She blinked, swallowing down the nausea curling up from her stomach.

People saw a version of the story—the chase, the confrontation, the way she refused to back down. But they didn't know what it had cost her. How much of herself she'd buried just to keep walking, keep smiling, keep functioning.

She kept her gaze forward as her friends walked ahead, laughter slowly returning to their voices. No one asked anything else. No one realized she wasn't breathing right. *If only you knew,* she repeated to herself. *If only anyone knew what it's like to survive something no one saw happen.*

And for now, she'd keep it that way. Because survival, in its quietest form, sometimes meant holding your truth like a blade. Just in case.

The night was quiet by the time they pulled into the gravel driveway of the Airbnb. A faint mist curled around the trees, and the porch light cast a soft glow across the worn wooden steps. No one said much as they stepped out of the car, the laughter from the bar still clinging to them like smoke—faint, but comforting.

The house was tucked back in the woods, quiet and removed, like it had been waiting for them to come and fill it with something old and unfinished. They kicked off their shoes, shrugged out of jackets, and instinctively made their way to the living room, where the fireplace waited behind a pile of kindling and logs with a full ceiling skylight above.

"I got it," Max said, crouching down to start the fire. Sparks caught quickly, flames licking up into warmth as the room slowly filled with a flickering orange glow.

Cora curled into one corner of the oversized couch, legs tucked beneath her. Across from her, Brillia poured hot cider into mismatched mugs they found in the kitchen cabinet. A throw blanket draped across their laps, and soon the others joined—quiet, close, cocooned in the kind of silence that doesn't need filling. They didn't need to talk. Not much. Just small words here and there.

"Same stars," Selah murmured, staring out the window. "We're under the same stars we were back then."

Jensen nodded, eyes on the fire. "Yeah, but we're not the same."

"No," Cora said. "We're not."

The flames crackled, casting shadows across the walls like memories dancing just out of reach. Someone put on a quiet playlist— slow songs that hummed in the background like the steady thrum of a heartbeat. For a while, they just sat, sipped their drinks, and let the years melt away. There were stories they hadn't told each other yet. Scars they hadn't revealed. But not tonight. Tonight was for neither confessions nor ghosts. Tonight was just about being together again.

Brillia eventually rested her head on Jensen's shoulder. Max fell asleep in the recliner, arms folded across his chest. Rowan was sketching absently in a notebook no one asked to see. Cora sat still, eyes fixed on the fire, MJ's face flickering in and out of her thoughts like a reel on loop. She didn't cry. She didn't need to. The fire was enough to keep him here with her, if only for tonight.

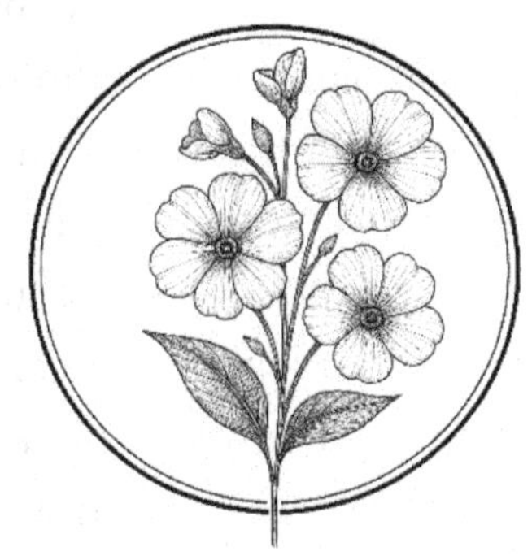

Chapter 15

The Vanishing Point

"And all that remained was her echo."

The café-style hall buzzed with the soft clatter of ceramic mugs, the hiss of an espresso machine, and bursts of laughter echoing from small clusters of former University of Delaware classmates. The late morning light streamed through the tall windows, casting warm beams across armchairs and round tables scattered with pastries and name tags.

Lady Gaga's *"Born This Way"* played quietly from a corner speaker—nostalgic enough to make Cora smile, yet low enough to keep the conversations flowing. It transported her straight back to her college years. A mixture of comfort and polite curiosity lingered in the air, as old acquaintances exchanged updates over cinnamon lattes and blueberry almond croissants.

Cora cradled a cappuccino in both hands, the warmth grounding her as she fielded questions about where she'd been, what she'd been doing, and whether she ever planned on coming back. She had on a cream knit midi dress, cinched at the waist with a tan belt, casual but elegant. Over it, a soft, rust-colored trench-style cardigan draped effortlessly down her arms. Her boots—short suede ankle boots with a heel in a muted taupe—were practical but polished. A stack of thin gold rings shimmered subtly with each movement, and her hair was loosely waved, parted to the side, effortlessly tucked behind one ear.

She smiled and nodded in turn, letting the conversation wash over her like background music, her mind half in the moment and half somewhere else.

Then her phone buzzed.

Cora glanced down, her heart stalling when she saw Harlyn's name flashing across the screen. She never called unless it was urgent. Stepping away from a group of old classmates, Cora pressed the phone to her ear. "Hey, what's up?"

The panic in Harlyn's voice was instant and ice-cold. "Cora—it's Avalina. She's missing."

The words didn't register at first. "What?"

"The zoo—she was at the zoo with the pre-school, and—" Harlyn's voice cracked. "—she's gone. They have the whole place on lockdown. Police are everywhere."

Cora's blood turned to fire. "She's gone?"

"They were in the petting area, and when the teachers looked away for a second, she was just… gone. Security is sweeping the entire zoo. No one's leaving or coming in until they find her."

Cora didn't hear the rest. The phone nearly slipped from her fingers as the cafeteria spun. She grabbed the nearest chair for balance, her breath coming too fast, too shallow.

"Cora?" Harlyn was still talking, but Cora was already moving, weaving blindly through the crowd. She had to get out of here. She had to get home.

She ran straight into Rowan. The concern on his face was immediate. "What's wrong?"

"Avalina—she's missing," Cora choked out. "The zoo—she—" She couldn't get the words out, couldn't breathe.

Rowan didn't hesitate. "We're leaving. Right now."

Just then, Selah and Jensen appeared from the far side of the room, their smiles fading the second they saw Cora's face.

"Cora?" Selah's voice rose slightly as she stepped closer. "What happened?"

"She's pale," Jensen murmured, already moving behind Rowan to steady her. "Is it Avalina?"

"She's gone," Cora whispered, eyes darting between them, still struggling to make sense of it aloud. "At the zoo. I have to go."

Selah's hand flew to her mouth, eyes wide with panic. "We're coming with you."

Jensen nodded firmly. "We'll take my car—Rowan, get her in. Brillia, grab the bags. Max, call the Airbnb and have them get our things to the airport."

No one argued. There wasn't time. It was a blur after that—Selah grabbing their coats, Brillia hustling to gather essentials, Max moving steadily beside them with phone in hand as Jensen called ahead to coordinate with local law enforcement.

Cora tried calling Harlyn back, but the call went straight to voicemail. Every second felt like an hour. The drive to the airport was agonizing. By the time they arrived, Rowan had already booked them on the next flight to Montana.

Cora barely remembered getting on the plane, only the feel of Rowan's steady hand gripping hers as they took off. Her body was on the plane, but her mind was already in Montana, at the zoo, frantically searching every shadow for her daughter.

She whispered a silent prayer. *Please, please let her be okay.*

Cora's heels clicked sharply against the polished airport floor as she rushed through the terminal, her heart pounding louder than the overhead announcements. They had landed in Kalispell, Montana, just after 11 p.m., cutting short her college reunion the moment she got the call that Avalina was missing, and it was a grueling day of travel.

The scenic drive to Bigfork, normally breathtaking with its winding roads and glimpses of Flathead Lake, blurred past her in darkness. The quaint town, known for its art galleries and summer tourists, felt foreign now. It was just after midnight, and the zoo had already been shut down for hours. It was only blocks from the boutique, so Harlyn asked Cora to meet her there. No one was sleeping tonight anyway.

As they pulled onto Electric Avenue, the charming shops and cafes stood in eerie silence, their cheerful window displays dim and lifeless. They parked hastily in front of her boutique. Inside, the store was a mess—papers scattered, lights left on, as if someone had rushed out in the middle of a thought. Harlyn stood in the center, her face streaked with tears, her expression crumpled and broken.

The bell above the boutique door chimed, but it didn't match the disorder spinning inside Cora. The sound was far too delicate, too ordinary, as if the universe hadn't gotten the message that everything had just tilted off its axis. Cora's head jerked up. Harlyn's body was frozen behind the register, but her heartbeat was like it was trying to punch through her ribs. She'd been pretending to function, but her hands had been shaking. Every breath she took felt like it might be the one that unraveled her completely, and she couldn't bring herself to leave the shop.

"She was there one moment, and then she wasn't," Harlyn sobbed, her voice cracking under the weight of panic. Her fingers trembled as she reached for Cora, clutching her arm like it was the only thing keeping her upright—something real in a moment that didn't feel possible.

Cora didn't flinch. She couldn't. Her body had gone still, every muscle locked in place as if any movement might shatter the fragile thread holding her together. Her heart thundered in her chest, but her face stayed calm—too calm. Shock had settled in like frost.

Avalina was gone.

She wrapped an arm around Harlyn automatically, but her own legs felt foreign, ready to give out at any second. The boutique blurred around her edges. The sound of the wind outside. The faint hum of a distant car. Even the way Harlyn was breathing—it all seemed far away, like it was happening through a pane of glass.

Inside her, something had cracked. And in its place, a low, familiar terror had begun to rise.

Then Gemma stepped in, not with her usual sunlit smile or easy warmth, but with her face drawn tight—grief and fear etched in the lines around her mouth. Her eyes scanned the shop like she half-expected to see Avalina's shoes by the rug or hear her laugh from the back room. Miles followed close behind, his shoulders squared, jaw clenched. He looked like he'd walked through fire to get there.

Everything in Cora went still. The world hadn't stopped—but she had. Because deep down, she already knew what they were going to say. Her mind fought to outrun it, to deny it. But her body told the truth. Avalina was missing. And everything was about to come undone.

"Hey," Gemma said gently, her voice like a blanket.

Cora straightened, startled by the sound of the door. "It's… midnight."

"We know," Miles said quietly. "We couldn't sleep."

"We heard," Gemma added, stepping closer. "We just wanted to see if you needed anything. Anything at all."

The mention of *need* nearly broke her. Her mouth opened, then closed. What could they possibly give her that would matter if Avalina didn't come home?

Gemma rested her hands on the counter, her face soft with worry. "We saw the flyers. Heard the chatter. I thought—I hoped it wasn't true. But Harlyn told me this afternoon."

"She's gone," Cora whispered. "I left town for some stupid, pointless college reunion and now my baby is gone."

"Hey, no," Gemma said quickly. "This isn't your fault." She reached across the counter, gently gripping Cora's wrist. "What do you need? Do you want us to help call people? Repost flyers? Watch the shop while you rest?"

"I can't rest," Cora said, pulling her hand back. "Not until she's in my arms."

Gemma blinked hard, then said, "Then let us help you look."

Cora stared at them. Just a few weeks ago, their connection had been fragile, built on bizarre encounters and the awkwardness of neighboring businesses. But somehow, that odd arrangement had become something more—an unspoken loyalty, a strange, beautiful kind of friendship that appeared when she needed it the most. Now they stood in her boutique like anchors in a life that was drifting away.

She nodded. "Okay."

Miles took out his phone. "Send us everything you have. Photos. Any leads. Even small things. We'll follow everyone."

As they turned to leave, Gemma looked back. "She's coming home, Cora. She has to."

Cora wasn't sure if it was a promise or a prayer, but she clung to it like it was oxygen. Her mind raced, piecing together the fragments of information. The serene town of Bigfork, with its vibrant community and scenic landscapes, now felt like a maze of unanswered questions and growing fears. Cora sat at the center of it all, surrounded by a patchwork army of loyalty and urgency—Jensen, pacing with his phone pressed to his ear; Selah, quiet but steady, typing out updates for the search team; Brillia and Max, huddled by the boutique window with maps and marked-up flyers; Rowan, perched near the door, eyes on every shadow that passed. Gemma and Miles brewed coffee like fuel for soldiers, handing out steaming mugs as if they were weapons of hope. Harlyn, worn thin but refusing to collapse, organized contact lists and called out check-ins like she was commanding her own unit.

It wasn't chaos. It was coordinated desperation and a collective refusal to let the dark hours swallow Cora whole. The boutique had become a war room. Flyers, Post-its, laptop cords, half-eaten bagels, and hand-drawn timelines cluttered every surface. No one left, and no one folded.

Determined, Cora stepped outside as dawn finally crept in, her gaze fixed on the horizon. The tranquil waters of Flathead Lake glistened in the distance, a cruel contrast to the storm inside her.

She closed her eyes, drawing in the crisp morning air, and in the silence, she whispered softly, *"Gram, show me the way."*

A calm steadied her breath, as if the gentle presence of her grandmother had slipped beside her, a quiet guide in the breaking light. She wouldn't stop. None of them would. Not until Avalina came home.

The first hint of sunrise streaked the sky in pale pink and ash-blue, brushing the rooftops of Bigfork with soft light. The town was beginning to stir—paper carriers on bikes, a dog barking in the distance—oblivious to the war waging inside the boutique. Cora stood at the door, arms wrapped around herself, scanning every car that passed, every unfamiliar figure on the sidewalk. Her body was exhausted, but her mind refused to rest. Inside, the others had gone quiet, not from defeat—but from focus. A tired sort of discipline.

Then Jensen's voice cut through the stillness. "We've got something."

Everyone froze.

Cora turned, heart lurching as she stepped back inside. Jensen held his phone out, speaker on. "That was Detective Salone. They picked something up on the zoo's rear lot cameras—past the employee exit."

Rowan leaned in. "What kind of something?"

"A woman," Jensen said, jaw tight. "Wearing a rugged coat. She's holding a child's hand. They vanished behind the feed blind spot near the maintenance building around 10:17 a.m. yesterday."

Cora's knees buckled, but she didn't fall.

"Did they get a clear look at her?" Selah asked.

"Not yet. But it's enough to launch a full-scale sweep of the zoo grounds again. They're calling in the dogs."

Max was already grabbing his keys. "We're going down there."

"No," Cora said, voice suddenly firm. "*I'm* going down there."

Rowan moved beside her. "We're not letting you do this alone."

She nodded, the fire returning to her chest. "Then let's go. Every second counts."

The war room emptied in an instant. And as they piled into cars under the rising sun, Cora's fear didn't vanish—but for the first time in hours, it had direction.

"I'm coming for you, Avalina," she whispered, steeling herself for the search ahead.

The car hadn't even come to a full stop at 8:00 am when the zoo opened. Cora jumped out, slamming the door behind her as she sprinted across the cracked pavement of the zoo entrance. Her lungs burned from the flight, the drive, the screaming silence that had filled every second since she got the call: Avalina is missing.

The zoo, once a place of weekend joy and sticky ice cream cones, felt foreign now—every family, every sound a threat, and every moment a ticking clock. Police cars lined the curb while staff in khakis and radios moved in hurried clusters. But Cora didn't see any of them. Not really. She saw *the gate*. And just beyond it, caught on the metal fencing like it had been reaching for her: Avalina's brave bow. A pale ribbon, its ends dusty and wrinkled, fluttering faintly in the breeze. Cora froze. The world around her fell away. Her knees buckled, and she sank to the pavement.

"No, no, no," she whispered, reaching for it like it might dissolve if she touched it too hard. Her fingers curled around the satin as sobs overtook her chest, raw and shattering. She held it to her heart like it was a lifeline. It was *hers*. Tied that very morning before the field trip. Harlyn had smoothed Avalina's braid, kissed her cheek, and whispered: *"Brave girls wear brave bows."*

And now it was on the ground. Discarded and lost. Just like her daughter.

"Ms. Atler?" She looked up, her eyes red, heart crumbling, to see a zoo manager approaching with a grim face and a folder in hand. Behind him, two officers whispered near the map kiosk. But all Cora could do was hold up the ribbon.

"She was wearing this," she said, voice cracking. "She never takes it off. She never would."

The manager nodded solemnly, but before he could speak, the sound of footsteps scattered behind her.

Cora turned to see her army—Jensen, Selah, Brillia, Max, Rowan, Gemma, Miles, and Harlyn—already spreading out across the zoo grounds without instructions. Jensen headed toward the rear service roads with one of the officers. Brillia snapped a photo of the ribbon and started showing it to every parent she passed. Selah and Max went straight for the petting area, retracing Avalina's last known steps. Rowan peeled off toward the east lot, eyes sharp and jaw locked. Gemma and Miles fanned out near the snack shacks and restrooms, checking behind fences and under benches. Harlyn stayed near Cora, fielding texts and coordinating with the growing number of volunteers who had shown up just to help.

They moved with a silent understanding, like soldiers dispatched across enemy lines. No one waited for orders. No one questioned their place. They were fighting for Avalina. And Cora—gripping the ribbon like a lifeline—knew she wasn't alone in this war.

The manager knelt beside her. "We've reviewed security footage. We're doing everything we can. Would you be willing to walk us through your daughter's habits? Favorite things? Favorite animals? Anywhere she might have wandered off to?"

Cora nodded numbly, rising to her feet. She wrapped the ribbon around her wrist like armor. Because brave girls wore brave bows. And Cora was going to be brave now, too. Her voice wavered as she tried to answer. "She loves foxes. And dragons. Her favorite color is pink. And anything with glitter." Her throat caught. "Sometimes she hides when she's overwhelmed. Or pretends she's on a secret mission. She loves art. She has nightmares."

The words came out hollow, like she was describing someone else's child. And then—something flickered in her memory. Ava's dreams. Her visions. Ava whispering to corners and giggling at empty spaces, talking to someone who wasn't there. Cora had chalked it up to her daughter's vivid imagination.

"She talks to someone," Cora added faintly. "Or… used to. An imaginary friend, I suppose. I thought it was imaginary, anyway. But now… it feels silly to even bring that up."

But it didn't feel silly anymore. It felt like she'd missed something— something crucial hidden in plain sight. She gripped the ribbon tighter. *Brave girls wore brave bows.* But brave mothers didn't ignore what scared them.

Cora stood outside the boutique later that afternoon, her phone trembling in her hand as she tried to process the most recent conversation with the local authorities. No new leads. No confirmed sightings. Just waiting. Endless, hollow waiting. She wasn't alone. Behind her, the boutique lights glowed dimly, and her army had returned—Jensen, Selah, Harlyn, Brillia, Max, Gemma, and Miles—all there, all still holding the line. Rowan had stopped by his house to check on his kids.

Some sat in the front windows, scanning the street for unfamiliar faces or official cars. Others stood quietly, phones in hand, eyes darting at every alert. They spoke in low tones, sipped coffee they no longer tasted, and waited. Not because they had to, but because they refused to let her face this alone.

A shadow passed across the sidewalk, and she looked up to see Lincoln. She hadn't seen him in over two weeks. But now he stood in front of her—his face pale, lips tight, eyes frantic.

A few fat raindrops began to fall, tapping softly on the pavement, quickly turning into a steady drizzle that blurred the edges of the world around them.

"I heard," he said, breathless. "Cora, I just heard. I came as soon as I could."

She stiffened. Her arms folded across her chest like armor. "I'm waiting to hear from the detective. Will you stay with me, please?"

"Absolutely, Cora… anything," Lincoln said, his voice steady despite the storm gathering overhead, as they both walked back inside.

A knock sounded at the door. Sharp and deliberate. Cora stood quickly, pulse picking up speed, and crossed the store. When she opened the door, Detective Salone stood there with his badge glinting at his belt, rain speckled across his shoulders. His expression was calm, but with that particular kind of weight Cora had come to recognize.

"Cora," he said with a short nod. "I'm sorry to show up unannounced. We have an update."

She stepped aside without a word. Detective Salone stepped in, the door closing behind him with a soft thud.

"We pulled security footage from the zoo parking lot," he began, voice steady. "It's grainy, but it's clear enough. Around 10:21 a.m., Avalina is seen walking hand-in-hand with a woman. Late twenties. Light build. Most distinct feature is hot pink hair, worn in a messy bun. She was driving a silver Honda Civic, late model. No plates visible from the rear angle, but we're working on enhancing the video from a nearby traffic camera."

Cora pressed a hand to her mouth, her thoughts racing. "Did Avalina look scared?"

Tate Salone paused. "No. That's the strange part. She didn't struggle. She didn't look distressed. If anything… she looked like she trusted her."

A heavy silence settled over the room.

"She knew her," Cora whispered.

"Maybe," the detective said carefully. "We're working through known associates, pulling anyone in your circle with that description. But Cora—do you know anyone matching that?"

Cora shook her head, but her mind was already scanning faces, fragments, possibilities. Hot pink hair. A Civic. Trust.

"She's not one of my friends," she said slowly, almost to herself.

Tate Salone's jaw tightened. "We've increased patrols and put out an APB. I need you to let me know immediately if you remember anything, no matter how small. A barista. A vendor. Someone who smiled too long."

Cora nodded, mind spinning. The idea of someone hiding in plain sight—earning Avalina's trust just long enough to take her—made her stomach turn.

The detective's phone buzzed. He glanced at it. "We're running down the car now. I'll call as soon as we have more." Then he was gone.

Cora stood there, staring at the space he'd occupied, her hands balled into fists at her sides. Hot pink hair. A Civic. Avalina leaving without a fight. Cora then opened the door to find Rowan standing there—rain-speckled, tense, his chest rising and falling like he'd been holding his breath the entire drive over. His eyes found hers instantly, glassy with worry.

"Any updates?" he asked, voice rough.

She nodded and stepped aside. *"Come in."*

As Rowan stepped through the doorway, Lincoln pushed himself up from the arm of the couch. Their eyes locked, and something in the air between them went tense, stretched tight like a wire. It was recognition. Lincoln felt it coil low in his gut. The man standing in the doorway wasn't a stranger. He was the one who'd danced with Cora that night in the boutique. The one she leaned into, smiled up at like he was safe. The one Lincoln had watched from the shadows, uncertain why it had bothered him so deeply then, but now he understood—it wasn't jealousy, it was knowing.

And now, seeing his rain-speckled figure, his furrowed brow, the way he avoided Lincoln's eyes altogether, it settled something. Rowan looked right past him, like he hadn't been part of anything. Like he didn't matter. But Lincoln did. And this time, he wasn't stepping aside.

Cora folded her arms tightly across her chest. "The detective came by just now."

Rowan's eyes flicked up, finally acknowledging Lincoln, but only to glance past him. "What'd he say?"

"They got surveillance footage from the zoo parking lot," she said. "Avalina's seen walking off with a woman. Late twenties. Slender. Hot pink hair, pulled into a messy bun. Driving a silver Honda—plates weren't visible."

Rowan froze, just for a second. But it was enough. His face didn't shift much. Then he moved, casually, slowly, toward the fireplace. "Pink hair?" he said, like he was repeating something foreign.

"Yes," Cora said, watching him closely now. "Do you know anyone like that?"

He gave a short laugh, but it didn't touch his eyes. "Um… no. No one I can think of. That's… wild." He rubbed his jaw and turned his back to her, staring into the street. "You'd think someone like that would stand out."

"She did," Cora said. "Enough for Avalina to walk away with her. No fear. No hesitation."

Rowan shifted. Just barely. But she saw it—shoulders tightening, neck stiffening like a vice was turning slowly.

"That kind of trust doesn't come out of nowhere," she added, voice sharper now.

He turned around, slower than before. "I'm sure they'll figure out who she is."

Cora narrowed her eyes. Something in her gut twisted.

"I'm just trying to make sense of it," she said, "because it sounds like Avalina knew her. And the only people Avalina knows with pink hair are characters in her sticker books. Not someone who drives a Civic and waits in parking lots."

Rowan looked at her, jaw tight. "Maybe it was a stranger. Kids are trusting sometimes. Wait, did you say Civic?"

"Yes, and she's not *that* trusting," Cora said coldly.

There was a long pause between them. The kind that didn't belong in a room that used to feel safe.

Rowan blinked. "Cora, there's something I need to tell you," he said as the boutique grew still. "I wasn't honest with you regarding my ex-wife, Vanessa. She is alive, and I'm worried it was her who took Avalina."

Cora took a slow breath. "What? You said your ex-wife was dead. You told me she died. Complications. Medication. That's what you said."

He nodded slowly, but his eyes didn't meet hers. "Yes. That's what I told you. But you don't understand. I had to have her committed. She wasn't safe for the kids to be around."

Cora stepped closer, voice low. "Rowan. If that woman is her—if she's alive and took Avalina—you *lied*."

He didn't respond. Not right away. Then finally, Rowan looked up, guilt heavy behind his eyes. "It's complicated."

"No, it's not!" Cora snapped. "You lied about her being dead!"

He opened his mouth to speak, but no words came. Just silence. Thick. Final. Cora took a step back. "Get out."

"Cora—"

"No. You don't get to be here right now. Not when the woman who has taken my daughter is your wife, and you stood here acting clueless."

Rowan's face collapsed into regret, but he didn't argue. He knew. She could see it in the way his hands clenched at his sides, like he could keep the truth from spilling out any further. He walked out the door without saying another word.

Cora stared at the door, her heart at war with itself. Logic told her to push him away. Rage screamed that he didn't deserve even an ounce of trust. But somewhere in the chaos, the mother in her… the desperate, hollowed-out version… knew that finding Avalina mattered more than any personal grudge. Before she could respond, a car screeched to a stop at the curb. The door flew open, and Dax burst out.

"Where is she?" he demanded, eyes already misting with tears.

"She's gone," Cora managed. "I think it was Rowan's ex—she took her."

Dax's hands flew to his mouth. "Oh my God."

Without hesitation, Dax rushed to Cora and wrapped her in a fierce, shaking hug.

"We're going to find her," Dax whispered into her ear. "No matter what. I'll tear this entire town apart if I have to."

Lincoln stepped with urgency and clarity, the calm in the storm. He locked eyes with Rowan as he stood outside on the walk, his jaw tightening. "This isn't about history or mistakes," Lincoln said evenly. "It's about Avalina. So we move fast, we move smart. No egos. No pasts."

Selah nodded too, pulling her phone out. "I've got friends in Missoula. I'll get her photo circulating everywhere. If she's on a road, a bus, a back trail—someone's going to see her."

In that fragile moment, beneath the weight of betrayal and heartbreak, they became a team—fractured, uneasy, but united by the love for one little girl who was everything to Cora. Cora's legs gave out before she even reached the counter, bracing herself to call the detective with the news she had just received. She crumpled to her knees, her fingers clawing at her scalp like she could dig out the terror forming behind her eyes. She couldn't scream. She couldn't cry. She just shook, violently, as if her body was rejecting the moment altogether.

Lincoln dropped to the floor beside her, pulling her into him without hesitation. She collapsed against his chest, every ounce of strength pouring out of her. He didn't say, *"It's going to be okay."* He didn't make false promises. He just held her, firm and steady, like an anchor in the middle of a hurricane.

"She probably knew where we lived," Cora finally said, the words barely audible. "Where I worked. She watched us. I should've seen it. I should've known. Oh, my God, I did know! I saw a woman with bright pink hair standing here on the street once. Harlyn and I thought she was a homeless person!"

"No," Lincoln cut in gently but firmly. "This isn't on you. She's unwell, and Rowan should've protected you both from her. This is not your fault, Cora."

She sobbed into his chest, the weight of blame splintering against the steadiness of his voice.

Across the room, Jensen and Selah exchanged a brief, guarded look. Neither spoke, but the unasked question hung quietly between them: Who exactly was this Lincoln, and what part was he playing in Cora's life now?

"We'll get her back," he said, pulling back enough to meet her eyes. "I have a friend at the department—he owes me more than a few favors. We'll get her picture to every patrol in a hundred-mile radius. And we'll find Avalina."

Cora nodded, but the panic still pulsed beneath her skin. "What if she hurts her?"

Lincoln's eyes darkened, his jaw clenched. "Then I swear to you, she'll never see daylight again."

Twelve hours later, after police leads and agonizing silence, Cora sat on Lincoln's couch, staring at the door as if Avalina might magically appear. She hadn't eaten. She hadn't blinked in minutes. She was a statue carved from fear. Lincoln returned from the kitchen with tea she wouldn't drink, a blanket she didn't ask for, and a flashlight, just in case the power went out as a storm began to roll in deeper. He didn't speak much, just stayed close, steady.

Then, at 4:13 a.m., her phone shattered the silence with a sudden ring, sharp and urgent. She fumbled to answer, heart pounding so fiercely it echoed in her ears.

"It's the police," the voice on the other end said, steady but kind. "We've found Avalina."

For a moment, time stopped—her breath caught, her hands trembling so violently she nearly dropped the phone.

"She's safe," the officer continued. "Scared, crying, but unharmed. We're bringing her to the station now."

The weight she'd been carrying—the crushing fear, the endless waiting—collapsed in on itself. Cora sank, knees hitting the floor as tears streamed freely, this time flowing not from pain but from a flood of overwhelming relief. Her body trembled as sobs racked through her, the tight coil of dread finally unraveling. She was whole again, if only for this moment.

Lincoln drove her to the station, gripping the wheel so tight his knuckles turned white. She couldn't stop shaking. He reached over once, grabbing her hand and holding it against the center console.

"I've got you," he whispered. *"No matter what happens next."*

When Avalina ran into her arms at the station, sobbing into her neck, Cora broke down completely. But she didn't crumble alone. Lincoln stood behind them, watching and protecting. When Avalina finally fell asleep in the backseat on the drive home, Cora reached over and gripped Lincoln's hand again.

"Thank you," she whispered. *"For letting me fall apart."*

"You didn't fall," he said. "You bent. You cracked. But you didn't break. Vanessa will be locked up for a long time now. She won't be able to hurt anyone else."

She looked at him then—really looked—and in the wreckage of it all, something solid had been built between them. And in that quiet understanding, she found the strength to believe she could keep moving forward—one unbroken step at a time.

Chapter 16

Letting Go To Hold On

"Sometimes the hardest part of holding on is learning when to let go—because only then can we grasp the life waiting just beyond our fear."

The boutique was still the next morning. Cora sat at her desk in the back, staring blankly at her planner. Nothing on the page made sense. Appointments. Book shipments. Storytime schedules. All of it felt too normal for the kind of ache still blooming in her chest. Avalina was now home, safe, and sleeping with a new nightlight and the door cracked open. But Cora wasn't okay—not fully. Her body had come down from panic, but her mind was still trapped in those empty hours, waiting for the phone to ring.

She didn't hear the door open later that afternoon, but she felt his presence, as always. "Hey," Lincoln said softly, stepping into the back room. "Didn't mean to sneak up on you."

She looked up, offering a faint smile. "You didn't. I'm just… spaced out."

"I figured." He leaned against the doorway, arms crossed casually, like he belonged there. Like he *wanted* to be there. "So… I have a wild idea."

Cora raised an eyebrow. "Oh?"

"I'm thinking… late lunch."

She blinked. "Late lunch?"

"Yep. Normally, it's the meal where people eat food in the middle of the day. Ever heard of it?" he teased lightly.

A genuine laugh slipped out before she could stop it, and Lincoln grinned at the sound.

"I don't know if I'm good company," she admitted.

"Don't care," he said. "I'm not looking for a comedy set. I run my own show. I just figured we could sit somewhere that's not filled with paperwork or worry. Maybe get you something besides granola bars and coffee."

She hesitated. "You sure you're not just trying to distract me?"

He stepped closer. "Cora, I want to be with you. Even if we sit in silence. Even if you don't eat a bite. I just… want to be near you. That okay?"

Her chest tightened. Not from pain, but something warm. Gentle. A tenderness that had nothing to prove and no expectations. *"Yeah,"* she said softly. *"That's okay."*

"Good," Lincoln replied with a small smile. "There's a diner in town. Real local. You'll hate their wallpaper but love their fries."

She grabbed her bag and stood. "Fine. But if the wallpaper's floral, I'm deducting points."

He held the door open for her after Harlyn strolled in, already chuckling. "You'll survive. And hey, we'll make a game of judging it together."

Cora stepped into the sunlight, the weight of the past few days still lingering. But she felt a little lighter with Lincoln beside her. It was just lunch, but maybe also a start. They stepped into Rita's, a cozy diner with exactly the kind of wallpaper Lincoln had warned her about— faded roses and roosters in gold-trimmed frames.

"Oh wow," Cora murmured, eyes scanning the walls. "It's like someone's grandma threw up on this place."

Lincoln laughed. "And yet somehow, their grilled cheese will change your life."

They slid into a corner booth, tucked away from the few other patrons. The waitress—an older woman with a name tag that read *Minnie* and a voice that sounded like gravel—poured them both water without asking.

"Y'all want menus, or you regulars?"

"We'll take menus," Lincoln said with a smile, and Minnie gave them a knowing nod before wandering off.

Cora ran her fingers over the edge of the laminated menu. "You come here a lot?"

"Used to. When things felt too loud."

She nodded. "Makes sense. This place has that… 3 a.m. in a good dream kind of feel."

They ordered grilled cheese for Lincoln, soup and half a sandwich for her, though she knew she probably wouldn't finish it. But it felt good to say yes to something. To anything.

Lincoln leaned forward, resting his arms on the table. "You sleep at all last night?"

She shook her head. "Avalina couldn't settle unless she was touching me. So she curled up against me like a puppy. Every time I moved, she flinched. I just… stayed still."

He softened. "That's love."

"That's exhaustion," she muttered, then paused. "But yeah… it's love, too."

Millie returned with their drinks and a plate of fries Lincoln didn't order but clearly expected. He pushed them toward her.

"They're therapy fries," he said. "Try one."

She smiled faintly and picked one up. It was hot and perfectly salted.

She let out a small sigh. "Okay. Fine. That was unfairly good."

"See?" he said. "All part of my master plan. Distract you with carbs and heartburn."

Cora laughed again, then caught herself. Her eyes dropped to her water glass.

Lincoln noticed. "What?"

"I just… forgot what it felt like. To laugh. To feel something besides panic." She looked up. "I don't want to let myself enjoy anything. It feels wrong."

"It's not wrong," Lincoln said gently. "It's human. And it doesn't mean you're forgetting what happened. It just means you're still here. Still breathing. Still trying."

She studied him for a long time. "Why are you so good to me?"

Lincoln tilted his head. "Because I see you, Cora. I see the way you fight for her. I see the way you carry all this weight and still get out of bed. And because… if I were Avalina, I'd want *you* as my mom."

Her throat tightened. No one had ever said something like that to her, not like that.

She reached across the table, brushing her fingertips against his. *"Thank you,"* she said quietly.

They didn't rush the meal. They didn't talk about the worst parts of what had happened. But in that little booth, surrounded by tacky roosters and the smell of burnt bacon, Cora felt something new unfurl inside her. It was peace. And maybe—just maybe—a little hope.

The sun hung low over Bigfork as they pulled away from the diner, golden light spilling across the windshield. Lincoln had rolled down the windows, letting in the breeze that smelled like pine and something faintly sweet—maybe from the orchard up the road.

Cora sat in the passenger seat, her head leaning back against the window, eyes half-closed.

"Full?" Lincoln asked, glancing at her with a smirk.

"More than I thought I'd be," she murmured. "Your therapy fries worked."

"Told you," he said. "They've got a ninety percent emotional success rate. FDA pending."

She chuckled softly, turning her face toward the wind. It lifted strands of her hair across her cheek. Lincoln reached out on instinct, brushing one back. She didn't flinch. She didn't pull away. Instead, she just looked at him. There was a weight in her eyes, but it wasn't crushing anymore. Just heavy with everything she'd survived.

"I hated going to that reunion," she said quietly. "Every second I was there, I felt like a fraud. I was smiling for people who didn't really know me anymore. And the whole time, I was trying not to think about how far I'd come… or how far I hadn't."

Lincoln kept his eyes on the road but listened with full attention.

"Then the call came," she continued, voice tighter now. "That Avalina was missing. And suddenly, none of it mattered. Nothing. I was on the next flight back, and I kept thinking… *This is it. I'm going to lose her. I'm going to be too late.*"

"You weren't," Lincoln said gently. "You got to her. You survived this, Cora, and it will never happen again."

"Avalina's different. She has these crazy nightmares, and she sees things…things I never told her about. I can't imagine how scared she must have been…and I can't imagine not being there for her during one of her episodes," she said, her voice cracking. "There's just been a lot going on. You kept me grounded. You helped me hold it together. And you didn't let me fall apart even when I was already halfway there."

Lincoln was quiet for a moment, then reached over, his hand finding hers where it rested in her lap. "I didn't help you," he said. "I just stood beside you while you saved her. I always will, if you let me."

The road curved gently around the lake, and the sky cast reflections in the water, like something out of a dream.

Cora looked out, her hand still in his. "I don't know if I'm ready."

"You don't have to be," he said. "You just have to keep showing up. I'll meet you wherever you are."

They pulled up outside her house, the porch light already on, even though the sun hadn't fully set. Cora didn't move right away. She looked at their joined hands, then at him.

"Want to come in?" she asked softly. "Just for a minute?"

Lincoln smiled. "Only if there's a second round of fries in there."

"No fries," she said, returning the smile. "But I've got wine and a couch that could use some company."

He turned the key, shutting off the engine. "Sounds perfect."

The house was quiet after Harlyn left, except for the sound of Avalina's giggles echoing through the hallway. Cora stood in the doorway of her daughter's bedroom, arms folded, one shoulder against the frame, watching Lincoln sitting cross-legged on the rug. Avalina was draped in a blanket like a queen, a stack of books beside her, and a flashlight in her hand as though she was running the show.

"Again!" she squealed, pointing the flashlight at him like a command.

Lincoln grinned. "Alright, alright. One more story. But then—it's tickle tuck time."

Avalina squealed again, already wiggling with anticipation.

He picked up the book—*The Snoring Hippo and the Jungle Parade*—and cleared his throat dramatically.

"Once upon a snore, in a jungle made of snores," he began, his voice deep and theatrical, "there lived a hippo who could *not* stay awake... unless someone tooted a kazoo near his ear."

Cora covered her mouth, stifling a laugh as Lincoln made kazoo noises with exaggerated effort. Avalina howled, falling sideways onto her pillow, her face buried but still grinning. He read through the story with sound effects, voices, and wild gestures. When he reached the end, he set the book down carefully on her nightstand.

"Alright, your majesty," he said, rising to his feet. "It's time for... the official tickle tuck. Cora, you ready for this?"

Cora raised a brow. "You're on your own, buddy."

"Coward," he whispered with mock betrayal before launching into a goofy, offbeat dance.

He swayed his hips, spun in a circle, then tiptoed toward Avalina with his fingers wiggling in front of him like claws. *"The Tickle Tuck Monster is comiiiiiing...!"*

She shrieked, laughing as he pounced, tickling her sides and chanting, *"Tickle tuck! Tickle tuck!"* as if it were part of some sacred bedtime tradition.

Cora's laughter joined Avalina's, and for the first time in what felt like ages, the house didn't feel haunted by what had happened. It felt... alive. Lincoln finally stopped and flopped onto the bed beside her, both of them breathless.

"You win," he said dramatically. "I'm officially tickled out."

Avalina reached up, wrapping her small arms around his neck. *"You're funny,"* she whispered.

He smiled, touched and humbled all at once. "You're braver than any kid I've ever met."

He tucked the blanket up around her shoulders, pressed a hand gently to her forehead like a soft promise, then stood and looked at Cora. She took his hand, guiding him out of the room as Avalina drifted off, her flashlight still clutched in one hand. Out in the hallway, the soft click of Avalina's bedroom door behind them felt like a seal—one that held in all the laughter, all the trust Cora hadn't dared imagine she'd let into her home again.

She leaned into Lincoln, her voice barely above a whisper. *"She really likes you."*

It wasn't casual. It wasn't filler. It was weighty, trembling on the edge of surprise.

Lincoln met her gaze, then slowly brushed her arm. "I *really* like her," he said. Then softer, with that steady heat she hadn't yet learned how to brace for, *"And her mama."*

Cora exhaled like she'd been holding something in for longer than she realized. She hadn't planned to let anyone in like this—not again, not after Rowan. But there it was. No fireworks, no grand declarations. Just comfort. Quiet and earned. And maybe that was what surprised her most—that Lincoln didn't ask to be let in. He simply belonged there.

A pause passed between them, full of all the things they didn't need to say just yet.

"How about that drink?" she asked, her voice quiet.

"Only if you do the tickle tuck next time," he teased.

She smiled. "Deal."

They walked to the kitchen together, the house quiet but full—finally full—in a different, beautiful way. The kitchen was dimly lit as Cora moved around, grabbing two wine glasses. Lincoln leaned against the counter, watching her. She was doing something small and familiar, but there was an undercurrent of restrained tension in her movements, a hesitance in how she didn't quite meet his eyes.

"Do you want red or white?" she asked, her voice steady, but there was a fragility there that he caught immediately.

"Red's fine," Lincoln replied. He watched her pour the wine. He wanted to ask, wanted to push, but he held back—waiting, patient.

She handed him the glass, her fingers brushing his as she placed it in his hand. He could feel the weight of the silence between them.

"I was in an accident. I don't remember a lot of things from before," Cora began, her voice low, almost a whisper. "There are gaps… dark, empty places. Lucky for me, I used to write everything down in journals…everything that happened with Ava's father—and those pieces are slowly coming back… I have had my fair share of lies, violence, manipulations. I thought I was just… running from it."

Lincoln stayed silent, giving her the space to keep speaking. He hadn't expected her to open up this soon. He could feel the heaviness in the air.

"I can remember some things clearly now," she continued, her eyes staring into the swirling steam of her tea. "His eyes. How he could look at me and make me feel like I was the only one that mattered. But then there were other moments. Things he said, things that happened that I can't even see anymore. Like a fog rolled in, and it's all… smudged."

Lincoln took a slow sip of his wine, his gaze never leaving her. "It's like your mind's protecting you."

She nodded, looking at the glass in her hands, as if it held answers she couldn't quite grasp. "It's not just about Declan, though. It's like… I'm living in a cloud. I go through the motions, but nothing feels real. We lived in Colorado, and I thought that if I left it all behind, moved to Montana and started fresh, it would get better. And maybe it did; I just don't remember. Every time something triggers a memory, I'm just left… lost. I can't trust myself. I don't even trust my own thoughts anymore."

Her voice cracked on the last part, and she quickly turned her face away, wiping her eyes before he could see.

Lincoln set his cup down and moved closer, standing beside her. "Cora," he said softly, his voice full of quiet conviction. "You're not lost. Not anymore."

She shook her head, wiping her eyes again, but this time, she didn't pull away when he gently cupped her face with his hand. *"You don't get it,"* she whispered, her breath shaky. "How can I find my way when I can't even remember the path? I don't even know who I am sometimes. I thought I'd found myself in Avalina, but now I'm scared… scared that one day, I'll wake up and I won't even recognize myself."

Lincoln's thumb brushed across her cheek. "You are not your past, Cora. You're not Declan, and you're not the fear that lingers in the corners of your memories. You're a mother. You're a fighter. You're someone who's been through more than most could bear, and yet—look at you. You're still here. You're still fighting."

Her breath caught in her throat. "But I don't feel strong. I feel like I'm just pretending. Like any second, the fog will swallow me whole."

"I get it," Lincoln said, his voice low, soothing.

Cora closed her eyes for a moment. She hadn't realized how much she needed to hear that until it was spoken aloud. It didn't fix everything, but it was a lifeline—a reminder that maybe she wasn't as alone as she felt. She opened her eyes again and looked at him, her gaze soft but searching. "I don't know what this is between us, Lincoln. I don't know if I'm ready to let anyone in. But I'm scared. And I don't want to be scared anymore."

He leaned closer, his voice steady. "Then let me help you, Cora. Let me be here when the fog feels too thick, when the memories are too heavy. You don't have to figure this out by yourself."

For the first time in a long while, Cora felt the weight in her chest loosen, just a little. She didn't have all the answers. She didn't know where this was headed or what the future held. But in this moment, she wasn't running. She wasn't alone.

Lincoln's hand lingered on hers for just a moment longer before he gently squeezed it, his gaze steady and full of understanding. "I'll be right here," he said. "Always."

Cora sat down at the kitchen table, her hands wrapped around her glass. For a moment, everything felt still—like the world outside had faded, leaving only the two of them in this small, quiet kitchen. It should have been unsettling, but instead, there was a strange peace settling in her chest. It was a peace she hadn't expected. A peace that made her feel both terrified and safe at the same time. She exhaled slowly, her gaze falling to her tea once more. Her fingers traced the edge of the glass, and for a brief moment, she found herself lost in thought.

"I hate how much I've let my past control me, " she said, her voice softer now, the tension in her shoulders beginning to loosen. "It's like every time I start to move forward, I get pulled back into the same memories. Same fears. Same mistakes."

Lincoln watched her, his expression open, patient, but there was something in his eyes. It was something she couldn't quite place. Understanding, maybe. Or maybe something more, something that made her heart beat faster than it should have been. His presence landed in her chest, and for the first time in ages, she felt a flicker of something other than fear—something that felt like… trust.

She let out a quiet laugh, but it was almost self-deprecating. "I'm not sure I even know how to let go anymore."

"You don't have to let go all at once. But when you're ready… I'll be here," Lincoln said, leaning against the counter again, his voice low but steady.

She then looked up at him, her eyes locking with his in a way they hadn't before—not like this, not with the kind of vulnerability she'd been too afraid to offer anyone for so long. But something inside her was shifting, the cloud lifting, even if just for a moment. A spark of something both terrifying and exhilarating igniting in her chest. She felt it then, a deep longing—a pull toward him, toward whatever this was between them. It wasn't love, not yet, but it was something real. Something tangible.

She stood up slowly, her knees suddenly weak beneath her, her heart racing. She took a step closer to him, then another, until she was standing just a few inches away. She could feel his presence, his warmth, like he was a lighthouse in the storm that had been her life for so long.

"I don't want to be scared anymore," she murmured, her voice barely a breath, but full of quiet resolve.

Lincoln didn't move, but his eyes softened, understanding written in every line of his face. "You don't have to be. Not with me."

She reached up, almost on instinct, brushing her fingers lightly over his arm. It was a small gesture, but it felt huge—like a promise, like something that could grow into something more. For a moment, neither of them moved, the silence between them comfortable. Then, with a deep breath, Cora pulled away slightly, as if realizing how close they had gotten, how much her heart had shifted in just those few moments.

"Sorry," she murmured, stepping back. *"I just—"*

Lincoln reached out then, his hand gently grasping her wrist, stopping her before she could retreat too far. "You don't have to apologize," he said softly. "You're allowed to feel whatever you feel."

Cora swallowed, her throat tight. She nodded slowly, her chest tight with all the emotions she hadn't yet sorted through. But there was something in her now that felt like a beginning. Not an end. Not a full resolution, but the start of something she hadn't expected. For the first time in a long time, she wasn't alone in the fog. She was standing in it, yes, but Lincoln was there with her. He wasn't asking her to leave the fog behind; just to take a step toward the light.

For a moment, neither of them moved. Then, as if the universe had decided it was time, Lincoln leaned in slowly, his face softening, his eyes locked with hers. The distance between them seemed to shrink in the blink of an eye, and before she could even process what was happening, his lips brushed hers—lightly at first, testing the waters, like he was waiting for a sign from her.

The world spun, just for a second, before she let herself sink into it. The kiss was tender, warm, and for the briefest of moments, everything outside of this kitchen didn't matter. It was just them—just the soft pressure of his lips on hers and the feeling of his hand resting gently on her waist.

Then, just as quickly as it began, Cora's balance betrayed her. She stepped backward too quickly, the heel of her shoe catching on the rug beneath her. Her legs wobbled, and she let out a surprised gasp as she pitched forward. Lincoln's arms shot out to catch her, but the momentum sent them both tumbling onto the kitchen floor, laughing. Cora landed with a soft thud, her head resting against Lincoln's chest, her body pressed against his. They both paused, eyes wide, laughter bubbling up between them like it was the most natural thing in the world.

"Oh my God," Cora gasped between laughs, her voice breathless. *"I'm sorry! I'm so sorry!"*

Lincoln's chuckles rang out, his hands still wrapped around her waist. "Well, that wasn't quite the graceful moment I was imagining, but I'm not complaining," he teased, his voice light and amused.

Cora looked up at him, still in a tangle of limbs, her hair tousled and a smile breaking across her face. "I can't believe I just fell into you."

He grinned, brushing a loose strand of hair from her cheek. "Funny. That's exactly how we met, remember? You tripped on the sidewalk, practically landed in my lap."

Her eyes widened in horror. "Oh my god, I forgot about that."

He leaned closer, eyes twinkling. "I didn't. Starting to think falling into me is your signature move."

She let out a breathy laugh, her forehead resting against his. "Guess I'm consistent."

Lincoln nodded, his voice quieter now. "Yeah. But this time feels different."

And it did. The chaos had quieted, replaced by something slower, steadier—like maybe falling wasn't such a bad thing after all. He flashed a mischievous grin, eyes sparkling like a power ballad's final note.

"Well," he said, voice dripping with rock-star charm, "if you're gonna fall, I'm damn glad it's into me—because babe, I'll catch you like the encore you never saw coming."

She rolled her eyes, laughing again. "So smooth, Lincoln."

He raised an eyebrow, still holding her close. "Hey, I try." He paused, his smile softening. "But in all seriousness… I'm not going anywhere, Cora. Not tonight. Not ever."

She looked up at him, her eyes meeting his in that same unspoken way they had before. Slowly, her laughter subsided, leaving behind something quieter, more tender. She reached up, brushing a stray lock of hair from his forehead, her fingertips lingering on his skin.

"Okay," she whispered, her voice steady despite the fluttering in her chest. *"I think I'm starting to believe you."*

Lincoln smiled, his hands gently cupping her face as he leaned in again. This time, the kiss was slower as if time itself had softened to let them stay in this moment. It wasn't like their silly, tipsy kiss outside McGillicuddy's, all laughter and nerves and the thrill of not knowing what came next. That kiss had been impulsive, born from curiosity and cocktail courage. But this—this felt different. There was no noise but the easy rhythm of their breathing and the soft hum of something finally being heard. As they pulled away, their foreheads resting together, the sound of their shared laughter lingered like a new promise. And in that gentle stillness, Cora realized that the fog wasn't gone, but maybe, just maybe, she was learning how to see the light through it—with him.

The quiet of the kitchen settled in after their laughter had died down, but the energy between them was different now, yet somehow more profound. They were tangled on the floor, their bodies still close, the world outside seeming far away. Cora could feel the heat of Lincoln's body against hers, his breath soft and steady in the small space between them. She pulled herself up slightly, resting her elbows on the floor beside him, but she didn't move away. His hand was still on her waist, his touch warm and comforting, like a constant in a world that had felt so unsteady for so long. For a moment, they just stayed there silent, neither one of them knowing exactly what to say next. The kiss, the fall, the laughter—it had been a beautiful mess. But now, there was a stillness, a kind of quiet aftershocks as if they were both trying to piece together the newness of the moment.

Lincoln finally broke the silence, his voice low, gentle. "You okay?"

Cora nodded slowly, her heart thumping in her chest. She could feel her vulnerability, but it didn't feel like something she needed to hide. Not with him. "Yeah, I'm good. Just…" She searched for the words. "Just trying to catch up with myself, I guess."

Lincoln gave her a small smile, his thumb brushing her skin as if he were reassuring her without saying anything more. "I get that. I think I've been doing a lot of that myself lately."

Cora looked at him, curiosity flickering behind her eyes. "You have?"

He nodded, propping himself up on his elbow, his gaze thoughtful. "I don't know if it's because of everything I've seen with Avalina… or if it's just the way life works sometimes, but I've been thinking a lot about… what matters. What we hold onto, and what we let go of."

Her heart skipped a beat as she realized he was talking about something deeper, something more than just the kiss, more than just the laughter. She watched him closely, trying to understand.

"You don't have to explain if you don't want to," she said quietly, suddenly aware of the tension that had settled back in. But there was something in his eyes that made her want to understand. She needed to understand.

Lincoln hesitated, his eyes flickering to the ceiling as if gathering his thoughts. "It's not about needing to explain. I guess I just… I think I'm starting to see that what I've been holding onto isn't always what I need. I've been running from things, too. From the mess I've made in my life, and from the parts of me that aren't exactly… pretty."

Cora blinked, surprised. Lincoln, who seemed so put together, so confident, was admitting to flaws? She hadn't expected that. But in a way, it made him feel more real. More human. And somehow, it made her feel less alone.

"I think," he continued, "I've been hiding behind a lot of things. Work, distractions, pretending everything's fine when it's not. And I think… maybe I've been waiting for someone to come along and help me figure it all out."

Cora's heart fluttered at his words. She wasn't sure what to say, how to respond. But she felt the pull again—the desire to let him in, to give him something real, even if it scared her.

She took a deep breath, letting it fill her chest, grounding herself. "I know what you mean," she said softly. "I've spent so long trying to fix everything that's broken… and in the process, I think I've forgotten what it means to just *be*."

Lincoln reached out then, his hand brushing against hers, as if he was silently offering her the space to take whatever she needed from him. She didn't pull away this time. Instead, she turned her hand to meet his, their fingers intertwining with a sense of quiet certainty.

"I don't know what comes next," she whispered, her voice steady but vulnerable. *"But I think... I think I want to figure it out with you. If that's okay."*

His eyes softened, and he squeezed her hand gently. "It's more than okay. I think that's exactly what I want too."

For a moment, they just looked at each other, the weight of the past still lingering in the background but not so overwhelming anymore. The air between them was no longer heavy with what they couldn't change. It was lighter, infused with the possibility of what could come next. Cora didn't feel like she was just moving through the motions, running from her past. She felt like she was stepping into something new. The future wasn't clear. There were still memories to face, ghosts to battle, but there was also something she hadn't had before: a sense of direction. A path she could take, with Lincoln by her side.

The days after that moment on the kitchen floor passed in a quiet blur. Each time Cora saw Lincoln, there was a lightness to her step. It was like the weight of the world had been lifted, even if only a little.

She hadn't fully figured out what it all meant, this feeling that was growing between them, but she couldn't deny it anymore. And she didn't want to push it away.

As the days turned into weeks, Cora found herself letting go little by little. She didn't rush it, didn't try to push past the fear or the uncertainty. But she allowed herself to lean on Lincoln more, to trust him with pieces of herself that she hadn't shared with anyone else. And in return, he gave her space when she needed it and showed up when she didn't even realize she needed him.

One evening, they found themselves at her place, sitting on the porch, the night still and calm around them. Lincoln was sipping his coffee, his hand resting casually on the arm of the chair. Cora glanced at him from across the small table, her heart full, but a little nervous too.

"I was thinking about taking a trip," she said suddenly, surprising herself with the words. She hadn't really talked about it before, not even to Selah, but the idea had been brewing in her mind for a while. "To see my dad and Ava's grandmother. Back in Colorado, with Avalina."

Lincoln raised an eyebrow, curious. "Is that something you've wanted to do for a while?"

Cora nodded slowly, the idea of it making her both excited and apprehensive. "Yeah, but I don't know if I'm ready. There's still so much I'm holding onto, so many things I haven't worked through yet. But maybe… maybe it's time to start letting go. Avalina will be turning four, so I thought a little birthday trip would be nice."

Lincoln smiled softly, his eyes meeting hers. "I think it's time. I'll be here when you get back."

The warmth in his words settled deep inside her, and she finally felt like she was moving forward—not alone, but with someone willing to take the journey alongside her.

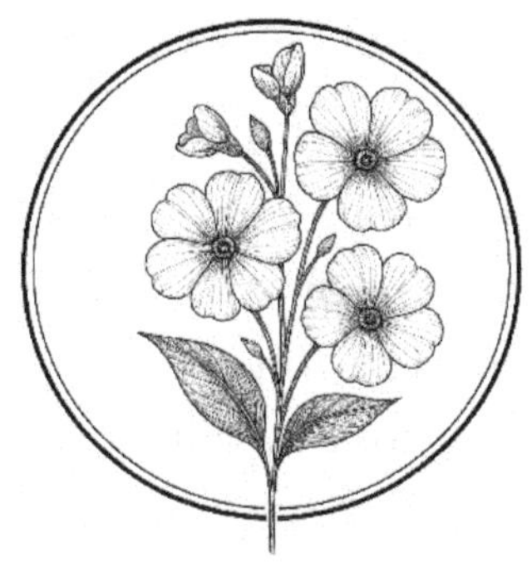

Chapter 17

Echoes At The Threshold

"The past whispers softly at the edge of every door—sometimes we must stand still long enough to hear what it has to say before stepping inside."

Cora had been mulling it over for days. The idea of taking Lincoln back to Pine Brook Hill with her felt right, but she still hesitated. Pine Brook Hill was home, but it also carried so many memories— some good, some painful. Yet, she realized that sharing this part of her life with Lincoln, letting him see where she'd grown up, the places that had shaped her, might be exactly what they needed. It wasn't just about her past but about inviting him into the future they were trying to build together.

The Fall Festival was just around the corner, and it was a tradition that had been a part of her childhood. The crisp autumn air, the smell of pumpkin spice and cinnamon, the sound of kids laughing as they ran through the carnival games—it was a piece of her heart, and she wanted to share it with him, and it would be Avalina's first time there.

It was late afternoon on a Sunday when she decided to ask. Lincoln had stopped by to check on her after a particularly long day, and they were sitting on the porch, the fading light of sunset painting the sky in shades of gold and purple. The wind had a slight chill to it, and Cora wrapped herself in a cozy blanket, feeling more at ease than she had in weeks. Lincoln leaned back in the chair next to hers, sipping his coffee. There was an ease between them now, a comfort in the silences and the small moments. But today, she had something important on her mind.

"Lincoln," she began, her voice a little tentative, "so…about this festival in Pine Brook next weekend. It's… kind of a big deal around there."

He turned his head, giving her his full attention. "The festival, huh? Sounds like fun."

She smiled softly, but there was a vulnerability in her eyes. "Yeah, it's been a tradition for years. I grew up going, and… well, it's something that always makes me feel like I'm really home, and I haven't been back to it in years."

Lincoln's eyebrows furrowed slightly as he took another sip of his drink. "You're inviting me, aren't you?"

Cora bit her lip, her fingers playing with the edge of her blanket as she gathered her thoughts. "Yeah. I think I am. I've been thinking about it a lot. I know it's a lot… There's history there, both good and bad. But I also feel like it's something I want to share with you."

Lincoln set his cup down slowly, his gaze steady on her. "You don't have to explain yourself, Cora. I'm not going to push. If it's something you think we should do together, I'm in."

Cora felt a wave of warmth at his words; the certainty in his voice was a balm for her nervousness. "I just want you to see it. To see the place that shaped me—and the people who are part of my world."

He nodded, a soft smile tugging at his lips. "I'd like that. I think it would be a good way for me to get to know you better. Your real world, not just the one here in Bigfork."

Her heart fluttered at the thought. "I feel like I should warn you about the town, though. I also feel like there is just so much to me, sometimes I worry you will walk away. Yes, it's where I grew up…but my life there was so sheltered, and when I came back from college, when my Gram died, I discovered so much about it that I hated…"

She paused, her voice catching as a sudden memory flickered—her grandmother's paintings at the auction. Intimate portraits of couples, not always touching, but always tethered by brushstrokes that hinted at open marriages, hidden truths.

"I'm rambling," she said, blinking herself back into the moment. "I guess it just feels right, having you there."

Lincoln chuckled, the sound light and warm. "Well, I'm not one to turn down a good festival. I'll take your word for it that it's a big deal. And no shame on a town, Cora….the town is not you. And everyone has a story…me included, so I am not in the least bit worried."

Cora laughed, the tension easing from her shoulders. "It's the event of the year in Pine Brook. Trust me. There will be funnel cakes, hayrides, a petting zoo, and this ridiculous pie-eating contest that my grandpa always won."

He raised an eyebrow, intrigued. "Pie-eating contest? Sounds like my kind of event."

Her smile widened. "Oh, you'll fit right in then. And we can go see the fall leaves, have some cider, maybe even take a walk by the lake. I have booked a hotel the first night, but plan on Ubering out to Nadine's estate and staying there over the weekend so she can have time with Avalina. It'll be… fun."

Lincoln's smile softened into something more tender, his eyes meeting hers with a sincerity that made her chest tighten. "I'll be there, Cora. Wherever you need me."

She could feel the weight of his words, the promise in them. She felt something settle in her heart, a quiet peace, as she realized just how much she wanted him by her side, in Pine Brook Hill, surrounded by her past but also looking forward to their future.

"Thank you," she whispered, feeling a mix of gratitude and something deeper. "I think it'll be good for both of us."

And so, it was decided. The fall festival in Pine Brook Hill would mark a new chapter in their connection—a moment where they stepped fully into each other's lives, where Cora let Lincoln see the places and people that had made her who she was.

On Friday, the silence in the car enroute to the airport was easy, companionable—until Lincoln tapped the steering wheel and said, *"Oh, hell yeah."*

Cora looked up from her phone. "What?"

He turned the volume up just as the unmistakable opening riff of *Smooth Up In Ya* by Bullet Boys came blaring through the speakers.

Cora blinked. "Is this… what I think it is?"

Lincoln nodded with a crooked grin. "You're welcome."

She laughed, shaking her head. "This song sounds like a bad pickup line with a mullet."

"That's *exactly* what it is," he said proudly. "Vintage sleaze rock. Pure art."

"Art?" she scoffed. "It sounds like someone spilled baby oil on a guitar and called it a personality."

He shot her a look. "Blasphemy. This is peak 1988 energy. Leather pants. Teased hair. Too much cologne. Zero shame."

Cora leaned back, smirking. "So basically… your dad in college?"

Lincoln chuckled. "Minus the leather pants. Plus better taste in women."

Cora muttered, sipping her coffee. "The title alone is basically an HR violation these days."

Lincoln chuckled. "Honestly, I respect the commitment. The song doesn't even try to be subtle."

Cora leaned forward, grinning. "If you start air-guitaring the solo, I'm getting out."

"Don't tempt me," Lincoln warned. "I've got the hair flip ready and everything."

As the plane touched down and they shuttled into Pine Brook Hill, the golden leaves and crisp air greeted them. Cora felt a wave of nostalgia wash over her. The town hadn't changed much since she'd left, but in some ways, it felt like a lifetime ago. She wondered how much of it had shaped her, how much of it still lingered in her bones. Lincoln's presence beside her was a comforting anchor, and as they drove through the familiar streets, their windows cracked open to let in the bite of the autumn breeze, Cora could feel the weight of her past settle gently behind her. This wasn't just a visit; it was a step forward. It was about more than sharing memories. It was about creating new ones together.

But tucked in the back of her mind was a fragment that had clawed its way free during the reunion. Amidst the forced laughter, the awkward small talk, and the fake smiles, a memory hit her like a brick wall: MJ. Declan. The fire.

It wasn't just an accident. It was arson. Manslaughter. The moment Declan's name was whispered, the world tilted, and the truth she'd buried threatened to shatter the fragile peace she'd fought for.

MJ hadn't simply died in a tragedy—he was taken from them by a man who set the flames, who destroyed lives with the strike of a match. Avalina's father.

Cora remembered it all in a single, searing flash: the blaze spreading, the screams, the sirens—how it unraveled her piece by piece, how she survived when so much was lost. The memory pulsed beneath her skin now, raw and aching, a relentless ghost she could neither outrun nor forget.

They drove quietly past Boughton Bridal, and Cora whispered a soft hello to her Gram and MJ, her voice catching in her throat. She didn't have the heart to stop in. Not yet. She would save that story for another time.

Lincoln reached over, his hand brushing hers. "You okay?" he asked softly, sensing her shift in energy.

She looked up at him, offering a small but genuine smile. "Yeah, I'm good. Just a lot of memories. But… I'm glad you're here."

And with that, they stepped out of the car, ready to experience Pine Brook together. Ready to face whatever memories—and future moments—lie ahead. Just Cora, Lincoln and Avalina.

Cora pulled her sweater tighter around her shoulders as the mountain breeze rolled off, cool and steady. The sun was just beginning to dip below the tree line. Lincoln walked beside her in silence, his hands tucked into his jacket pockets, their steps falling into rhythm over the graveled path. She could feel the question forming in his mind—the one he hadn't asked yet, the one she'd been dodging.

"I need to tell you something," she said finally, voice low as Avalina scurried off in front of them.

He glanced over, eyes steady. "Okay."

She stopped walking. "I was married to a man who I thought I loved with my whole heart. He didn't end up being a good man. He is Ava's father, and he is in prison. I know this sounds awful but it's true. She just thinks she and I are in her little, tiny world. I mean, one day I suppose she will…"

Lincoln stayed quiet, but his posture shifted. His brows pulled together, not in judgment—but in concern.

Cora took a shaky breath. "Between him, this town, my college past and Rowan, I just don't seem to have good luck by my side."

"Ok, I understand what you are going through with little Avalina…But let's start with this town. Tell me about it."

"Pine Brook Hill," she said. "Ok. Well, I am just gonna say it. It's a lot. This town had a secret society of open marriages/open relationships…or it did when I was growing up. Um, let's see… I never knew my mom. She committed suicide over it. Ava's father was raised in a home where it was normal, and he completely threw me under the bus more than once. He tried therapy, but he was a deceptive man, and he just couldn't be helped." Cora sighed, looking into the void as she paused for a brief moment. Then she continued, "My good friend MJ died in a fire downtown at my bridal boutique, and it was because of Declan. He lied his way out of the charges, of course. Then, one day, I get a knock at my door and it's a police officer telling me my sister has died. A sister I never knew I even had. Her name was Fallon Avaline. I named Ava after her. Anyway, long story short…Declan was helping cover up her murder. I know this is crazy, but I want you to know."

Lincoln didn't speak right away. He stepped closer instead, his expression softening as he looked at her—really looked at her. *"Cora,"* he said gently, his voice low and sincere, "that's not just a lot. That's a damn avalanche. And you've been standing in it this whole time, still finding ways to breathe." He reached for her hand, curling his fingers around hers like an anchor. "Thank you for telling me. For trusting me with this. I can't imagine what carrying that has felt like, but I need you to know something—I'm not going anywhere."

He brushed his thumb over the back of her hand, gaze locked on hers. "You're strong as hell. Not in the fake, tough-it-out kind of way. The kind of strong that grows from surviving every blow and still choosing to love your daughter fiercely and show up for your life."

A pause, a breath. Then a crooked grin tugged at the corner of his mouth.

"But just for the record…" he added, eyes twinkling, "if this town ever decides to revive the secret society thing, I'll only join if I can do it in a bandana and leather pants like an '80s hair band reject. Preferably with wind-blown hair and a fog machine entrance. That's my only condition."

Cora smiled as she pretended to kick dirt up with her shoe.

He nudged her playfully. "You smiled. That's all I wanted."

Cora looked at him then, her chest tight with the weight of vulnerability and the strange relief that came with it.

"I'm still me," she whispered.

"I know," he said. "And I like you just like this."

Cora looked away, blinking toward the water, unsure if she was about to cry or laugh—or both. The silence stretched between them, a little too long, a little too fragile.

Lincoln cleared his throat. "So…how's the memory with being back here? If I ever say something dumb, like really dumb, you might forget it?"

She turned to him slowly, her lips twitching despite herself. "Possibly."

"Well, that's the best news I've had all week," he said, grinning. "I've been practicing and I've got a whole arsenal of terrible dad jokes I've been saving for someone who can't fully hold them against me."

Cora let out a soft laugh.

"Like, did you hear about the guy who invented Lifesavers?" He nudged her with his shoulder. "They say he made a mint."

She groaned, covering her face with both hands. "You're actually doing this."

"I warned you. It's part of the *Lincoln McAlister's Charm Package.* Deep loyalty, killer playlists, and jokes that make you question every decision you've made in your life."

"Do they all come this bad?" she asked through a smile.

"Oh, worse. You haven't even heard the one about the skeleton who couldn't go to the dance."

She gave him a sideways look. "I'm afraid to ask."

"He had *no body* to go with."

She burst out laughing this time—genuine, loud, the kind that cracked something open in her chest she hadn't even realized was locked away.

"See?" he said, eyes lighting up. "Laughter is medically proven to help with memory retention. And also, incredibly helpful when you're trying to impress a beautiful woman who keeps surprising you."

Her smile softened as she looked at him. "You're a lot."

"I know. It's exhausting being this delightful."

"But thank you," she said, "for not making it feel heavy."

He reached for her hand again, lacing his fingers with hers. "Some things are heavy, Cora. But that doesn't mean we can't laugh while carrying them."

She squeezed his hand, the warmth of it grounding her. And for once, the blank spaces didn't feel so scary. They walked a few more steps before Cora spoke again, her voice quieter now—measured, like she was walking barefoot through memory shards.

"There's something else," she said, "since we're being honest."

Lincoln gave her space, letting her lead. "I'm listening."

She exhaled slowly, eyes fixed on the ripples in the water. "After the accident… after Declan… I swore I'd never trust anyone again. And then I met Rowan."

Lincoln's jaw tensed slightly at the name, but he said nothing.

"He was gentle, patient. He had two kids from a previous relationship. I believed everything he told me because… I wanted to. I was so tired of feeling guarded all the time. He made me feel safe."

She blinked up at the sky, like it might offer her clarity. "But he lied. She hadn't died. She wasn't gone. She was very much around… just… conveniently hidden. Estranged, sure—but not out of the picture. Not to him. And definitely not when he showed up at my boutique and started unraveling everything."

Lincoln's brows furrowed, his mouth opening slightly. "Wait—he never told you?"

"No," Cora said, shaking her head. "Not until I confronted him that day. Not until she forced the truth into daylight. She wasn't just an ex. She was angry. Obsessive. And he kept her a secret like a bad habit he couldn't quit."

Lincoln swore under his breath.

"I let him into my life—into Avalina's life," she said, the guilt flickering in her eyes, "and I didn't see it. Not until it was too late."

"You didn't do anything wrong," Lincoln said gently, "you trusted someone. That's not a flaw, Cora. That's just… human."

She gave a half-smile, one heavy with regret. "It's harder to know who deserves my trust now."

Lincoln stopped walking and turned to face her. "I'm not going to tell you to trust me. That's something you'll decide when—and if—you're ready. But I will say this: I don't have a secret wife. Or, any ex-wife for that matter."

A laugh broke out of her despite the heaviness, and she shook her head. "That's a very low bar, Lincoln."

"Hey, I clear it proudly." He grinned. "Also, not into the upside-down pineapple life, in case you're wondering."

Cora looked at him, truly looked, and something in her chest loosened. Maybe it was the way he didn't push her, or the way he gave her pain enough room to breathe. Maybe it was just that he showed up—silly jokes and all—and didn't flinch when she unraveled.

"I'm not good at doing this slow," she said. "I either build a wall or dive in headfirst."

"Then let's build something around both of us. Even if it's slow," Lincoln said. "You don't have to dive. And you don't have to hide. I'll be honest with you, Cora—I don't have a long résumé when it comes to relationships. No marriage, no kids. I've spent a lot of years learning how to show up for myself, but not a lot of time learning how to do that with someone else." His voice dropped, softer now. "But my Mama raised me right. She taught me how to listen, how to own up when I mess up, and how to treat a woman like she matters—because she does. You do. And if you give me the chance, I'll learn everything I can about how to love you the way you deserve."

Then his lips curved into a small, self-deprecating smile. "I may not be great at braiding hair or assembling dollhouses yet, but I've mastered the art of bedtime snacks and I make a mean dinosaur noise, in case

Ava's into those." He shrugged, still smiling. "I'm not perfect, but I'm willing. And you won't have to do any of it alone."

She nodded, her fingers brushing his. "Okay. But you better keep the dad jokes coming. I mean, how do they come so naturally anyway?"

"Oh, I've got years' worth stored up. It's how I start up every board meeting after I throw a flying Elmo onto the table."

They kept walking—two people carrying heavy things, choosing to share the weight, one step at a time.

Later that evening, the air had cooled to that perfect early autumn temp—warm enough to keep the day alive, soft enough to feel like something new was beginning. They stopped at a little walk-up ice cream shack on the edge of the park, string lights tangled around its overhang like fireflies caught mid-laugh.

Cora ordered Avalina her favorite: vanilla swirl with gummy bears and candy eyes—two of which Avalina immediately plucked off and stuck to Lincoln's cone when he wasn't looking.

He feigned horror, then acceptance. "Guess I'm eating a creature now."

They found a bench just off the playground path, tucked under an old cottonwood tree. Avalina ran toward the swings with her cone in hand, expertly stealing bites between skips. The streetlights were just starting to hum on, bathing the park in a golden glow that made everything seem quieter than it was.

Lincoln sat beside Cora, one arm slung across the back of the bench—not touching her, but close. Close enough.

"She's amazing," he said, watching Avalina kick her legs higher with each swing. "A wild little light."

Cora smiled, soft and tired in that kind of way that only came after a day full of too much feeling. "She is. She saved me, in a lot of ways."

Lincoln looked at her then. Really looked. "And you're doing such a good job, Cora, even when you think you're not. Especially then."

She didn't speak for a moment. Just took a bite of her cone, let it melt a little on her tongue. "Thank you. I'm not used to letting anyone help carry the weight," she said.

"Then maybe," Lincoln said, his voice low and steady, "you've just been waiting on the right person."

Across the park, Avalina shouted from the slide, "Look, Mama! I made the ice cream monster scream!" Her cone had collapsed slightly in the heat, dripping like melted eyeballs down her hand.

Cora laughed—really laughed—shoulders finally releasing the last of their tension.

Lincoln leaned in and said, "Told you. Candy eyes are cursed."

"Thanks," she murmured, accepting his words and tying her hair back with trembling fingers. She glanced at him, the weight of a memory pressing on her.

For a moment, her mind drifted back to Gram's cozy kitchen, sunlight spilling over the worn table where her grandmother had sat, hands folded like a prayer.

"Gram used to say the past comes back like a storm. You don't have to face it all at once, but you can't ignore the thunder forever. I feel like there are so many missing pieces in my storm."

Cora swallowed the lump in her throat and met Lincoln's steady gaze.

"I had this… flash," she said quietly, voice barely above a whisper. "A memory of Declan's laugh. It was cold, sinister—like he knew exactly how much pain he could cause and enjoyed it. It echoed in my mind like a warning I couldn't shake."

Lincoln's eyes darkened with understanding. "That kind of laugh… it's not something you forget."

She nodded, the weight of it settling heavier than ever. "No. And it's like it's still with me, haunting the edges of everything I try to remember. You probably think I'm insane," she admitted.

"I think you had a memory come back that your brain buried for a reason," he said softly, "and I think anyone who'd hear what you just said and walk away isn't worth a damn."

She closed her eyes and leaned back against the wall, her voice barely audible.

Lincoln looked at her like she was a puzzle he wanted to solve gently—not pick apart. "You don't have to tell me everything tonight," he said, "but if you want to… I'll listen."

There was a long pause. The kind that felt like a door being opened, just a crack.

"Do you believe people can fake love that well?" she asked.

He nodded. "Yeah. But I also believe some people don't know what real love looks like until they're standing in front of it."

They stood there, neither rushing the silence. Just breathing. Just *being*.

After a few more minutes of silence, Cora pushed off the tree, wrapping her arms around herself. "Can we walk a little? I don't want to go to the hotel yet."

"Only if we make it dramatic and pretend we're in a music video," Lincoln said, slipping his hands in his pockets, "I'll be the misunderstood lead singer. You can be the girl with a tragic past and great hair."

She snorted unexpectedly. "I do *not* have great hair right now."

"Disagree. It's got that post-panic, wind-tousled thing going. Very… 'emotional indie film at Sundance.'"

They walked along the sidewalk, quiet again for a few steps, her laughter fading into thought. She finally said, "Declan told me he loved me right after they took him. After MJ. He cried, said that it was an accident. I wanted to believe him. I *needed* to."

Lincoln looked over at her. "You ever hear of Stockholm Syndrome's slightly lesser-known cousin? Rock Bottom Romance? Happens when the worst person you've ever met kisses you right and suddenly you're writing wedding vows in your head."

She gave him a sideways glance. "You're making that up."

"Entirely. But tell me I'm wrong."

She didn't. Instead, she sighed and kept walking.

"I don't know what's real anymore. That memory—him laughing. It felt real. It was real. But then what does that make everything else?"

"Fake," he said simply. "Or at least… not the version you deserved."

They stopped at the edge of the little park, the swings swaying idly in the breeze. She leaned on the metal post of the jungle gym. "It's weird. I've spent so long trying to forget, and now that I'm remembering, it's like—there's this girl inside me, screaming. And I don't know how to let her out without losing myself again."

Lincoln leaned beside her, close but not crowding. "Start with telling me her story. The version you remember. And if you get too deep, I'll interrupt with a deeply inappropriate fun fact about hair metal bands. Like how Twisted Sister once opened for Metallica and nobody clapped."

She smiled faintly, eyes glassy. "That sounds terrible."

"It *was* terrible. And yet, somehow not as messed up as what you've been through. So, if you can survive Declan and a repressed murder memory, you can definitely survive my weird facts and emotional support walk."

Cora sank into the swing like it was instinct. The metal creaked beneath her, and the chains groaned as she rocked, barely moving.

Lincoln plopped into the swing next to her with a dramatic sigh. "Okay, serious talk. But I will be swinging like a child the entire time because I find emotional vulnerability much easier with momentum."

She laughed under her breath, then went still. Her fingers wrapped tightly around the chains. "MJ wasn't just my friend. He was my anchor. The one person who knew everything. We met at the University of Delaware."

She swallowed hard. Lincoln didn't speak—just listened. His swing clicked back and forth softly beside hers. "Declan didn't like him. Said MJ was too close and too involved. But MJ was the only one who saw through him. I should've listened."

Lincoln leaned his head to the side. "I once dated a girl who threw my TV out a second-story window because I watched The Notebook without her. We don't always pick the right ones."

Cora gave a hollow chuckle, blinking away fresh tears.

"Declan didn't throw my TV. He just isolated me. Slowly. Cut me off from MJ, from anyone who could keep me grounded. He was so good at sounding concerned—like it was love."

She kicked at the sand beneath the swing with her toe, her voice growing quieter. "The night MJ died was the night of our engagement. He was just there one moment, then gone the next."

Lincoln's voice was gentle. "And you blocked it out."

She nodded. "Declan laughing, standing there like he was proud of what he'd done. And I didn't remember before. I didn't even *try*."

Lincoln bumped her swing with his. "Hey. You survived. That's not a weakness. That's instinct. Your brain did what it had to. But now you're ready."

She looked at him, eyes wide and full. "Do you think I can actually bring the truth to light? That it'll matter now?"

"I think," he said, "that anyone who can go toe-to-toe with repressed trauma has what it takes to burn it all down and rebuild."

"You're kind of the weirdest guy I've ever met."

He grinned. "And yet, the top ten best emotional support swingers. Admit it."

She didn't answer, just leaned back in the swing and closed her eyes, letting the stars flicker above her as the memory settled—not gone, but named. Lincoln didn't say anything else. He just kept swinging beside her, quiet and steady. They sat on the swings a while longer, the autumn wind teasing at their hair. Cora's breathing evened out, and she was no longer gripping the chains like a lifeline. Instead, she watched the stars like they were finally giving her permission to look up.

"You know… this is gonna sound like a curveball, but hear me out."

Cora gave him a tired side-eye as she watched Avalina go down the tall slide in the near distance. "Are you about to tell me more hair band trivia?"

"Tempting. But no. I was just thinking—you ever consider writing any of this down? Like… all of it?"

Cora blinked. "You mean like journaling?"

"More like a memoir," he said, kicking at the sand. "Not just for you—but for someone else. Some girl out there who's stuck where you were. Who's trying to love someone who only loves control."

Cora was quiet. The idea hovered in the air like fog—unexpected, but not unwelcome. "I'm not a real writer, I just dabble in children's books, Linc," she said softly.

"Um, I believe I just saw your first children's book as a NY Times Best Seller? And not to mention, you just made me feel like I lived a whole horror movie in under five minutes," he replies. "Your story's in you already. You just need to give it a spine."

She swallowed hard. "You really think it could help someone?"

"I *know* it could," Lincoln said. "Hell, you helped me tonight—and I was just the guy with the Motley Crue playlist and a flair for bad timing."

That pulled a real laugh from her this time. She shook her head, then looked down at her hands. "What would I even call it?"

"That's easy," he said, grinning. *"The Girl Who Remembered.* Oof. Too on the nose?"

She smiled, eyes glassy. "It's not bad."

"Or maybe," he added gently, "you just call it Yours. Because for once, it will be."

She nodded slowly, the idea anchoring itself in her mind like it belonged there. "I'd need someone to keep me honest," she said. "Someone who calls me out when I try to run from the hard parts."

Lincoln raised a hand. "Volunteer tribute… I will happily annoy you into finishing it. I've got a ton of useless band facts and zero boundaries when it comes to snack motivation."

Cora leaned her head against the swing's chain. "Thank you, Lincoln."

"Anytime. Just promise when you're famous, you won't forget your emotionally available daiquiri buddy."

She reached out, hooking her pinky with his. "Deal."

The last of the ice cream was long gone, but the sugar-high energy still buzzed in the distance with Avalina's laughter. The night had settled in like a blanket—warm, familiar, and just strange enough to feel new.

"But, hey…let's talk about tomorrow…Do I get to wear a flannel and pretend to be a farmhand named 'Dusty?'"

Cora gave him a sideways glance. "Only if you agree to do the hayride and not mock the scarecrows."

"Done," he said, without hesitation.

As Avalina ran ahead toward the playground tunnel, Lincoln leaned closer, just enough so that only she could hear him. "So what's the plan after we check into the hotel tonight? Still full speed ahead tomorrow?"

Cora let out a slow breath, half a laugh, half a brace-yourself sigh. "Oh yeah. Big day. Pumpkin train, face paintings…. And then…" she gives him a look, "you're officially meeting my dad. Dax."

Lincoln arches a brow. "The fire detective?"

She nods. "And his fiancée, Isla."

"I should probably iron my flannel," he muttered.

"Oh, and my ex-mother-in-law Nadine will be there too."

He blinked. "Wow. That's… okay. Deep breath. Anyone else?"

"She's bringing who we think is her new girlfriend. Alora."

He paused, then grinned. "Wait. Nadine has a girlfriend now?"

Cora nodded. "They've been best friends for years. Apparently, one wine night and a shared loathing for toxic men might have turned into true love."

Lincoln let out a low whistle. "Honestly? Power couple energy."

Cora laughed again, and he saw a flicker of something lighter in her—maybe even a glimpse of peace. "I warned you this wasn't going to be a quiet weekend."

He nudged her knee gently with his. "Cora… I've faced down a preschooler hopped up on candy eyes. I think I can handle your dad, his fiancée, and a surprisingly romantic ex-mother-in-law."

She narrowed her eyes playfully. "We'll see. If anyone asks, you're just here for the cider donuts."

"Dusty the flannel-wearing farmhand, here strictly for the donuts," he said with mock seriousness. "Got it."

"It's going to be weird seeing old faces. Some of them know what happened with Declan. Others just… pretend not to."

Lincoln shrugged. "Then we bring new energy. You, me, and a soon-to-be-four-year-old sugar monster with a tiara. They won't know what hit 'em."

Cora laughed, then reached over and linked her pinky with his again. And for the first time, being home didn't feel like a step backward. It felt like planting a flag. Like reclaiming a chapter she never got to finish.

Chapter 18

The Name She Gave It

"To name a story is to claim it—to turn pain into meaning, and silence into a voice that refuses to be forgotten."

The sun hadn't risen yet, but the pale lavender light was already seeping through the gauzy curtains. Cora stirred beneath the covers, tangled in the warmth of sleep and the sharp clarity of something new—a thought that had slipped into her dreams and stayed there, waiting for her to wake.

Her eyes blinked open slowly. There it was. A title. Clear as a bell.

Becoming Cora: A Memoir of Shadows, Survival, and Rising Again.

She sat up in bed, heart beating a little faster—not from fear this time, but something close to excitement. Or maybe courage. She reached for the journal on her nightstand, the one Lincoln bought her at the gas station as a joke because it had a glittery unicorn on the front. He'd said, *"Trauma looks better with sparkles, trust me."*

It had made her laugh at the time. Now it made her feel brave. She opened the first page, the pen already tucked neatly into the spiral binding like it had been waiting. At the top, she wrote the title in shaky script:

Becoming Cora: A Memoir of Shadows, Survival, and Rising Again. A memoir by Cora Atler

The words looked small, but they held weight. The kind Cora had run from. The kind she was ready to chase. She could almost hear Lincoln in her head: *"You start writing, I'll bring the snacks. And if you cry, I'll pretend I didn't see it while Googling facts about Bon Jovi's hair."*

Cora smiled to herself and looked out the window as the sky warmed above the rooftops. Today, she'd write the first page.

This Isn't the End of Me

It was still dark outside. The quiet in that way it only gets before a child wakes up—when the air feels like it's holding its breath. I used to dread this hour. It's when the memories crept in, the ones that didn't have names yet. The ones I pushed down so deep they stopped knocking. But now they're rising. And for the first time, I'm not afraid.

I remember his laugh—MJ's. The way he'd lean back like the sky was in on the joke. The last time I saw him, he was smiling. That's what I've clung to all these years. A smile, frozen in my mind like a photograph. But now I know the truth. What followed. What I blocked out. And who took him from me.

Declan.

Even writing his name feels like shaking glass loose from my chest. He told me I was safest when I was quiet. That love meant protecting him from the truth. That everything MJ said was meant to ruin me. And for a long time, I believed him—because believing him meant I didn't have to face the truth about myself.

I know better now.

This story isn't going to be neat. Or linear. Or palatable. But it's mine. And if I don't write it down, I'll keep living inside the echo of someone else's version of me. I want Avalina to know who I really am— not just the mom who makes pancakes in funny shapes or reads her bedtime stories with the voices. I want her to know the girl I was. The one who survived. The one who forgot. The one who is remembering.

And maybe—just maybe—this story will find someone who needs it. Some girl who's staring at the mirror, trying to decide if she's crazy, or just being lied to most carefully.

This isn't the end of me.

It's the beginning.

……

The soft, reluctant groan of the bedroom door's hinges broke through the hush of early morning, pulling Cora from the tangle of her thoughts. Her fingers, mid-sentence, froze over the page of her journal. In one swift, practiced motion, she closed it with a soft thud and slid it beneath her pillow, the scent of ink and paper briefly lingering in the air.

Tiny footsteps padded across the hardwood floor, uneven and muffled. Cora looked up just in time to see Avalina appear in the bathroom doorway—her silhouette backlit by the muted light creeping. Her curls were a wild halo, tangled and untamed, framing a face still marked by the tenderness of sleep. She clutched her beloved stuffed fox, its fur worn at the seams, and blinked up at her mother with heavy-lidded eyes.

"Mommy," she whispered, her voice a hush of morning breath and trust. *"It's morning now."*

Cora's chest softened. She opened her arms without a word, and Ava climbed into bed, worming her way beneath the covers and curling into her mother's side. Her small body radiated warmth, the faint scent of syrup and baby shampoo rising from her skin like a memory. Her fox was tucked safely between them. Cora pressed a kiss to the top of her daughter's head, letting her lips linger there for a moment as they curled up in the hotel bed, the soft hum of traffic outside barely touching the quiet inside their little cocoon.

"It is very early, Little Wren, but guess what," she murmured, her voice low and secretive.

Avalina shifted under the covers, her cheek warm against Cora's arm, eyes fluttering open just enough. *"What?"* she whispered, her voice scratchy with sleep.

"We have a big day today."

Ava blinked. "A birthday day?"

Cora nodded. "In one more day! But first, we are driving to see Nana Nadine."

Ava's gasp was dramatic and entirely awake now—one small hand flying to her chest like she'd just heard the most incredible news in the world. "Then, I get to see the pumpkin train?" she asked, eyes going wide.

Cora smiled. "And caramel apples."

Ava sat up halfway, the blanket falling off her shoulder. "And the pony rides!?"

"Only if the pony says yes," Cora said, feigning seriousness.

Ava giggled, already imagining it. "I'm gonna ask really politely."

"I think that helps your chances."

Cora's smile lingered. "We're meeting Grandpa Dax and Isla there, too."

"And who else?" Ava asked, sleep still clinging to her voice.

"Alora," Cora said gently. "She'll be there too. They brought you a present. I peeked—there's glitter involved."

"Of course there is," Ava said, as if that were the most obvious truth in the universe.

Cora let out a quiet laugh, brushing her thumb across Ava's hand. "And Lincoln will be there. But only if we let him wear flannel."

Ava's eyes sparkled. "Can I call him Farmer Lincoln?"

"I think he's secretly hoping you will."

She watched her daughter's smile stretch across her face before she tucked herself back beneath the blankets, clearly satisfied with tomorrow's birthday vision. Cora glanced over at the adjoining door that connected their room to Lincoln's—two separate hotel rooms with one door between them. It had been a quiet, mutual decision. They hadn't said much about it, but they didn't need to. They were keeping things simple, slow. Honest. Not confusing Ava with anything new just yet. Just close enough to feel like something was beginning. Just separate enough to honor the space they were still gently exploring.

Ava's breathing began to slow again, her body curling in like it always did when she was finally still. Cora reached over, letting the early morning settle in, soft and steady. For the first time in weeks, she felt a hush of relief in the quiet. The dark dreams that once shook Avalina awake night after night had eased, fading like storm clouds chased off by dawn. Her drawings—those haunting scenes of the cemetery and the man in red—had stopped, too. Cora didn't know why, and maybe she didn't need to. She was just thankful. Thankful for a morning like this, for peace, however temporary. She closed her eyes and let herself breathe in the stillness beside her daughter, grateful for the moment's mercy.

She whispered one last thing before closing her eyes. *"Sweet dreams, Ava-girl."*

The morning sun slipped through the thin hotel curtains, casting soft gold stripes across the foot of the bed. Cora was finally awake, lying still, listening to the steady hum of the air conditioner and the soft rustle of Avalina turning in her sleep beside her. She'd always been a morning snuggler—curled in close like a kitten, arms tucked in tight.

The hotel room phone rang quietly, a gentle chime that felt almost out of place in the stillness. Cora reached over, careful not to jostle Avalina, and picked up the receiver. "Hello?"

"Room service," came Lincoln's warm, teasing voice. "Special delivery of waffles, orange juice, and someone who looks extremely rugged in plaid."

Cora smiled instantly, rubbing sleep from the corner of her eye. "How'd Farmer Lincoln sleep?"

"Like a rock. Woke up ready to herd pumpkins and chase sticky children. You two hungry?"

She glanced at Avalina, who was now stirring, her hair a wild halo on the pillow. "I think I've got a girl here who would trade her left sock for a chocolate chip pancake."

"Perfect. I already scouted the buffet downstairs. Pancakes, waffles, even tiny boxes of cereal with cartoon mascots. It's basically kid heaven."

Cora laughed softly. "Give us ten minutes and we'll meet you down there."

"Take your time. I'll grab a table by the window. I figured we could start the day slow—before the chaos begins."

She could hear the smile in his voice, the steadiness that had become something she didn't realize she'd been needing. "Thanks for calling," she said quietly.

Lincoln paused, then added gently, "Thanks for letting me."

They hung up just as Avalina stretched with a sleepy groan and blinked up at her. "Was that Lincoln?"

"Yep," Cora said, brushing hair off her daughter's forehead. "He says there are waffles downstairs and a table with our names on it."

Avalina gave a sleepy, satisfied smile, as if the universe had confirmed something sacred. "He's funny," she said. "He told me my fox has 'main character energy.' I don't know what that means, but I think it's good."

Cora's laughter bubbled up from somewhere deep. She tightened her arms around her daughter, her heart full to the brim with a kind of quiet, aching joy. "Hey, almost-birthday-girl," she said, brushing Avalina's curls back from her face. "Why don't you go get that special pre-birthday outfit we packed?"

Avalina jumped off the bed and scampered across the room. Cora sat there a moment longer, staring at the wall. The memories were coming faster now. No longer hints. No longer shadows. They were clawing their way to the surface. And she was finally ready to face them. Cora stood by the window, her fingers tracing the outline of the curtains as she dialed her dad's number. She hadn't talked to him much lately—not since the last visit, when things had been tense. But this felt like the right moment, like the world had shifted again, and it was time to let someone else in on the change.

The phone rang three times before he picked up. "Cora? Everything okay?"

His voice was steady, the familiar warmth of it pulling at something deep in her chest. She swallowed, fighting the tremor that had crept into her voice. "Hey, Dad. I'm—yeah. We're okay."

"Good. You sound a little off, though. You sure?" he asked as he switched the call to FaceTime.

Cora took a deep breath. "Actually, I think I'm starting to remember things."

There was a pause on the other end, the sound of shuffling papers. Then she saw his face. "Remember things? What kind of things?"

She leaned against the counter, eyes drifting to the calendar on the wall. "People. Places. And… moments. But not just the good ones. It's all coming back now. Declan. MJ. The night he died."

Dax's voice softened, and she watched him rub a hand over his face, trying to process. "Cora… I don't know what to say. That's a lot to handle."

"I'm okay. I really am," Cora reassured him quickly. "It's just—everything's coming back. And it's not easy. But I think I'm ready to face it. The truth."

Another pause. Then, in his familiar, reassuring way: "Whatever you need, kiddo. We're here. You don't have to do this alone."

She let out a shaky breath. "We're actually here for the weekend. For Avalina's birthday. We'll be staying at Nadine's estate starting tonight."

There was a soft laugh on the other end, and she could almost see him smirking. "Of course you are. Nadine will be thrilled. It's good to hear you're home. I was beginning to think you'd never come back here after everything."

Cora closed her eyes for a moment. "It's time. It feels like it's time. I need to be there for Ava. And maybe… for me, too."

"We'll buzz over," he said, voice steady. "I'm glad. And if you need anything, anything at all, you know where to find me."

Cora smiled faintly. "I know, Dad. I know. We would love for you guys to join us for the big birthday celebration at the festival tomorrow."

As Cora was ending the call with her dad, a soft rustling noise came from the room. She froze. A familiar, carefully controlled voice drifted in. "You're here in Pine Brook Hill?"

Cora's eyes slowly focused to see Isla standing there, her posture always impeccable, like a woman who had mastered every room she entered. She was leaning against the doorframe, arms crossed, watching her with that unreadable expression.

Cora's heart did an odd flutter at the sight of Isla. She was, after all, her father's fiancée—someone she should be able to trust, yet someone who'd always felt like a delicate barrier between herself and Dax. Isla was… different. Too polished. Too composed. Everything Cora hadn't been, or ever wanted to be.

"Yeah," Cora said, brushing a stray hair from her face. "Avalina's birthday is this weekend. We're staying at Nadine's."

Isla's gaze softened, just a touch. "That sounds… lovely. But you're sure you're ready for it?"

Cora hesitated. "Ready for what?"

"The memories, " Isla said quietly, her eyes flicking to the side as if searching for the right words. "I know how difficult it's been for you. After… everything."

Cora felt a sharp pang in her chest—like being pierced by an unspoken truth. She didn't want to get into this now, not with Isla. But somehow, it felt like the words were already halfway out.

"I'm remembering more," Cora admitted softly. "Things I tried to forget. People I didn't want to remember."

Isla's expression remained neutral, though her lips pressed together for a brief moment. "It's good," Isla said, her voice almost too calm, like she was measuring each word carefully. "Facing the past… it's how we heal."

Cora wanted to tell her to stop. That Isla didn't understand. She wanted to say it—*you can't know what this feels like*. But instead, she just nodded, swallowing down the growing lump in her throat.

Isla stepped forward slowly, her gaze briefly flicking over Cora's face. "If you ever need anything," Isla said, almost too casually, "I'm sure your father and I can help."

Cora tensed, instinctively crossing her arms, not wanting the closeness Isla was offering, not knowing if it was real.

"Thanks," Cora said, her tone clipped, pulling herself back into the familiar armor she'd worn with Isla all these years. "I'll keep that in mind."

Isla tilted her head slightly, as if she were considering something, but then her eyes softened again. "I'm just saying… sometimes the people who think they know what's best for us are the ones who hold us back the most."

Cora blinked, not fully understanding the weight of Isla's words. But for a brief moment, it felt like something unsaid—something buried beneath the surface—had just been unearthed. Isla didn't wait for a response. She turned and left, her heels clicking softly on the hardwood floor as she disappeared into the next room, leaving Cora with the strange feeling that she wasn't just talking about the trip to Pine Brook Hill.

She leaned against the hallway wall, her fingers still curled tightly around the ceramic mug, now lukewarm and forgotten. Cora's pulse throbbed in her temples. She squeezed her eyes shut, steadying herself with the cool touch of plaster behind her. No more running. No more pretending the past was some distant country she'd never return to.

This weekend, she thought *in Pine Brook Hill. I'll ask her. I'll look her in the eyes and I'll ask her what she knows.* Not in anger. Not with fire in her throat. But because she needed peace. She deserved peace. Not the kind you fake with smiles and surface-level forgiveness, but the kind that comes when shadows are dragged into daylight and the truth is finally given a name. She pressed a hand to her chest, grounding herself. *One step at a time, Cora. Just one honest question at a time.*

And if Isla flinched, if her mouth twitched, if her voice cracked— Cora would know. She wasn't the same fragile girl who'd fled to Montana in the dark. She was a mother now. A survivor. A woman reclaiming the past that once tried to bury her. And she was done being afraid of the answers. The road curved gently as they crossed into town after breakfast in the hotel lobby, the mountains casting long shadows over the valley. In the back seat, Avalina's face was pressed to the glass, her breath fogging up the window.

"Are we here, Mommy?" she asked, eyes wide as saucers.

Cora smiled in the rearview mirror. "We're here, baby. Home for the weekend. We are going to stay at Nana Nadine's."

She wasn't sure why the word *home* caught in her throat. Maybe it was nostalgia. Maybe it was dread. Maybe it was both. The gates of Nadine's estate opened slowly, the crunch of gravel under tires oddly soothing. The house loomed ahead—gorgeous, sprawling, intimidating. Like it had witnessed things it didn't speak of.

Lincoln glanced over from the passenger seat. "Okay, you weren't kidding. This is like… 'Gone with the Wind' meets 'Clue.'" He gave a low whistle. "Are there secret tunnels? Please tell me there are secret tunnels."

Cora laughed, but it came out thin. "Only in the hearts of the people who grew up here."

He didn't push. He just nodded, picking up on the tremor behind her voice the way he always did, then reached into the back and grabbed Avalina's plush fox. They parked under the carport, the front door already swinging open. Nadine stepped out in a wide-brimmed hat and sunglasses, as if she were expecting paparazzi—or ghosts.

"You brought the sunshine," she called out, arms opening dramatically. "And a very tall man!"

Lincoln grinned and tipped an invisible hat. "Lincoln. Tall. Mostly friendly."

Cora scooped Avalina into her arms as Nadine pulled her in for a tight hug. "She looks just like you," Nadine whispered, her hand brushing Avalina's curls.

Cora's heart twisted. She didn't have the energy to unpack that yet— not with her father and Isla pulling up behind them in Dax's pickup truck. Dust kicked up in slow motion. And there she was. Isla. Stepping out of the passenger side with grace and style, and those same damn heels clicking on the driveway. Cora's stomach tightened.

Her father waved. "There are my girls!"

She waved back, smiled for Avalina, who was already squirming to run into her grandpa's arms. But her eyes didn't leave Isla. And Isla… wasn't looking at her. Not yet. She was adjusting her sunglasses, her mouth tight. She knew something was coming. Maybe she felt it too.

Cora reached for Lincoln's hand. He squeezed it without a word. She was ready.

Cora stepped onto the wraparound porch with Avalina on her hip, her shoes clicking against the worn wood. Nadine was already sweeping her into a one-armed hug, the other arm extended—gracefully, naturally—toward Alora. Alora. Still so statuesque. Still wearing linen like a second skin and smelling faintly of gardenias.

They were standing close. Too close to be just two women who used to share afternoon tea and gossip about other people's grandchildren. And then Cora saw it. Their hands. Lightly linked, fingers brushing, like something they'd done a thousand times before and never had to hide. It was so simple. So elegant. So them. Dax was right.

Something clicked into place in Cora's mind—something warm and somehow familiar. She remembered Nadine's arm resting gently around her shoulder, offering silent comfort. Alora's gentle smile came to mind, soft and reassuring. Oliver had always been... well, loud. Commanding. The kind of man who left no room for quiet or gentle things. Now, with him gone, the whole house felt different—quieter, softer. It was as if the house itself had finally exhaled.

Nadine pulled back just enough to study Cora's face. "You alright, sweet girl?"

Cora nodded. "Better now. It's good to be back."

"You look like a woman who's seen too much and survived all of it," Alora said, stepping forward to stroke Avalina's cheek. "Just like your mother."

Cora didn't flinch at the mention of her mother this time. Instead, she watched as Nadine reached again for Alora's hand, lacing their fingers with practiced ease. And Cora smiled. Because whatever else this weekend was about to bring—Isla, her dad, the memories clawing their way out of the dark—something was grounding in seeing love bloom again. Even here. Especially here.

"I think the house missed you," Nadine said, pushing the door open. "And so did we."

Nadine's heels tapped softly up the grand staircase, her voice floating back toward Cora and Lincoln as she led them down the long, gleaming hallway. "You'll be in the west guest suite—best view of the orchard," she said with a wink over her shoulder. "It's the same room you stayed in that summer we first met, Cora. Still has the mural you and Alora painted on the closet wall."

Cora gave a soft laugh, remembering the paintbrush slipping from her fingers, the scent of turpentine, Alora sketching stars in the corner while Nadine brought them lemonade. "I didn't think that mural survived," Cora murmured.

"We never had the heart to paint over it," Nadine said simply. "Felt like covering up a memory."

She opened the double doors, revealing a room soaked in amber light. The bed was wide and tall, draped in velvet and linen. There was a vintage bed tucked to the side with Avalina's name already hand-stitched into a pillow, as if Nadine had been waiting for them all along.

Lincoln let out a low whistle. "This is a *guest* room?"

"It's Pine Brook Hill, darling," Nadine said, smoothing the bedspread. "Everything's always a little dramatic."

Cora stepped to the window, brushing aside the gauzy curtain. The orchard stretched endlessly beneath a fading sun, golden leaves fluttering like confetti in the wind. Something about it made her eyes sting—beauty tangled with memory.

"Late supper will be served in the main dining hall," Nadine said, her voice warm but measured now. "Around eight. You'll hear the bell. Dress if you like. Or don't. We're more about spirit than formality these days."

She paused at the door, Alora now waiting in the hallway. "Settle in, sweetheart," Nadine added gently. "You're safe here. Whatever's coming—face it, rested."

And then they were gone, the doors softly closing behind them. Cora let out a breath she hadn't realized she was holding. Lincoln dropped his bag beside the closet and sat at the edge of the bed, glancing at her.

"That wasn't weirdly comforting at all," he joked.

Cora smiled, but her fingers were already drifting to the window latch. "No…it was."

She looked back at the pull-out bed for Avalina. At Ava's pillow. At the mural they'd painted once when she first met Declan's family.

So much had changed. And yet something about being here again—right *here*—made it feel like maybe Cora could start facing it all. As soon as the door closed behind Nadine and Alora, Lincoln flopped backward on the bed with a dramatic groan, arms stretched like he'd just survived a ten-day expedition. "Alright, this place is… like the haunted mansion meets a retirement catalog. Do you think the towels here judge you if you don't use all the forks at dinner?"

Cora laughed as she stepped out of her boots. "Only if you eat dessert first."

He sat up and grinned, reaching into his duffel. "Which is why I come prepared."

With a flourish, he set down his IronFlask bottle and pulled out a case of Miller Lite.

Cora blinked. "Wait. You had…are those… road sodas?"

"Damn right they are. You think I was getting into a seventy-minute Uber ride through winding mountain roads without some courage?" He handed her a bottle as if it were a love offering. "Classy people call it *proactive hydration.*"

She took it with a grin, popping the cap with a satisfying *snap*. "You smuggled beer like a mom sneaking snacks into a movie theater."

"Exactly. It's about the journey. And the buzz."

They clinked bottles gently, the bendy straws bobbing like little flags of surrender.

"To arriving alive," she said, sipping.

"To arriving with prepared ambitions," he added.

Cora curled onto the armchair by the window, the beer light and fizzy on her tongue. She watched Avalina snuggled in her travel blanket, already dozing in the little bed with Mr. Whiskers tucked under her arm.

"Thank you," she said quietly. "For making this… easier."

Lincoln didn't say anything for a moment. Just smiled. "I'm not here to fix the past, Cor. I'm just here to make the present suck a little less."

She laughed through her nose, that ache in her chest loosening just a bit. "Well," she said, lifting her plastic flute, "mission accomplished."

The dining hall smelled of roasted rosemary, aged wood, and something sweet—maybe apples and clove. Candles lined the length of the long mahogany table, flickering gently as if even the flames were whispering. Mismatched chairs surrounded it, collected over generations like stories only Nadine and Alora remembered how to tell. Nadine stood at the head, wearing a velvet shawl draped over one shoulder and holding a ladle like a scepter.

"Soup's hot, wine is poured, and there's honey butter on the table," she announced. "This is not a negotiation."

Lincoln leaned toward Cora as they sat. "I feel like we've walked into a fairytale where the witches are stylish and the food actually slaps."

Cora tried not to laugh too loud. "Be careful. Nadine's spells are mostly just guilt and garnishes."

Avalina climbed onto a cushioned chair beside Alora, who passed her a tiny, hand-painted bowl of pear soup. *"This is what princesses eat,"* Alora said, her voice low and melodic.

Avalina beamed. "Do they have toast?"

"Only the cinnamon kind," Nadine chimed in, sliding a plate of golden triangles across the table.

It was all so soft. The room breathed with warmth. No raised voices. No ghosts in the corners. Just stories flowing like wine.

Lincoln, cheeks already flushed from his second glass, bit into a biscuit and sighed. "Okay, I'm joining this family. I don't care how. I'll start as a gardener. Or a guy who labels the pantry spices."

"You'd never survive Nadine's kitchen," Alora said dryly. "She labels her herbs like war medals."

Everyone laughed, even Avalina, even though she didn't get the joke. She just giggled when her mama did, her sticky hand reaching for Cora's under the table. Cora squeezed it gently. She looked around the table—at these women who had known her before she'd known herself, at Lincoln sipping wine like he belonged here, at Avalina chewing cinnamon toast with wonder in her eyes—and felt something unfamiliar. Stillness. Maybe even peace. For tonight, at least.

As the soup bowls were cleared and the wine turned a little more golden in their glasses, the room eased into a slower rhythm. Avalina had curled up on a nearby chaise with her fox in her arms, her cinnamon toast half-finished on a napkin beside her. Cora was just taking another sip when Nadine leaned her elbow onto the table and tilted her head, eyes steady.

"How's the memory coming along, honey?" Nadine asked, almost offhand.

Cora looked up slowly, the spoon in her hand pausing mid-air. She nodded faintly. "It's getting better…. Bits and pieces."

Nadine watched her closely, her voice lowering just enough to feel like a test. "Is that how it's been lately? Just… flashes?"

Cora's stomach tightened. She caught Lincoln watching her, quietly respectful, not jumping in.

"Some things are coming back," she said cautiously, placing her spoon down. "In weird ways. Smells. Songs."

Alora smiled gently. "Memory's a patient creature," she said. "It doesn't need permission to slip back in."

Nadine reached for her wineglass, and her next words came a little too lightly. "And have you remembered anything about the boys? About—"

Cora's hand shot out, a subtle but firm motion, her voice a sharp whisper. *"Not in front of her."*

She glanced toward Avalina, who was watching the chandelier above her with sleepy wonder. Just a child, untouched by the fire of that name. Declan. Cora's breath caught in her throat. Even hearing it implied made her ribs tighten.

Nadine's mouth softened, and she nodded. "Of course. Forgive me."

Cora exhaled slowly and reached for her wine again. "Later. We'll talk."

The room settled into a heavy silence, thick with fragile hope. Outside, the wind whispered against the windows, carrying with it the weight of everything they hadn't yet faced. Inside, they waited—each holding onto the fragile thread of comfort that had somehow woven itself between them.

Chapter 19

Cracks In the Armor

"The armor didn't shatter all at once—it cracked in silence, letting the echoes slip through. And with them came the memories she'd sworn she'd buried for good."

Upstairs, the guest suite glowed with low lamplight. Cora sat at the edge of the bed, brushing Avalina's curls from her forehead, the familiar lull of pine and lavender drifting in through the open window. Avalina blinked up at her, heavy-lidded, Bunny tucked beneath her chin.

"Mommy," she murmured, her voice soft and curious, "Was that lady my grandma, too?"

Cora smiled, heart caught somewhere between ache and awe. "No, sweet pea. Just an old friend who loves you already."

"She smells like flowers and pie."

"That's how you know she's magical," Cora whispered, kissing her daughter's brow.

Avalina's lashes fluttered once more, and then she was gone to dreams. Cora tucked the blanket higher, lingered a moment longer, and then eased away.

Downstairs, the fire in the main hearth was dying slow, orange coals glowing like memory. Cora stepped quietly through the French doors and onto the side terrace where Nadine sat alone, a shawl wrapped around her shoulders, a bottle of red between two glasses. She didn't say anything, just poured. Cora sank into the chair beside her, pulling her cardigan tighter around her arms. A moment passed between them, crackling with old ghosts.

"You were going to say something at dinner," Cora said softly, accepting the glass.

"I was," Nadine said. "I didn't want to be the one to place shadows where there should be light."

Cora stared into the firelight flickering against the terrace railing. "I remembered something," she admitted. "Something small. Declan and Gareth. A voicemail… an argument. And then… silence."

Nadine didn't flinch. Just sipped her wine. "That silence has been your armor."

"It's cracking," Cora said, her voice trembling. "And I don't know what I'll find beneath it."

"You'll find her," Nadine said gently. "The version of you that survived. And the one who's still healing."

They sat in silence, the kind that only years could hold. Then a shadow passed across the doorway. Lincoln. He stepped out, hands in his pockets, not wanting to intrude. "I can give you two space," he said.

"No," Cora said quickly, standing. "I'm done with space."

She walked toward him, the wineglass still in hand. He met her halfway, eyes kind, grin lopsided. "Want to take a walk?" he asked. "I need to check if the stars are different here or if it's just that your town has no streetlights and a suspicious number of deer."

Cora nodded. "Let's find out."

The gravel crunched softly beneath their steps as they wandered past the edge of the estate, where the land rolled out into quiet fields and distant pines. Above them, the sky stretched wide and wild—an ocean of stars, scattered without pattern, like memory.

Lincoln looked up, then over at her. "Okay, confirmed: the stars here are brighter. Either that or Nadine slipped something into the soup."

Cora chuckled, hugging her arms. "It's not the stars. It's the quiet."

They walked a little further, past the weathered fence line and into the soft rise of a hill. Lincoln let the silence be, didn't rush her, just kept beside her like the moon itself.

After a few moments, Cora spoke, her voice barely more than breath. "I was sitting on the floor. In a house I didn't recognize. Holding my phone. Declan had just left—slammed the door so hard a picture fell."

She stopped walking, turning her face to the sky, eyes blinking fast. "I remember overhearing his brother Gareth's voice. He sounded scared. Really scared. And then someone else grabbed the phone. There was shouting. A scuffle. And then nothing. Just breathing. Like someone was hiding."

She turned to him now, eyes wide, raw.

"That's the night everything started unraveling. The night I knew something was off. One week later we were on an exclusive trip and then he was back in prison. I didn't even see it coming."

Lincoln swallowed, stepped in gently. He didn't try to fix it. Didn't offer platitudes or promise it would all make sense. He just reached out and took her hand. They stood there for a long time, the stars flickering above them like signals from some place not yet remembered.

The night air was thick with silence, the kind that only the mountains could afford. Cora's heart was still pulsing with the aftershocks of the memory she'd shared with Lincoln, the truth sitting raw in her chest like a tender bruise. For a moment, the world felt a little bigger, the weight of it softer in the quiet of the open field.

But then, the crunch of gravel reached their ears. Cora turned to see Alora walking up the hill toward them, her figure glowing in the dim light of the stars. The way she moved was fluid, like someone used to dancing with the earth itself.

"I thought I might find you two here," Alora said, her voice light, but with that underlying knowing that always made Cora feel like she was seen. "I'm starting to think this is the only place in Pine Brook that doesn't have a 'keep out' sign."

Lincoln grinned, leaning back slightly. "Guilty as charged. You're interrupting our star-gazing."

Alora raised an eyebrow, a soft smile tugging at her lips. "I'm not interrupting. I'm just… adding perspective."

She stopped beside them, looking out over the sprawling valley. Her gaze drifted to Cora, soft and understanding. "There's something about this place," she murmured. "Something in the air that helps you see things a little clearer. I think it's because it's been around for so long. It knows how to hold memories."

Cora swallowed, her throat dry. Alora wasn't wrong—Pine Brook Hill had a way of making memories feel alive, like they were breathing just beneath the surface.

"I'm remembering more," Cora said quietly, not sure how to say it any other way. "But not the easy stuff. The hard parts. The pieces I buried."

Alora nodded, her expression steady. "Sometimes, the hardest memories are the ones that need the most space to breathe."

"You sound just like Gram," Cora said softly.

"Well, I learned a lot from your Gram. We all have."

Cora squeezed Lincoln's hand again, grounding herself in the moment. It felt like Alora wasn't just talking about memories—they were talking about healing. About what it meant to return, not just to a place, but to yourself.

"I'm scared I'm not ready to face all of the memories here," Cora admitted, the words falling out before she could stop them. "I don't know if I'm strong enough."

Alora's gaze softened, and she reached out, placing a hand on Cora's shoulder. "You've been strong enough this whole time. Maybe it's not about being ready. Maybe it's just about taking it one step at a time. One breath."

The three of them stood in that quiet for a moment, the sound of the night around them—chirping crickets, a distant owl, the rustle of leaves in the breeze. The stars above twinkled a little brighter, as if in agreement. After a few more moments of silence, Cora's chest felt lighter, but the weight of the night's truths lingered, unspoken but still buzzing in the quiet. She looked over at Lincoln, then back at Alora and Nadine, who were sitting on a weathered wooden bench nearby, their heads close together in a soft, intimate space that felt like something sacred. Their laughter, low and gentle, floated over to her— sweet, untangled. For just a moment, it felt like a world where things could heal at their own pace, where love could settle softly, without need for explanation.

Cora took a slow breath and then leaned toward Lincoln, her voice soft. "I'm going to head in. I think I need to sleep on all this."

Lincoln nodded, not pushing, just understanding. "I'll head on up, but you know, when you want to talk about something more important, like why there's a *suspiciously* good bottle of whiskey in the fridge…I'm here."

She smiled, feeling the warmth of his words, then glanced over her shoulder at Alora and Nadine. The two women were sitting close, their arms around each other, a quiet love between them that didn't need words. The glow of the lanterns in the distance made them seem like figures from another time, just for a moment—a flash of peace Cora had once longed for but had been afraid to claim.

"I'll leave you to your night," she said quietly. "I'll see you in the morning."

As she reached the edge of the terrace, she paused for a moment, glancing over at the bench where Nadine and Alora sat—holding hands, nestled together in the quiet darkness. Cora felt something soften in her chest. Maybe it was hope. Maybe it was the slow realization that there was more to life than fear, more to healing than running. She didn't know yet. But for the first time in a long time, she was ready to figure it out.

The heavy oak doors of the estate creaked softly as Cora entered, the warmth of the house wrapping around her like a familiar blanket. She took a few more steps into the foyer, her mind still swirling with everything she'd spoken aloud and everything she'd kept buried deep.

The house was quieter now, the night having settled in like a slow exhale. Lincoln made his way up to the guest suite, and she paused as her eyes caught the glint of something framed on the console table by the stairs. It was a photograph—one she hadn't seen in years, but one she could never truly forget.

There she was, smiling, radiant, in a sun-drenched courtyard with Declan, the Mediterranean breeze tugging at her hair, the world feeling wide and full of possibility. They were on their honeymoon, in Greece, their wedding just a few days behind them. It was *their* moment—the moment before everything had started to unravel.

Cora's heart stuttered in her chest as she reached for the frame, the edges cool in her palm. The picture of her and Declan, so full of hope and joy, now felt like something out of reach—like a life she used to know, a version of herself that no longer existed. She stared at it for a long time, her fingers tightening around the glass. Her chest was tight, the flood of memories too much to carry in that fragile moment.

And then, just as suddenly as the pain had hit, it softened, like a tide pulling away from the shore. *"Not yet,"* Cora whispered to herself, her voice breaking the silence like a fragile thread.

With a quiet resolve, she set the frame down carefully, gently, and opened one of the drawers in the console table. She slid the photo inside, closing the drawer with a soft click. It wasn't that she wanted to forget—she couldn't. Not yet. She couldn't let Avalina see it. Not now. Not when her little girl still deserved to see only the joy and the safety that *this* moment promised.

Cora stood there for a beat longer, her hand resting on the drawer as if grounding herself in the decision. *"Not yet,"* she whispered again, the words both a promise and a shield.

She exhaled and turned away, heading for the staircase, a slow smile crossing her lips despite the heaviness she carried. It was the first time that she'd taken an active step to protect her daughter from the ghosts of the past.

The soft creak of the stairs beneath Cora's feet was the only sound as she made her way upstairs, the house now wrapped in the stillness of the night. The long hallway stretched before her, the dim light from the sconces casting faint shadows on the walls. As she approached the guest suite, she could hear the faint hum of Avalina's soft breathing through the door, followed by the quiet rustling of sheets.

When she opened the door, she stopped in her tracks.

Lincoln was stretched out on the bed, his long frame sprawled awkwardly, but there was a softness to the scene—his hand outstretched, resting gently over Ava's small, curled-up fingers. Avalina, deep in slumber, was curled against him, her little hand clasped so trustingly around his. The two of them—familiar strangers in a way—looked so peaceful, like they had somehow drifted into this moment without even meaning to.

Lincoln's chest rose and fell with the rhythm of sleep, his face relaxed, almost childlike in its stillness. Avalina's head was nestled against his shoulder, her own hand tucked firmly into his, as though she had always known he would be there, providing warmth and comfort. Cora stood there for a long moment, watching the two of them, her heart shifting in her chest. She didn't know when it had happened—when Lincoln had become someone she could trust like this. But seeing him with Avalina, so effortlessly protective and kind, it hit her in a way that words couldn't touch.

She took a quiet step forward, not wanting to disturb the scene before her, but needing to be close. Her fingers brushed the doorframe, steadying herself as she inhaled the quiet peace of the moment.

"I didn't mean to interrupt," she said softly, almost to herself.

Lincoln stirred slightly at the sound of her voice, blinking open his eyes slowly. His expression softened when he saw her standing there in the doorway, watching them.

"You didn't," he said quietly, his voice hoarse with sleep. "We just... crashed out. She insisted on holding my hand. Apparently, it's the only way she sleeps these days."

Cora's heart swelled, a soft laugh slipping past her lips as she approached the bedside. "She's a little thinker, isn't she?"

Lincoln nodded, still smiling, his gaze lingering on Avalina's sleeping form. "She's got that look about her. Like she knows things. Things I'm only starting to understand."

Cora lowered herself to the edge of the bed, her eyes taking in the scene—her daughter asleep, safe, and so deeply trusting. She reached out gently to stroke a strand of hair from Avalina's forehead, her voice barely more than a whisper.

"She's been through a lot, Lincoln. More than any child should."

"I know," he said softly, looking over at her. "But she's tough. You've raised her well."

Cora's heart twisted at the weight of those words, at the quiet acknowledgment of the journey they'd both been on.

"We're just getting started," she whispered, more to herself than to him.

They sat there in silence for a long moment, the three of them in a cocoon of shared stillness, the quiet of the night wrapping them in its embrace. Cora stayed with them, just watching, letting the peacefulness of the moment fill the spaces that had been too empty for so long.

Finally, with a deep breath, she stood up, leaning over to brush a soft kiss across Avalina's forehead.

"I'll let you two sleep," Cora said quietly. "Goodnight."

Lincoln gave a slight nod, his eyes still warm and tired. "Goodnight, Cora. I'm glad we're here."

As she slipped out of the room, the door clicking softly behind her, Cora stood in the hallway for just a moment longer, her heart full of an unfamiliar kind of peace. She felt it then—maybe, just maybe, they were finally where they were meant to be.

Chapter 20

Beneath the Scar

"Beneath every scar is a story too painful to say out loud… until it demands to be heard."

Morning light slipped through the sheer curtains of the guest suite, painting gentle shadows across the walls. Cora's eyes blinked open, her body reluctant to rise. She lay still for a moment, absorbing the quiet of the house—a peaceful rhythm she hadn't known she'd been missing.

A faint sound carried from downstairs—laughter, and the unmistakable sizzle of something cooking. The smell of something sweet, warm, and comforting wafted through the air, teasing her senses. Cora pushed the covers off her legs and swung them over the edge of the bed. Her feet met the cool floorboards, and she stood slowly, stretching her arms above her head.

She heard Lincoln's voice as she descended the stairs—a low, friendly hum of a man clearly in his element, comfortable and unhurried. The kitchen door was open, and the laughter was louder now, accompanied by the playful clatter of pots and pans.

"I'm telling you, Mickey Mouse pancakes are the best for birthday mornings," Lincoln's voice rang out, light with humor.

Cora stepped into the kitchen, still in her soft, blue bathrobe. Avalina, already up and in her matching robe, was perched on a barstool at the counter, watching Lincoln with wide, excited eyes as he worked at the stove. A grin broke out on Cora's face as she took in the scene before her.

Lincoln stood over the stove, a spatula in hand, expertly flipping pancakes into perfect little circles. The one in his skillet already had two round eyes and an oversized smile—a pancake Mickey Mouse, with a perfectly placed dusting of powdered sugar.

"Happy Birthday, Little Wren," Cora said lightly, her voice still soft with sleep.

Lincoln turned, that easy grin of his lighting up the room. "What can I say? I'm just trying to make *friends* with the Birthday Princess. You should see her face when I do the ears just right."

Avalina giggled, clapping her hands. "Mickey pancakes! Mickey pancakes! Don't forget the *whoop* cream!!"

Cora chuckled softly and walked over to the counter, resting her palm on the smooth granite surface. She took in the warmth of the room, the light spilling across the floor, and the simple comfort of this morning—one that felt soft, like a new chapter quietly unfolding.

But then, the scent of pancakes, the sight of the skillet in Lincoln's hand, and the soft laughter of her daughter triggered a flash of something in her mind—something she hadn't expected.

For a split second, Cora's vision blurred, her gaze unfocused. She saw the kitchen in her old apartment, dimly lit by the light of the moon. There, in the middle of the night, Declan was standing at the stove, flipping pancakes with the same ease, the same smile. The light glinted off the stove, casting shadows on his face as he hummed to himself, a low sound that had always been soothing to her. She saw him then, the way he had been back before everything had gone wrong—before the lies, before the tension had sunk so deep that even moments like that one had started to feel forced.

The image faded quickly, as quickly as it had appeared, leaving Cora standing in the present, the laughter of Avalina and Lincoln filling the quiet space.

"You okay?" Lincoln asked, his voice gentle, noticing the sudden shift in her expression.

Cora blinked, shaking the moment off, her heart pounding just a little faster. She didn't want to linger on it. Not now. Not when there was warmth here, a small, new beginning.

"Yeah," she said softly, her voice steadying as she smiled at him. "Just a memory… from a long time ago."

Avalina looked up at her, her wide eyes filled with innocent curiosity. "What's a memory, Mommy?"

Cora leaned down to Avalina's face, her fingers lingering for a moment. "It's something we hold in our hearts. Sometimes it's happy, sometimes it's not… but it always stays with us."

Avalina tilted her head, nodding as if she understood. "Like Mickey pancakes?"

Cora smiled, a warm, full smile. "Exactly like Mickey pancakes."

She straightened up, glancing over at Lincoln, who was finishing up the last of the pancakes, his easy charm back in place. There was something about him—something steady—that had begun to feel like it could belong to her. She didn't know if it was right, or if it was even *real* yet, but for the first time in a long while, she felt like maybe there was more ahead of her than just memories. Maybe there was a future. Maybe it was okay to take small steps toward it.

The crisp autumn air wrapped around Cora as she stepped out of the estate. The vibrant colors of fall were in full swing—burnt orange, deep reds, and sunny yellows filling the trees and ground. It was the kind of morning that felt like a breath of fresh air, like something important was starting to shift in the world.

Boughton Street had been transformed into a street fair for the festival, the quaint business district now a full-on fall carnival. Street vendors lined the sidewalks, each booth brimming with colorful displays of baked goods, seasonal crafts, and more treats than Cora could count. The street itself was a patchwork of warm golden leaves, a carpet laid out for the parade of townspeople and visitors to enjoy. And then, there were the smells—rich, sweet, and impossible to ignore.

"Look, Mommy! There's the French silk pie booth!" Avalina exclaimed, pointing to a stand draped in bright orange and black decorations.

Cora laughed, squeezing her daughter's hand as they strolled closer. "I think there's a French silk booth on every corner, honey."

Lincoln grinned, glancing over at Cora. "I don't know, I've heard the pie's pretty legendary around here."

They walked past one booth after another, the air thick with the tempting aromas of French silk pie, French silk ice cream, and even French silk coffee. The rich, creamy scent of chocolate wafted from the pie stands, luring festival-goers to line up for a taste of the famous dessert that everyone claimed was the best in the state. The scent mingled with the crisp autumn air, the sweetness of cinnamon, nutmeg, and the unmistakable allure of butter. Children in colorful scarves ran by, clutching balloons and cotton candy, while local musicians played cheerful folk tunes from a nearby stage. The sound of laughter, chatter, and distant carnival games created a happy, bustling background.

As they passed one booth after another, Cora found herself caught up in the festive atmosphere. The golden sunlight seemed to pour from every corner, mixing with the colorful banners and the clinking of mugs filled with hot cider. The world felt lighter here, a place where she could let go of the weight of the past and simply enjoy the present.

"I swear," Lincoln said as they reached a pie stand, "if they serve pie with a scoop of French silk ice cream, I'll just collapse in happiness right here."

Avalina nodded enthusiastically, already ready for the challenge. "I think I can eat both. Maybe even three!"

Cora shook her head, laughing as she joined the line behind Avalina, who was bouncing from foot to foot, impatient for her sweet treat. The fall festival was everything she remembered about Pine Brook Hill: the comfort, the small-town charm, the traditions that made the place feel like home even after all the years she'd spent away.

The line for the French silk pie stand was long, but Avalina didn't mind one bit. Her excitement was contagious as she bounced around, pointing at everything from the pumpkin patch to the spinning Ferris wheel at the edge of the festival grounds. Lincoln and Cora exchanged amused glances as Avalina's energy never seemed to slow.

"I want to go on the big ride, Mommy! The one that goes whoosh into the air!" Avalina exclaimed, her eyes sparkling as she pointed toward the Ferris wheel.

Cora chuckled softly, a warm sense of nostalgia washing over her. This was exactly the kind of carefree day she had hoped for when they arrived in Pine Brook Hill—a day filled with laughter, pie, and simple fun. The perfect beginning to a birthday. But it was hard to ignore the flicker of hesitation in her heart. She pushed it down, wanting to enjoy the day with Avalina.

"You're braver than me," Cora said with a teasing smile. "I think I'll be staying on the ground for that one. What do you think, Lincoln?"

Lincoln gave a dramatic sigh, rolling his eyes. "I guess if she *insists...*" He kneeled to Avalina's level, offering her a wide grin. "Alright, kiddo, we'll do the Ferris wheel. But only if you promise not to scream so loud that you make the whole town think there's a tornado coming."

Avalina giggled and nodded vigorously. "Deal! But you have to promise you won't scream either!"

Cora raised an eyebrow at Lincoln, but he just shrugged, standing up and offering a smirk. "You're on, Ava. Let's go make a memory."

With Avalina leading the charge, they made their way toward the rides, the sounds of carnival music and excited chatter filling the air. Avalina was already pointing out the next adventure—spinning teacups, a towering carousel with brightly painted horses, and of course, the glowing Ferris wheel that beckoned them from the distance.

But before they reached the rides, Avalina's voice cut through the air with a new excitement. "Look, Lincoln! The pumpkin launching contest!" Avalina exclaimed, her face lighting up as she saw the large catapult set up in the center of the square. A huge crowd gathered around.

Lincoln stopped in his tracks, looking at the large contraption with raised eyebrows. "Pumpkin launching? Now that sounds like my kind of fun. What do you think, Cora? Should I show these folks how it's done?"

Cora couldn't help but laugh at the glint in Lincoln's eyes. She could see that gleam of competition forming in his expression, and it made her wonder just how far he'd be willing to go for a little bit of glory. She gave him a teasing look. "I don't know… Are you sure you're up for it? You might launch a pumpkin all the way into next week."

Lincoln gave a pout, placing a hand over his heart in mock hurt. "You wound me, Cora. I'm a professional pumpkin launcher." He winked at Avalina. "What do you say, kid? Think I've got it in me?"

Avalina, already halfway to the sign-up table, nodded enthusiastically. "Yes! I *know* you can do it! Please, Farmer Lincoln, please!"

Cora smiled, watching them both. Lincoln's easy-going nature had quickly won her over, and now it was clear that he was fully embracing this little piece of their world. She shook her head, but there was a warmth in her voice as she spoke.

"Alright, alright. Go show 'em what you've got. Just don't come back covered in pumpkin guts, alright?"

Lincoln grinned as he jogged over to the contest table to sign up, Avalina skipping happily beside him. Cora followed at a slower pace, taking in the moment—the small-town charm, the genuine laughter, and the way they were all starting to fit together, piece by piece.

When it was finally Lincoln's turn, he flashed a grin at Cora and Avalina, giving them a thumbs-up before gripping the lever with confidence. The crowd watched in anticipation as he tugged the rope, sending the pumpkin flying through the air with a satisfying whoosh. It soared high, then dropped with a soft thud into the pumpkin patch a little further away from the target zone, but the crowd erupted into applause nonetheless.

"Not bad for a rookie," one of the contest organizers called out with a grin.

Lincoln stood, looking proud of his efforts, and waved over at Cora and Avalina. "I'll take second place if you'll give me a prize for enthusiasm," he shouted over the applause.

Avalina clapped enthusiastically, her face beaming. "That was awesome! You're the best, Farmer Lincoln!"

Cora couldn't help but laugh, her heart light as she joined them near the contest area. She watched as Lincoln took a playful bow, the joy on his face infectious. The morning stretched out ahead of them, filled with pie, rides, games, and laughter. Cora knew this was the start of something new for them, something she didn't fully understand yet, but was finally ready to embrace. The little family of three walked hand-in-hand toward the next adventure—the spinning teacups, the towering carousel, and the soft rustle of leaves underfoot. They were creating memories, and for the first time in a long while, it felt like exactly what they needed.

Just as they passed a group of teenagers playing ring toss, Cora stopped dead in her tracks. There, right in front of her, stood Sebastian—his unmistakable, warm smile shining brightly just as she remembered. His arm was wrapped around the waist of a woman Cora didn't recognize. She looked happy, her laughter bubbling over as Sebastian pushed a stroller, and inside, a small baby slept peacefully. Cora's heart skipped a beat, and for a moment, she stood frozen, unsure of what to say. It had been years since she'd seen Sebastian—since the mess of her own life and all the ties that had unraveled.

The sound of Avalina's voice brought her back to the moment. "Mommy, what's wrong?" Avalina asked, tugging gently on her arm, sensing the sudden tension in her mother.

Cora forced a smile, squeezing Avalina's hand. She could hear Lincoln's voice from behind her, walking up just as Sebastian turned to spot her. His gaze softened when he saw her, and for the briefest second, Cora swore she saw something in his eyes—a recognition of the past, but also a tinge of sadness.

Sebastian cleared his throat and took a step forward, his smile never fading. "Cora," he said, his voice warm but a little hesitant. "It's… it's good to see you."

The woman at his side looked up, noticing Cora for the first time. Her smile was bright, friendly, and completely unaware of the history between them. "Hi! I'm Vera," she said, holding out her hand.

Cora shook Vera's hand, forcing a smile as the words felt strange in her mouth. "It's nice to meet you, Vera." She glanced at the stroller, where the baby slept peacefully. "And this little one…?"

"Oh, this is Bryar," Vera said softly, looking down at the baby. "He's our world. Sebastian's been an amazing dad."

The mention of *"dad"* hit Cora harder than she expected. She bit her lip, her heart heavy with thoughts she wasn't prepared for.

Sebastian glanced at her, then back at his wife. "Bry is about six months now. How's Montana? It's been a while, huh?"

Cora nodded, but her mind was elsewhere. Her eyes caught sight of Avalina's eager face, waiting to move forward. It was almost as if she were a bystander to her own emotions in this moment.

"It's good! This is my friend, Lincoln, and this is little Avalina. Her birthday is today," Cora said softly, the words coming out quieter than she intended as the two men shook hands. She felt a flicker of something—the past, the pain, the life they might've shared had things turned out differently.

For just a second, she saw it again. The worn wood of her Gram's staircase, creaking beneath her bare feet as she raced up, laughing— breathless and sixteen, with Sebastian chasing close behind. He had nearly tripped over the last step, arms outstretched, grabbing for her waist like catching her was the most important thing in the world. She remembered the way they'd collapsed in a pile of tangled limbs on the old quilt in the loft, the smell of dust and sunshine and his cologne all mixed into one long, perfect afternoon. Back when it was easy. Before promises broke. Before time split them into strangers.

Now here he stood—polished, polite, with Vera at his side and a child who looked just like him. And she? She stood next to Lincoln, her daughter's hand in hers, the memory of that loft softening and burning all at once.

Sebastian studied her for a moment, then glanced at Lincoln, who had approached her side, his presence steady and comforting. "Well, happy birthday, little one! It's good to see you, Cora," Sebastian said, his tone carrying a mix of warmth and something else—regret, perhaps. "Maybe we can catch up sometime. You know, it's been too long."

Cora hesitated, wanting to say more, to ask how he was truly doing, to ask about everything. But she knew better. It was a moment of closure she wasn't sure she was ready for, not yet. "Maybe," Cora replied with a soft smile. She glanced down at Avalina, who was already tugging Lincoln's hand, eager to go to the next booth. "It was nice meeting you, Vera. And good to see you both."

Vera waved brightly, her smile wide and open. "It was great meeting you, Cora. Take care, alright?"

With that, Cora, Avalina, and Lincoln continued on their way, but Cora's mind lingered on Sebastian, Vera, and the little boy who looked so much like his daddy.

As they walked away, the silence stretched between them for a beat too long. Lincoln cleared his throat. "So… that wasn't awkward at all," he said, raising his brows. "I give myself a solid B-minus for standing there like a decorative houseplant."

Cora let out a soft laugh, the weight on her chest easing just a bit. "You were more like a really supportive ficus," she said, bumping his arm gently. "Very grounding."

Lincoln glanced over at her. "Okay, but—real question. Should I be emotionally preparing for a string of exes with unresolved feelings to start appearing out of the woodwork? Because if that was the opening act, I'm bracing for the heartbroken high school boyfriend who still writes sad songs about you in his garage."

Cora smirked. "If he shows up with an acoustic guitar, we run."

"Deal," Lincoln said, grinning. "Unless he's got snacks. Then we negotiate."

As they walked, Avalina chattered excitedly about the next ride, oblivious to the emotional encounter her mother had just experienced. Cora took a deep breath, trying to shake the weight of the moment, and found solace in the warmth of Lincoln's steady presence by her side. Still, as they made their way through the crowd, the sight of Sebastian and his new life lingered in Cora's mind, leaving her to wonder about what could have been. But she couldn't dwell on it for too long. Not today. Today was about making new memories, even if some of the old ones still haunted the edges of her thoughts.

Avalina tugged on Lincoln's sleeve, her voice full of excitement. "Lincoln, can we go on the teacup ride next? Please?"

Cora smiled softly at the sight of their easy rapport, but her eyes drifted toward the festival clock as she checked her watch. It was getting later, and they still had plans to meet up with Dax and Isla.

"We need to get going, sweetheart," Cora said, her voice filled with gentle authority. "We're supposed to meet Grandpa Dax and Isla at the craft booth so you can get your face painted."

Avalina's eyes lit up at the mention of face painting, and she tugged on Lincoln's hand eagerly. "Come on! Let's go! I want a butterfly this time!" Avalina said, practically hopping on the spot.

Cora laughed softly and glanced over at Lincoln. He grinned at her, shaking his head in mock defeat. "I'm at your service, Ava," he said. "Lead the way, kiddo."

The three of them made their way through the festival, weaving through the crowd toward the craft booths. The scents of roasted almonds and fresh kettle corn mixed with the crisp autumn air, and the sound of children's laughter and carnival music surrounded them like a familiar, comforting blanket. As they neared the craft booths, Cora spotted Dax and Isla standing near a table piled high with handmade scarves, candles, and other local crafts. Dax's deep voice carried through the crowd, and Cora could see him laughing with Isla, her head tilted slightly in that way she always did when she was deep in conversation.

Avalina, her energy never faltering, darted ahead, already calling out to her grandfather. *"Grandpa Dax! Grandpa Dax!"* she yelled, and the two of them turned toward her at the same time, their faces lighting up.

Dax knelt to greet his granddaughter, a wide smile crossing his face as he scooped her up into his arms. "Hey, pumpkin! You ready to get your face painted?" he asked, giving her a big kiss on the cheek.

Avalina nodded enthusiastically. "Yes! I want a butterfly! And maybe some sparkles!"

Isla smiled warmly at Cora as she approached, her eyes flickering briefly to Lincoln before settling back on Cora. "Hi, Cora. It's great to see you again," Isla said, her voice soft but warm. "How's everything going?"

Cora offered her a small smile, her tone casual but sincere. "Good. Really good, actually. It's been nice to be here… just kind of… settling into things."

Isla gave her a knowing look, a quiet understanding passing between them, before she turned her attention to Avalina, who was now happily talking about all the things she wanted painted on her face. "She's a handful, isn't she?" she said with a gentle laugh. "But in the best way. You're lucky."

Cora smiled, her eyes softening as she watched Avalina run over to the face-painting booth, her enthusiasm infectious. "Yeah," she said quietly. "I am. She's my world."

As they watched Avalina sit down at the face-painting table, Cora felt a sense of peace settle over her. The heaviness of the encounter with Sebastian lingered in the back of her mind, but at this moment— this moment with her family, old and new—was exactly what she needed to ground herself in the present. The festival buzzed around them, and for just a moment, Cora allowed herself to take it all in. She was here. She was present. And maybe, just maybe, things were starting to feel like they could be okay again.

The afternoon wore on, and the festival was in full swing. Avalina's face was now adorned with a colorful butterfly, sparkling accents dusting the edges of her cheeks. Her excitement was practically contagious, and she bounced from one booth to another, dragging Lincoln along to check out all the fun activities. Cora, Dax, and Isla lingered behind, chatting casually while Avalina led the way, chattering excitedly about the face painting. But then, as they passed a booth selling caramel apples, Avalina suddenly stopped dead in her tracks. Cora, not noticing immediately, continued her conversation with Dax about the craft booths, but Avalina's quiet voice broke through the din of the festival.

"Mommy, there's the man again," Avalina said, her words strangely calm and matter-of-fact.

Cora froze, her smile faltering. "The man?" she asked, confused. She glanced down at Avalina, who was pointing toward a man standing near a popcorn stand.

The man in the red coat stood there, just as he had earlier, watching them from a distance. His expression was unreadable, and for a brief moment, Cora thought she saw him tilt his head, almost as though he had been waiting for them to notice.

Avalina tugged on Cora's sleeve. "He's the one who smiled at me when I said I wanted to go on the ride. He always watches."

Cora's stomach twisted. "Ava, we don't—" she began, but her words trailed off when she saw the look on Avalina's face—genuine confusion, not fear. Just an odd certainty, as though Avalina knew exactly who this man was.

Isla, standing beside her, followed Cora's gaze and caught sight of the man in the red coat. He was already turning away, melting into the crowd like he hadn't been there at all. But something about him—the deliberate pace, the subtle glances—made Cora's blood run cold. He wasn't just some passerby.

Her breath caught as the memories came flooding back—her book signings, her boutique in Big Fork. She brushed it off at the time, writing it off as a strange but harmless passerby. But now, under the golden hue of the carnival lights, she could see it clearly. Same build. Same unnerving calm. Same red coat. This wasn't random. He had followed them.

Dax's eyes flicked toward her, reading the shift in her posture like a warning sign. His tone dropped, low and deliberate. "Is something wrong, Cora?"

She barely managed a nod. "That man… he's been near us before. In Big Fork. At my shop."

Lincoln lingered for a moment, watching Dax shift position like a trained protector, now standing between the group and the crowd behind them.

"Did I miss something?" Lincoln asked quietly, stepping in close to Cora.

Cora's voice was tight. "I think he's been watching us… longer than we knew."

Lincoln's jaw tightened as he scanned the thinning crowd. "Yeah. I've got that feeling too."

Dax's eyes narrowed. He'd seen enough. Following the direction of Cora's frozen stare, he locked onto the man in the red coat for just a moment—just long enough. His entire demeanor changed. Calm but firm. Controlled, but sharp.

"Alright," Dax said, clapping his hands lightly and stepping in. "Let's go grab some kettle corn and head toward the hayride. I think it's about to start." His voice was too casual. Too precise.

He moved quickly, positioning himself between the man and the group without drawing attention. Isla caught on immediately and began guiding Avalina in the opposite direction, her voice cheery as she asked about caramel apples and cotton candy.

Lincoln lingered for a second, watching Dax's body tighten ever so slightly as he scanned the crowd again.

Cora shook her head, though her heart was pounding in her chest. "I don't know… I just… something doesn't feel right. We should probably keep moving."

Avalina, oblivious to the tension, skipped ahead, eager to see the next booth. "Come on, Mommy! Let's get some cotton candy!"

After a few more laps around the carnival booths, Avalina was practically buzzing with excitement, ready to run off and explore the playground that sat at the edge of the park downtown. She spotted the swings and immediately bolted toward them, with Lincoln following behind to give her a push. Cora, smiling softly at the sight of Avalina's boundless energy, walked toward one of the nearby benches, grateful for the moment of quiet. She took a deep breath, letting the cool autumn air fill her lungs, and as she looked around, her eyes found Isla sitting with Dax at another bench, talking quietly but with a relaxed demeanor.

Cora's pulse quickened. There was something she needed to ask Isla—something she couldn't ignore anymore. Her mind kept circling back to the past, to those flashes of memory, to the moment she had overheard Isla on the phone saying Vinny's name, how she recognized Cora in the photo from freshman year. She had to know more.

With her heart pounding a little faster than usual, Cora slowly made her way over to Isla, who was now leaning back against the bench, her hands clasped in her lap. Cora hesitated for a second, then gathered her courage and softly cleared her throat.

Isla looked up and smiled warmly when she saw Cora approaching. "Hey, Cora. Everything good with Avalina?" Isla asked, her voice light.

Cora nodded, her smile polite but her mind racing. "She's fine. Playing on the swings with Lincoln."

There was a slight pause before Cora spoke again, her voice quiet but firm. "Isla… do you think we could talk for a minute? In private?"

Isla raised an eyebrow, a flicker of curiosity crossing her features. She stood up slowly, her movements fluid and unhurried, before nodding with understanding. "Sure. Let's step over here," Isla said, glancing toward Dax, who was deep in conversation with a few locals nearby, completely unaware of the subtle shift between the two women. They walked a little farther down the park, away from the noise of the carnival, until they reached a quieter spot near a small grove of trees. Cora could hear the sound of children playing in the distance, the faint laughter of Avalina and Lincoln drifting over to them.

When they were out of earshot, Cora turned to face Isla, her gaze serious. "I need to ask you something. Something that's been bothering me for a while."

Isla, sensing the weight in Cora's voice, nodded slowly, her expression softening. "Of course. What's on your mind?"

Cora swallowed hard, the words feeling heavier than she'd anticipated. She had spent so much time avoiding this conversation, but now that she was here, it felt impossible not to say it.

"The day I left for Montana… I remember overhearing you talking on the phone. You said his name—Vinny." Cora took a deep breath, steeling herself. "I need to know what that was about. And why you didn't tell me. I know he is your nephew, but I need to understand what is going on."

Isla's face remained calm, but Cora could see the brief flicker of something in her eyes—was it surprise? Guilt? She wasn't sure, but it was enough to make her stomach tighten.

"Cora," Isla said, her voice soft but steady. "I… I didn't think it was my place to tell you. I was trying to protect you from all of that. From him." She paused, looking down at the ground for a moment before meeting Cora's gaze again. "Vinny was part of your past. A part I knew you didn't want to revisit."

Cora felt a sharp pang of confusion and frustration. "Why didn't you tell me? Why didn't you warn me that he might still be out there, connected to the same people I'm surrounded by now?"

Isla's lips pressed together in a thin line, and she took a careful step forward, her expression softening with empathy. "Because I didn't want to reopen old wounds, Cora. I know how much you've fought to move on from that life… from Declan… from everything connected to him. I thought if I stayed quiet, it would keep you from falling back into the mess of that world. I never wanted to be the one to drag you back there."

Cora's mind was spinning, the weight of Isla's words crashing over her. She couldn't quite process it all yet—Vinny's name, Isla's secretive behavior, the dark corners of her memory that had started to resurface.

"But you knew, Isla, " Cora whispered, her voice trembling slightly. "You knew everything. And now… now I'm starting to remember things. Things that are making everything harder to understand. Things about Declan. Things about… about Vinny. And I need to know. I need the truth."

Isla's face softened, her eyes full of regret and understanding. She hesitated before speaking again, her voice barely above a whisper. "I'll tell you everything, Cora. I promise. Just… please, let's sit down. This is going to take some time."

Cora nodded slowly, trying to steady her breath, her mind already processing the fragments of the past that were beginning to piece themselves together. She wasn't sure if she was ready to hear all of it, but she knew she couldn't back away now.

Isla led her to a nearby bench, and as they sat down together, Cora could feel the heavy weight of the truth that was about to unfold. Isla seemed hesitant at first, her hands clasped tightly in her lap. The weight of Cora's question hung in the air between them, and for a long moment, there was silence. Then, finally, Isla spoke, her voice low but filled with emotion.

"Cora, my family… they were part of something much darker than I ever wanted to admit. They were connected to a crime family in New Jersey—a family tied to everything that went wrong in your life… and mine." Isla's voice faltered, but she steadied herself. "I was young when I realized the depths of it all. My brother, Rocco, was always around, always trying to prove himself to them. And he—" Isla paused, her breath catching, before continuing. "I think Vinny's succumbing to it all. He's getting deeper into their world, and I've seen him slip, Cora. He's changing in ways I don't recognize anymore. It's part of the reason why I went into law enforcement."

Cora's pulse quickened at the mention of Rocco. It wasn't just the name—it was the fear in Isla's eyes, the realization that this man had a hold over so many lives. Her mind flashed back to that moment at the estate, when she had first heard Vinny's name when Isla took the call, and the unsettling sense of dread that had crept over her.

"I don't understand," Cora murmured, her voice trembling. "You stood in my home, and you saw my photo, and it clicked. Why didn't you say anything then?"

Isla's eyes filled with regret, her expression pained. "I didn't want to pull you back into that world, Cora. You were trying to figure it all out—your life with Declan, everything that happened. I thought… I thought keeping you away from all of this would be the best thing. But now… now I realize that wasn't the right decision. I should've told you sooner. I just… I didn't want you to be involved in the mess again."

Cora shook her head, frustration building. "But I *was* involved, Isla. You didn't have to drag me back into it. I was already there—when I went to the reunion… I ran into Vinny. The way he looked at me, the way he spoke. He… he seemed like he was trying to hide something."

Isla's face went pale, and she clenched her fists tightly in her lap, looking away as if the thought of Vinny brought physical pain. *"You ran into him at the reunion?"* she whispered, her voice barely audible. "Cora… I'm so sorry. I never wanted him to come back into your life— not like that."

Cora could feel her heartbeat pounding in her ears as the pieces started to fit together. Vinny's return, Isla's silence, her memory lapses—it all felt like a jigsaw puzzle with missing pieces. The fragments were starting to align, but the bigger picture remained clouded in shadow.

A memory jolted forward like lightning—violent, jagged. She remembered the pressure of his body, the stale air of the room, and the way time had folded in on itself. He had attacked her. She couldn't recall the lead-up, couldn't remember his voice or his words—but she remembered the panic. The raw, animal instinct to survive. She'd reached for the knife from the drawer. Her hand had closed around it without hesitation, and in one quick, terrified swing, she slashed it across his face. She could still hear the guttural noise he made as blood streamed from the gash, the way he stumbled back, clutching his cheek.

No one had believed her when she tried to bring it up—not even herself. Not when she woke up crying. Not when she caught herself checking locked doors twice. Not even when she found the red box beneath a loose floorboard in her old apartment—worn, dusty, and sealed tight. She didn't know what she was looking for when she opened it, just that her hands were shaking. But the memory never came. Only that familiar heaviness in her chest and the unshakable sense that something bad had happened—something she'd forced herself to forget.

Until now. The scar. It all clicked into place with terrifying clarity. The man who had attacked her was Vinny—the one she had sliced and escaped. It wasn't a nightmare or a hallucination. He was real. And he had come back. And now, in the chaos of the fairground, the memory pulsed alive beneath her skin.

"When I first met you," Cora said softly, regaining her composure. "I didn't know who you were. I didn't even know about your family, your connection to all of this. But now, hearing this, I feel like… like I've been caught in something I didn't even understand."

Isla's voice quivered with guilt as she met Cora's gaze. "I never wanted to drag you into my mess, Cora. My family… they're dangerous. They're dangerous to everyone, especially now that Vinny is getting more involved. I don't know if he's still trying to prove himself to them or if he's completely lost himself, but I'm scared. And I didn't want you to be a part of that. I couldn't let you fall into the same trap I did."

Cora felt her chest tighten as her mind raced with the weight of the conversation. Her relationship with Declan had been tangled in lies, deception, and dark secrets. This wasn't just about her—it was about protecting Avalina from the same darkness that had haunted Cora for so long.

"Vinny," Cora repeated, her voice a little stronger now, "I need to know, Isla. Is there anything else I need to remember? Anything that's still hidden from me? I can't keep running from this."

Isla looked down at the ground, then back up at Cora, her eyes filled with both sadness and resolve. "I don't know everything, Cora. But I promise, I'll help you remember. Whatever it takes. I'll tell you what I know, what I've been keeping from you all this time." She hesitated for a moment, then added quietly, "But be careful. Vinny isn't the same person anymore. I don't know if I can protect you from him, not anymore."

Cora took a deep breath, trying to steady her racing heart. But memories came crashing in like a wave—sharp, uninvited.

But the worst part wasn't the broken glass or the sting in her jaw—it was Avalina, sitting cross-legged on the floor, crayons scattered around her. She'd drawn a house, a crooked sun, and in the corner…a small red box. Inside it, a stick figure with a purple smudge along its arm. Cora hadn't asked how she knew. She didn't have to. Avalina had seen the bruises. She'd known all along.

After the blood and the silence, after she crumpled to the floor in tears, Vinny had cried that night too. Swore he could change. Promised he'd never raise a hand again. So, he took her to his family's cabin by the lake—a so-called fresh start. He cooked a huge Italian meal, made her laugh for the first time in days. They drank wine by the fire. They made love. She wanted to believe him. Then the next morning came. Her keys were gone. She remembered the way her stomach dropped, how cold the air felt against her skin as she stood barefoot by the door, realizing she wasn't leaving—not without help. She had called Jensen. Called Selah. Told them she didn't feel safe. And they came. Just in time to see Vinny drag the body to the trunk. Vinny disappeared after that. Vanished. Like he never existed at all. And there were pieces to this story she never shared with even the best of friends. She just couldn't.

Cora blinked back into the moment, her voice low. "I can't stay in the dark anymore," she said to Isla. "Not when the past keeps dragging itself back, no matter how many times I lock the door."

As Isla nodded, a faint, distant sound of laughter from Avalina echoed through the park. Cora glanced back toward the swings, where Lincoln was still pushing Avalina high into the air, her laughter lifting in the crisp autumn air. For the first time in months, Cora felt a slight spark of hope. She wasn't alone in this—she had Isla, she had Lincoln, and most importantly, she had Avalina. No matter what secrets from the past came to light, Cora was ready to face them.

But as she turned back to Isla, the knot in her stomach tightened. The shadows were growing longer, and the truth was only just beginning to unravel. Cora's thoughts were still tangled with the conversation she'd just had with Isla when Avalina's voice pierced through the heavy silence. The little girl was running toward her, her face bright and eager, her pigtails bouncing with every step.

"Mommy! Mommy! I'm thirsty!" Avalina exclaimed, her eyes wide with excitement. "I want a lemonade shake-up! And I want to check out the Tumble Bus and the Boogie Bus! They're right next to the Bookmobile!"

Cora blinked, momentarily caught off guard as the weight of Isla's words settled deeper in her chest. But then she saw the pure joy in Avalina's eyes, the excitement radiating from her like a sunbeam, and for a moment, the world seemed to shift.

"A lemonade shake-up?" Cora repeated with a soft laugh, kneeling to Avalina's level. "Well, I guess we can't pass up on that, can we?"

Avalina nodded eagerly, her tiny hands grasping Cora's arm with determination.

"Please, Mommy! Please! And the Bookmobile has the best books!" Avalina bounced on her feet, tugging Cora toward the cluster of carnival booths, the colorful Tumble Bus and Boogie Bus nearby, their bright paint jobs nearly glowing in the afternoon sun.

Cora smiled, her heart lightening with the simple joy of Avalina's excitement. For a moment, all the questions about her past and the complicated relationships she was trying to untangle seemed to fade away. It was just her, Avalina, Lincoln, Dax and Isla enjoying the simplicity of the fall festival.

She glanced back at Isla, who was standing a few feet away, her gaze following them with a mix of concern and quiet understanding. Cora could feel the weight of their conversation still hanging in the air, but she knew she couldn't focus on it right now—not with Avalina so happy.

"Okay, sweetheart," Cora said, taking Avalina's hand and standing up. "Let's go get that lemonade shake-up, and then we'll see about the Tumble Bus and Boogie Bus. Sound good?"

Avalina's face lit up even more, if that was even possible, and she pulled Cora toward the lemonade stand with all the energy of a newly acclaimed four-year-old who knew exactly what she wanted. Lincoln followed behind them, chuckling to himself as he jogged to catch up. As they reached the lemonade stand, Cora felt the familiar stir of contentment settle in her chest. The bright orange and yellow flags waved in the breeze, and the air smelled of popcorn, cinnamon, and the crisp fall leaves. It was a world far removed from the heavy conversations and the darkness of the past she had been revisiting. It was a moment of lightness, a moment of escape.

Avalina eagerly handed her a few crumpled bills she'd gotten from Lincoln earlier, ready to buy her drink. "One lemonade shake-up, please!" Avalina said, her eyes wide as she looked up at the vendor.

As the vendor made the drink, Cora watched Avalina's face glow with excitement, her thoughts briefly leaving the shadows of her past. But as the vendor handed the drink over to Avalina with a bright smile, Cora's eyes once again flickered toward the Tumble Bus—a brightly painted, old-fashioned school bus transformed into a mini gym. And just beyond it, the Boogie Bus—the one that looked like a mobile disco with lights and music blaring—drew in crowds of children eager to dance.

"How about we check out the Tumble Bus first?" Cora asked, holding the lemonade shake-up in her hand as she offered it to Avalina. "Then we'll head over to the Boogie Bus. Deal?"

Avalina's face lit up as she took the drink, her excitement nearly bubbling over. "Deal! Deal!"

Cora smiled, feeling a fleeting sense of peace. Even if the rest of the day was going to be tangled with questions and hard conversations, this moment—this simple, perfect moment with her daughter—was worth it. As they walked toward the buses, Lincoln by their side, Cora's thoughts briefly flashed back to the conversation with Isla. The secrets she was beginning to unravel about her past were far from over. But for now, she let herself take in the scene around her—the laughter, the music, the buzz of the festival.

The day had been full of laughter, fun, and nostalgia. The fall festival had been a brief escape for Cora, a reprieve from the heaviness that had followed her for so long.

"Mommy," she whispered, eyes lighting up with sudden realization. *"I'm four now."*

Cora kissed her forehead. "Yes, you are, birthday girl. Lincoln has a big surprise. We've got a ginormous balloon to catch."

Avalina gasped. "A *real* balloon? Like in the *sky*?"

"A real hot air balloon. Just us, up through the Rockies," Lincoln said, brushing Avalina's curls from her eyes. "And after? Pizza at BloNo's Pizza Garage."

"With the racecar tables*?*" Avalina squealed.

"The very ones," Lincoln added, stretching with a yawn.

They stepped out into the crisp mountain air just as a vintage Jeep from the estate rolled up to the corner to take them to the balloon site. Nadine was inside and had packed a woven basket with pastries and thermoses of cocoa, which sat waiting on the front seat.

"Best birthday ever," Avalina declared as they climbed into the back seat, her voice already full of awe.

Cora nodded, heart thudding in rhythm with the slow pulse of wonder that this—this moment, this new day—was real. She leaned over and whispered to Lincoln as Avalina bounced excitedly between them. "This is the kind of memory I want her to keep forever."

Lincoln grinned. "Then let's float it right into the sky."

And with that, they set off toward the mountains, like the first spark of a brand-new chapter. The basket creaked softly beneath their feet as the flame roared to life above, sending a wave of heat into the early morning chill. Slowly, gently, the ground began to fall away. Trees turned to tufts, houses to dollhouses, and streets into sleepy ribbons of gray. The rising sun spilled gold across the landscape, casting long shadows over fields and rivers that shimmered like glass.

The world grew quiet up there—no car horns, no chatter, just the occasional hiss of the burner and the gentle rustle of wind against canvas. The moment the balloon lifted from the earth, Avalina gasped—hands clutching the edge of the basket, her curls bouncing as she peeked out over the world below. *"We're flying!"* she squealed, her voice full of awe.

The fields became patchwork quilts, the roads like trails for ants. She pointed at every tiny car, every speck of a cow, every shimmer of water as if discovering treasure. Avalina's fourth birthday crown— pink, glittery, slightly crooked—caught the sunlight, and for a moment, she looked like a little queen ruling the skies. Beside her, Cora watched with a hand over her heart, overwhelmed by Avalina's joy. But it was Lincoln who made her catch her breath. He stood close—one hand steadying her waist as the basket shifted gently in the breeze. "She's never going to forget this," he murmured, his voice low and warm against her ear.

Birds flew below, and the horizon seemed endless, a watercolor blend of blues and pinks. You could see the curve of the Earth if you squinted just right. It felt like floating in a dream—weightless, peaceful, untethered. The people below went about their lives unaware, while up in the sky, time felt suspended. Hearts beat a little slower, breaths came a little deeper. It was magic—not the kind with spells and wands, but the kind that wrapped around you in silence and space and made you feel beautifully small. The sky stretched endlessly around them, a soft canvas of sunrise hues.

Lincoln's eyes looked piercing in the glow, and when Cora turned to face him, the world seemed to pause. A flock of birds passed just below, wings slicing through gold-tinted clouds. Avalina laughed and waved. And as the balloon drifted higher, carried by nothing but air and fate, Cora let herself lean into Lincoln's side, her hand finding his. Up there in the quiet sky, with her daughter wide-eyed at the world and Lincoln's heartbeat steady against her arm, Cora let herself believe in magic again.

The balloon drifted higher, brushing the clouds like a whisper. Avalina clutched the side of the basket, her wide eyes filled with wonder. "I can see the whole world, Mama!"

Cora smiled, tucking a loose curl behind Avalina's ear. *"Almost,"* she whispered. "Look over there—see those little chairs hanging in the air?"

Avalina squinted, then lit up. "Ski lifts!"

"And that jagged line along the horizon?" Cora pointed. "That's the Rocky Mountains. I used to go there with my Gram when I was your age. We'd eat snow straight off the trees and pretend we were snow monsters."

Avalina giggled and mimicked claws.

Lincoln stepped beside her, his hand warm at the small of her back, grounding. "You okay?"

She nodded, too quickly. "Just… remembering."

The moment he turned to point out something to Avalina, Cora's gaze dropped to the trees below and her breath caught. Somewhere, just beyond that range, was the cliff. The one her mom drove off when Cora was two. The one no one really talked about.

They said she couldn't handle her life. That her silence had swallowed her whole. Up in the sky, Cora swallowed hers too. She smiled for Avalina. She leaned into Lincoln. But deep down, in the quiet place no one could reach, she wondered how far she'd come from that edge—and how close she sometimes still felt.

The balloon drifted higher, carried by wonder and wind. And for a moment, with Avalina's laughter filling the air and Lincoln's hand brushing hers, Cora let herself believe that maybe she wasn't her mother. Maybe, just maybe, she was healing.

When the balloon safely graced the ground, Avalina hopped out, her sparkly tutu slightly catching on the ropes, a glitter crown slightly askew on her curls. They drove to the pizza garage where Dax, Isla and Alora were waiting. The pizzeria was a little hole-in-the-wall spot that smelled like dough and childhood and tomato sauce dreams, and Cora couldn't have picked a better place if she tried.

"Birthday girl gets all the pizza she wants," Dax said, holding his third slice hostage behind his back as Avalina tried to grab it from his hand.

"Not fair!" she giggled, bouncing in her seat between Cora and Nadine. "That one has extra cheese!"

"Well," Lincoln said, eyes twinkling, "then it must be for the queen."

Cora laughed, leaning her head against his shoulder. Across the red-checkered table, Dax was recounting one of Avalina's early birthday meltdowns to Lincoln and Alora, who were doubled over laughing.

"I'm telling you," Dax said, shaking his head, "she screamed bloody murder when the frosting wasn't pink enough."

"She was two," Cora defended, laughing. "And very opinionated."

"She still is," Alora added, raising her soda glass like a toast.

The waiter brought out a tiny cake with a purple number four candle on top, and the whole table burst into an off-key but enthusiastic version of *Happy Birthday*. Avalina clapped along, beaming, her round cheeks red and pink like little apples.

And then, when the song ended and the candle was puffed out, Nadine pulled a gift from her tote. Wrapped in cream floral paper with a gold ribbon, it looked almost too pretty to open.

"This one's from me," she said softly, sliding it to Avalina.

A hush fell over the table—not intentional, but reverent. Avalina tore through the wrapping, slow at first, then faster when she saw the polished wood beneath. She lifted the lid, and the first gentle notes of *You Are My Sunshine* spilled out into the room, a soft lullaby that pulled something ancient and tender into the open.

Avalina's little hands froze on the box as she listened, her lips parting, eyes wide with wonder. *"It sings,"* she whispered.

"It does," Nadine said, blinking back tears. "Your mama used to sing that to you when you were still in her belly."

Cora reached across the table, placing her hand over Nadine's, her voice thick. "I did."

Avalina hugged the music box to her chest. "It's so pretty," she said again, her voice soft like a secret. *"Thank you."*

Lincoln gently pressed a kiss to Cora's temple, whispering, "You okay?"

She nodded, blinking fast. "More than okay."

Dax cleared his throat and raised his glass of root beer. "To Avalina. The bravest, spunkiest, most pizza-loving four-year-old we know."

Everyone clinked glasses. And as the music box wound down, its final notes hanging in the air like the last bit of daylight, Cora looked around at the people she loved—the family she'd built from broken pieces—and knew they'd given Avalina something her younger self never had. Roots. Joy. And a song that would never leave her.

As everyone began to rise from the table, carrying to-go boxes of pizza, laughter rang out into the parking lot. Cora wasn't out there long before Dax followed, hands tucked in the pockets of his worn jacket. "Got a second?" he asked, his voice low.

She nodded, and they walked together across the gravel to where his truck was parked. He stopped beside the tailgate and looked at her with a seriousness she recognized instantly—something between concern and preparation. Without a word, he pulled a small brass key from his pocket and placed it in her palm.

She looked down, then back up at him. "What's this?"

"There's a storage unit on Maple Ridge Road. It's mine. Has been for a long time," he said, eyes fixed on hers. "While you're here… if you're ready…there might be answers waiting for you there."

Cora didn't speak right away. The key sat warm in her hand, deceptively simple for the weight it suddenly carried. "What kind of answers?" she asked quietly.

Dax looked away for a moment, jaw tight, like he was choosing every word with care. "Ones I should've given you a long time ago. About your mother. About Fallon. About why things happened the way they did."

Her stomach turned, the ache of old wounds flaring.

He reached out and gently closed her fingers around the key. "You don't have to go. Not if you're not ready. But if you are—everything I couldn't bring myself to say is in there."

Cora held the key tight in her hand, the metal pressing into her skin. "I'll think about it," she said softly.

Dax nodded once, then pulled her into a brief, strong hug before heading back toward the house. She stood there for a moment, the porch light flickering above her, the hum of laughter drifting through the windows behind her. The key stayed curled in her hand. Waiting.

Chapter 21

The Moment the Air Held Its Breath

"It was the moment the air held its breath—when fear loosened its grip, and she let herself fall into him, whole and unguarded."

They returned to Nadine's estate after the whirlwind of a day. It had been everything little Avalina could have ever dreamed of. She crashed early after her bubble bath in the enormous jacuzzi tub. Cora had watched her little girl, all clean and rosy-cheeked, wrapped in a fluffy towel as she drifted off to sleep. She looked so peaceful, so unaware of the shadows that lingered in her mother's world.

Cora tucked Ava in carefully before she quietly slipped out of the room. As she closed the door, she paused for a moment, letting the calm wash over her. She needed this peace, needed to reclaim what she could of herself before she had to dive back into the turmoil. She walked down the hallway, drawn by a quiet pull toward the outside. The cool evening air was inviting, and as she stepped onto the porch of Nadine's estate, she found Lincoln standing by the railing, looking out at the sprawling grounds.

Their eyes met as she approached, and he offered a small, tired smile. His posture was relaxed, but there was something in his gaze that suggested he, too, seemed weighed down by thoughts.

"You okay?" Cora asked softly, her voice barely rising above the evening's stillness.

"I'm fine," Lincoln replied, his voice low but warm.

Cora stepped closer, her hands lightly resting on the railing beside him, her gaze sweeping over the quiet estate grounds. The distant chirping of crickets, the rustle of trees in the wind—it all felt so peaceful. Yet there was a quiet tension in the air, the kind that lingered between two people who had formed an unexpected bond.

The silence between them wasn't uncomfortable, but it was heavy with meaning. Cora's mind was still wrapped up in everything Isla had told her, the conversation about Vinny and the secrets that had come to light. Yet, something felt calming about being with Lincoln again, the closeness they had found helping ease the tension that had followed her for so long.

Lincoln stood close enough that she could feel his warmth radiating toward her. She glanced up at him, her heart fluttering unexpectedly in her chest. His eyes were softer now, the usual intensity in them replaced with something gentler.

"I think you are doing great…being here," Lincoln said quietly, his voice barely a whisper against the night air. "After everything."

Cora looked at him, the weight of his words sinking deep into her chest. She hadn't expected this moment to feel so vulnerable—so raw. Her past with Declan and all the things she had buried had been complicated, but Lincoln felt different. She felt like she could trust him.

"Thank you," she admitted, her voice low, "It feels like I'm supposed to be here, even if it scares me."

They stood there for a moment, the world around them slowing, the noise of the day fading away. It felt like they were suspended in time, two people who had come to understand each other in a way neither had anticipated. Without a word, Lincoln took a small step closer, reaching out to hold her hand. His touch was gentle, almost tentative, as though he, too, was unsure about how to bridge the gap that had formed between them. But there was an undeniable pull, a magnetic force drawing them together once again.

Cora's breath haltered as their faces drew closer, and for the first time in a long while, she felt the weight of everything—the past, the pain, the love—fall away. She wasn't sure who moved first, but in an instant, their lips met in a soft, tentative kiss. It was a kiss that spoke of everything they'd lost and everything they could still find in each other. For a moment, there was no past, no secrets—just the two of them, remembering what it felt like to be whole again.

The kiss deepened, more urgent this time, and the world around them seemed to fade even further away. Cora felt herself being pulled into the moment, the weight of everything slipping away as they gave in to the connection that had once been so undeniable.

And just beneath the night sky, with the moonlight casting its soft glow around them, Cora and Lincoln found each other again. In that moment, they were more than just the fragments of their broken past—they were two souls reunited, if only for this brief, fleeting moment.

They pulled away slowly, both breathing heavily, their foreheads resting against each other. Cora's heart was pounding, a mixture of emotions coursing through her, but she felt something she hadn't felt in a long time—peace.

"Cora..." Lincoln whispered, his voice raw. *"I..."*

But Cora simply shook her head, pressing her fingers to his lips for a moment. She didn't have the words yet. The past was still there, lingering in the shadows. But for now, she allowed herself to be in the moment, to feel what was in front of her, not what had already been.

"Let's just stay here for a while," Cora said softly, her voice trembling slightly.

And so, they did. Beneath the mountainous sky, they stood together, letting the night wrap around them, finding solace in the quiet.

The night settled deeper around them, the stars above casting their soft, ethereal glow over the two of them. The air was cool, and the scent of earth and leaves lingered in the air as Cora and Lincoln stood close, still catching their breaths from the kiss that had swept them both into the present moment.

Lincoln gave her a lopsided grin, his gaze lingering on her with a knowing warmth. "So," he said, breaking the peaceful silence, "how's that memoir coming along?"

Cora laughed, the sound soft and genuine, as the tension in her shoulders began to ease just a little more. Lincoln had this way about him—one that was both sincere and effortlessly funny, always able to lighten even the heaviest of moments.

"You know, I'm still trying to figure out if I'm writing a memoir or a psychological thriller," she said with a playful shrug, her eyes twinkling.

Lincoln let out a short laugh, his eyes sparkling with amusement.

"I'd say it's a thriller. You've got the perfect setup—mysterious past, unresolved tension, and a twist that no one saw coming. Add a plot about a woman trying to outrun her own shadow, and boom, bestseller."

Cora chuckled, feeling a little more at ease in his company, the weight of everything lifting, even if just for a while. It was nice to laugh again, even if the future still held so many uncertainties.

"You're not wrong. Maybe you should be my editor," she teased.

Lincoln raised an eyebrow, a playful smirk creeping onto his lips.

"Well, I could use a side hustle," he said, feigning seriousness. "But I'd probably make a better character in your book, don't you think? I'd be the charming, mysterious guy who swoops in to save the day—and maybe steals a few hearts along the way."

Cora rolled her eyes, laughing more freely now, her worries momentarily forgotten as she enjoyed the ease of their conversation. "Well, you've definitely got the charm part down," she said, nudging him playfully with her elbow.

Lincoln grinned wider, stepping a little closer to her, his expression softening. "Just making sure I'm not giving you too much material for the psychological thriller part."

They both laughed again, and in that moment, Cora felt something she hadn't allowed herself to feel in so long—lightness. The kind of carefree, easygoing joy that comes from being with someone who understands the weight of your past, but isn't afraid to help you laugh through it.

"You know," Cora said after a pause, her voice quieter, "maybe I will write about this. About… about finding peace in the middle of all the crazy."

Lincoln's expression softened, his eyes searching hers. "I think you're already doing it, Cora."

The moment was tender, quiet, and just perfect. Cora felt a sense of gratitude for Lincoln—for his patience, his humor, and the way he had managed to make her feel understood when everything else had seemed so complicated.

"Thanks, Lincoln," she said quietly. "I needed that."

He smiled at her, his eyes reflecting the soft glow of the moonlight.

"Anytime."

And for just a little while longer, they stood there beneath the stars, the world around them fading into the background, leaving just the two of them—laughing, talking, and taking solace in the quiet moments.

The walk back toward the estate was slow and quiet, filled with shared smiles and the occasional brush of their fingers as they strolled side by side beneath a moonlit sky. When they reached the grand entrance, the glow of the fire beckoned like a warm invitation.

Cora tugged her vibrant teal *Melly* hoodie tighter around her body, the oversized sleeves bunching at her wrists. Lincoln, in his deep marigold version of the same hoodie, gave her a wink as he pulled a bottle of red wine from the tote he'd swiped from the kitchen on their way out.

"You're just full of surprises," she said, smirking.

"Years of daiquiri-based improvisation have prepared me for this moment," he replied with a grin.

They settled into the cushioned chairs beside the fireplace, their faces flickering with light and shadow as flames danced and cracked between them. Lincoln popped the cork with a quiet flourish and poured them each a glass into two mismatched mugs he'd also pilfered—one with a faded cartoon cow and the other proudly displaying *World's Best Mom*.

Cora chuckled when he handed her the cow. "Well, I guess it's better than 'Grandma.'"

"Hey, I was going for *nostalgic vintage.* That's practically Pinterest-worthy," he said, raising his mug in a toast.

"To firelight and funny hoodies," she said, clinking hers against his.

"And to remembering who we are," Lincoln added, softer this time.

They sipped, the wine warming their insides while the hoodies wrapped them in fleece and memory. Ava was asleep upstairs, the estate was still, and the stars above them winked like secrets waiting to be told.

Cora tucked her feet up beneath her and let her eyes drift across the fire. Something about the way Lincoln looked just then, relaxed and silly in that hoodie, with sparks from the flames reflected in his wine-dark eyes—it made her heart ache in a good way.

"This… is one of the safest moments I've had in years," she said quietly.

Cora got up and stood at the threshold of the room, the soft hum of night pressing in from the hallway behind her. The flicker of firelight danced across the walls, casting golden shadows that reached toward her like warm hands. Lincoln stood across from her, his eyes holding something steady and quiet—like he had been waiting, but would never rush her.

She turned slowly and reached for the French doors, easing them shut with a soft click. The hush that followed felt sacred. Lincoln stepped closer, his hand brushing her cheek with a gentleness that made her breath slow. She leaned into his touch, her eyes never leaving his.

"I don't want to pretend," she whispered. "Not with you."

"You don't have to," he said, his voice low, steady. "We're right here. Just us."

Their mouths met in the middle, slow and searching—tentative at first, as if neither of them wanted to disturb the fragile thing forming between them. It wasn't just a kiss; it was a quiet exchange of everything they hadn't yet said aloud. His lips were warm, patient, brushing against hers like he was learning the shape of her. Lincoln's hands anchored her in a moment she hadn't known she needed. Her fingers slid up his chest, resting over his heart—steady, strong, thudding as if it had been waiting for this moment just as long as hers had.

Clothes were shed in hushed motions, not hurried but intentional. Each layer peeled away like a truth finally spoken, like letting go. They pooled around their feet and trailed across the rug like a map of trust, with scattered secrets left unhidden. Behind them, the fire murmured and flickered, casting a soft amber light that danced across her bare skin and caught the vulnerability in Lincoln's eyes. He looked at her like she was something sacred. Like he didn't just want her—he wanted to honor her.

He laid her gently on the thick rug in front of the hearth, his lips moving from her mouth to the hollow of her throat, then lower, tracing the curve of her shoulder, the line of her collarbone, the quiet places where she carried sorrow. Where the past still clung like ghosts. Cora exhaled slowly, her fingers slipping into his hair, pulling him closer—not out of desperation, but surrender. Her heart opened in the way only trust could allow. No armor. No performance. Just her. Just him.

It was perfect. Their bodies moved with hunger and hesitation, tenderness and need. It was real. The kind of intimacy that rewrites old pain and touches not just skin but memory. When they finally came together, it felt like belonging. Like returning to something they'd both lost along the way. The fire warmed the room, but Lincoln's hands— his mouth, his breath, his presence—warmed something deeper. Something that had been untouched for too long. And when the wind whispered against the French doors behind them, brushing cold against the glass, Cora didn't flinch. For the first time in years, she wasn't afraid. Not of love. Not of being seen. Not with him.

Just as the fire crackled into quiet embers and their second mugs of wine sat half-drunk on the edge of the fire pit table, a sound pierced the still night.

Avalina's voice, high and frightened, carried out through the open kitchen window upstairs. *"Mommy!"*

Cora was on her feet in an instant; she sprinted, grabbed her clothes, threw them on haphazardly, and ran up the stairs. Lincoln was right behind her, their cozy comfort instantly traded for adrenaline. They reached the guest suite at the same time, Cora fumbling with the handle before rushing inside. Ava sat upright in the big bed, her cheeks flushed, her little fists rubbing sleep from teary eyes.

"Sweetheart," Cora whispered, crossing to the bed and scooping her daughter into her arms. *"It's okay. I'm here."*

Lincoln crouched beside them, his hair tousled and hoodie sleeves pushed back, his eyes wide with concern. "Was it a dream, bug?" he asked gently.

Avalina nodded into her mother's neck. "It was the man in a red coat," she murmured, barely audible. "He said he was going to tell me… but I didn't want to know."

Cora looked over Avalina's shoulder at Lincoln, her heart racing. The words lodged in her throat like glass. She felt the chill crawl up her spine, that familiar edge of panic creeping in—but before it could settle, Lincoln leaned forward with a soft grin and a voice like a bedtime song.

"Well," he whispered, tucking a loose strand of hair behind Avalina's ear, *"you don't have to know anything you're not ready for. And no red coat gets to tell you otherwise."*

Avalina nodded slowly, her little hand clutching the fabric of Cora's shirt. But Cora wasn't breathing. Not really. Because this wasn't just a nightmare. This was her past clawing its way forward—leaving fingerprints on the one person she swore she'd never let it touch. She'd fought so hard to bury the trauma, to keep it from leaking into the bright, safe world she had built for Avalina. But here it was again. Wearing red. Whispering in her daughter's dreams. What if he hadn't just followed her? What if he had always meant to get to Avalina? That thought alone nearly made her buckle.

Cora blinked hard, fighting the sting in her eyes. Lincoln's hand found hers—steady, warm, anchoring her to the present. He didn't say anything. She could see it in his eyes: he knew. And in that silence, Cora vowed one thing—whatever it took, she would not let the darkness touch Avalina again. She would dig through every buried memory, expose every hidden scar, and face down every red coat that came for them, because love wasn't just soft and safe. Sometimes, it was fire. And this time, she would burn the past before it stole anything else.

"Okay, I think I know exactly what's going on," he said. "This is what happens when you leave your bubblegum on the bedpost at night."

Avalina turned her head just enough to peek at him through her lashes. "Huh?"

Lincoln nodded, keeping the tone light and conspiratorial. "Oh yeah. True story. If you stick your gum there thinking you'll chew it again in the morning? BAM. You get the weirdest dreams. I once dreamed I was a pirate… and my parrot was actually a piece of toast."

Ava blinked. "Toast?"

"With peanut butter. And every time it said 'squawk,' a crumb hit me in the eye."

Cora giggled despite herself, brushing Avalina's hair from her forehead.

"That sounds awful," Avalina said, but the smile tugging at her lips told another story.

Lincoln threw up his hands. "See? Lesson learned. No gum on the bedpost. You get haunted by toast parrots and strange dream dudes in red coats."

Avalina let out a sleepy laugh that crumpled into a yawn. Her little body melted back against Cora's. "Will you stay with me?" she asked, voice small again.

"Of course," Cora whispered.

Lincoln didn't say anything—he just tugged back the covers and flopped down on the other side of the bed with a theatrical sigh. Cora slid in with Avalina curled between them, her tiny hand resting on her mother's heart, her foot tangling with Lincoln's leg.

The room quieted again. The moon filtered through the gauzy curtains, casting soft shadows across the wall. Cora listened to the rhythm of her daughter's breathing slowing, steadying. Then she glanced over at Lincoln, his eyes already drifting shut, a gentle smile still playing on his lips. *"Thanks,"* she mouthed.

He didn't answer, but his fingers found hers over Avalina's belly, and the three of them drifted off like that—tangled in warmth, laughter, and the slow, healing magic of a night spent together.

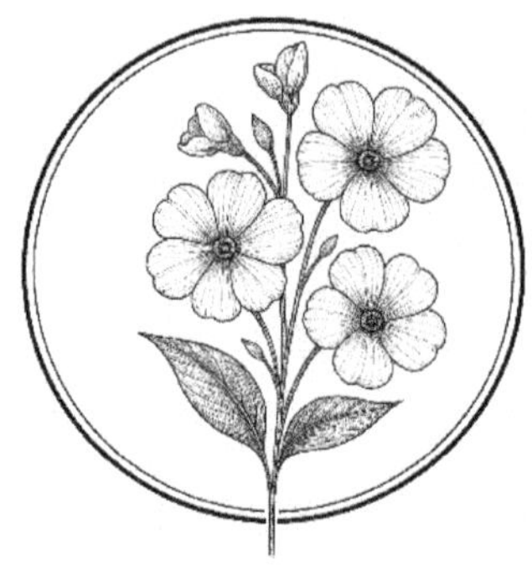

Chapter 22

What The Mountain Remembers

"You can bury the past beneath a thousand tomorrows, but the mountain remembers. Every scream, every goodbye, every secret whispered into the wind—it holds them all."

The tires crunched over gravel as Cora pulled into the overlook. The wind met her before she even opened the car door—sharp, salty, familiar in a way that made her skin prickle. It was the same wind that had carried her mother's final breath. And though Cora was only two when it happened, she swore the cliffs still held the echo of it.

She stepped out slowly, white roses pressed against her chest, petals trembling with each gust. The air smelled like pine and something colder beneath it all—like endings.

She didn't have memories of her mother. Not real ones, at least. Just photographs, stories, and that one video where she was giggling in her mother's lap while bubbles floated around them. Her mother's voice in that video was high and sweet, full of life. And then, one day, it wasn't.

Cora walked to the edge, where the cliffs stood exactly as they had for twenty-six years—unyielding, jagged, honest. Selah had once said closure isn't something you find. It's something you choose. And Cora was finally choosing. She knelt and laid the roses down on the rocky earth.

"I don't remember your laugh," she said quietly, staring at the horizon. *"I don't remember your touch, or how your hair smelled, or what your favorite song was. But I've spent most of my life missing you like I did."*

A gull called somewhere above, sharp and distant. *"I used to imagine you would come back,"* she admitted. *"That this was all a mistake. That you were out there watching me from somewhere. And now, I guess part of me still wants to believe you are."*

Her voice wavered, but she didn't stop. *"People tell me I look like you. That I laugh like you. Sometimes I wonder if the sadness I carry is yours too. If grief can live in a child's bones before they even know what it means."*

She stood and pulled a single rose from the bouquet, tracing a fingertip over the petals.

"I brought these because I read once that white roses mean remembrance. And even though I don't remember you... I remember the feeling of wanting you."

She held the rose out over the edge, her hand steady.

"I wish you could see Avalina. I think you would've been the kind of grandmother who danced in the kitchen and stayed up too late telling stories. You left before I could understand you. Before I even knew what it meant to lose something."

The wind picked up then, sudden and soft like a breath against her back. She let the rose go. It tumbled down the cliffside, petal by petal, a whisper of love delivered too late and right on time.

"I'm still becoming," she whispered, more to herself than anyone. *"And I hope, wherever you are, you see that. I hope you know I've survived."*

Cora stood there a moment longer, letting the ache live beside the peace. Then she turned and walked back to the car—not healed, not whole, but somehow closer. But as her boots crunched along the gravel, something made her pause. A flash of red.

The air was sharp with pine and ash. The peace she'd just grasped unraveled like smoke in her lungs. Then she saw him. Just beyond the curve of her bumper stood a man. Still and watching. A red jacket clung to his frame like it had grown into him, the hood drawn low, casting his face in deep shadow. But she didn't need to see his features to know. She always knew.

Her heart began to pound, a slow, suffocating drumbeat inside her chest. His head tilted—methodical, curious, as if memorizing her all over again. She couldn't move. Couldn't blink. The only sound was the whisper of wind combing through the trees and the distant roar of water far below the cliff's edge. Then he took a step forward, slow and deliberate. The mist around him shifted as if even the fog didn't want to touch him.

"You were in the car that day," he said, voice rising. "Here. On this mountain. Your mom—she set Fallon down… and she was going to take you with her." He nodded like it was the most casual truth. "I jumped out of the car," he said, voice calm, almost bored. "Didn't wanna die that day."

"But she did," Cora said, anger breaking through the disbelief.

Hudson Winslow's head tilted again, like he was deciphering her reaction. "She chose Dax. She chose Fallon. Not you. Not me. But she left Fallon on the side of the road like a stray dog. And I—" he pressed a hand to his chest "—I pulled you out. That was the only good thing I ever did."

"Who are you? You don't get to talk about her," Cora hissed.

"I'm Hudson. I watched you grow," he continued. "Saw her in your smile. The way you walked. And every year, you looked more like her, less like Dax. I kept you safe. All these years."

The name hit Cora like a jolt—*Hudson*. She blinked, her mind racing back to Noah, the photographer. He'd told her once, his voice low and careful, *We have a past.* Said his father's name was Hudson, a name wrapped in shadows and warnings she'd never fully understood at the time. Had he tried to warn her? Was this the man?

Cora's lip curled. "You weren't protecting me. You were haunting me. Lurking and watching. Following me around like a curse."

Silence spilled between them, heavy and wet. Her voice cracked when she spoke again. "Why didn't you take care of Fallon?"

He looked down at his boots, the mist curling at his ankles. "Because I knew she wasn't mine to keep."

He looked back up, eyes gleaming under the shadow of his hood. "But you… You were mine the moment your mother drove off that cliff. I figured you'd come."

"It was you. You sent the box of old toys, the music box," she replied.

He nodded his head. "I wanted you to remember." He paused before continuing. "I didn't think she'd actually do it. I didn't think she'd leave us. She wasn't right, Cora," he said, voice thin with something close to nostalgia. "Plagued by two men in love with her. She left us both. But you—" he paused "—you were the one I couldn't let go of."

"You never wanted Fallon," she whispered, and the words hurt worse than she expected. "She waited for you her whole life. Waited for someone who never wanted her. If I had known about her, I would've taken care of her." Cora's voice broke now, jagged with rage. "You watched me grow up. You stood outside my shop. You followed me through streets, through cities, through years. For what? Guilt? Control? Some sick version of love?"

Hudson's voice was quiet. "Because you were the only thing I ever got close to getting right. I didn't know what to do with a newborn."

"You don't get to say that. You don't get to claim any part of me or dismiss Fallon as if she wasn't good enough."

"You've got her eyes," he murmured as he flicked his cigarette.

"And Dax's heart," Cora snapped. "I am not your daughter. I am not your second chance. I am not your redemption."

He looked at her for a long moment, then nodded. "But you came here. That's something."

She shook her head. "It's closure."

She turned, walked to the car, her keys clenched in her trembling hand. At the door, she stopped, casting one last look over her shoulder. "You disappear," she said, voice like iron. "Today. For good. Because if I ever see you again, it'll be in a courtroom. Or a grave."

Hudson didn't move. Just stood there, a shadow wrapped in red, his expression unreadable. Something in his eyes cracked—but she didn't wait to watch it fall. She opened her door and slid behind the wheel. And this time, she didn't look back. The engine hummed beneath her, but it took a moment for her hands to stop shaking long enough to shift the car into drive. Gravel crunched beneath the tires as she pulled away from the overlook, her knuckles gripping the steering wheel white, her jaw clenched against the sob rising in her throat. She didn't look in the rearview mirror.

The trees blurred past, tall and skeletal in the dying light, and her breath began to stutter as tears spilled freely down her cheeks. Silent at first—then all-consuming. Her vision blurred, and she blinked fast, wiping at her face with the sleeve of her sweater, trying to breathe through it. But the weight of everything—the truth, the twisted past, the knowing—was too much to carry all at once.

At a stop sign halfway down the mountain, she let the car idle and glanced down, needing something—*anything*—to anchor her. Her keychain dangled from the ignition, swaying slightly with the movement of the car. Among the usual jingling keys and an old grocery club tag, her eyes caught on the small, brass key.

Dax had given it to her. *A backup,* he'd said, pressing it into her palm. *In case something ever happens to me. Or if you need answers, I'm not ready to give yet.*

It opened a storage unit on the edge of town. At the time, Cora thought it was just another one of his overly cautious habits. Something about keeping old case files, family things he didn't want in the house. She hadn't thought twice about it. Until now. Until today, when every buried truth felt like it had claws.

Cora sat there, her breath fogging the window, one hand brushing over the key as if it might burn her. It felt heavier now. Like it had been waiting for her all this time. Her tears had slowed, but her chest still ached, raw and torn open. She smoothed a wisp of her hair away, turned off the hazards, and whispered to herself, barely audible within the stillness inside the car: *"Alright, Dad. What are you hiding?"*

She put the car in gear and turned toward town—toward the answers. Ready or not. The sky had dimmed to a pale gray, the quiet hour between afternoon and evening when everything felt suspended. Cora pulled into the gravel lot behind the row of storage units on Maple Ridge Road, her tires crunching over loose stone. Her fingers tightened around the brass key in her lap, the one Dax had pressed into her hand with words she hadn't stopped thinking about since.

If you're ready…there might be answers waiting for you there.

She wasn't sure if she was ready. But she was there. The unit was near the end of the row—unremarkable, with a dented blue door and a rusted handle that looked like it hadn't been touched in years. She climbed out of the car slowly, the key cold now between her fingers. Her heart thudded as she slid it into the lock, half-expecting something to stop her.

Nothing did. With a soft clunk, the lock released. The metal door groaned in protest as she rolled it upward. Cold air rushed out as if the unit had been holding its breath. A single, bare bulb hung from the ceiling, swaying slightly as if disturbed by her presence. She pulled the chain, and dim yellow light flickered to life.

The space was small but meticulously organized. On the left, a row of metal filing cabinets, all labeled in Dax's unmistakable handwriting

Case Notes, 1994–1998... Personal: Veda... Hudson Winslow.

Her breath caught at the sight of his name.

To the right, an old cedar chest sat closed beside a small table stacked with composition notebooks and Polaroids. A pair of lawn chairs had been placed awkwardly beside it, like someone had once intended to sit and sort through memories but couldn't bring themselves to do it. Boxes lined the back wall. Some were marked with Sharpie:

Court Documents, Fallon—Medical, Letters (Unsent).

Cora stepped in slowly. She ran her fingers along the edge of the chest, then across the top file cabinet drawer. Everything here felt frozen in time—waiting for her. She wasn't sure what she would find. But something told her, once she opened the first drawer, there would be no turning back. And maybe that was the point.

Cora kneeled in front of a battered cardboard box labeled *"Fallon"* in faded black pen. The box sat atop a stack of unopened crates, waiting for her attention for far too long. Inside were scattered belongings consisting of faded photographs, notebooks with worn covers, and folded neatly at the bottom…a sealed envelope.

Her fingers brushed the paper, her heart quickening. The envelope was yellowed but neatly addressed in Fallon's handwriting:

To Cora….for when you are ready

Cora's hand shook while she broke the seal and unfolded the letter.

Dear Cora,

If you're reading this, it means I'm gone—and the past has found you, the way I always feared it would. I wish I had more time, more courage, and more chances to say the things I've kept buried. But I hope this letter gives you even a fragment of the truth you've deserved all along.

I tried to find you. After I got stable—when the noise in my head finally quieted and I could breathe again—I needed to see you. To know you were real. I didn't want to barge in and wreck the life you had, so I reached out to Dax. I thought maybe he'd help me find the right way to reach you. But he told me... not yet—that you were healing. That your world had finally started to feel safe. And I didn't want to be the reason it cracked open again. So, I waited. And while I waited, I watched from the edges—hoping you'd find answers in your own time.

Hudson Winslow isn't just a name. He's a wound that never closed. My father. The man Mom feared. The man who twisted her love into fear and silence. She tried to protect us from him. Her death wasn't just a tragedy, Cora. It was a choice—after one last desperate attempt at trying to save us.

Dax... he is your real dad. He protected you, even when it meant keeping the truth from you. I don't blame him. Not anymore. I wish I'd been stronger. I wish I'd come for you sooner.

But more than anything, I want you to know—you are not alone. You never were. We all carry the weight of where we come from, but it doesn't have to define where we go. You are light, even if you've lived in shadows. You are everything Mom hoped you'd be. And more.

If Hudson ever comes for you—stand tall. You are not his. You never were. Remember who you are. Remember who loves you.

Please be gentler with yourself than Mom was with herself. Than I was with me.

With all my love,

Fallon

The letter slipped from her hands, fluttering to the concrete floor like it was made of something far more fragile than paper. Cora sank to her knees beside it, her sobs breaking free in sharp, uneven waves. She pressed a hand to her chest, as if that could keep her heart from shattering all the way through. Fallon's words echoed within her—*I tried to find you... I watched from the edges... You were never alone.*

All those years of emptiness, of wondering, of feeling forgotten—rewritten by the truth. Not erased, but rewritten. The ache didn't lessen, but it shifted. It wasn't just grief now—it was knowing. It was love, late but not lost. And as the tears poured down, Cora finally let herself feel it all. The sorrow. The rage. The relief. The longing. She let it wreck her—because for the first time, it felt safe to fall apart.

She stayed there on the cold floor, knees drawn in, surrounded by dust and secrets and a letter that changed everything. The storm inside her had finally broken—but in the stillness that followed, she found something else waiting beneath the wreckage. Clarity.

Cora had carried the weight of too many ghosts for too long. But she wasn't a child anymore, or a victim of her past. She was a mother now. A woman. A survivor. And she would choose strength, not for herself, but for Avalina. So her daughter would grow up rooted in love, not haunted by fear. So Avalina would never have to question if she was safe, or worthy, or wanted.

And she would choose love. Not the kind that wounded or disappeared, but the kind that stood steady in the storm. The kind Lincoln gave without conditions. She would let him in—not just into her life, but into her heart. Fully and fiercely. Because he deserved it. Because she deserved it too.

As the tears slowed and the dust settled around her, Cora picked up the letter, pressed it gently to her chest, and whispered a silent promise. She would carry the truth. She would carry the love. And she would not look back. She would write it all down—every fracture, every flame, every moment she chose to survive. She would turn her pain into pages and give it to the world, not as a warning, but as a voice. The voice she once needed. The voice other women still do.

Epilogue

The studio lights were warm and bright, casting a soft glow over the set of *Morning Rise*. The skyline of the city shimmered through the windows behind them, sunlight spilling through like a quiet promise. Cora sat on the tufted cream couch, her fingers laced with Lincoln's, the cover of her memoir propped perfectly on the coffee table between them.

Becoming Cora: A Memoir of Shadows, Survival, and Rising Again.

The host smiled warmly as she turned toward them. "Cora McAlister, your memoir is already climbing bestseller lists, and the response from readers—especially young women—has been nothing short of extraordinary. What made you decide to share such a personal story with the world?"

Cora offered a soft smile, one shaped by both grace and grit. "For a long time, I was afraid of my own story. Afraid it made me weak. But then I realized the strength wasn't in avoiding the pain—it was in facing it, and turning it into something that might help someone else. I wrote this for every girl who's ever been silenced, or scared, or unsure she deserves better. I wanted them to know they're not alone—and they never were."

The host, Malita Cole, nodded, visibly moved. "It's powerful. The red poppy on the cover of your memoir is already a universal emblem of courage, remembrance, and resilience, the kind of bravery that persists even after hardship. Its fragile petals don't make it weak; instead, they prove that beauty can survive in even the harshest conditions. It's the perfect flower of strength, much like yourself. And Lincoln, you've been by her side through this. What has it been like, watching her step into the spotlight and share something so vulnerable?"

Lincoln leaned toward the mic, his expression softening. "It's been… inspiring," he said after a pause. "I've watched her carry things most people would never have the strength to talk about, and then transform all of that into something that helps others feel less alone. When she says *'Be brave enough to bloom,'* it isn't just a slogan—it's the way she lives. She's proof that even after the hardest seasons, you can choose to rise, to stand tall, and to open yourself to the world again."

The audience sat in silence, the weight of his words hanging in the air before breaking into heartfelt applause.

Lincoln smiled, his hand tightening around Cora's. "She's the bravest person I've ever known. I didn't fall in love with the part of her that survived—I fell in love with the part of her that kept choosing to."

Cora turned to him then, eyes shining, and leaned her head against his shoulder for just a moment.

"Cora, your memoir has struck a deep chord across the country. But your book tour—it's become more than just readings and signings. It feels like a movement. Is there a name for it?"

Cora glanced down for a minute, then looked back up, her voice strong. "Yes. It started with a hashtag—#DareToRise. At first, it was just something we printed on stickers and bookmarks. But then women started using it. Sharing their own stories. Not just rising out of what broke them, but rising with one another. That's what this is really about—rising now, not later. Not when it's convenient. Now."

She paused, her eyes scanning the audience before settling back on Malita. "Honestly?" she continued, her voice steady but full of emotion. "I thought I was just sharing my story. But every stop on the tour became something bigger. Women—so many women—came forward. Not just to say they read the book, but to say they felt it. That they saw themselves in it."

"They brought their own stories," Cora continued, "their hurt, their healing, their hope. Some stood in line for hours just to hug me. Some whispered secrets they'd never told anyone else. I didn't expect that kind of honesty. That kind of connection."

She paused, brushing a loose strand of hair behind her ear. "I realized the tour wasn't about me anymore. It became a space for women to be seen, to be heard, and to stop apologizing for surviving. We cried together. We laughed. We held hands. And city by city, it felt like this quiet revolution of women reclaiming their power."

Malita reached over, touched her hand. "That's beautiful. And now, there's been a lot of speculation—but would you like to share the news everyone's hoping is true?"

Cora glanced at Lincoln, her eyes bright with emotion, and then back to the camera. "We are…" she said, a soft smile spreading across her face. "We're expecting a baby. Avalina's going to be a big sister."

Cheers erupted from the crew behind the scenes. Lincoln chuckled and reached for her hand as they stood together.

"And," Cora added, her voice firm with purpose, "this memoir—it's just the beginning. I wrote it for the woman I used to be, but I'm sharing it for every woman out there still searching for her voice. I want to be the voice I needed. And I won't stop showing up."

Malita leaned toward the camera, smiling as the studio lights glowed around her. "You heard it here first, America! *Morning Rise* is confirming—it's time to **RISE NOW**."

Applause swelled from the audience, and Cora could feel it in her bones: this wasn't just a moment—it was a movement.

Cora wasn't just promoting a book. She was starting a revolution of truth and tenderness, one woman at a time. As they walked off set hand in hand, the applause behind them felt like more than clapping—it felt like a promise. Cora's mission extended beyond marketing. This was about making an impact.

The studio lights dimmed behind them as they walked through the backstage doors and out into the morning. Beyond the glass, the city was just waking up. Sunlight spilled over rooftops, traffic hummed in the distance, and life moved on—unaware, but somehow perfectly in tune with theirs. Cora glanced up at Lincoln, her heart full, her hand still in his. She had survived the fire. Now she was walking into the light. And this time, she wasn't walking alone.

Lincoln stretched as they stepped into the sunlight, his voice low and teasing. "You know, I was just thinking… for someone who has been chased, stalked, ghosted, and emotionally detonated— life's gotten suspiciously calm."

Cora raised an eyebrow, amused. "Suspiciously?"

He smirked. "Yeah. I mean, no more awkward couples with secret drama, no more cryptic stalkers, no one trying to drag you into emotional karaoke. It's just…you and me now." He paused, then added with a grin, "Honestly, it's starting to feel like we're livin' on a prayer over here."

She groaned, but her smile widened. "If you start quoting Bon Jovi, I swear—"

"I'm just sayin'," he said, eyes twinkling. "You used to have a front-row seat to a twisted rock ballad. Now we're more like… acoustic Poison. Still got the hair, just less venom."

Cora laughed, the sound light and real. "Acoustic Poison?"

He leaned in, kissed her temple. "Every rose has its thorn, baby. But we've done the thorns. I'm ready for the roses."

She looked up at him, eyes soft. "Me too."

They walked forward, hand in hand, the sun rising behind them, casting its light like a spotlight. And if life ever started playing power chords again, at least this time, they'd face it together, in tune.

Speaking of Memoirs……..

Coming Soon

Live, Lust, Repeat — A Memoir by Chrissy Curry

An unapologetic journey through desire, discovery, and the fire that makes us feel alive.

I'm thrilled to announce something deeply personal, wildly intimate, and years in the making—My memoir, *Live, Lust, Repeat,* is coming soon. This isn't a story about romance or attraction. It's about *lust* in its richest, rawest form— Lust for life. Lust for truth. Lust for freedom. Lust for *yourself.* In these pages, I explore what it means to wake up to your own longing in the quiet hours, the messy seasons, the untamed moments of becoming. I write about what it means to want more—and to reach for it unapologetically. This is not a memoir about being perfect. It's about being alive—fully, boldly.

If you've ever dimmed your light to keep the peace…

If you've ever mistaken survival for living…

If you've ever felt the stir of something wild just beneath the surface—This book is for you.

Stay tuned for cover reveals, tour updates, pre-order details, and a few seductive surprises along the way.

With fire and gratitude,

Chrissy

Love Wide Open Series

Book 1

Open Fire: The Flames of Betrayal

Book 2

Open Promise: The Tides of Deception

Book 3

Open-Ended: The Echoes of Redemption

Please visit www.chrissycurry.com

Children's Books by Chrissy Curry

Daisy Doodle is NOT Tucked In at Night

Wonders of the Sea

Savy Elf Saves Christmas

Just One More

Simply Ask Away

LOVE IS Where You Are

Will You Still Remember

Listen With My Little Hands

Zadie Zebra Zips Out Another AHHH-CHOOO

The Kindness Egg Hunt

Gramma's Love

Madness On the Farm

Pumpkin Paws and the Halloween Hunt

COMING SOON...

The Keeper of Christmas Spirit

Adventure Day at CC's

Learning Time at the Zoo

When the Little is No More

Twinning with You

Smoocharoonie

It Shaped You

You CAN Do Big Things

All Aboard the Potty Train

Please visit www.chrissycurrykids.com

Acknowledgements

To the women who need a little encouragement, a gentle push, and just enough love to set you free: May you rise into the woman you were always meant to be. And may you always *rise,* no matter what.

To my readers and loyal social media family: Thank you for showing up with open hearts and eager eyes. Your messages, shares, reviews, and unwavering support have breathed life into these pages and me as a writer. Whether you've been here since the first line or just found your way to my stories, I'm endlessly grateful for your presence. Every comment, every post, every moment you spent with my characters—*thank you*. You make this journey matter.

To my Danny (Slade): Thank you for cheering me on every step of the way, and for your classic line: *"When ya gonna write this book, Woman?"* Look where we are…Lil Wifey has written three novels now. Your humor and wit have been the perfect antidote to my stress as I wrap up this series. And let's be real—no one can touch your 80s hair band knowledge. You're one of a kind, and I'm so grateful to have you by my side. You will forever be my Lincoln McAlister.

To my daughters, Savannah and Sadie: Or as I lovingly call you, *SAVADIE* (because saying your names together was the only way to get your attention!) Being your mama is the greatest honor of my life. I've cherished every single step of our journey together, and I'm constantly in awe of the strong, beautiful women you've both become.

You will always be my greatest joy… and my most important work. May you forever *RISE*.

To Aynslee and Lauren: Thank you for bringing your beauty, heart, and unique flair to every content video you create for *The Love Wide Open* series. Your creativity blows me away, but it's your love and support that mean the most. I'm so lucky to have you on this journey with me.

To my daughter's bonus mom, Erin: Thank you for always cheering me on every step of the way. Thank you for being our hype girl and loving my girls like they were your own. We're so lucky to have you in our lives.

To My Baby Sista Kelly: I can't wait until you get that Bachelor of Nursing degree so you can finally sit down and read my work!

To all the indie bookstores carrying this series: Thank you, from the bottom of my heart, for believing in me as an author. Seeing my work on your shelves, right alongside the very best, is a feeling I can't quite put into words. Your support means everything.

To Teri, Leah, and the amazing crew at Wordsmith Bookshoppe in Central Illinois: Thank you for the love, the hugs, and your wholehearted support. You've made your shop feel like home, and there's truly no better place to spend a Saturday. You'll always be one of my favorite stops.

To D.J. Maughan: Bestselling author of *Idaho Fall* and all-around gem—Your review, your kindness, and the way you championed my work meant more than I can put into words. Thank you, truly.

To Danielle Steel: You lit the spark, and I'll always be grateful.

And lastly, most importantly, thank you to Nathan, Michael, and Glenn at Hemingway Publishers. Your guidance, belief, and steadfast support have meant everything to me. Thank you for seeing my dream not just take shape, but *rise*.

Hey there, lovely reader,

If you made it to the end of the LOVE WIDE OPEN series, first of all, thank you. Truly. Whether you binged it in a weekend or savored it in stolen quiet moments, I'm so grateful you gave these characters a home in your heart. If the storyline made you feel something—laugh, cry, scream into a pillow (I get it), or maybe text your best friend with a "YOU HAVE TO READ THIS"—I'd be so honored if you'd leave a quick review on Amazon or Goodreads. Stories like this one are meant to help us rise, to feel seen, to feel strong, to feel like maybe we're not as alone as we thought, and if it did any of that for you, I'd love to hear about it. So, if you have a second and a kind heart, I'd be forever grateful for your voice.

With all the gratitude and caffeine in the world,

Chrissy.

About the Author

Chrissy Curry is an award-winning author who lives with her husband in Central Illinois, though their hearts belong to St. Petersburg, Florida, where they spend their anniversary each year. She has two adult daughters, three adult bonus children, and a beloved golden doodle, Daisy. In her free time, she crochets cuddle cloths for NICU babies in the Midwest. She began her writing career with Children's Books. Her dream is to fill as many doctors' office waiting rooms and emergency rooms as she can with little books for tiny humans. She plans to continue her dual-genre writing technique with more children's and dark romance/psychological thriller titles to come!

Lincoln McAlister's Playlist

"Every Rose Has Its Thorn" – Poison

"I'll Be There For You" -Bon Jovi

"Home Sweet Home" – Mötley Crüe

"Smooth Up In Ya"- BulletBoys

"Heaven" – Warrant

"Is This Love" – Whitesnake

"Love of a Lifetime" – FireHouse

"Don't Know What You Got (Till It's Gone)" – Cinderella

"I Won't Forget You" – Poison

"Wonderful Tonight" – Eric Clapton

"Mama, I'm Coming Home" -Ozzy Osbourne

"Love Bites" -Def Leppard